he & She

Wayne Clark

he & She

Wayne Clark

Published by Wayne Clark YUL/NYC

ISBN: 978-0-9921202-0-7

Printed by CreateSpace

Cover design/page composition by Nell Chitty, Toronto, ON.

For

S. K. R.

Acknowledgment

Very is often a word that can be deleted without any loss of meaning, but not in this instance. I wish to say a very special thanks to Bob Stall, the finest editor I have ever worked with, both for his unnerving skill and his constant encouragement.

CONTENTS

PROLOGUE

THOUGHT had become pointless. There were no opinions worth forming, for he could no longer express them, even had there been someone still in his life to express them to. There were no decisions to debate in his own mind for there were no actions he was capable of taking. There was nothing worth learning because he could never use the knowledge. He had never learned how to change a tire. His were flat now, permanently. That was something he knew without having to be told or to read it somewhere.

Feelings were now irrelevant, too. Since he could no longer act on desires, he stopped desiring. Occasionally he sensed vague shifts in his moods but he suspected they were random chemical spills from the brain. Chemicals don't beget images as desires do, little movies he could at least pretend to be living in. He had spent most of his life living in the movies his mind produced, satisfying self-serving fictions adapted for the screen from the world he actually lived in, a world he was ever reluctant to impose himself on.

But now the screen was blank. No credits had rolled by at the end. His name didn't appear anywhere. He could no longer recall hearing anyone ever say his name. He could speak it in his mind, but that was now pointless, too. He didn't need a name anymore.

The only thing left to him in life was masturbation.

Even there, he could not produce emotional desires, or even soulless B-movies. He needed external images, a magazine, a picture, in color. He recognized what he saw, a woman, but if he closed his eyes a moment, all that appeared on his eyelids were flickering spots, white-on-black, or uneven lines and blotches, the herky-jerky end to a silent movie.

When he masturbated to the picture in the magazine, arousal was long in coming. His left hand was a virgin at first, after the stroke, but he persevered most of the time. His world had been reduced to sensation, and there wasn't much of that with his entire right side paralyzed. Masturbation was the only sensation he could command.

He couldn't control what the nurses did to him. There were always two of them now, changing him, turning him on his side, cleaning him. Every time he saw them approach he felt the only other sensation, besides arousal, he now knew. Irritation, annoyance, resentment. He had become so irritated once that he struck at a nurse with his left arm, hitting her on the shoulder. A report had been made. The nurse had been trying to use a hoist to place him in a wheelchair. Now there were always two nurses, and they never tried to get him out of his bed again. The therapists no longer visited either.

Someone would leave the magazine on his lap. No name. Just the face, somehow familiar. After the face left, he would have to carefully reposition the magazine next to him on the bed, on the left side. Since he was propped up in bed, he could look down on the pages, flipping slowly through them until his eyes fixed on an image.

With his palm flat, he would press the gutter of the glossy page, hoping it would stay open. He would then move his hand under his pajamas to his flaccid penis, and slowly set to work. Masturbating was tiring, or was until he at last began to feel aroused, because he had to try to keep his left arm positioned over his chest as much as possible so he could have an unobstructed view of the image. At first he had tried placing the magazine on his right side. Angrily he realized his left arm couldn't reach the right-hand page to turn it. Grabbing what he could of the magazine, he'd hauled it across his body.

Anger, resentment, arousal, the high and low points of his day, interchangeable in the end because they at least registered on the graph as experience. Whether the curves and dots were positive or negative was immaterial. At least they had not flatlined. He was alive, though all but comatose. Black dots on a flat black line are invisible.

When he died after two years on that same bed, a nurse remarked to a passing physiotherapist that at the end of life our sexuality outlives the rest. Memories, meaning, love, they vanish long before.

CHAPTER 1

Musical Debut

YEARS after the fact, Kit Cayman would tell people he never forgot the exact, precise, dead-on, eureka-and-then-some feeling of freedom that whisked him into the street the day he quit his job. It wasn't true, but it wasn't a big lie either. He had survived on his own. It felt right. The money didn't matter most of the time, which was probably for the better.

When he had work, he got up at dawn. It had become a habit over the years, even during droughts, which were more common in a freelance translator's life than the tsunamis of work. He would be at the keyboard before taking his first sip of coffee. Instant-on was his way of piling up sandbags against the usual flood of random daydreams and unfriendly self-interrogation. By the time he'd built up momentum, usually not long after killing coffee No. 2, he was OK. He would lock into the translation on his screen and the hours would fly by. On days without work, drinking coffee in the relative quiet of the early morning often became the best part of his day, the only time when optimism stood a chance. Optimism wasn't natural to him, he'd decided.

If there was no work today, it would be the fourth straight day. But it was early. Most of his clients were still commuting to work.

The girl in bed beside him, curled up and facing away from both him and the gray morning light, didn't budge as he got to his feet and began edging his way around the bed, squeezing between it and the trunk, to get to the kitchen. As he got to the other side of the bed he saw her face for the first time in daylight. He remembered the purple hair, bob cut in uneven lengths. In the club last night, it appeared candy colored as he looked down from the stage, but now there was nothing for the hair to reflect.

After measuring the beans into the coffee grinder, he stood in the doorway between the kitchen and bedroom with the grinder in his hands. He pressed the On button and watched the girl's face. She was lying on her right side. At the sound of the grinder, her left shoulder twitched once, nothing more. He counted slowly to five, the time that seemed to create the best grind for his French-press coffee maker.

When the grinder stopped, she suddenly turned to her other side. The rotation took some of the sheet with her, baring the lower left side of her back and one rounded buttock. For a moment he studied the tattoo on her right arm, the one pressing the sheet to her body. It ran from her wrist to her shoulder, an elaborate light green, yellow and rose-colored vine growing more entwined and thicker as it climbed.

On the floor beside the bed was a small black skirt, a black corset and torn black stockings. "Do they buy them that way?" he wondered. On top of the pile were two large silver hoop earrings, a chrome-studded black leather bracelet and a beaded black lace choker. How did women manage to be neat even when high and horny?

As the coffee brewed, he returned to watch her sleep.

Kicking himself mentally, he realized he could have coffee any morning but he couldn't have someone like her every morning. He slipped back into bed. Just as he was about to place his hand on her hip, she rolled over again, turning her back to him. Was it unconscious, or was she awake? He decided not to find out. He realized he was still tired as well. The night had ended only three and a half hours ago. It was only caffeine addiction that got him up. He closed his eyes and recalled the evening.

It was the second time that he'd linked up with a woman while playing in public, but the first time didn't really count, he now decided. When he was a waiter in his twenties and a month of stingy tips left him ten or twelve bucks shy of rent money, he took to the streets with a flute and a hat for anyone who wanted to lighten their load of pocket change. Once, a young woman from somewhere in North Carolina took him to her cheap hotel room where they shared a bottle of wine as supper. She had to return home the next morning. She wrote once, saying she'd found a recording of the Bach cantata he was playing when she first saw him. He included his phone number in his short reply but he never heard from her again.

The encounter had faded badly in memory, as if the images had been drawn in charcoal. By comparison, he had a feeling the encounter with Selita would endure like a tattoo. She had been witness to his real musical debut. After she followed him home, he knew for certain that "musician" would have more sex appeal than "word professional" on a business card.

Now that he was working for himself, he was almost always in his apartment. It was music that got him out of the apartment last night and it was possibly music that got this girl into his apartment this morning. Until recently music had been his secret, one he thought he should keep to himself, like sexual fantasies that would evaporate if tested in the outside world.

He played decently but it was only while playing alone

in his room that he would pretend he was a real musician. He was self-taught and intimidated by the genius of the musicians he loved, just as he was by the monster skills of young musicians coming out of university jazz programs. He had a bookshelf full of jazz theory and exercises, volumes of transcribed solos by the greats, some analyzed to death bar by bar. Each time he bought one he'd come home excited, believing it would reveal the secret to improvisation that so far eluded him, but most of the time the material seemed so dry he'd pour himself a Scotch and put the book aside.

If he wasn't too frustrated he'd put on a Jamey Aebersold or Bob Mintzer play-along CD and crank it up full volume. The CDs came with sheet music, the head and chords, and a dynamite rhythm section he could hide behind when it came time to solo. Some days he felt he'd "gotten it," he'd felt the music in his fingers. Emboldened, he would blow over the rhythm section as he was intended to do. If he felt particularly elated, he imagined one of them nodding approval to him as he put down his horn afterwards. They'd even call him by name sometimes, and of course he knew their names from the CD credits.

When he once told a neighbor friend about musicians on CDs talking to him, his friend said he regretted not having a number handy for a shrink.

It was during one of those play-along sax sessions that he had met his upstairs neighbor, who'd heard the music coming from below. While pausing to find a fresh reed, he heard a knock at the door. The man introduced himself as LeBron Jackson. He'd only just moved in. Kit extended his hand.

"Kit, Kit Caymen," he said.

"I play bass," LeBron said. "Didn't know you played, too, K-Man."

The name stuck, although most of the time LeBron just called him K.

LeBron was tall, and as skinny as a soprano sax.

"Who are you playing with?"

If he was disappointed with the answer, that the horn was just a hobby, it didn't show.

They spent the rest of the afternoon listening to music, comparing tastes. As they drank, the bass player's ear seemed worth more than all the books combined, particularly when he said things like: "It's not always nearly as complicated as you think. You don't not play simply because you don't have all your scales and chords down."

He told K how on certain pieces you could play a single five-note scale through the entire piece and you'd sound fine. "You'll get bored with those five notes," he'd said, "but you'll be making music."

In the following weeks they started playing simple pieces together, other times just common R&B horn section licks which LeBron would sing to him, or they'd dig out some old recordings. At LeBron's, they spent afternoons with Sly and the Family Stone, Otis Redding, The Temptations and James Brown. Some days they confined their sleuthing to anything Motown. Any nugget would do, and LeBron would have him playing it far more quickly than if he'd tried to pull it out and polish it himself.

The more time he spent with LeBron the bolder he got in the face of oppression, what LeBron called the tyranny of theory.

"Just effin' play, man. Just let your fingers find what's in your head, and if there's nothing in your head, take the horn out of your mouth and sing it, anything, then wing it. Keep playing but hang tight with that little idea that spilled out of your mouth when you weren't thinking. Play it long enough and it will turn into something, and then it will be in your head. It will be yours, something you can use every which way."

LeBron's head always seemed to be into playing, unlike his. There were days when the horn weighed a ton around his neck. He was going through the motions.

LeBron would simply stop playing. If this happened a couple of days in a row, LeBron would stop answering his door for a while. One day, when LeBron finally let him back in, LeBron was wearing a Mets hat, the blue one. Although it was gray and cold outside, the Mets were playing their home opener.

"You ready to play?" LeBron asked. "It's too bad you're a horn player because some days you'd be better off if somebody just axed off your head. But you need your mouth to play, not like bass players."

LeBron took off his ball cap and pointed it at him.

"When a real hitter steps to the plate, and some pitcher is going to throw a ball at him faster than a Charlie Parker tempo, that hitter, he's got to stop thinking. If he's thinking, he's wearing handcuffs. It's not the time to think because there is no time to think. Thinking's got to stay in the batting cage. Same with your horn."

They didn't end up playing that day. They talked and sipped and listened to the ball game.

Some days he almost regretted turning on his computer in the early morning and finding an urgent request for a submission on a translation job. But he wasn't making enough money to say no. He had learned that he wasn't a good enough or committed enough actor to pimp himself as the translator — correction, adapter — every big-bucks corporation needed.

At the beginning, a good decade ago, right after being fired from a job at what he called a translation factory, he made a million phone calls and sent out at least that many letters. One hundred thousand and two of the recipients promised to keep his contact information on file, two of them said "Let's meet," fourteen requested he send samples of his work or do a test, and seven of them sent him jobs within the first four months of freelancing.

One of them made him think he'd need a bank account in the Caymans to hide all his money. A woman he'd studied with at NYU had gone on to specialize in medical translation. The agency she worked for was suddenly swamped. Would he be interested in bailing them out? After confessing that he'd never translated a medical document, she assured him the job wouldn't be too technical. It was not actually a document, she said. Instead it was four hours of taped lectures and workshops at a medical convention. There was no French transcription to work from.

"You'll have to work from the tapes. You can charge your top rate."

Not really knowing what he was getting into, he said yes. At first blush, four hours of tapes should be worth a fortune to a man who sometimes wasn't sure whether he should think of himself as a freelancer or simply unemployed.

When the material arrived, the first few minutes of the first tape resulted in more than an hour of rifling through dictionaries. Play, Stop, Rewind, FF became so tedious he was overjoyed when background noise, audience applause or laughter allowed him to dismiss portions as "inaudible." The job took him three seven-day weeks of hours far longer than he ever put in at the conveyor-belt translation agency.

By the end, he had become familiar with much of the vocabulary. His confidence grew as he went back to the first pages and used Search and Replace to hide the ignorance with which he started the job. He did a rough calculation in his head of how much money the job would bring in based on what he'd done so far. When the figure topped $10,000 he paid a nurse friend $100 to quickly read through the text to make sure there were no horrific errors in medical terminology.

"Thank you, NYU," he wrote in his journal. "You're moving me to Easy Street."

It was to be the last five-figure contract he ever got. The medical translation agency never called back, although their name looked good in the list of clients on his website. Out of the one million approaches he'd made that first year, he now had seven clients he could call regulars. Only one of them ever kept him working full-time for more than a month or two.

When that happened he rarely picked up his sax. LeBron worked at night, mostly as a musician, so they rarely saw each other. It was probably for the best, he would think. He never managed to dump the feeling that he was a musical pretender.

Then one Saturday in December, LeBron knocked at his door. He had a CD in one hand and a bottle of beer in the other.

"You ready to make your debut?" he asked. "Star Search has chosen you, my man."

LeBron sat down on the radiator by the window and laughed at his friend's petrified expression.

"An easy gig, a fun gig. I promise. What's the term I'm looking for? Yeah, fifth wheel. You'd be like a fifth wheel, a fifth horn, not really needed. Thought you might like it, you know. You'd finally become one of the really cool people, not just some closet word freak."

Kit put LeBron's CD into his computer's optical drive and plugged in the external speakers. After listening to the opening cut, all he could say was a silly, "Fucking ferocious funk, Batman."

"Want to play it on stage?"

"I'd be lost before you got to the bridge."

"Don't worry. We don't need you. We've already got four horns up there. I'm just asking if you want to get a taste. You can join in on whatever you learn between now and next Thursday. One piece, two pieces. Doesn't matter. We've already played some of what you just heard, only slower and in little bits. If you get lost, just pretend. If you get back on the horse, go for it. If not, no matter. No one's going to hear you, no one's going to be watching you.

"But," LeBron added, "if you have any thoughts about soloing, we shoot you. The only thing is that you don't get paid. You're just sittin' in, as my guest."

When the gig arrived, LeBron wouldn't let K have a drink before the first set. The club, a former disco-funk hall in Crown Heights in Brooklyn, had looked seedy until the lights were lowered. Now it was half full. He guessed it might seat several hundred people.

The piped-in reggae and soca stopped and the band was announced. His knees were shaking as the leader counted out the tempo for the first number. They stopped shaking the instant he heard how big the band's sound was.

He couldn't help it. He climbed aboard and rode the rhythm. The horn section was sparring and he was part of it, landing musical jabs right to the gut, getting more and more insistent before culminating in a glorious ensemble uppercut that launched the trumpet solo.

Christ, he'd done it. He cradled his horn and looked back towards LeBron, whose eyes seemed to be glued to the floor. LeBron played the electric bass with his feet close together and swayed, like a tall narrow skyscraper in an earthquake.

It was then that he looked down from the low stage and saw the girl with the candy-colored purple hair. Her eyes were closed. When she opened them they were looking straight into his.

Her name was Selita.

After the set, she asked, "You ever get to solo?"

"Nope. I prefer duets." He couldn't believe he said that, laid down a move on her. Not a moment's thought went into it. Had he become smooth all of a sudden?

She raised an amused eyebrow.

"Drink?"

Before she could reply, LeBron tapped him on the shoulder. He was squatting at the end of the stage.

"Well, word pro?"

"I'm changing professions. Right here and now."

LeBron laughed, eyeing the girl for a second as he scanned the room.

"Well, word man, gotta tell you now that I tagged you as a fool the first day I met you. Now I know for sure. By the way, you did fine."

"How do you know?"

"Because I couldn't hear you. If I did I would have known you were messing up."

"It's time for a drink, LeBron."

"You earned it. Have two if you want, K-Man. You might not want to come up for the second set, though. Boss has thrown in a new piece, one I haven't shown you. He wants to cut loose on it. Your call."

"We'll watch. I'll be in better-looking company," he said, looking at Selita. "Let's get that drink," he said to her.

"Before we do, can I touch your horn?" She said it innocently, but LeBron reacted immediately, as if she'd uttered an old musician's joke.

"OK, on that note, I'm outta here," said LeBron, unfolding his six feet six and a half inches. "Enjoy."

There were tables available but Selita said she wanted to dance, drink in hand. Like LeBron when he was playing, she fixed her eyes to the floor as she danced. He wondered whether she was doing that just to let him watch her body move to the music without the embarrassment of being caught staring. Her face made him think of a woman he'd seen in a hip-hop video but he couldn't attach a name. The more he looked at her, he realized she was a few years older than the woman in the video, her face slightly wider at the cheek bones. Some faces take you to the eyes, others to the lips. Hers had options.

He wanted to leave with her before the second set was done so he wouldn't end up drinking too much, but he couldn't because his alto was still on stage, on a sax stand, its two hues of bronze conflicting brilliantly under the stage lights.

Tonight seemed to vindicate the indulgence. That

horn had been his one splurge after getting the agency job when he graduated. It took him three and a half years to pay it off in addition to the remaining debt from a long-ago vacation to Barcelona, an extravagance on a waiter's salary that would have been disappointing for the most part had it not given him the idea that mastering a second language and becoming a translator might be his passport to a real career. He was already in his late twenties at the time, too old to pretend he was just waiting for something better to come along.

After the final set, LeBron accompanied them back to Manhattan, then parted ways a few subway stops early, at 6th Avenue and Spring Street, LeBron saying he had some business to attend to. The sound of the train doors opening drowned out a joking remark about going for a spring roll.

As for Selita, she had never mentioned where she lived nor asked where they were going. It seemed irrelevant now that she'd come this far. When they arrived at 34th Street Penn Station, she got off with him. She accepted his right arm. His left held the black sax case.

As he put his head back down on the pillow the following morning, he was glad he hadn't had a coffee to jolt him into the day. The last thing he saw was Selita's left shoulder. He reached over and covered it with the sheet. As he closed his eyes he felt the sudden infusion of sleep chemicals. At this hour on a weekday morning, when everyone else was trying to revive their corpses for work, sleepiness could be the sweetest high of all. It overtook him before he could replay the previous night.

It was a slight jiggling of the bed that woke him. He hadn't moved. He was still on his right side. He opened his left eye — the other was sunk in the pillow — and saw Selita seated at the foot of the bed with her back to him. She was juggling three differently colored balls, soft ones like hacky sack balls. She dropped a ball every two or three rotations, — not that he could have done better — but she was determined, picking up the errant one and going right back at it without the slightest change in expression, as if klutzy was part of the human condition and not something to beat yourself up about.

As he watched her he began to replay the night. It was the best sex he'd had in years. He'd been seeing a woman off and on for a good decade but the feeling of sexual satisfaction was off and on as well. Rarely did making love rescue him, if only momentarily, from existence. He'd long ago lost the lifetime guarantee on erections. In consequence, mostly unconsciously, he had all but stopped initiating, which only compounded the problem. He wished sex shops sold a magic potion that paralyzed men's minds for the time it takes to make love. It would outsell Viagra and Cialis combined, he thought.

What bothered him now was that sex last night had seemed so uncomplicated. He tried to figure out why. If something was uncomplicated it must have a complicated reason. No answer came to mind. He continued to watch her slender arms operating in turns like pistons, gently pumping the balls into space. Then he realized she made love the same way she juggled. When she dropped a ball she barely lost a beat. She was determined to learn to juggle, and last night she was determined to make love to him. She may even have been determined to do so as far back as when their eyes met at the club. She didn't ask if she could come home with him, nor did she wait to be asked. She just did.

A nice, tidy answer, he thought, but he was addicted to complicated. Why had he not complicated their love-making, or even derailed it, by mentally rating the readiness of his erection, or asking himself, "Did that come from me or was she mostly responsible?" He recalled her playing with his cock and balls but couldn't remember whether he was aroused much before that. It mattered because more and more his erections were foreign manufactured. She was cute as hell, he acknowledged, but looks never seemed to be enough, not the way they had been in his twenties and, to a lesser extent, his thirties.

Eventually, she completed seven rotations of the three balls without dropping one. He thought he espied the hint of a smile before she resumed, as calmly determined as before. It was then that he realized last night was perfect because she had taken him. She had not spoiled a second with even a perfunctory nod to the usual male ego. She played him.

He tried to filter what happened through his memory of a night when a woman he had met in a bar had somehow, while sitting with a table full of other women, reached deep down inside him and found assorted fantasies, not only submissive ones but masochistic ones. She played the nascent urges like a virtuoso all evening.

But while Selita made love to him, he realized he hadn't imagined her getting rough with him, or spanking him, or any of the other fantasies he was starting to rely on to stay turned on. Did the night represent another shade of masochism? After playing sax on stage with a kick-ass horn section in a funk band, he had been silently kidnapped by a pretty woman with purple hair. She didn't have to point a gun at him. In fact, she hadn't said a word. Total submission. It was kink without the accoutrements. He couldn't have asked for more.

As that thought occurred to him, she reached back without looking and squeezed his left big toe.

"Thought I smelled coffee. A long time ago."

She'd been awake, feigning sleep when he'd tip-toed to the kitchen. He looked at her and wondered whether she was aware of everything around her in life, including how to make him do anything she wanted.

"My intentions were good," he said. "But while I was waiting for it to brew, I looked at you there in bed and got horny."

"But you didn't do anything about it," she replied, looking at him as if awaiting a full explanation, like a teacher expecting to be told the truth behind the dog-ate-my-homework story.

"You turned your back."

"I've never heard that excuse before from a horny man."

He considered for a moment, then confessed, "I hadn't realized at that moment, but I wanted you to make love to me, not the other way around."

"But you realize that now?"

"Yes."

As convoluted as his own words seemed to him, the answer seemed to satisfy her. She flipped the balls at him and reached for her corset. He dropped two of the balls and missed getting a good look at her lovely ass as she bent over to get her clothes.

He poured out the old coffee and put on water for a new pot. She deserved better than coffee reheated in a microwave.

While the water boiled, he also got dressed. After pressing the coffee, he made the bed, a necessity in a tiny apartment if there was company, and sat down before his laptop to check for email. Selita was in the bathroom. He heard her singing over the sound of the tap but couldn't distinguish any words.

He saw he'd received a translation job due by end of day. He swore under his breath. Overall, business had been bad for months. Every now and again a tornado would whirl through, forcing him to hold on to his keyboard for dear life, and then it was sixteen, seventeen-hour days, during which he would neither make the bed nor get dressed because he never knew when sleep would insist.

He debated replying:

"Sorry. On deadline with another job for this aft. Let me know later if you can't find anybody for today. I'll be all yours tomorrow."

Whenever he could, he left the impression that clients were lined up for his services. If he turned a job around in record time, they might think he'd given them priority, done them a favor.

Selita was suddenly beside his chair, her hand on his shoulder, her eyes on the screen.

"No good porn this morning?"

"Worse," he said. "Work."

"Wish I had some," she said, retrieving her juggling balls from the trunk.

Fantasies expressed in daydreams can sometimes seem to last ages, he thought. They end and you look around you. There's no one else in line. The bus you had been waiting for when you started fantasizing has passed. It is already halfway down the block.

Other times, like now, as he looked at her back just a few feet in front of him, the feature-length film rolls by faster than a conscious mind can see. Before Selita had put the third ball in her purse, she had become his grateful secretary in his mind. She wore bra and panties as she lay on the bed, on her tummy, propped up on her elbows reading a book, waiting for him to dictate part of a translation while she typed, a make-work scheme allowing him to pay her a small sum that he could deduct at tax time as a subcontracting expense. A dream of an arrangement that lasted a full cozy winter. It had passed through his imagination, full blown, in two seconds, maybe less.

"Got time for breakfast?" he asked.

"Do you?"

"Not really." After a moment, he added, "But you're welcome to stay if you'd like."

The words had come out as if he were indifferent to her decision. He was afraid she'd say "Sure," yet that was what he really wanted to hear.

Just then he heard LeBron's voice in the stairway, then a woman's voice complaining.

"Too many damn stairs for a girl with no sleep."

"Whose damn fault is that?" answered LeBron,

teasingly. "C'mon, girl, one more flight."

By the time the voices died away, replaced by the sounds of shoes on the floor above, LeBron's apartment, Selita had put her own boots on.

"Got train fare?" she asked.

He gave her the change he had in his pocket, more than enough. For a second he thought of giving her his MetroCard, anything to increase the chances she would come back some day. Then pride said no.

"Thanks," she said, and gave him a light kiss on the lips.

She looked small going down the stairs.

While she knew where he lived, he had no idea where she lay her head at night. Afterwards, she frequently popped in and out of his memory. Sometimes he would think about being swallowed whole by her love-making. Sometimes he'd see her sitting at the end of the bed. He'd see her motionless bare back and twitching shoulder blades. Atop that, the purple hair. Atop that, like fireworks rocketing skyward, the juggling balls.

Once, in a dream, those balls danced above words scrolling across the bottom of his mind, like the balls once used in silent movies to rhythmically point to lyrics to help an audience sing along. The words in his dream were gibberish. There was nothing in them to understand, let alone sing. But he could feel the balls each time they ricocheted off the bottom of his mind. It was as if they were pinging, like a submarine sounding, trying to map deeper waters. The dream suddenly nudged him clinically awake but he felt he was still eavesdropping on his own subconscious. It was yakking away about how she had choreographed every dance step that night, and how he had submitted to her, an absolute stranger, without a word. She had collared him and he had never strained at the leash. She had confirmed that somewhere down there, there was a submissive itch that needed scratching.

CHAPTER 2

First Sighting

ALMOST a year later, he found himself reminiscing once again about Selita. Though he hadn't seen her since what he called the one-night affair, he couldn't think about her without smiling. He'd lived a lifetime then in not quite twenty-four hours. In the intervening year he'd left his forties behind, and as mathematically illogical as it was, that fact of fifty made the night with her seem a lifetime ago.

At the time, LeBron had whooped and applauded several times upon hearing the details of all that had transpired after he'd left them on the subway. Since then, LeBron seldom wasted an opportunity to tease him about Selita. "K-Man, you never played better than you did that night," he'd say, pretending to be talking about music. Other times, he'd discreetly pick something off the floor — a sock, a slipper or, from the bedside table, a bottle of sleeping pills or a paperback — choose his moment carefully and suddenly toss the object at his friend. Most of the time K would fail to catch it. "Selita would have caught that," LeBron would say, referring to her juggling skill.

Could less than a year really have made that much difference? He'd been dropping the ball for years. That night with Selita was the exception. For the first time in ages, he'd felt like a man, a lover. He'd felt young. Who wouldn't have? First, he'd become a real musician that night, on stage and kicking ass, after telling LeBron time and again he was demented for trying to convince him he could be one. But, in retrospect, what was even more rejuvenating was that Selita had lassoed him, not the other way around. The role switch animated something he'd felt before but could never nail down or give a name.

Now the pixie dust was far beyond its expiration date, and even the best days of his life seemed like party balloons with leaks that were audible if he closed his eyes. Suspicions nagged, itches persisted. A formless something was always missing, or, he thought at times, it was there, like a black hole in space, a measurable mass if you knew the formula but invisible until it passed close to a star.

By evening, he realized he'd done nothing all day except let his mind meander from here to nowhere and back again. Selita was the only tangible. He'd formulated no real thoughts, ones born of the impulse to logic and connections. It was like traveling through the European Community, with no borders, no passport stamps, no photos with time stamps on the back.

While he surfed the Internet, darkness had fallen. The skies over New York were not particularly clear that August night, yet suddenly, somehow, a mouse click triggered his inner Copernicus. What that absent-minded click unveiled was a new universe. The nag, the itch, the whatever, it had form. His mind didn't have to tell him. He knew. The missing something was indeed something, or possibly someone, to orbit around.

The moment he first laid eyes on her, or at least

her image, inches away from him, right there on the Internet, he felt her presence so intensely it was as if she had had walked into the room, headed straight for him, gently grabbed his crotch and, her face inches from his, said, "Hello."

That first Internet image engraved itself in his mind, and every pixel was to remain in place, illuminated, welcome or not, for the rest of his life.

Some dating agency advertised on television that one out of five relationships began on the Internet. He had found that hard to believe. In the days when he went to bars in the hope of meeting a girl, there was no Internet. Having now stumbled over fifty, he told himself he qualified as an old dog when it came to learning new tricks. Anyway, he wasn't looking for a date or a girlfriend.

Though he had been in a relationship for years with a younger woman named Alana, and although he made his living with words, he never knew how to describe it.

LeBron had never even met Alana. He once asked why.

"Simple. You're never here when she's here. You're always out playing somewhere at night."

"We've known each other a long time, K," LeBron answered. "If I was out playing every night like you say I wouldn't be living in this dump."

When that didn't get a response, LeBron asked: "Afraid I'll steal her from you?" As LeBron said it he whipped his ball cap forty-five degrees off center like a young dude on the make.

"The truth," K said, "is she's not here that often. Her place is a lot bigger, with a real bed."

After a moment, his eyes met LeBron's and he confessed.

"Actually, she's never been here."

"In all this time? What is it, a decade?"

"Yeah. Don't really know why. Kinda like my independence, I guess. Besides, she's way up in the Bronx."

LeBron straightened his ball cap and shifted it to the back of his head.

"Independent. Like a cowboy. Just him and his nag and the lone Prairie."

"Exactly, you got it, LeBron. That's me."

"Maybe she's not the right girl for you?"

"No, no. I really like her. Wouldn't still be with her after all this time if I didn't, would I?"

Maybe LeBron bought the logic, maybe he didn't, but he didn't press the matter and his friend was happy he didn't.

The truth was, the longer he stayed in the relationship the more it became habit. Would he rebel first, would she? They never talked about it, at least not with each other. But something had to give. Dumb instinct told him that. The relationship no longer held out promise. There were no images floating around of hand-in-hand happiness in old age. And he knew he probably wasn't fueling her hopes for the future either. They'd just had another argument over nothing, a stupid comment, as stupid as in lighting a cigarette while pumping gas. Now, he couldn't even remember the words that ignited her.

When he looked ahead he mostly saw more of the same. He knew why he stayed. Notions like nice, cozy and rooted had sabotaged his instinct to escape. Rooted, he thought, was not far removed from the word mired. The problem was, especially at his age, it was always easier to say what he wanted to escape from rather than escape to. At times he wondered if he were a congenital malcontent. Perhaps. Or maybe he was just too dumb to see the good things in life.

"It's not bullshit, you know," LeBron had once said. "Stop and snort the flowers. Seize the moment, K-Man. That's where you should be living."

It made sense but when he tried he always tripped over the niggling notion there was something else in life, something he was missing. How could he keep his eye on the moment and look out for the big picture at the same time?

He always thought spontaneous people, people living in the present, probably didn't fear dying when their time came. They never stopped to think whether they were wasting their lives. Spontaneity must be genetic, he thought, and he'd lucked out.

The relationship with Alana had started spontaneously enough. On the night it began, he hadn't expended a single thought about past or future. But the present moment soon had competition.

The relationship had been an odd one from the outset, one that in fact seemed to have ended after the first test flight. There were no sparks until much later and even those first ones seemed to be generated by the friction of mutual suspicion that hovered over their horniness. When talking to each other, each claimed to be a card-carrying agnostic when it came to believing in the joys of setting up house. Nevertheless, they cared for each other. They both knew that and, with time, the sparks came more often. With time, enough sparks had accumulated that they could lay claim to a shared and intimate past, not that they ever talked in those terms.

They also never talked about seeing other people. He assumed she did, just as he would from time to time during periods when he felt he and Alana were drifting apart. He couldn't count the times he felt he didn't matter to her. Within a span of just days she could run from hot to cold for no apparent reason. The relationship was wearing thin. At first he enjoyed thinking of her as his girlfriend. But now he used the term mostly for conversational convenience, or subterfuge when he didn't want others, or even himself, looking too closely at his life.

As much as he loved those days with LeBron — baseball, beer, blended Scotch and music stealing the hours like an afternoon at a cinema that still offered newsreels, cartoons and feature presentations — he managed to keep his defenses manned, not so much against an invasion by LeBron but against the temptation to allow his deepest fears to escape.

Life had become same-old so fast he sometimes thought there should have been a red consumer-alert label on his birth certificate. He was only middle-aged, well, maybe quarter past middle-aged, but he had learned too well that when boredom is allowed to be present long enough, it assumes squatter's rights. In no time at all, it's part of the family, no longer merely a roommate you can give the boot to and replace with something better. He was no longer afraid of the thought that he would have to make his move soon. He'd have to leave her.

It was while rehashing that thought that his spasming mouse finger stopped clicking. On the screen was a single static image, poised and suspended somewhere in a digital universe. It spoke to him. It said he wasn't dead yet.

CHAPTER 3

Cha-ching

HER body faced the camera but her head was in profile, her right. She was seated, the bottom of the photo framed by her tiny black-corseted waist. Black lace cupped her breasts, and the corset nudged them upwards, tastefully yet tastily. Or at least that is how he now remembered it, although much later it was to become an image he couldn't bear to look at. It never left his head completely. It was too deeply engraved. He couldn't do anything about that but he learned to stop opening the digital copy on his computer. He renamed the photo, putting the letter Z before her name so it would never appear near the top of directories. He'd never see the name by accident. He'd have to scroll down to see it.

The black corset set off pale skin that he learned later became deep, dark brown after the slightest exposure to Central American sun. Long sylphine arms. A pianist's fingers resting on her lap. A ballerina's neck. Haughty nose, or maybe just a proud one, and long black hair pinioned with hair sticks. Her hair suggested geisha, but only for a moment. In the next second he realized this must be a representation of an Egyptian princess, a princess from thousands of years past, ruling over thousands, with dark, dark eyes that never blinked.

A mutual friend swore years later that she told him she was a Moroccan Jew, but she wasn't. She was Canadian, although for the longest time he thought she was American, born in Maplewood, New Jersey. She once even told him she was born in Romania and brought to New York as a child. She never said she had Gypsy blood but he liked to believe she did, although it contradicted that first image he'd seen of her. Even when she smoked a cigarette, she was still ancient Egyptian royalty. He often liked to wonder what her old soul had once been up to, even when, for a period of years later, he hated her.

What she was, he and the mutual friend agreed, was the best, most sensual dominatrix they had ever met. Until meeting her, he thought he would grow old reminiscing endlessly about the greatest World Series games in history. Instead, had he survived until old age, it would have turned out to be that dominatrix in particular, and perhaps all the dommes he met later.

As long as he looked at that particular photo of the Egyptian princess — there were other photos on the site, which he also tried to animate by staring hard at them for minutes on end — the idea of contacting her seemed inevitable. Deep down, he felt a certainty that denied him any choice.

Yet, seconds later, running roughshod over that certainty was the plodding part of him that denied anything intuitive. The rational part of him was waving an admonishing index finger. If you punch in this stranger's number on your cell you will wash out the bridge between you and the woman you refer to as your girlfriend.

Dial the Egyptian princess's number and he would jettison eleven years of shared existence with someone he didn't really mind. For what? The moment he stopped looking at the photograph on the screen, he realized he didn't know.

Maybe his bellyaching was no more than a bad habit born of mindless repetition. People did that to themselves, compulsive complainers who wouldn't recognize a sunny day if it gave them sunstroke.

The debate lasted for hours and got nowhere. When he presented the case for the defense, he made a lot of the fact that he'd made it on his own in life. He worked for himself, and that made him freer and less beholding than most people. And, on average, he made a get-by living. As far as he knew, no one hated him, even after a half-century on earth.

The prosecution's case was simple: the defendant had let himself grow numb to life.

When he got tired of circles, his mind limped into limbo. It was then that little flickers of vaguely remembered sensations and imaginings appeared, flashing like pin pricks in the dark, popping up here, disappearing, and popping up somewhere else, sometimes closer to the forefront of his mind, sometimes more distant, like the flashing dots in a field of vision test.

The image of this young woman, all by its inanimate self, was brightening those flickers of light, lifting the fog that was obscuring a vague and never-explored urge that had been toying with him on and off as long as he could remember. Sometimes it simply entered his mind and he would play with it for a while. Other times he'd see a woman on the street, or on a cinema screen, who would suddenly blow on this undefined urge, and like a dying ember it would start to glow. These women didn't necessarily resemble each other physically, but they triggered the same response. It was as if they knew him, or something about him, but he didn't know them. Was that what happened when he chanced upon the image of the Egyptian princess? He could only wonder.

He wanted to tell himself that calling the young dominatrix couldn't possibly end life as he knew it. He'd see her, see what all the temptation was about and carry on as before with his everyday life. But instinct kept poking its nose in when the guards weren't looking, and it told him he was going to go down a very long hole.

Once again, he tugged his eyes away from the screen and told himself he was too old to shed his skin. Leave the ho-hum the way it was. Don't rock the boat. It was low to the water line but it floated. It was real and better than nothing. Despite his age, he felt like a kid who desperately wanted to run away from home and would if only he knew with certainty that he could find his way back in case it got cold outside. How could he consider selling himself out for a pocketful of pixels on a computer screen? Besides, he'd learned it was best to never leave the bar stool unless your foot knew where the floor was.

But even with his eyes off the screen, she, that woman, her image, they were still tickling the nameless notions inside him. He liked that kind of tickling. It was like champagne. It made him giddy, giddy enough to think a life-altering event would be just what the doctor ordered. He wanted to transform his life. There was no doubt about that, none. It had to be done.

However when he looked outwards and cast his eyes around his room, the same small Chelsea flat he'd occupied for almost twenty years, he realized he had no idea what he wanted to be transformed into. If he did, he could tinker away at it quietly over time with nobody being the wiser. But he didn't know, and he didn't have a hell of a lot of time. Perhaps he would have to be shoved over a cliff and come to in some kind of Shangri-La-like valley, the kind that sometimes took shape in the bottom of a glass. If a precipitous cliff wasn't the answer, someone would have to appear out of nowhere and kidnap him, yanking him by the ear. Pretending to kick and scream, he would let himself be propelled out of the bar, out of his living room, or out of the cab he took home some nights when walking was problematic.

A dominatrix. A decision-maker by definition, he

thought. The buck stops there. Who better to shove him over a cliff? She would pick up the pieces and reassemble them for her own ends.

As he stared at the laptop screen for the thousandth time, he realized that handing over the controls was the last true craving left to him, one he hadn't even known really existed until he saw her image.

A daydreamer, yes, but nearly always pragmatic, and always blind to any notion of destiny, he assumed he had controlled most of what happened in his life. He did not practice a profession that migrated to money, but he had the control to teach himself to never seriously dream of wealth or the things it could buy. When he had money he spent most of it and felt relieved for having done so. No money, no decisions to make, no temptations to urgently hog tie and turn his back on.

If his life was running out of gas, he was responsible. He knew he held those controls. He was at the wheel. What he would rarely concede, and this only while drinking, was that while he may indeed be at the wheel, he didn't steer very well. The only corrective action he tended to take in life was to duck. He never quite figured out how to step out of the line of fire, or boldly dash to the top of a new hill with new horizons. He laid low as a rule. Very occasionally, during some particularly messed-up period when life was exceeding his limits, he'd complain that he didn't elect this life, and he wished someone, for Christ's sake, would seize upon his record of mismanagement and vote him out of office. "Here! Take the goddamn wheel. Let me squeeze over to the passenger side. Move! Move!"

Yes, he thought, that's what he was craving more than anything. Someone, take me for a ride. Then cha-ching. Why not pay someone to drive?

Suddenly he realized why he couldn't take his eyes off the woman on the screen.

CHAPTER 4

Contact

HE first contacted her by email, as she requested on her dominatrix website. She wanted to know about her prospective clients: their sex, their fantasies, their expectations, their limits, their experience in the BDSM world, their cleanliness, their sobriety, their manners. The queries were presented in a form on her site. Copy it into an email message, fill it in and send. If you do not receive a reply in the next few weeks, the instructions read, it means I am not interested in seeing you. Do NOT try to change my mind.

It was not until much later that he learned how impossible it was to change her mind.

On a humid Saturday night in early September, intermittent rain softened the sound of traffic outside his window as he began to fill in her application form. Within minutes, he had run out of room. He did several rewrites, starting afresh, but concision could not contain nearly a lifetime of murky imaginings and frustrated desires that were coming into sharp focus only now, as he typed. He was coming face to face with his fantasies in black and white on the screen of his laptop. He felt an erection beginning.

As he usually did whenever he felt happy, sad, angry or excited — in short whenever he realized he had a pulse — he got up to pour himself a drink. A joint would have been healthier but he had never smoked and the idea of smoke in his lungs evoked childhood nightmares of suffocating.

As he was filling in the form, a passing thought came back a second time and gave him pause. He sipped his Scotch. As he began to debate the thought, his erection subsided, but the thought didn't. What, he wondered, would his solitary life be like if acting out his fantasy ended up killing the fantasy? Quashed it, squashed it. Smithereens are forever. What if he couldn't for a moment tolerate the pain he had dreamed of receiving from the hand of a beautiful woman? He saw himself tied hand and foot to a bench being chastised by Egyptian royalty. The voices in his head simultaneously sounding "yay" and "nay way, man" were so numerous they amounted to hubbub, an audience, thumbs up and thumbs down as his Egyptian Princess flailed away, not breaking a sweat, lost in the measured rhythms of strap and paddle that ratcheted up her own pleasure. The young princess's lips betrayed a slight smile but her dark eyes were bold and solemn, a regard appropriate to an affair of state.

Life took flight so easily in fantasy.

Drink in hand, he sat down again before his laptop. He reread the information he had entered into the form. He was verbal, too verbal, always was, especially at the wrong times, so much so he suspected he would demand to make a speech before going through with a dare to bungee jump, or while hunched at the open cargo door of a Cessna when the time came to graduate from skydiving class. A simple "goodbye" would not suffice. If he kept talking kismet would just have to wait.

If his Egyptian Princess truly wanted to know who

it was requesting permission to come aboard, he would tell her. Two hours, several Scotches and five thousand words later, he closed his laptop. He had not stepped off the edge, he had not hit Send. Instead he lay on his bed and masturbated. He drifted off to sleep with the thought that he was a new man.

. . .

The description of his fantasies that had tumbled out the night before stood up well in the morning light. Hemingway would have been proud, not because of the writing but because he had kept his mouth shut until he was sober.

She will never read all that, he thought as he fiddled with the text, but that wasn't what mattered at this moment. The excitement last night was that he was pre-paring to step out of the Cessna. The excitement this morning was the suspicion that self-discovery might be blinking back at him from between the lines. Although he had written word after word with more pauses for a drink refill than for thought, there remained a cogency about it all this morning. Had he somehow flushed out his real self? When was the last time a keeper thought, a shiny silver bullet of insight, had remained lodged in his mind the morning after? No, this morning he knew he was onto something that promised change.

He opened his Internet browser and called up her page again. Absurdly, as he looked at her photo, he felt he was getting to know her. It was as if they'd spent all of yesterday evening together and were now sharing crois-sants and café au lait for the first time. He switched back to his email program. He then realized the feeling of familiarity was derived entirely from the mini daydreams that imposed themselves between keystrokes the night before, constructions fabricated with eager projections about a complete stranger whose gaze at the moment of the photo was fixed somewhere far beyond the camera's field of focus, and certainly not on him.

Abruptly, he pushed back his chair and got up. Rather than hit Send, he decided to bask a while longer on the sunny plane of being where possibilities rank higher than immediate realities. Because it was morning, when his mind tended to be sharpest, he poured his first drink of the day. He wanted to experience his newly discovered self rather than think about it. Scotch was a nearly sure antidote to thought, much faster and far less fragile than meditation. In fact, meditation irritated the hell out of him.

When he awoke in the late afternoon, while on his way from sofa to bathroom, he hit Send. By now, he was too mind dead to believe the email would lead to anything. He'd still be him tomorrow morning. He brushed his teeth and turned on the TV. Maybe he'd order in Chinese later. At the moment, decisions of any kind were not on the menu.

After sending the message to her, he kept his hopes in check by telling himself his overture likely would fall on deaf ears. Nobody has ever written a song about keeping the lid on anything, on hope, love, despair. Sinatra would have scoffed at the idea. But that's what he knew he must do. Anything that was truly desirable in life remains unattainable. By their late twenties that's what almost everyone suspects. In their late thirties they get morose about it, and in their forties, sane people conclude that second best will do just fine. I'm OK, you're OK, care for a drink? You had to keep the lid on that crock pot of experiences thrown together over the years. Keep the lid on and pray that, allowed to simmer, they would eventually impart flavor and life to one another, turn the whole mess into a hearty stew, rich enough to make you forget it was concocted from commonplace ingredients. Take the lid off prematurely and the flavor evaporates, the stew dries up.

If this stunning dominatrix replied, he thought, the experience would not end up in the crock pot. Even if she said no, not interested in you or your fantasies, it would not be a commonplace experience, at least for someone with his track record. It would go down as the first step of a walk on a marginally wild side.

To be realistic he had to also accept that she might not reply at all. Maybe people with time on their hands and enough money to pay for a domain name weren't at all what their Internet sites said they were. Maybe they just wanted to see what people admit to desiring, and have a little laugh at their expense. Maybe his chosen one (he had done his research before stumbling upon her) didn't look at all like her pictures. Maybe she was doing a PhD in post-Kinsey kink and wanted to mine people like him, who never would have dreamed of adding kinky to their CV.

Afternoon turned into evening and vanished without him leaving any trace of having lived those hours, not even a scribble, a note to self, the beginnings of a grocery list. He hadn't dirtied a dish. On the old steamer trunk he used as a coffee table, the magazine article on therapeutic uses of music, which he started to read several days earlier, lay still open at the first page. At some point he had fallen asleep once again on the sofa, dressed. Though he had been in a deep sleep, a single ping-like sound from his computer woke him. Just as his unconscious could jostle him awake seconds before the alarm clock sounded, it could ignore the all-night traffic outside his window yet detect something as muted as a mail notification from his computer.

For a moment, he lay on his left side, motionless but with his eyes open, letting the shadows in the room reveal the familiar shapes that would orient him. His first thought was that he should have eaten. He felt weak. His second thought sprung him upright. He looked at the laptop on the desk to his right. The screensaver flashed the time in six-inch-high figures, 2:13 a.m. Suddenly he needed badly to have a piss, but he stopped at the computer anyway. He jabbed his middle finger at the track pad to banish the screensaver. The mail program appeared. Even on his worst days he emptied his inbox before drinking seriously, before going to bed. Less to wade through on a fragile morning after. He leaned as far forward as his bursting bladder would allow, hoping to decipher the sender of the email. A blur. His right hand swept the desk in search of his glasses. It collided with a glass of water, not knocking it over, but spilling some of its contents. He couldn't hold it any longer and quick-stepped his way to the bathroom.

As he washed his hands and face afterwards, his one and only thought was that rejection was waiting for him in the living room. She'll say simply no, she'll say there are enough flakes in her life without him, she'll say she's not accepting new clients, she'll say she likes 'em younger, she'll give him shit for imposing a novella on her, which she didn't bother to read, it earning him automatic dismissal on the grounds of inconsideration.

Staring at himself in the mirror, he decided to catch his breath and march to the scaffold in a dignified manner. Perhaps prepare some coffee to sip on the way. Berlioz's *Symphonie Fantastique* started to play in his mind, but he quickly rejected the temptation to listen further. The march to the scaffold was almost heroic, patently, absurdly melodramatic in his situation. A simple *no* from an absolute stranger did not require a soundtrack. Grinding the coffee beans drowned out the vestiges of Berlioz. He forced himself to remain in the kitchen until the water had come to a boil and the coffee had brewed.

At last he sat down at his laptop. He still couldn't find his glasses. Probably waking his neighbors in the apartment below, he twisted his chair around without getting up first. Not wanting to put the light on, he slowly felt his way over the top of the trunk. His fingers found the glasses. Putting them on, he turned back to the computer.

Hell. The sender's name, it wasn't the dominatrix's. If it were daytime, he would have quickly deleted it as junk mail and moved on. But it was 2:30 in the morning and it was the only message in his inbox. He was up, awake, a whole pot of coffee awaited. He took a sip and clicked.

CHAPTER 5

Clues

I must thank you, sincerely, for your lengthy response to my questions...they usually get nothing but the most short and succinct replies.

I am most interested in your fetishes, unitards/tights and spanking as well..you need not fear being ridiculed or hysteria- I don't need to raise my voice to make you obey.

Sadly, I only own one piece of clothing that could be considered a unitard...and it's more of a body suit of lingerie than anything else. So, if you would like me to wear a unitard, you will have to choose one you like and gift it to me. And boots...well i have boots that stop just below the knee, so if that isn't satisfactory...well... you get my drift.

I extended my vacation- (i'm having too much fun here) so I shan't be back in new york until the thirtieth of september.

If you would like we can set up something upon my

return or schedule something now for that day.

Again, I thank you for your honesty and candidness.

It's always appreciated.

His Egyptian Princess had signed the email with what he decided to call her *nom de fouet*, her professional name. Later, it became a name he could not bear to pronounce, or hear others use, and even long after she stopped working as a professional dominatrix her name still had a haunting habit of forming on strangers' lips in the BDSM world.

As for her real name, he had been able to guess it before they even met face to face. At the time she received his email, she was out of town on vacation, in San Francisco, functioning, for the most part, unless opportunity presented itself, in vanilla mode. Inadvertently, she had replied to him from a personal email account. The sender's name he saw on his screen was a cleverly playful but transparent corruption of her actual name. It was years later when he first told her he had known her name all along. She was horrified, not because he knew it — they had liked each other instinctively and become friends early on — but out of fear that she had made the same mistake with other submissive suitors. She thanked him for not telling her at the time, sparing her years of worrying that vanilla friends and family knew her secret.

She was in no way ashamed of what she did — it was but one of her two selves, she said — but she never ceased to be amazed by people's reactions to the fact that she loved tying people up and toying with their pain threshold. She became aroused to varying degrees most of the time, as did some of her paying victims. Few were the ones who, once initiated, didn't return to her or some other professional woman on a fem-domme pedestal. Yet among the few people, mostly girlfriends, she confided in, revulsion appeared on the most unexpected faces, among them a young, pretty and defiantly free-minded stripper and tripper. The wall that woman built separating vanilla and kink was high. If there was such a thing as zoning regulations in a community of friends and acquaintances, the stripper's wall was in violation.

Contrary to her domme name, her real name had become one he suspected he would utter aloud or silently, with a virtuosic range of intonations, at least once a day for the rest of his life. No soundtrack would have to accompany the utterance. He rejected any notion that he was sliding into melodrama territory.

She had written that she would be back in New York on the "thirtieth of september." That left him three weeks to contemplate his dream role before stepping on her stage. The impending realization of what had been weightless and full-blown in fantasy meant parsing the role he would soon be playing on that stage. To do that, he needed to flesh out the character she had become in his mind.

She sounded anything but mercenary, but that appearance is easily enough manufactured before the prospect of new business. If the Internet picture was recent, he knew she was young, and the email seemed to confirm it. She was articulate but had a young person's disdain for punctuation and capitalization. She was informal in a friendly way yet felt comfortable dropping a haughty "shan't" into the equation he was trying to solve. It did, however, suggest determination and command. She knew what she wanted. She was not someone to be swayed easily about anything. He would have to be on his best behavior. She could send someone packing in very few words, polite words. She could dominate without raising her voice. All to the good.

He moved on to the next clue. What was he to make of the phrase "the thirtieth of september." People whose formative years were spent in Internet chat were too impatient for full sentences. They embraced ellipses, fast-forwarding to the next thought or some irresistible digression that couldn't wait for a paragraph of its own.

They wore abbreviations and acronyms as naturally as freckles. They did not spell out "thirtieth," ever. And more often than not, "september" would be "sept." She wanted to impress her prospective client, he concluded. She wanted to show she could handle "old-speak" when the occasion called for it.

Years later, her use of language was one of the first things to jump from memory. She did speak well, although her writing always slipped into texter-spell. She had heaps of vocabulary at her disposal, which perfectly suited an appearance that was fine-boned, delicate and sophisticated even in T-shirt and jeans. What quite delighted him, though, was something that seemed spontaneous at the moment but in time betrayed itself as a habit. For her, the issuing of an emphatic "fuck" was a daily imperative. And she did not care who was within earshot. Bad girl, bad girl. He never knew what she was going to do.

As September wore on, his step grew lighter. He knew he was walking in the right direction.

As he awaited her return to New York, he continued to find his own history revealing itself as if written by someone who knew him better than he did. The nameless notions that had once drifted through his mind like mini-moons in search of something to orbit were rapidly gaining definition. He knew now there was almost a lifetime of inevitability about the urge to see someone like a dominatrix, a domme. He could now name the notions and file them away for later when he hoped to have enough pieces of the jigsaw puzzle to prove his life had some shape or direction.

He now knew that while his recently revealed desire to be dominated by a woman was fueled by elaborate subtleties, his willingness to fall off a cliff sprung from his groin. He longed for lashings of libido but nothing did the trick. What was left of his libido couldn't rescue him from dull sex. When he was young, libido was shorthand for being alive. Now it needed rescuing.

Other mental files had begun to grow fat from the moment he made the decision to contact her. A key turned in his memory and a door opened. From that point on the urge to relinquish control rode a wave of domination and spanking fantasies tossed about with images of his body and soul being plundered by women who could possess him in an instant. They stripped off everything until he became an object, their object.

He acknowledged now that he had loved fem-domme images since adolescence. Before he even knew the term, he had zeroed in on them like a heat-seeking penis, but with a difference. These physically beautiful and beautifully disdainful women were a challenge then, creatures to conquer. If he had to spank them to tame them, he would. Then, his ire up, he'd give them the best fuck they'd ever had. It was never making love. It was fucking. How had he forgotten those fantasies? Was he that old?

He had maintained that conqueror myth about himself for years, astonishingly forgetting that the first time he ever had sex it was the woman, a little wisp of a thing, who took him, all six feet of him. She really took him, coming out of nowhere on a Saturday afternoon at her apartment, one room, with a single bed that doubled as a sofa, one chair, a small table, and an upright piano.

She had just faultlessly played the first four bars of the bridge to a bossa nova song popular at the time, *Desafinado*. He had said he loved that bridge, and her reply was to get up from the bed and sit down at the piano. Without the slightest hesitation, she ripped off the four bars and a little more, her ear invincible. It was an ear she shared with two brothers, both professional jazz musicians in Boston. Not long afterwards, she fucked him. She initiated, she finished, she conquered. What had just happened? He didn't say that aloud, but he certainly wondered then. He was so naive he didn't know whether that's the way it usually worked between men and women.

Despite all the wondering at the time, he never ended

up doing the math he was doing now in his life. The number of times he had truly conquered a woman, from the beginning of the scene until curtain, across three decades, equaled zero. He had had his moments in the topsy-turvy heat of passion, but those moments were reactive for the most part. When he started to do the calculation, basically to ascertain how tall he stood in the saddle, he honestly thought his conquering side would dominate. When he put the calculator aside he realized he was the saddle. A bottom, not a top, as he learned to say later in BDSM-speak.

Though he was seventeen when the tiny twenty-three-year-old piano player introduced him to sex, it was the only taste he was to have for years to come. It had happened out of the blue. He had no alphabetized filing system of experiences to place it in. He had had no experience of the heart, although he thought he was eager for it. He wanted to be a grown-up as soon as possible and he thought the faster he could accumulate trunks full of emotional successes and failures, the faster he would be entitled to claim the mantle of adulthood.

Though it was not an experiment he could share with his peers because of his choice of music, he realized early that he could emulate adult emotions by combining Scotch and music. He had laid claim to an album belonging to his parents. They praised his taste because the music was of their era, not his. It was a Frank Sinatra album.

When he sat in his attic room and listened to it, the stolen Scotch slipped down his throat barely noticed as he slipped easily into the image on the album cover. He wore Sinatra's trench coat and hat, and sat at the bar, glass of whisky in one hand, cigarette in the other, at quarter to three in the morning, and asked a barman apparently named Joe to set 'em up yet again. The album title alone was so emo, multiplied by a factor greater than his mental computing capabilities, there wasn't the slightest possibility of mentioning it in conversation with his contemporaries. *No One Cares.* No album would ever bear that title again. The world had become too cynical by half when talking about feelings.

Before he had any experience with life worth communicating let alone memorializing in song, a time when in fact he really didn't know a damned thing about life, he judged that Sinatra had nailed it, life. Over time, as the needle re-engraved that LP, he learned how to deepen the appreciation of life with Scotch, and his teenage self, impatient to grow up, began to long for the day he would be jilted and jaded, and forever have the right to wear melancholy like an undershirt. "Been there, man." Adults on the next bar stools would look him in the eye and say, "I think we played on the same team on that one, bud," and offer to buy the first round. "Life's a bitch, ain't it." No answer required. A barely detectable nod or two would do.

In later years he wondered whether he had programmed himself too well. Each time he lost at love, or even unromantic sexual attraction disguised as love, the drama was increasingly not worth the price of admission. It afforded him no cachet with his bar friends. His experiences were all too commonplace. For a while, as the years went by, he occasionally contemplated the notion that the sheer number of his relationship failures might eventually warrant him a higher bar stool than the men and women in his entourage, although they were falling by the wayside with time. But the subject bored everyone, himself included. Ballads and Old Blue Eyes lost their appeal.

By the time he entered his fifties, it was as if his top had stopped spinning. When it had been spinning fast enough to be perfectly perpendicular, it looked like it was made of silver. It glittered. But when it started to slow down the glitter gave way to splotches of silver paint that appeared solid only at high speed. His top wobbled drunkenly from diminished momentum, then fell on its side. A couple of horizontal, lop-sided pirouettes later, it ceased to move. It was in the shadows of this interregnum that the image of his Egyptian Princess first appeared, on the cusp of condescending, but attentive and so beautiful, and so welcomed.

. . .

On September 27, he received another email from her:

Change of plan. Have to see someone in Montreal before going home... not really sure when I'll be back in NYC. Caught a seat sale on a direct flight from SF to Montreal...just tooooooo good to pass up. Love that city. Not as much as SF because of the fucking winter though. Sorry if I've messed up your plans. I do want to make a session happen soon. Be patient. Be well. I'll let you know.

Unable to hold his breath any longer, he hailed a cab and went to a liquor store. Walking there would have taken barely fifteen minutes. He had not noticed it was a beautiful morning.

. . .

He drank all afternoon, passed out and dreamed he was drowning in a wave pool surrounded by scores of shrieking children. His legs pedaled and his arms conducted a silent orchestra but he couldn't stay afloat.

When he awoke for good around 11 that evening, he drank as much ice-cold water as he could gulp down. When he felt the advance of nausea, he stopped. He turned on the television. Jay Leno was interviewing someone he didn't recognize. K felt short of breath. His rib cage weighed him down. It barely budged when he tried to breathe. He lay back down and the weight was gone. If he stayed still, and calm, he could breathe.

The young man on the screen was an actor, a Canadian, and Leno was saying, "Montreal, you know, it's just got to be the most beautiful city on the continent." The actor, now living in L.A., agreed.

K hadn't thought of Montreal since the city lost its Major League Baseball team. In a day or two she would be flying to that city. He tried to picture her on the plane, wearing the same black corset with the little bits of black lace cupping her breasts. She was on the starboard side of the plane, her head turned to look out the window. In his mind, he was in the seat behind her, and if he pressed his head against the cabin wall, he could once again see her right profile. This time she blinked, not often, but now and again.

Too hungover to sustain the flight of imagination, he clicked through channels. He had arrived at CNN. He forgot about his Egyptian Princess immediately. Katrina filled the screen. All night he watched, and cried. He didn't know for whom. People clung to rooftops and tree limbs, praying they wouldn't be carried away to their deaths. As he stared at the New Orleans nightmare, he treaded water, too. It was what he had done with most of his life.

By daylight, he had recovered enough to go out for breakfast. He felt empty, indifferent, not in a hostile way, just too tired to care about anything, not even his Egyptian Princess. His depressions always outlasted his hangovers.

CHAPTER 6

Obsessions

DURING the next week, fully recovered, he thought of his Egyptian Princess too often. He knew that, but anything that filled the void was not to be judged. He had never been truly obsessed with his current girlfriend, just unconsciously addicted to a need for female company, and not just for sex. If he had to choose between living the rest of his life with either his male friends or his female friends, and with no sex involved, he suspected he would quickly choose to die with women.

The undiagnosed addiction to his current girlfriend had been a long time forming. It required months of gestation. They had met at a party, collapsed into bed just before sunrise and had barely conscious sex. Later that day, after tentatively drinking half a glass of orange juice, she said "Call me." He suspected that she too was merely assuming that the sex had been at least OK. He was glad she wrote her name, Alana, below the phone number she passed to him as he stepped out into the daylight.

On this early September day, hearing a plane overhead, he wondered whether it was Montreal-bound from San Fran. Again, he tried to picture her sitting at a window seat, in profile, eyes right. This time he tried not to breathe as he pushed his head toward the space between the back of her seat and the wall of the cabin, coming within inches of her face. Suddenly he realized it couldn't be her flight. If it was, it was on a latitudinally challenged flight path from the West Coast, Montreal being virtually due north of New York City. He thought of the pilot who once overshot Minneapolis by a couple of hundred miles. That flight originated in California as well. The whole crew missed the target. Did it have something to do with California, or had they been obsessing about something, like him?

Today he was working on deadline, a ridiculously tight one. But he still found time to direct his browser back to her page as if to make sure she was still there. He had bookmarked the page as Egypt, as if it were a travel destination. His client called for the second time that morning wanting to know when he would get his translation. It had been promised for yesterday at the end of business. Clients never understood that while a translator might knock off three hundred words in an hour, some terms, one single word, could take an hour or more to track down. This client was a new, much-needed one since the recession.

"By noon?" the client pleaded.

At that very same moment the browser search for "Egyptian Princess" took 0.14 seconds to produce 439,000 hits.

"Yeah, by noon, absolutely. But I can't work if I'm on the phone. OK?"

Why was he using a euphemism to name his bookmark? Should he create another one to sit next to it on the bookmark bar called Skiing, Colorado? Visitors were rare. Why didn't he name it dominatrix? Or Trix? Or domme? Or spank me? Ouch! Or Brave New World?

BNW? He liked that one, but then he realized he was mixing up Huxley and Dvorak. He had meant the symphony. He knew he had to see her. Hers was the new world. There was no stopping now. The motor was running. Like a lawnmower whose motor turns over on the thirteenth angry, sweating yank, you don't turn it off to go back to the house in search of your sunglasses.

Almost a week later, he still thought of the email he wrote her as the most liberating thing he'd probably ever done. When she shelved their rendezvous plans in order to go to Montreal, he immediately started drinking, but with a difference. He was determined to keep his hopes up. After several drinks, he actually gave himself a pep talk, out loud, right there in his living room, which was also the only real room in his apartment, apart from a bathroom and a five-by-eight-foot kitchen. If he started to get sullen, he stood up and tried not to sound like Tom Hanks as he exclaimed, "There's no crying in baseball!"

He could not have known that in the coming months his Egyptian Princess was to astound him by declaring she couldn't stand Tom Hanks as an actor. Those were her words. She didn't say, "I don't like Tom Hanks." She said, "I can't stand Tom Hanks." She often said things that made him wonder whether she was just yanking his chain.

"You must be the only person on the planet who doesn't like Tom Hanks," he replied. After she later shut him out of her life, the only Hanks movie he would allow himself to watch was *In a League of Their Own*, mostly for the drunken admonition about crying. Damn straight.

He finished the translation, prepared his bill and sent the two documents off as email attachments. In a spreadsheet record he kept of projects, he boldfaced the date the invoice was sent. It was next to the Date Paid column. He wanted to keep an eye on it. New clients in a big hurry for a first translation were often the slowest to pay. Some just disappeared. Not often, but it happened. He couldn't insist on a partial payment in advance when the client pleaded at 9 a.m. that he needed the document translated for a meeting just four hours away with his company's biggest client.

It had been years since he'd actually met a client. Face-to-face encounters had gone the way of faxed and couriered documents. Digitize or die, a bumper sticker if there ever was one. The arrangement suited him. Most of the time he found meetings awkward, afraid his business-like armor would crack and reveal the existential vagrant underneath.

When he had work, he had learned to plunge into it, often before dawn, praying to make headway before thoughts crept in and sent his mind trolling for a new direction in life. When he had a lot of work, he never drank. The days at the keyboard passed quickly enough. Every few hours he popped up his calculator application and computed his earnings to that point, number of words translated multiplied by his per word rate, or number of hours by his hourly rate. One day — it was still a record — he made just over $1,000 working eighteen and a half consecutive greed-driven hours for a client willing to pay the emergency rate applied to night work and weekends. The client also was willing to excuse the occasional terminological sloppiness. The main thing was that the document be comprehensible for an English-speaking client.

A few more days like that and he wouldn't have to worry when the next project might come his way. However, until now, until having allowed the image of an Egyptian Princess to animate his all-but-dead libido, he had no idea what he could spend surplus money on. He lived cheaply, to the extent that was possible in New York, as a buffer against obsessing about the next contract.

He turned off his phone. The invoice he had just emailed would pay more than half the rent for his fourth-floor walk-up in Chelsea. It was rent-controlled. He had lucked into it when a cousin decided to follow a woman to France. He never heard from him again, but three years later a mutual friend reported having seen him in a line at the Shake Shack on Eighth. He had apparently lost the woman and gained weight.

He had some thinking to do that afternoon. In truth, the thinking would likely be fantasizing. But, God, he was dying to be decisive about something. Do something irrevocable. Take a leap. Wake up tomorrow and know, without looking, which way his compass pointed.

That evening, only mildly drunk, he figured he had just the thing. Instead of waiting for her to return from Montreal, he would arrange to be baptized into a world encapsulated in one of the English language's most space-efficient abbreviations, BDSM. Each part of the definition seemed to be coupling with the next: bondage and discipline (BD), domination and submission (DS), sadism and masochism (SM). Tomorrow, maybe. His Egyptian Princess would not find him a virgin. She would not find him tentative in yielding to her ways, not that he really knew yet what they were. She could plunge right in and top away to her heart's content. After a couple more drinks, he was thinking she would look at him as the find of the decade. He would be her very own jewel of the Nile, or jewel of the Hudson, or the East River, or the Harlem River for that matter. Putty, putty, putty. Pure joy, she would think. Shit, I'd beat his ass for nothing!

What did his ass look like? As he got drunker, he realized he didn't really know. It was one of those things you think you know but don't. He had glimpsed it in profile but never the way she would see it. He stood up and walked to the tiny bathroom. He dropped his pants to his ankles and tried to turn around far enough to look at his ass in the mirror above the sink. There wasn't room to back away far enough to see his ass. He would need something to stand on. He had an armchair and a desk chair, but even the latter would not fit between sink and toilet.

Dictionaries. He had lots, some two to three inches thick. He took an armful from their shelves in the living room and piled them on the black-and-white tiled floor of the bathroom. When they were three layers high, he placed his right foot on top. The height should be sufficient to view his ass. But as he raised his other foot, the left, the glossy dust jack of the *Oxford Concise Dictionary, 2001*, ripped, sending his foot knifing painfully into the side of the shower stall. With his pants hobbling him at the ankles, he would have fallen to the floor had he not managed somehow to grab the rim of the sink on the way down.

He sat on the toilet seat until the throbbing subsided. He no longer felt high from the Scotch. He no longer felt up to juggling all the images he'd concocted for his new life. In less than a minute, they had popped like soap bubbles. Without standing up, he pulled his pants off the rest of the way, dropping them to the floor to his left, half in the kitchen. He then stacked the dictionaries in front of him, crumpling up the torn *Oxford* dust jacket and tossing it near the kitchen garbage bin.

After climbing into bed he turned on the TV with the remote. He thought it would turn his mind off but it managed only to subdivide his thoughts, like an avaricious real estate developer. Separately, none seemed so grand anymore. The inspiring vista of his re-invented self had disappeared, all because after five decades of life he didn't know you can't see your own ass.

CHAPTER 7

While Waiting

K WAS standing at the kitchen counter, phone braced to his ear. He stopped frothing the hot milk for his first coffee of the morning when the answering machine kicked in on the other end of the line. Mature female voice, measured, scripted phrases:

"You've reached your final destination. This is where you get off. We are sorry to inform you that the station-master had to deal with a late arrival last night and is still sleeping. Please call back later for updated arrival and departure information."

Cute. Sexy.

He whipped up the milk some more.

The second number also ran afoul of an answering machine. Why was he calling dominatrixes this early in the morning?

"If you think the number you've just dialed is really the number you wanted to dial, that means you have not completed Step One. If you've got my number, you've seen my webpage. If you've seen it, you know I don't accept phone calls from people I don't know. If you want to know me, fill out the application form online and I might call you. Then we can move on to Step Two."

The third answering machine message was shorter. A smoker's voice:

"Hi, it's me. It's too friggin' early. Go masturbate. Do something. Later, please."

Before crashing the night before, he had had the presence of mind to scribble a note on the small pad of yellow lined paper he kept on his desk. He no longer used the desk for working. Though his posture suffered, his endurance was greatly enhanced when he worked from his old wingback chair, using a TV table as a desk. As he wrote the note, his hand paid no heed to the lines, but his words were legible the next morning: "Line up domme. Talk to Alana." One. Two. That's all. Do those two things and the sluice gates would clank open. He'd ride the current to a new life.

It wasn't too early to call Alana but, unlike last night, he wasn't sure what he wanted to say to her.

. . .

If he was indeed going to start afresh at quarter past mid-life, trading in something that was too well known for an unknown, it seemed sensible to make a clean slate of things, jettison the safety nets. Yes, that was what Alana represented to him, a safety net, woven haphazardly over the years.

He couldn't remember exactly when they met eleven years ago. The hangover of that first night lasted several days. Out of politeness, and an uncertain curiosity about what really happened between them, K had called Alana the following evening. She sounded as rough as he felt.

"I'm OK," she said. "Yeah, yeah. Not the first time," she joked about the hangover.

But she didn't say much beyond that. He had been hoping she might say something descriptive about the night, even, "Hey, man, I guess that was kind of fucked up." She would laugh, and he would laugh, and he'd say something like, "OK. Just checking. See you around." And that would be that.

But no. She offered nothing more and he filled the eventual silence with a pathetic, "I'll call." It was stated more as a question. Though he was hungover still, and had virtually no memory of the night with her, his male ego needed to hear some degree of female approval. It didn't have to be, "Yeah, I'd like that." He would have settled for a "Whatever." Not affirmative, not negative.

Instead she said nothing for a long second, then "Ciao."

She was pretty, which complicated things. He never got a permanent feel for how much he found the rest of her interesting. At times, even now after what constituted the longest relationship of his life, more than a decade, he found her surprising and courageously off-the-wall. Other times, she seemed mired in the same quicksand he was.

He had been married once in his early twenties. He hadn't bothered to tell his parents until after the fact. His mother was usually incoherent, even at the breakfast table. She was addicted to prescription drugs and cigarettes. Once she burned his cheek while trying to give him a little kiss to send him off to school, forgetting she had a cigarette in her mouth. His father had tuned out his wife so long before, he forgot he also had a son. His father spent little time at home, which was just as well since he was a prick.

The secret marriage lasted less than two years. She split because she wanted children and he didn't. At least that's what she claimed. She went back to California, where she was born. He suspected she was having second thoughts about a boyfriend she'd dumped, someone she had known in high school. His name had come up too often in conversation.

Until he met Alana, relationships never lasted long enough to legitimately be defined that way. They became the norm and he had grown tired of hoping to find something promising. By the time he found Alana, or she found him — he couldn't recall who led, who followed — he no longer had any expectations. After their second or third night together, long after their first meeting, he realized she had at least one habit he found endearing: She promised nothing.

She wasn't the kind of person who smiled a lot, even when being introduced to people for the first time. She always gave the impression she would let you know later whether she approved. Which, to the borderline milquetoast he was becoming, was very much like an order to stop trying to be cool and get off your ass and try to impress me. He hadn't tried in ages.

Later he learned she had an eye akin to an artist's. She drank in impressions, appraising, not judging. And he learned that she did smile from time to time, often at unexpected times, as if surprised that something he said actually dovetailed with her way of seeing the world. But it annoyed him that she didn't praise him, didn't seem to really need him for much of anything. Yet she called occasionally, not as often as he called her, but she did call.

So it was the nice ass, a very nice ass, in fact, and her chestnut eyes that drew him to her door. When he thought of those two features, he could convince himself that it was a normal sexual drive that took him across town and all the way up to the Bronx and not a need for company, not the need to be needed. He knew a reasonable number of people, but his circle of friends was at best half what it was in his late twenties, and half again what it was not so very long ago in his forties.

If he felt more passionately, he might feel some possessiveness about her, but he didn't. The relationship had been going on so long, it didn't feel vulnerable to attack. Besides, he sometimes told himself, where was it written that there was something wrong about hanging with somebody just to hear a familiar voice even though you didn't always listen to the words? Or share a bottle with on a rainy evening, or slouch on a sofa masturbating each other just because any sensation was sometimes a whole lot better than no sensation? At times, he had to admit, there was tenderness in their kisses when the evening came to an end.

They rarely went out. She liked loud music. He didn't. Sometimes he and Alana planned to go out but changed their minds when they got together after work.

"Do you want a drink before we go?" One or the other would ask the question. It wasn't the alcohol or the joint that depleted the desire to go out. Early in the day, a concert sounded exciting. By early evening, tired of having to bear down to fish work demands out of the fast-flowing stream of daydreams and pressing life questions, the prospect of going out would begin to feel much like work.

She was a graphic artist whose job description had morphed into one that didn't even include doodling on the back of envelopes. When the screen printing company hired her at the age of twenty-five, she had visions of discovering her inner Warhol. The company thought her artistic side would come in handy. The company grew but the bright future they painted for her never materialized. Most of her days were spent pricing and purchasing inks. She never once shouted to her friends over the club music: "Hey, guess what I did today!"

Sometimes they joked as one of them poured a second or third drink at her apartment, on what had started out as a club night, that the only time over-priced bar drinks weren't over-priced was when you hoped to score. Endorphins and pheromones and whatever other chemicals that might tango with the cocktail more than made up for the price.

Chase and be chased. That's how they had met, at a party. They scored each other that night. But as they sat on her lumpy sofa years later, he inwardly acknowledged that the memory was scarcely worth toasting since neither could remember the actual moment they met, nor much else about the evening. He suspected the same thought had occurred to her. So by mid-evening, one of them would crumple up the club-listings page in the paper.

Off would come the shoes and they'd just hang. Sometimes they'd make out. But now that the chase was over, all twelve hours or less of it, Alana did all the initiating. Some nights he saw the impatience on her face when he responded with perfunctory caresses, as if he were petting a cat, someone else's cat, just to show he liked cats. Sometimes she would suddenly stop, angry.

"Fuck! I hate my job." she would say, instead of cursing him.

K would be already braced for the blow to his ego, and when it didn't come he would feel relief for himself more than concern for her unhappiness. It wasn't that he didn't care at all. He had become chronically gun shy.

Alana was lonely, too, he suspected, and less independent than when they first met, when he couldn't tell if she gave a damn whether he ever knocked on her door again. Maybe she too dropped casual references now and then to "my boyfriend," the mention serving to at least temporarily plug one of the slow leaks in her existence. Perhaps because she was much younger, he didn't think she felt her ship was in danger of sinking. She wasn't looking to be rescued, and she wasn't looking to set up house, which was a plus in his mind.

The older he got the more he saw his apartment, not that it even had room for two people, as an oxygen chamber. Like a whale surfacing, he'd have to return frequently to breathe.

But even there, alone, he wasn't at peace. As he got older he started to see his existence as a garden hose bought on sale at Wal-Mart. It had more leaks than Alana's. Water barely dribbled out the nozzle now. The problem wasn't Alana, the problem wasn't just getting old, it was everything. All those holes, too many to plug, too much to think about. He was tired of looking at himself.

. . .

When he set eyes on the Egyptian Princess, her eyes fixed, unblinking, on some kind of private eternity, he instantly wanted to see what she saw. There was something out there after all. As dark as her eyes were, they were not dull like the mirror told him his had become. They shone. She wasn't gazing at the same world he was.

He caught himself. He was about to launch feature-length daydreams about a woman he'd never even met. He had other things to do today.

As he finished his last coffee of the morning, he checked his email. His new client from yesterday had written back saying only, "Got it. Tks." That was enough to greatly improve the odds of eventually being paid.

He decided to have breakfast out and think about what he wanted to say to Alana. He hadn't spoken to her in several weeks. When he called after a silence that long, he usually felt he should have a reason to offer, either for not having called, or for calling now. However, this time, he couldn't blurt out on the phone his reason for not having called.

"Hi, Alana," he'd say. "Sorry but I came across this image on the Internet, a woman. She kind of looked like an aristocrat from ancient times, you know, some kind of goddess in an Egyptian temple or palace. She blew me away. Anyway, shit, I think I'm low on battery. Just to finish that thought, it turns out she's really a dominatrix. That's all I've been thinking about, I mean, that's why I haven't called."

As he walked over to Ninth Avenue he found a slightly damp copy of *The Village Voice* clinging to the side of a stoop. He picked it up and took it with him to the diner two blocks from his apartment. There might be something going on at a club, he thought. He could phone Alana and ask if she'd like to go. If she did end up wanting to go, which he hoped she wouldn't, they'd meet downtown and probably go back to her place afterwards. He could tell her about his idea. He would tell her he wasn't dumping her. No, not at all. Just experimenting, he'd say. He'd tell her, "You have to do that every once in a while to make sure you're still breathing."

"I don't even know where the idea came from," he'd add, disclaiming any responsibility. "It was just chance. Was browsing, and bingo..."

By the time the bacon and eggs arrived, he was starting to warm to another idea entirely. What if, he thought, as he used his fork to bulldoze a crescent-shaped space for ketchup at the edge of the home fries, what if Alana had some of the same urges he did, or better yet, complementary ones? The idea had never occurred to him. If he had a lifetime of secrets, albeit almost forgotten, so could she.

When he pushed his plate aside no more than ten minutes later, he was full physically and less hungry emotionally for the new world he had imagined earlier that morning. It was Alana's image that now hovered along the perimeter of his mind, not those of the dominatrixes he was trying to hook up with before seeing the Egyptian Princess.

Alana began looming larger in the silence of his slightly hungover mind. She was not looking directly at him, which was often the case when they were actually in the same room. Right now he wished he could tap her on the shoulder to get her attention and say, "What do you think about S&M?" Get it out, get it over with.

Why leap off the deep end when the shallow end was in sight. Maybe a kinky Alana was the shallow end. Maybe he could become the man he now knew he was, a saddle not the rider, without making waves, without losing her.

As a boy he had dreamed, not just imagined, that he had come into possession of Tom Sawyer's raft. Had he come across it by the shore, lashed to a tree, and stolen it? He could no longer remember. But his body remembered every sensation as he lay on his back under a warm, early-evening sun and drifted downriver. Huck Finn wasn't there either. No one was at the oar, which didn't concern him at all. He trusted the current. He had never felt that way about life again. Now, in real life, he was being taken in a direction not of his own charting. His Egyptian Princess was the current tugging him downriver. If it weren't for her, he would still be on dry land, withering. However before abandoning everything and floating out to sea he owed it to Alana to invite her on board.

He shifted sideways on the booth seat, resting his back against the wall and letting his feet dangle over the end of the bench seat. He sipped a tepid coffee and tried to imagine another Alana. He had never heard her use the word fantasy. He seldom used it either, and he never had with her for the simple reason that his mind was often overrun with them. It was a can he didn't want to open. He had never asked her if there was something else she would like to try for fear that she might take it as a complaint that their sex life simply wasn't fully recharging his battery anymore. The all-conquering male he long ago thought he was would not have hesitated for a second.

Suddenly he knew that the shame of that reality, a man tiptoeing through life, had to be eradicated. He had to decide. And he did. Instead of looking for a professional dominatrix to tide him over and initiate him before the Egyptian Princess returned to New York, he would boldly find out if Alana was the hidden treasure Tom Sawyer was looking for. He knew absolutely that if he didn't find out, he would face a lifetime of wondering what he might have passed up. He would ask her tonight, concert or no concert.

After paying at the counter, he stepped onto Ninth and walked north, thinking. What if she answered with a question:

"What do you mean by try something else?"

Dive in or wade in?

As he approached 34th Street he realized he had left the copy of the newspaper with the club ads in the restaurant. Damn. If they didn't go out first, he might have to jump right in and ask the question without them having had drinks first, or had their senses massaged or, as the case may be, pummeled by club music. Painful physiotherapeutic massage or dental work didn't bother him much. He knew that. But he couldn't tolerate being pummeled by music. He would do it for her, though, tonight, if it opened doors. Hers.

She was funny that way. Part of her would respond to soft and subtle, and part seemed to demand an assault on the senses. Lightly Latin or heavily metal. Both could open her doors, but despite the amount of time he had known her he knew he might as well be trying to read Braille when it came to picking up her signs. Her fault or his? Probably his.

As he walked he began to feel full of purpose. There was a revolution going on inside him. Once the fantasies were integrated into reality, he told himself, as if he were a psychologist who knew what he was talking about, they would become part of the whole instead of all of it. He would have plenty of himself left over to dispense unselfishly. Who knows, he might even be capable of loving somebody.

The judge was skeptical.

He turned at 35th for no particular reason, except maybe to walk into the sun. It was starting to feel warm on his face but it was still low enough in the sky to force him to keep his eyes lowered. They fell on a red newspaper box, *The Village Voice*. He bent down and took one, rolling it like a baton so he could carry it with his fist instead of holding it with his fingers. He was feeling aggressive. He was taking charge. The synchronicity of just then stumbling across the newspaper box didn't escape him. His plan for Alana was on track.

It didn't matter that not one concert listed in the paper appealed to him.

. . .

"Let's do it," Alana said, interrupting K before he had a chance to describe his second and third choices for the evening. "My head's killing me. I need a new job and a drink, not in that effing order."

They met outside Grand Central Station, two blocks from her office. They had time to kill, lots of it. She said she couldn't survive a crowded train ride home to the Bronx just to change, then get sweaty hauling ass all the way back down to the Lower East Side where they'd decided to go for the evening.

She was wearing a short silver skirt, and black leggings which disappeared into ankle boots with a ladder of lacing. As usual, she wore her black faux leather jacket. She'd had her black hair cut since he last saw her. Short and parted. A boy's haircut, completely baring the tattoos that climbed her neck. Her boss had once complained about them, so she had let her hair grow. K liked the long hair, but she looked so different now with the new haircut he felt turned on, or almost, an in-between state that tortured him.

He never knew how to describe his arousal in these situations. Once again he found himself wishing he could get a magnificent erection spontaneously, like an adolescent, right there in the middle of the street, at the mere sight of a woman with presence. Instead, all he felt was a stirring, which he had learned in his forties was more fragile than a soufflé. It was an embarrassment in bed. He or his partner would have to crank it up again. Once inside her, he was often good for a medium-long ride, occasionally attaining pile driver status.

It wasn't a hot day but it was humid. To kill time they walked slowly over to Madison Avenue and south. Alana was not in the mood for subtle and sophisticated, and the Shake Shack at Madison Square Park was her beacon during the twenty-block walk. The line at the stand killed another three-quarters of an hour but eating the monster burger construction and downing a vanilla shake while slouched on a shaded park bench restored her.

Too full to walk, they lay down on the grass. Before doing so, to avoid getting ink stains on her flashing silver skirt, she took K's newspaper and unrolled it. Squatting, she held it down on the ground it and quickly covered it with unused napkins. She had told him to lie down between her and the slight breeze so the napkins wouldn't blow away. As if landing a helicopter, she slowly lowered her ass onto them. As she did, his eyes fell high up her inner thighs, encased in black leggings. Despite being in public, Alana would have welcomed his touch, mostly because he initiated. She didn't know he had a fetish about tights.

As K lay beside her, he delighted in the sudden arousal he felt. But an erection wasn't on the horizon. Fantasies were supposed to enhance arousal, not dampen it. Why were his fantasies botching the job? Or were they? His testosterone levels were just fine, said his doctor. But you might try drinking less, he added, not having the slightest notion of how much his patient actually drank.

"Normally," K told his doctor, "I knock back anywhere from a mickey up to a twenty-sixer per week." A slip of the tongue, he would say if they ever analyzed his liver. He would then have been forced to confess he had meant to describe his daily, not his weekly, consumption. Working for himself meant no boss ever saw him tip-toe into the morning.

He loved looking at women. Artists made women. God got stuck making men. Men often seemed to have been punched out by machines, some of the machines leftovers from the old Soviet Union. Almost every day he saw a woman he could imagine sliding into, just like that, pants and panties down and zippity-doo. And her loving him for it. That was the version of his younger self he had latched on to, stamped and validated in his memory. Certified copy. Let the record show... But he knew now that was a lie. He needed something to hold on to, something workable, as a backdrop to the rest of his life, an image of himself turned on, erect and getting off. Now he was discovering he needed to redefine his sexuality in mid-life. The fantasies were nudging him, sometimes with irritation, impatience, as if he were an overly polite subway rider on a crowded train. Time's running out. Act now or forever hold your dick.

The frustration yielded a thought. Were his fantasies failing to give him an erection because they kept him focused on himself and not his partner? And if so, would they become his ally if he made her part of them? No more secrets. The thought excited him.

Alana had closed her eyes. K propped himself on his elbows. As he looked down at her, he tried to imagine those eyes growing big as he described the fun they'd have tying each other up, getting themselves turned on to the point of bursting, then turned over and paddled. Back to the coda, all eight bars repeated twice, then fading out, rhythm section only, the last dying strokes after orgasm.

"Gotta walk off that burger," Alana announced an hour later. He too was full. He'd stopped fantasizing after the first mouthful of fries and was happy to slip into their usual small talk. Eventually, Alana had dozed off. He felt a chill when he suddenly wondered whether after tonight he'd ever see her again. He wished he weren't sober but he had to be because he had his pitch to make afterwards.

They walked east, starting on 23rd Street and zig-zagging toward the Lower East Side in the vicinity of Rivington Street, to a club called Baby something. He couldn't remember. He picked it from the ads in the paper because he knew Alana liked the band now playing there.

Despite the early hour there was a small line outside,

no doorman in sight. When he got home that afternoon, he had checked the place out online. There were so many bad reviews he wondered whether the good ones were written by ringers, staffers or cousins of the owner. The place also cost more than he liked to pay, from doormen who improvised their prices depending on their mood and the attractiveness of bodies, to the price of drinks. As a real drinker, he long ago realized he would never make enough money to buy his way to even a slight buzz in a New York City bar. If he had to go, he usually arrived already at cruising altitude.

When they got inside, they took a table near the bar. Halfway through their first drink, Alana noticed the band hadn't even begun to set up. The first set was scheduled for 9:30. The DJ upstairs gave no sign of winding down. In fact the volume was spiking. After their first order their waitress never made eye contact, she must have pegged them as nursers, so Alana got up and asked a barman.

"Fuck," she said, dropping back into her chair. "Band's been cancelled," she shouted over the music. "Booked some big party upstairs. DJ's playing for them. Fuck us."

"You think they'd tell you when they let you in," she said as they walked toward the subway. He didn't tell her he'd also read that the staff was famous for not caring. Some online reviews even screamed out in capital letters, BANDS, DON'T PLAY HERE!

Nearly an hour later, they got off the 6 at 138th Street in the Bronx and walked toward Alexander Avenue. The jostling and sway of the train had calmed Alana, like a colicky baby absorbing vibrations on a washing machine.

"What can you do," she said, resigned. It wasn't a question.

K usually stayed overnight when he accompanied her home. He wondered if tonight he might find himself on a downtown train in the early hours of the morning.

CHAPTER 8

After the Bomb

IN ALANA'S eyes, K had dropped a bomb. In his eyes, considering that there had been almost a lifetime of gestation, he had simply laid an egg.

At first she just stared at him, not sure what she was hearing. An ultimatum, a relationship ender? Was he that bored with her and their sex life that he now wanted her to wave a wand and, presto-poof, morph her Bronx studio apartment into a pre-World War II Berlin cabaret, without the catchy music, just tights and paddles and straps and floggers — toys, he called them, as if they were something you'd find next to the Barbie and Ken collections at FAO Schwarz?

Her sofa wasn't long, but there was a wasteland between them. K sat at one end, kitty-cornered to face her but out of arm's reach, defensive. She usually found his face intelligent without being high-brow. Now it appeared Botox dumb and soap-opera defiant. Was this the real him talking?

Suddenly, she pushed herself up from the sofa and strode to the washroom, to the right, off the kitchen, shutting the door behind her and turning on the tap. He got up, too, and took a few steps in the same direction. She thought he was going to stop her to pursue the conversation.

"Let me be. I need a minute. Please!" she had said, hearing him get up off the sofa, but, turning, she realized he only wanted to get ice cubes from the freezer.

She looked into the mirror and saw her crying face start to emerge, like an earthquake tossing tectonic plates about, leaving a mess of colliding frowns, squints and pursed lips. She slumped to the toilet seat and burst into tears.

"You son of a bitch!"

By the time she returned, it was more than the minute she'd asked for, more like fifteen. While sitting on the toilet, their relationship had passed before her eyes. She flushed. She didn't want him to hear her crying, not over this.

The only time she had cried in front of him, it was not about their relationship. It was because that particular evening she had become overwhelmed with the notion that "Life just sucks, period. In fact, it super sucks." When that outburst came, they had been sitting on the same sofa but without the wasteland. She had leaned into him and the squeeze from his left arm told her he understood. Maybe that was the real reason for relationships, not love, not sex, just company. That's the part you don't want to lose, the presence of another body. Conversation was overrated, she thought then. If your heat sensors detected something, alarms didn't go off half-cocked. No night sweats about waking up old and alone. There will be someone to close your eyelids and maybe kiss your forehead.

K was no longer seated at the very end of sofa, and he had lost the acting-school defiance. In an apartment that small, he couldn't help but hear her crying.

He wanted to comfort her.

As she looked at him, he seemed sad that he had upset her, but then again, she thought, maybe he was just laying down his gentleman thing. What a funny old-fashioned term that was. I can open my own fucking doors, she thought. But that's what K was, even half-drunk, a gentleman. He could get angry and raise his voice. It was a big one. But he rarely cursed much beyond the occasional *merde*, the usage of which, she assumed, came from passing his working hours translating French to English. Anyway, he had explained, shit constitutes, or at least constituted, swearing in English but its translation, *merde*, didn't get your mouth washed out with soap. Even if he was giving her shit, she liked the way he would sometimes hammer that last syllable, *mer*-DUH! She also liked it because he made his point but she didn't feel threatened, which an angry guy could make her feel, especially one his size. The second time she woke up with him in bed — she couldn't remember the first time — his back was turned, and, still half asleep, she thought she was looking at the wall.

"What do we do now?" she said, still standing, looking down at him.

He looked at her moist eyes and felt guilty, not about what he had revealed to her but how he had phrased things. Until the tears he thought he was not much more than a lay to her, and not a reliable one at that. He shouldn't have said he refused to spend the rest of his life fucking without the fantasy, that's who he was, or at least who he'd become. No going back, he had said. He wanted to die doing it his way.

"Doing what?" she said. "Fucking? You mean spanking, don't you? It doesn't sound like fucking to me."

They're the same thing, he said.

"Sounds like you want to fuck the fantasy, not me." She was angry. That was not in his script. He should have made the fantasy sound like a side dish, or better yet an hors d'oeuvre, or an aperitif. If she found she liked it, he would have said, they could sometimes make a meal out of it, like tapas.

. . .

Since he was a teenager, he had bought tights from time to time, always while drinking. If he awoke some morning, horny as hell with no girlfriend to call, he would drink for breakfast, steeling himself to go shopping. Sometimes he would lose his nerve and return home, needing another drink to suck up the headache that came when his blood alcohol level dipped too low.

He would wear tights only at home, and not very often. He would have to be vaguely horny to begin with. He always pulled them up as tightly as he could but being careful not to tear. He loved the feeling of the cotton clutching his balls and prodding his anus as he walked. He experimented with spanking himself, using rulers or ping pong paddles, anything handy, wooden spatulas, hair brushes. But that soon lost most of its appeal.

He could never be a good Catholic, he thought. Self-flagellation didn't scourge him of anything. The first couple of blows were exciting, but only initially. Although a shrink might say otherwise, nothing in his life was propelling him to do draconian penance. There was no medieval torch burning within, drawing him closer and closer to deliverance as blows rained down on his back. No, pain without sexual domination hovering about him like a shroud was just pain. What would the pain transform itself into under such a shroud? For decades he had fantasized, but he still didn't know.

He had never lived out the fantasy. He had known the plastic-wrapped magazines from England as a late teen and a young man. The strange thing, as he learned early on, was that the fantasy mutated the moment he felt drawn to a beautiful young woman. He became a hunter, spear at the ready. What primal joy it was to feel it come to life at the first sighting of a lush head of hair bobbing fifteen feet ahead in a wave of pedestrians jostling their way to work. Sometimes, he would take his life in his hands and step onto the street, doing a high-wire act as he sprinted a few strides between curb and cars to gain ground on her, to see what the rest of her looked like, first and foremost from behind. If the behind passed muster, that would become the image that held his thoughts that day. He would caress it, squeeze it and ultimately spank it. He never used much of his strength. It was the sight of the buttocks bouncing and wobbling under the smacks, and growing pink, that turned him on. She might squeal at first, more out of surprise than pain, but if he did it right, massaging her behind between volleys of smacks, she wouldn't force her way off his lap. The need to enter her grew so quickly urgent that his beautiful women never suffered anything close to a real spanking.

While he knew he could never truly hurt them, for the game to work, she had to believe he would, yet trust him at the same time. How many women would walk that fine line? When he was very young, young defined as pre-Internet, he could only manufacture a guess. None, he guessed at first. But those magazines, he thought, they obviously had a market. But they all were aimed at guys. Where were the spanking magazines for girls?

As he grew older and relationships fizzled faster, he would go through the motions of sitting at a bar with his Sinatrafied cronies and pine for lost love, as if their actions had nothing to do with their having being dumped by wives, girlfriends and mistresses. A beautiful woman still got a lingering stare back from the hunter in him but he no longer dared pursue unless he had been boozing. Then he'd shoot himself in the foot, the alcohol fueling long-winded pronouncements and theorizing about this and that. It never took long for his prey to realize she was never going to get caught, no matter how high she hiked her skirt.

Alana had been an exception. She had yanked him against her body before his mouth had a chance to derail the ritual of hunter and hunted. He should have thanked his lucky stars. Sometimes he did give a nod in that direction but he knew the connection between them was akin to a wobbly rope-and-plank suspension bridge in a tropical forest where everything rotted fast. Secure? Maybe, maybe not. Either way, he never threw caution to the wind and galloped across in the heat of passion. No, instead he advanced tentatively, each hand clasped to its respective hempen handrail. Sometimes wisdom raised its hand midway and asked permission to suggest he turn back.

Year by year he felt a little more lost. His penis no longer pointed the way. The compass needle still spun madly at the sight of a gorgeous woman but never came to rest on a direction. It never stopped wigwagging long enough for him to know which part of him was responding. In fact, he had tired of the confusion. He had told himself he was never going to seek out a relationship again. Better to be alone and fantasizing.

Alana had fouled his plan and he never knew quite what to make of it. Vanilla was no longer the only flavor listed on the panel of the ice cream truck that circled his neighborhood. The advent of the Internet years before had answered his young man's questions. He learned he was no longer alone in his fantasies. Bulletin boards beckoned in the 90s, then chat rooms with all those # signs, and now, pick a kink, any kink, out of a Bettie Page shoebox, and there it would be, an URL for dedicated social networking sites. Hell, there were hundreds of thousands of him. He was practically normal, even better than practically normal because women abounded in these groups. The Internet allowed people, even in small towns where there was no possibility of anonymity, to get their kink on one way or the other.

The kids were lucky, he thought. Maybe his Egyptian Princess grew up thinking kink was just another flavor of sex, on the list right after jellybean ice cream and just before licorice.

. . .

Now on the sofa next to an angry and teary-eyed Alana, he saw that he was at a crossroads, live, in real-time, rendered speechless by taunting idioms: a bird in the hand was worth two in the bush, half a loaf is better than none. Despite the smudged makeup under her left eye, which was his bad, she looked hot tonight, much more than usual. In a flash, he wondered whether he had been blind all along. Or did she look beautiful solely because her tears showed she cared about him in some way, an affection that surfaced now in a moment of confusion, but may have underlain any number of seemingly offhand gestures in the past? There was no time for his mind to scan through all of those gestures to determine whether they added up to evidence of deep caring. Before he spoke, the last question to nudge, poke and scratch at his insides was whether he would sell himself out for a few crumbs of caring.

"I've got to have this, Alana. I really, really do." He chose not to sell himself out. It was too late in life for that. She just stared at him. She took a breath and let it out through her mouth. She was reasserting control, slipping on the Kevlar again. He sat up a little straighter, surprised at himself. He'd held his ground, and that was a step forward. He sensed it. Take me as I am.

He was hoping she would say something, albeit resigned, like, "OK, we'll give it a try." But she didn't. When she at last dropped her gaze, she stood and turned her back on him.

"I'm going to bed. Do what you want."

. . .

When he couldn't unknot his emotions, and subsequently tag them with a cause and a cure, he drank and became indifferent to them, or he made lists of options to convince himself he was responding logically. He needed to control situations, or abdicate, entirely. Middle ground was quicksand, no man's land. As he rode the nearly empty train back to midtown, he felt guilty for deserting Alana.

After she went to bed he had sat on the couch for what seemed the longest time, not twitching a muscle. In his head, he composed a list of options. The first was to pour just one more drink and stay, but a voice in his head warned against it. His effort to come out to Alana would end up being trivialized, if not negated entirely, if he got high and horny like any other guy. Anyway, booze and boners had been declining to cohabit for several years. If he woke her and tried to screw her, and couldn't, he risked even more disdain.

Option 2 began with the word "disdain" and a mental ellipsis. Was it reasonable of him to assume that disdain for him was what she took to bed instead of him? If so, if he was to climb into bed and do nothing except be there, beside her, so she would know he wasn't deserting her, would that decent gesture sit well in the morning? He was tempted by Option 2. He wanted to be decent. But as he sat thinking, he could not stop focusing on the fact that Alana had not reacted the way he had hoped, unequivocally enthusiastic. "Whoopee! Let's get it on. It's time you started cooking with spices, man. Bend over, mister!"

Enter Option 3, finish the booze and slink out into the night. He realized he had no idea what she thought about his ultimatum: spank me or lose me. When he had begun tabling his fantasy life before her, he feared he was merely laying an egg. Now he pictured that innocent little egg exploding in a microwave. He didn't want to be there when Alana woke up. The Latina in her didn't pull punches. Option 3 confirmed, the only safe one. Drink up, go. He had no idea what he could say to her if she woke up. If he just left, she might never get in touch. He would find out what he really thought about that if the time came. Or she might eventually get in touch to say:

"You can be such as asshole. Why didn't you stay over? We could have talked in the morning."

Having acted on the last choice in his list of options, he fell to counting the number of subway stops left before 51st and Lex. He would do the same on the short ride later on the E train to Penn Station, a short walk from home. This was habit for him, a comfortable mental retreat in any storm. Anything to keep uncertainty at bay. However, tonight there was some notion breathing down on the back of his neck, hovering about, making a nuisance of itself. As the doors opened at his stop, he stepped onto the platform and stopped. He felt free, and, for him, strangely certain about things.

Although Alana was clearly upset by his revelation — tears — and although she ended the night by literally turning her back on him and going off to bed, and although her final words, "Do what you want," perhaps betrayed a startling degree of indifference toward him, part of him wanted to selfishly dismiss those reactions as emotionality that could damn well wait until later. Details, please. This is an important turning point. He wanted to know what she really thought about his fantasies. A touch of turn-on here, a sprinkling of revulsion there, but on the whole...

By choosing to walk out he may have denied himself his first real-life feedback about what until that night had existed entirely within his mind. Technically, the first real-life acknowledgement was the email reply from the Egyptian Princess the week before, but she was a professional dominatrix and stood to make money from his fantasies. Thinking that she was truly interested was probably just another fantasy. He constructed them as easily and unthinkingly as a card shark shuffling a new deck.

Nevertheless he could say, and he did, aloud, as he walked home, "I've done it!"

CHAPTER 10

Treading Water

TWO days passed. On the first day, his morning list included, "Call Alana." A second item read, "Contact another domme??????" Then, contradictorily, he added, "Don't call A."

Guilt made him think he should call Alana. The part of his soul that he long suspected was aging faster than his body said, don't call. Isn't it supposed to be the other way around? His soul was parched. Souls had ways of talking. His wanted to shake him up, turn him upside down like a piggy bank to see if anything valuable dropped out. Now's the time, man, before you're too old to spend it.

By contacting the Egyptian domme a week ago and by outing his fantasies to Alana, he had succeeded in shoving and shouldering his jalopy of a soul to the top of the hill. By rights, all he had to do was hop in and let gravity take over. He now had momentum. There was no turning back.

He slid his coffee to the side of the desk and picked up a pencil, a 2B he had bought a year ago along with a sketch pad in the hope of teaching himself to draw. In that time, he had progressed no more than a hop and a skip from Stick Men 101. His inner eye was still blind. He rarely persevered at anything long enough to profit from momentum, the flip side of effort. But now he had momentum. He felt it in his legs last night as he walked the four flights up to his apartment.

After another sip of coffee, he tried to swat indecision like an annoying fly. He crossed out "Call Alana." He left "Don't call A" as the day's new priority. With the pencil he drew an arrow moving it to the top of the list, above "Contact another domme." Acting on the latter would cement his new commitment. Calling Alana might soften it. The familiarity of her voice might even make him blurt out something like, "Forget all that shit I told you last night. God knows where all that came from. Want some breakfast?"

. . .

Alana Sandoval. Likable, pretty. Most mornings, she still made an effort to ensure her prettiness showed. However, although she was younger than him, she was already in retreat from life. K speculated that Alana's premature retreat from the belief she could make something of her life was what attracted him to her. Something shared. He didn't dream anymore either. Maybe that was some sort of hidden magnet that drew them together every month or so in the beginning. Now it was probably simple habit erected over the years that was calling the shots, or an unconscious enforcement of some unspoken mutual security pact. They were two cars running near empty but as long as they stayed close to each other one could siphon off some gas from the other in emergencies. But they both knew they wouldn't make it very far down the road without a fill-up.

"This is not the way it was supposed to be," she had said early one Saturday morning while they sat on a stoop eating tamales they'd bought from a street vendor on the other side of 138th. It wasn't the food she was talking about. She'd grown up in the South Bronx eating Latin. She had zeroed in on these tamales before she had ever set eyes on K. She was talking about passing thirty and being bored to the point where "this here fuckin' plastic spoonful of food, it's the best thing that's happened all week, and maybe the week before."

She bitched about living in a tenement where the pipes rattled far more often than her bed. Was she complaining also about his tame love-making, or just his absence from her bed?

She bitched about being a graphic designer who didn't design anything. She loved to paint but no longer even owned a sketch pad, let alone paints. She sometimes made collages from everyday objects. The last one was composed of take-out containers, take-out menus, Watchtower pamphlets and advertising flyers left in the building's lobby, and her paltry pay stubs.

She once sprinkled a freshly glued collage the size of her coffee table with a potpourri of spices, then soaked the surface with half a can of olive oil cooking spray to keep the random-colored spices in place. In the morning, it stank. She took her pocket-sized camcorder off a bookshelf and hit record. She then placed it back on the shelf facing the collage. She took some wooden matches out of the top kitchen drawer. She kept them for lighting candles because she always ended up burning her thumb when she used a lighter. Her thought was to toss a lighted match onto the collage and film the flames. But before she lit the match she had to go to the bathroom. She took her cell with her to check for messages and saw that she was already almost late for work. When she returned home that night the camcorder battery had died. She had filmed a two-hour still of the collage, which still stank. She crumpled it into the garbage container under the sink.

One morning K sat her down on the sofa. She sank into its exhausted cushions. He sat on the edge of the coffee table facing her, their knees interlaced. Though it was almost noon, neither had dressed. She wore a black T-shirt she'd bought a couple of years before at a rock concert. The band's name had been laundered away. He wore only jogging pants.

K towered over her. For ten minutes he gave her a pep talk. If she weren't so down, she might have laughed at the clichés colliding like bumper cars at Coney Island. He said she had to take guilt by the horns and turn it into energy.

"Dare yourself," he said, "to put up or shut up. There's always a way to do what you truly want to do." The words came easily. He had used them on himself so often he didn't listen to them anymore, unless he was drunkenly making a list of Scotch insights. Solving other people's inertia was simpler.

"You're right," she said, simply, when he finished. For several seconds she stared at the face looking down at her. He was leaning forward, his hands back, reversed, grasping the edge of the coffee table like somebody about to dive into a pool.

She got up and led him to bed. She pulled him on top of her and felt his erection. Surprised, she grabbed on, making sure it wouldn't go away as it so often did. They made love quickly. He was in charge, attacking. Bumper cars, she thought.

She had been too happy the rest of the day to think about injecting her life with something she cared about.

He was a hard read. She knew he liked her body but he never made booty calls. There was always some other reason, a show for instance, her kind, or a new jazz CD, his kind. Or the arrival of a long-overdue check from one of his clients.

"That calls for a bottle of the good stuff," he would say.

. . .

Flies don't die easily. Even after a good swat, like a Federer forehand, their little legs can twitch. In a moment of inattention, K found himself debating again about calling Alana. As he began, he suddenly remembered a fleeting moment from two nights earlier. He usually brought Scotch for their evenings, but the night he dropped the bomb it was a bottle of Tequila that he put down on the table. Next to it he placed a small brown paper bag full of limes. The change to Tequila was enough of a break in the routine that Alana's eyes opened wide and she couldn't help smiling at him as he prepared their glasses. They were about an hour into the bottle, K guessed now, when the smile disappeared. He wondered whether he'd buy Tequila ever again. It was odd, K thought, how trivial details grew into symbols.

. . .

The morning after the confession, Alana didn't feel sad. She didn't feel angry, apart from being pissed off that K dropped his bomb and ran away. What she felt was cheated. He was not what she thought he was, not the man she thought he was. He was big, and in his own way handsome. Handsome, the barest dusting of salt in his black hair, but worn-down handsome, not so much by years but by resignation, and the drinking, too, she guessed.

She liked his big hands and his voice that hovered between bass and lower-range tenor. She knew that only because he had dragged her to a concert once at Carnegie Hall. He met her outside her office, flashed the tickets and didn't give her a chance to go home and change.

"Hell, it doesn't matter what you wear there," he said. James Taylor and Sting were singing with the Young People's Chorus of New York City. At the intermission she asked him where he would be standing in the choir if he were singing. That's when she learned what kind of voice he had. That night he was a take-charge guy. The Latina side of her liked that, the same side of her that didn't like it when she asked, "What do you feel like eating?" and he would answer, "Whatever you want."

Most of all she now resented one thing. Somewhere in those eleven years together he had owed her the truth. Now she finds out he wants her to take charge of their sex life, have him pull on tights, and spank him. Even tie him up if she wants.

"If you want," he'd said, as if he was being generous. No, she didn't want.

The only kinky thing she'd ever done was handcuff a guy to her radiator. But at least they were her cuffs. She'd pulled his clothes off, except the shirt. She had unbuttoned it but couldn't remove it because of the handcuffs. Hadn't thought of that. Except for the sleeves, he was all flesh, beautiful flesh, no white cotton tights between her and his body, like some kind of full-body straitjacket, but veil thin.

Now she realized she'd been stuck with a guy who dreamed of her spanking him while he wore white tights so she could see his ass get red.

"Fuck! Wasn't anything in this life the way it was supposed to be?"

She called her regular hair salon and booked an appointment for that afternoon. She then rummaged through her closet, pulling out combinations of tops and bottoms. She was going out on her own. Salt-N-Pepa was playing at The Paradise Theater on the Grand Concourse. Girls night out, she thought. Girl band. Girl state of mind. Screw men.

CHAPTER 10

Treading Water

THE third day of his new life held no promise. He hadn't the energy to make something of it. His Egyptian Princess was starting to flicker and disappear like a desert mirage. It was Saturday. Outside, it was gray, humid and uninviting.

Upstairs, LeBron had started playing his stand-up bass at 7:38 that morning. Either LeBron hadn't gone to bed yet or couldn't sleep because of the humidity. He knew his friend usually got up early, and he was clearly trying to play quietly, not that it mattered. Unlike the electric, there was something so deeply human about acoustic strings that telling LeBron to shut it down would be like telling himself to shut down. Nevertheless, the notes and footsteps from above were puncturing thought bubbles below with annoying accuracy.

He hadn't given in and called Alana. Feelings of embarrassment fought with a creeping sense of liberation. When he tired of trying to objectively assess where he stood in this instant of his life's evolution, his mind emptied for what seemed like minutes, but was in reality probably just a micro-second. A micro-second seemed huge because the chatter in his mind was often oppressive. He once imagined a single CIA analyst being tasked with listening to transmissions from a hundred spy satellites simultaneously. That was his head.

In that micro-second naked Alana draped herself over his knee. He was spanking her, not the other way around. Not hard but persistent slaps. She began to wriggle but she didn't try to slide off his lap. Her cheeks bounced and grew visibly pinkish. He no longer heard the bass upstairs as he began stroking his penis. He didn't finish masturbating because he suddenly imagined himself in bed with Alana, raised up on his left elbow looking down at her face. They had just made love. He liked her. He really did.

The debate wore on. Call Alana. Don't call Alana. On or off the carousel? When he stood on the edge, it seemed to spin faster. It was harder to think. Centrifugal confusion.

By late afternoon, he'd done everything but what he knew he should do. The floors were washed, the laundry done, the bills were paid online. He would dust another day, he decided, putting on fresh coffee. He hoped it would jack him up enough so a desire of some kind could kick in. He knew people who thirsted for life. He had to be on something in order to thirst. Alana, too. That made her comfortable company, someone you could fall asleep with, and it would be somehow alright if you didn't wake up. As long as you weren't alone, dying would be OK. He often thought that.

After one coffee, he called Alana. He wasn't going to retract his confession. He was simply going to ask if he could see her that night. He would act normal when he got to her place, as if the whole thing were no big deal, which, to him, it wasn't. He'd know soon enough whether he was still on the ride. Who knows, maybe she had thought about things and wanted to opt in.

That thought juiced him more than the coffee. He punched in her number. He seldom remembered how to speed dial. His fingers were too big for the cell's keyboard.

"Hola. Can't take your call now. Ciao."

The voice was bouncy. It made you feel your call was just one of a million things going on in her life at the moment, yet it was welcome. Since he'd known her she had never changed the message. Was she really like that at some point in the past, on top of life? Was he the one who had put the night cover over the bird cage? Silenced her singing?

He poured a Scotch. The notion came full blown because he'd had it before, about her and about previous relationships. He fell for young women who liked to laugh and tease, and had energy to burn. They wore hip-hop hats before hip hop and now, askew or ass up, brim to the eyes, daring you to set them straight. Almost always there was Latin in the blood somewhere, Mexican, French, Puerto Rican, and enough of it, he hoped, to crack his shell, wake him up. By the time the relationships died, the women weren't fearless and 25 anymore. The hats were in the cupboard. They no longer sang when they went from commode to closet picking out their clothes for the day. Had he done that? Was he that much of a shit?

Two Scotches later, the phone rang.

"This is Felina."

Shit. He'd wanted it to be his Egyptian Princess.

"You left a message a couple of days ago," Felina said. "I might consider seeing you but, as my message says, you have to fill out the online application first. Go to this site. Do you have a pen?"

He scribbled the URL across the bottom of a piece of sheet music lying on the steamer trunk. Prokofiev's *Sonata for Flute and Piano*. He could play very little of it at anywhere near the required tempos but it was the only piece he had that called for the D in the fourth octave. It took him forever to learn to hit the note, and, now that he could, he tested himself every once in a while, starting a few bars before and trying to be casual about it being on the horizon. Some days he managed it as if it were all in a day's work, like an Olympic ski jumper soaring foolishly into the sky and then landing on his feet and coasting to a stop.

Felina said she would keep an eye out for his application. The line was already dead when he finished scribbling and said thank you. Damn. He'd written the address at an angle, over a flurry of sixteenth notes. When he put the phone down, he wasn't sure he could read either the music or the URL with any certainty.

Looking toward the window he noticed that darkness had fallen. He exhaled slightly, relieved. It had become an unconscious response. Since he was a teenager he felt invisible at night, and free, or free-er. He used to go for walks through the neighborhood very late at night. In winter, he could go earlier because a coat with a hood and early sunset made recognition unlikely. If an acquaintance hailed him, he felt cheated out of something, as if the night had withdrawn a promise of revelation.

After trying several spellings of Felina's URL, he finally succeeded in calling up her page on his laptop. Like most of the dominatrix pages he'd seen, she welcomed prospective customers in the same breath she warned them that she was not in the business of pleasing them. The lucky ones might be allowed to see her at her pleasure.

His eye was becoming practiced, like that of a figure-skating judge espying a slightly asymmetrical arm position during a spectacularly fast spin that would have been perfect in the eyes of the uneducated.

The photo that anchored the page was shot from below, so the domme was looking down on visitors. Par for the course, but effective. The eyes on the better pages managed a challenging condescension. The poor ones parodied severity, or looked blank, as if a body and a crop were enough to ring up a sale.

The recipe usually included leather corsets, bras, bikini bottoms, some thick and studded, fit for a Harley Davidson on a warm day, others fine and soft and expensive like the domme herself. If the thigh-high boots were soft enough to cling to her skin, K would be halfway to pressing Enter.

K examined Felina's boots, trying to imagine their feel. Then, suddenly small like Jack and the Beanstalk, he climbed to the top of the boots and stood on the rim. If he stood on his toes, he thought for a moment, and reached as high as he could, he could touch her crotch.

Other dommes wore latex. That seemed to up the ante, but even if it did, he blessed them for escaping the bonds of black.

Felina's application form was a two-by-two sticky note compared to the novella the Egyptian Princess inspired: when, what, what not, experienced yes/no, have you read my rules? Not much else. He was glad. He was tired. He'd had only three — or four? — Scotches but he hadn't eaten since morning. He had written pages and pages to the Egyptian Princess. No, he corrected himself again, to the Queen, the Pharaoh. Why was there no feminine form for the latter? She was too beautiful to wear a male title. King Cleopatra would have captured no man's imagination. He sipped his Scotch, toyed with anointing her Empress, then returned to Princess.

He went back to the form on the screen. He had lost track of all time the night he wrote the Princess. Words had come easily. It was the Grand Confession, the Great Unburdening, a freaky and free-at-last kind of moment. Though it had turned out that 2,582 miles separated them that night, her in San Francisco, him in New York, as he filled in her form he felt he was whispering in a gloriously sympathetic ear across the Internet. In fact, he remembered imagining kissing that ear, and wondering what the many piercings would feel like against his lips.

Felina's earrings, black as night, dangled from her lobes almost all the way down to her shoulders. For the first time since finding the page, he noticed her eyes. They were blue. The earrings were wrong, they clashed. He filled out the form anyway. His answers were short: enter just a few words each, and tab on. Briefly, he wondered whether he should say more, then decided to do the exact opposite. He went minimalist. When? Tomorrow. What? Spanking. What not? Verbal humiliation. Experienced? No.

He then read the rules: If you arrive late, the door will be closed forever. If you arrive early, you will wait. If you smell of alcohol, tobacco or sweat, you will be turned away and you will lose your deposit — $50, paid online when making the appointment. If you try to touch my person (and "try" is as far as you'll ever get, believe me) the session will end immediately. There is no sex, no bargaining, of any kind. Don't even think about it. If you try to top from the bottom you'll find out what I'm like when I'm pissed off. Clear?

Yes.

He phoned Alana. Her phone was off.

He hit Enter.

. . .

For two more days he heard from neither Alana nor Felina. Now he didn't even want to hear from them, at least not immediately. One moment he felt he was suffocating in a world where aging, weight and booze had rendered him a sexual cripple. The next he felt he was agilely hopping aboard an express train already pulling out of the station toward a radical reincarnation of his sexual self.

He was never one to target middle ground. Life was too boring to settle for rationality. He told himself that most days, as if repetition would cut him loose. But on days when he was too tired of hum-drum to pretend he was anything other than what he appeared to be, he suspected the ritual was about as effectual as praying. There simply was no chariot of fire to hitch a whirlwind ride on. We were all just plodders with pretensions.

In fact, the chariot lost a wheel not long before. He had attended the American Translators Association's 50th annual conference. He was not a joiner but the conference was being held in New York, at the Marriott Marquis on Broadway in Midtown. For four days, he bathed in reminders that he was a professional, by definition a cut above. He had a name tag so his peers would know who he was, which, for those four days, made him feel he knew who he was.

On the final day, flush with craft insights and new avenues to explore from the sessions he'd sat through, and with his laptop bag full of brochures from language software companies offering the latest computer-assisted translation tools at irresistible discounts, he decided to do a little networking around the cash-bar at the closing reception. He recognized several people he'd met at the conference, and a few others he knew already.

It was there that he overheard himself being described. It was there that the conference flush evaporated faster than the double Scotch emptied.

"Capable, I suppose. I mean, he gets by as a freelancer, right? Walks a pretty straight line, I'd say, at least on the way to the bar, ha ha. Likes his nectar, which isn't a crime, of course, especially for a single guy his age. Loses it a bit, though, if you sprinkle religion or Republicans into the mix. Other than that, pretty M-O-R."

The man pontificating on K's life was an in-house translator for a bank. K suspected his English accent was affected. He was addressing a slim, middle-aged woman in a gray suit. Her blonde hair was straight, not a single wave. Her suit was pressed. When she turned slightly, he saw that her eyes sat on a pile of wrinkles. The eyes darted about the room as she listened to the bank translator. Her face was familiar but that's all. Did she represent a translation agency? Was she looking for soldiers? It didn't matter. After being reminded who he was, by someone who scarcely knew him, he no longer felt like dancing with potential clients. He took a cab home.

He had dropped his conference name tag atop a never-used glass ashtray filled with paperclips and pondered the fork in the road he had mapped by opening up to Alana.

Now, not long after finishing his morning coffee, chance gave him his out. An email informed him a job bid he had made several weeks ago had been accepted. It meant more than a few dollars. It was precisely the kind of translation project he needed to restore some notion of independence, which was the whole reason he had chosen to work as a freelance translator instead of remaining a language grunt shackled to a desk at a best-word-rate-in-town translation factory. The new job wouldn't make him rich, or anything resembling it, but he would be able to coast for a while, maybe a month or two, and say no to projects that would bore him or were laughably urgent.

The latter was the disease of the new century. Translate in two days a document that took two months to write, and if you can get it done any sooner we'd greatly appreciate it. We know you'll produce a quality document.

He never put a dollar amount to what was necessary to buy independence. It was more an attitude, one he borrowed from an older colleague years before.

"I've had some of the shittiest-paying jobs in the world," the colleague said, "but even when I was just starting out I always put aside a few bucks from each pay. I called it my 'Fuck-you money.' A boss gives me attitude, he gets my back and out the door I go, my fuck-you finger so high in the air it would make Huey Newton proud."

This morning's project would arrive in stages, the first part, the smallest, due in three days, the final part in eight. The confidentiality agreement between him and the client had already been signed and returned electronically. He was told he'd receive the text that afternoon at the latest. That meant he would have some time to kill. It was late morning.

He showered, dressed and stepped out into the hallway. The last thing he wanted was to start thinking about dominatrixes, or imagining Alana being reborn, eternally grateful to him for revealing her domme side. He wanted to play a little sax. He usually played only during the afternoon hours so as to not disturb anyone. There was no sound from behind closed doors in the hallway. He went upstairs to LeBron's door and listened. Nothing. Hopefully he wasn't sleeping. However, if LeBron had come home last night, he'd entered silently on tiptoes, which wasn't easy in size 14s.

Removing his alto from its case, he stuck a reed in his mouth to moisten it. It stayed there, like a cigarette, while he rifled through his sheet music. One voice said "Practice," while another said, "For God's sake, have some fun for a change. Feel good. If you think you can feel it, play it."

He pulled out a volume of transcribed Lester Young solos. They were for tenor sax, but he had been too lazy to transcribe them to the equivalent key for alto. He loved the ballads most of all. No wonder Billie Holiday loved Prez so much. He started with *I Can't Get Started* and felt better and better as he relaxed into the lines of the solo, his sound getting fatter and fatter. No one in the building had ever complained while he played standards. An hour later, he had gone up tempo.

His phone rang. It wasn't a neighbor bitching. It was his client, telling him he'd just emailed the texts to translate. He sat on the sofa and cleaned the horn, swabbing out the inside of the body and neck with pieces of cloth attached to a string for pulling them through the instrument. He used cigarette paper to absorb the moisture that collected on several pads near the top of the horn.

Happy to have shut his mind off for that hour, he spent an extra minute burnishing the brass before returning the alto to its case.

Work gave him a fantasy-free focus. It also had another benefit. He never mixed work and drinking. The tougher the deadline the better. Less time to think, no time for listening to old albums.

He called up the first text to translate. His personal record for working non-stop, not getting up from his chair even once to piss away the coffee, was six and a half hours. By supper time, not that he planned to eat, he had gotten into the groove. His mind had rarely wandered, but he was suddenly tired. He needed to get up and pace his ten-by-twelve universe.

K downed several handfuls of peanuts and changed into his bathrobe. He didn't want to eat a proper supper because digestion slowed his mind. He didn't want to shower again because awakened senses distracted him from his focus. He often worked like that, stopping in the small hours of the morning when his eyes stung and his head ached.

When he sat down again at his keyboard to start the evening session, he was amazed at how much of the job he had mowed down in the first stretch. He worked until nearly midnight. After making a backup of the text he'd translated, and before opening his bed, he calculated how much money he'd made that day. As he closed his eyes, he mentally calculated how much money he'd make in a month at that rate, then a year. It was an old habit, and it was silly because he didn't want to work that much and, more important, he couldn't physically work at that intensity much beyond a few days. But the habit at least worked as a sheep-counting exercise.

Three or four hours later he was making coffee for Round Two. Alana didn't call.

Felina emailed back after Round Three, but he dragged the message's icon into his Pending folder. His penis hadn't even twitched when her message popped up on his cluttered screen. He had browser windows open for two online terminology databases, and a third for Googling financial-world phrases he had translated, to verify that they were used in investment speak. By his left knee, at the foot of the bed, which he left open when working round the clock, were three specialized bilingual dictionaries: economics, accounting and finance. His bookshelves sagged under the weight of various dictionaries. Though their physical presence was still reassuring — he liked to pretend they contained an answer for every translation problem — the Internet had become by far his best and fastest source for terminology. Leafing through a thousand-page volume with print sized for younger eyes was no longer the joy of discovery it once was. It was tedious.

After Round Five of the project, he was wired. He thought he would never sleep a full night again. He would wake every few hours in need of coffee.

The sun had just come up. His life belonged to him again, not to a client. He had finished the project three days early, which meant he could invoice the client and potentially get paid three days earlier. Had he been more rational, he would have spread the project out and finished it in due course. He would have made the same amount of money, and he wouldn't be exhausted. Nor, he reminded himself, yawning as he sat in his work chair looking at the sunshine streaming in, would he be exhilarated. When life was flat he built pretend mountains to climb. He loved freelancing on those days when he made it to the top.

Before jumping overboard to freelance, he had started to hate his chosen career. After graduating from NYU, he quickly got a job with a translation agency within walking distance of his apartment. He sat squeezed into a room with 19 other translators who rarely uttered a word to each other all day long. They were required to translate a set number of words. Their portions of larger texts were assigned to them each morning, sometimes starting in the middle of a sentence, the agency manager's word processor having chopped the original text into 2,300-word segments. They were mostly business documents, reports prepared by branch offices of American companies in other countries. He and two other translators handled the documents in French. The language of the reports was uninspired, predictable, formulaic, the language businessmen are comfortable with, which meant he had to think like them while translating. He suffocated there for six years and nine months.

When he started school, he saw himself translating novels, spending days in search of the right phrase, just as the author would have. In his own way, he would be a writer too. Because he would be translating into English, more people in the world would read his words than the original author's. That dream died when a prof told him there was no money whatsoever in translating fiction. It was mostly done by academics because it looked good on CVs.

In subsequent years, the closest he came to that dream was translating two children's books, written by a woman from Quebec who'd followed her husband to New York for a job. She was publishing the books herself and paying for the translation out of her own pocket. He cut his rate in half to accommodate her.

He ended up so enjoying the process he would have done it for even less. He and the author didn't discuss deadlines. They discussed "getting it right." Later, he was proud to tell anyone who would listen that he was, even at his age, naive enough to believe that business should work that way too. Late at night he knew he didn't really believe that. If he were forced to work for a multinational corporation peddling a press release proclaiming to the world that sales of their genetically modified sunflower seeds had exceeded projections by three-quarters of one percent in the first quarter, he would be in a hurry to sign off on the sloppiest of translations and bolt out the office to get a jump on rush hour. He suspected businesses were eventually going to be satisfied with mangled-but-free machine translations, unconcerned whether the phrase "sales exceeded projections" was rendered as "sales overshadowed protrusions" or "sales outclassed outcrops" or "sales overreached outlooks."

As the morning turned into afternoon, he recharged himself with a shower and a meticulous shave. He wanted to enjoy his accomplishment a little longer. The choice to be made was either to sleep the day away or head out into the sunshine and hope to extend his day long enough to stand a chance of resuming a normal sleep schedule within the next couple of days. He thought of it as jet lag without jets.

Two hours later he sat at a café. His body was saying *no* to more caffeine after the five-day marathon. He sat at a floor-to-ceiling window seat. The bookmark in the novel he'd brought instead of the laptop had advanced only two pages. Overused eyes couldn't penetrate it.

He watched girls stream by, all shapes. Most of them kept him from nodding off. Stretching his neck, he looked up at the four-story brick building across the street. Graffiti covered the first floor. Two of the three tall narrow windows on the second floor proclaimed in block letters, "SEX MASSAGE." Vertical letters on each side announced "LAP DANCING." The bottom frame merely read "SEX" and for some reason bore the image of two crossed, checked starter's flags. The third window, on the left, proclaimed in slanted neon-red script, "Pussy Corps."

It looked inexpensive. He had never entered such a place. Would they offer afternoon specials? Then he imagined himself on the table, falling asleep mid-wank-off, and the girl's overly made-up face turning ugly as she said "Fuck you, mister. Party's over." Why would she care, he wondered, forgetting momentarily that he was still sitting at the café.

On his way home, he bought a frozen dinner and went straight to bed.

The next morning he saw that the frozen dinner was still in its plastic bag on the counter. It was no longer frozen. He tossed it in the white kitchen garbage container. As he did so, he realized he couldn't remember what the frozen dinner was. Whatever it was, it had looked good in the store. For a second he thought of retrieving it to read the now-soggy box, but he stopped himself. Knowing what he hadn't eaten couldn't have mattered less. So what if he'd been wasteful. The food was spoiled. Nothing he could do about it. And what could it matter beside the fact he had slept well?

Physically he felt good. But his mind seemed to want to pick a fight over nothing. It seemed to hold a grudge against him. It didn't want to gear down to saunter and help ease his way into the new day. It didn't want to cooperate. It was bitchy and sarcastic. It flicked images at him, made absurd associations. The frozen dinner, whatever it was, was an unknown soldier, tossed in an open grave and left there to rot. Where the hell was this shit coming from? He turned on the morning news to erect a wall of sound and images to dam the effluvia.

His mind subsided an hour later, after he had phoned Alana. He realized his subconscious wouldn't have been so bitchy had he made a list for the day. "Call A" would have been on it. It had been well over a week since he had spoken to her, more than time enough for her silence to amount to meaningful. It had become a statement.

After four rings she answered. He realized he had no idea what to say.

"I was worried about you. Been almost a week —"

"You were the one who split," she interrupted. "I didn't tell you to go."

"You said, 'Do what you want.' I thought you were angry."

"Yeah, I was. Really pissed off. How long have we known each other? What other fucking surprises do you have?"

"Why are you making such a big deal out of this? We all have secret —"

Alana cut him off again. "So why did you fuck off like that? Why didn't you call? What's the secret behind that?"

"Shit." Though he had expected she might be angry, he was annoyed that she was. "You're going to tell me you don't have secrets?"

"Yeah. I got secrets. I got one from the night after you fucked off. I went out and got laid. We just fucked and fucked. No one got their ass whipped." Then she added, "It was great," and hung up.

CHAPTER 11

Learning a New Language

FOR some reason, to him at least, endings weighed more than beginnings in memory. Alana now weighed a lot. He'd had no idea how much.

Break-ups, divorces, firings, failure to make the high school basketball team, and death itself outweighed the moments of discovery, possibility, triumph and birth, of someone, of something.

The only significant beginning, the last one he truly believed in, was the day he knew he'd never have to serve another table in his life, the day he graduated almost twenty years earlier. However, his faith in the future lasted about as long as having faith in cops investigating police misconduct.

By late August of the year he graduated from university, he had begun to suspect that rationalizations about the job would someday have a room of their own in his mind. In barely two months, he had gone from validation to trepidation. Walking out the door at NYU and almost immediately landing the job at the translation agency left him exhilarated. A made man overnight. The job validated the certification. He had a career. Getting paid for translating made him what the piece of paper itself didn't: a translator. Two days after the final semester came to an end, he mailed in a passport renewal application. He wasn't planning a trip. On the new passport, his occupation would read *translator* instead of *waiter.*

After high school, a temporary job as a waiter at a diner in Brooklyn metastasized into what had every appearance of becoming a career. It was restaurant to restaurant to bar to restaurant, sometimes two jobs at a time to make up for either the lack of shifts or the day shifts that brought in no tips worth counting. On three occasions he had taken jobs at call centers to make ends meet, feeling ancient seated next to kids working for date and dope financing. The most recent gig at an upscale bar-restaurant, on Nostrand Avenue near Park Place in Brooklyn, was good for tips and meeting girls, which was a priority then, a sexual priority, less complicated and more urgent than what came to replace it years later. The bar tips paid for most of his only trip abroad. He lost count of the number of times he and friends, examining their young lives, had said, "Damned if I'm going to spend the rest of my life here."

Darkly aware that his twenties had simply vanished, with little to show for all those days and nights, he had booked a flight: three weeks, off-season, to Barcelona. He chose the city as his backpacking base because a girl he knew slightly was planning on spending an entire winter in Spain. They had a friend in common. Although he had made no concrete plans, he told her one night in the bar that he was probably going to take off the following February.

"Tips are usually shitty in the New Year. Good time to split," he said.

"February?" She paused to mentally check her itinerary. "Yeah, we could hook up in Barcelona."

"Awesome."

She came to the bar a few times after that, with girl-friends or work colleagues. She usually greeted him by name and introduced him once as a "bud of mine." When he got to Spain the number she'd given him must have been for a phone that wasn't GSM compatible. At any rate, they never hooked up.

It was while in Barcelona, swept up in an unaccustomed whirl of energetic, educated, polyglot young people, that a new beginning took shape in a café on Carrer del Tigre near La Paloma. He'd made it his home base, a place to start the day with *café con leche* and *bollos*, and an afternoon refueling station after hours of exploring.

Shortly after ordering some tapas one day, he shook the hand of a young man who had just introduced himself as Alejandro. He'd first noticed Alejandro because his right shoulder was higher than his left, like someone who spent too much time cradling a phone between ear and shoulder. He came to the café every afternoon and they'd taken to exchanging *holas*. He asked Alejandro what he did for a living.

"Why do Americans always want to know what people do for a living? Does it make any difference?" the Spaniard asked in return.

"Because I don't like what I do for a living."

Alejandro seemed mollified by the sincere answer and said he was a translator. Over the next half hour, peppered with questions, he switched easily from English to French to Spanish as he described his work. Finally, after checking his watch, he rose and said, "*Hasta luego.*" Then, as an afterthought, he added, "I'm sure they need translators in New York."

Kit was disappointed when Alejandro didn't show up the next day. The afterthought had kept him awake half the night and he wanted to thank the Spaniard. He'd worked out what he would say in Spanish. "My future self wants to thank you in advance. I've decided to go back to school when I get stateside." His Spanish dictionary didn't provide a solution to the slang "stateside."

The café was a stone's throw from an elegant old ballroom he'd read about. On his fifth night in Barcelona he walked in to take a look. It was around 11 o'clock, relatively early by Spanish standards. At first glance, he felt he was entering some kind of history, but the young people he saw before him, as passionate and pretty and defiant as many of them were, seemed like graffiti on the wall of Le Louvre. He stayed anyway, for the Spanish experience. He was glad the night wasn't one of the raves he'd read about. He was beyond that. The crowd was almost suffocating but he enjoyed dancing with girls he couldn't understand. He also learned he didn't have their staying power. He was young in body but in mind the realization made him concede time was moving faster than he thought. He was gone by 3 in the morning, annoyed with himself. He'd read that many of the young Spaniards and most of the stoned North American tourists wouldn't clear out until around 5, in search of a bite to eat or a new friend's room. He'd assumed he'd be among them.

Part of him wanted to hurry home to research translation courses in New York. He wanted a career that might let him travel. Barcelona, even in winter, seemed full of people from somewhere else, people who would soon be on their way to anywhere else. The transience was attractive.

He didn't know much Spanish, other than one year of high school Spanish and what he was starting to pick up on the road. However, he'd twice had a chance to use his halfway decent French. For much of one wine-dominated evening, he talked to two young Frenchmen, who kept bringing the conversation back to Spanish women. They said there was a subtle difference between Spanish women and French women. The Frenchman sounded so unlike Americans, he thought. It seemed a discussion of the nuances was worth as much wine as the chase.

He bid them good night, hoping to get the chance to do original research before his vacation ended.

On the other occasion, he had met a slinky American girl from Rhode Island while walking on the nearly deserted La Barceloneta beach on a frisky gray afternoon. She was heading for Paris in two weeks. She had just discovered how inadequate her school Spanish was in the real world. She was afraid the same thing would befall her school French.

He immediately switched into French, confident he could say almost anything and she would think him fluent. He assured her they had time to get her French in shape to get by in Paris, and he assured himself he stood a reasonable chance of getting laid. At one point, while she wracked her brain to come up with a word-for-word French equivalent for "Hit the road Jack" — she was concerned she would have to fend off the advances of Frenchmen — he toyed with the idea of asking her if she had ever been made love to in French. If she hesitated, he would assure her the question was meant in the language-lab sense. If the idea brought a smile or a giggle or anything in between, he would whisk her off to an early dinner, an American suppertime for a change, not Spanish. But after half an hour of earnest French, she said it was too tiring. Maybe she just didn't have the foundation she thought she had. He tried to explain to her that the language would come more easily the next day, and more easily still each day before her flight. Maybe, she said, unconvinced.

Over supper of tapas only, he realized they had little to say to each other. In French, he could say anything and she would be interested because it was French. In English, Rhode Island didn't sound so interesting. They met one other time. She thanked him cheerily for his help, making it sound as if she'd made great strides thanks to him, adding that he had bent over backwards to be a patient teacher.

"I can't wait to get there," she said, adding that she

had to hurry back to the hotel and write a letter home about the Spanish portion of her travels.

"A letter on paper?" he asked.

"Yes, on paper. Maybe it will end up in some institution's archives someday." He had no idea what possessed her to think her European vacation might ever merit a memoir. She gave a little wave of her right hand to say goodbye.

He'd done well in French in high school and had augmented it by reading a handful of French novels, including some French erotica he'd found at a flea market. From then on, French study no longer seemed like work. The novels weren't much as literature, he decided on first read, but something made him read long portions of several of them a second time, and not only to perfect his French. It was the first intimation that there were new doors to pass through. The realization had excited him, although some inner censor told him that the very doors opening before him were doors that had to remain behind other doors, closed doors.

His flight home was via London, as it had been in the other direction, because it was cheaper than a direct flight. At Heathrow Airport's Terminal 3 he re-Americanized himself with a Big Mac. It was the first time he had ever encountered an utterly sullen McDonald's employee.

There were four hours to kill before boarding an American Airlines flight to JFK. He set to making lists. He hadn't made lists in Spain. Now he calculated that he had just enough cash to get home once he landed. He would need to buy milk, bread and coffee that evening. His Heathrow calculations confirmed what he had already guessed, that he had overspent his waiter's budget. Although the fact hadn't bothered him as long as he was in Barcelona, it annoyed him as he wandered the terminal to pass time.

Unconsciously, he started voicing his thoughts in French, tossing in the odd Spanish phrase here and there, exclamations and interjections he'd learned in Barcelona. It occurred to him the world seemed both larger and smaller because he knew another language. Foreign countries weren't really that foreign. He resolved to start studying translation that fall. Maybe NYU had a program. His next trip abroad would not be on a waiter's budget.

On the plane, he wondered whether his bookshelves at home still contained any of the French erotic novels that first began to give definition to what he was later to think of as a sexual alter ego.

CHAPTER 12

Renaissance

NOT long after returning to New York, buoyed by the born-again him and a seriousness that he thought probably happened to everyone when they turned thirty, he moved into a cramped apartment on the Lower East Side. The location was convenient for work and his classes at NYU. He shared the apartment with another waiter and his girlfriend. The couple mostly worked evening shifts. They slept in the living room. He slept in a windowless room that was probably once part of the living room before a landlord decided to illegally squeeze another dollar out of the place.

There were two feet to spare on either side of the bed and enough room at the foot for a chest of drawers. One night when it was too hot to sleep, remembering that heat rises, he tried to sleep on the floor between the bed and the wall. In that position, he couldn't see the crack of light under the door. In the absolute darkness, the wall and the box spring were so near his shoulders that he felt he was in a coffin. He was aging fast but not that fast.

Instinctively he shot his hand upward to see if the coffin was closed. When the suffocating feeling subsided, he returned to the bed and sweated. The entire apartment unit was tiny, and only livable for three people because he worked or went to class while they slept and screwed.

To work around his studies he tried to pick up as many weekend shifts as possible, but too often he got stuck with tip-starved day shifts and there wasn't much money left over to deflate his credit card bill from Barcelona. However the shifts were less onerous, he realized, simply because he knew he would soon be turning his back on them.

When that moment arrived the following spring, he looked up the word *omnipotent* just for the pleasure of reading a dictionary definition that could have been written expressly to describe the way he felt. He'd turned his life around in a year. He felt he could accomplish anything. When he landed a translating job shortly afterwards, he opened his dictionary to "O" once again.

It was the last time he let Webster flatter him. By late August of the year he graduated, when bars once again became places to drink in, not work in, and with only two months at the translation agency under his belt, his new life was becoming old fast. The job was a grind, so much so that he almost yearned for the molasses hours at the restaurant-bar when there were no customers.

At the agency he sat and he translated, hour after hour until his shift was done. They were not documents that told a story. They were business documents wordy reports written by some manager to justify his department's budget for the coming year, for example, letters from claims departments to clients justifying refusals of claims, email exchanges with head office, projections of corporate tax payments under revised tax legislation for foreign companies, or a legal department opinion defending the generosity of a golden parachute for a terminated executive. On a good day there might be a confidential human resource department investigation of a sexual harassment claim against an executive.

When the work did slow down, he mostly wanted to close his eyes to rest them. He would listen to the sounds of the office. There was little talking. He heard sporadic keyboard outbursts from around the room, as previously untranslated phrases got gunned down and new ones came into the line of fire. The sounds of desk chairs rolling over thin commercial carpet were muffled and short, but sometimes alarming for a moment, like a ship's hull complaining. The ringing of a telephone would force his eyes open and he'd roll his chair back toward his computer terminal, like a tired boxer inching back to the center of the ring for another round.

On a hazy Friday in late August he left the office two and a half hours early for a non-existent doctor's appointment. He had been working at the company for only two months and already he wanted payback for the drudgery. Though he was technically fresh out of school he was not a newcomer to the working world. He was thirty-four years old and his ego expected better treatment from life.

He walked several blocks south on Broadway and turned left onto 31st. He felt better already, playing hooky, playing rebel, the crime of the century, grand theft payroll hours. He had been planning to sit on a bench somewhere and watch everyone else living. Happy or sad, stressed or floating, didn't matter, but better than watching his own life. The plan was to wait until 5 o'clock, the start of a happy hour at a hotel lounge off Fifth Avenue.

He happened to be in front of the place one night when the skies unexpectedly released a torrential downpour. It was not a young people's bar but it was comfortable. He stayed an hour after the rain stopped, sitting near a curved granite bar and eavesdropping. Before he left, he'd heard French, Russian, Portuguese and accented English. Now, growing restless sitting on the city bench, he checked his watch. An hour and fifteen minutes seemed an eternity, happy hour or no happy hour. He walked the remaining few blocks.

The lounge was almost empty, except for a table of seven women, mostly blond, in their twenties and thirties. He sat at the bar, just several feet to the right of their table. He didn't have a clue what language they were speaking. Not understanding was sometimes comforting, white noise, like the air-conditioning, or Latin at mass. He kept his jacket on not because the air-conditioning was set particularly high but because his shirt undoubtedly betrayed the sweat of a humid August afternoon. He'd wait.

At one point, one of the women said something in perfect English. Not knowing the context, he didn't understand why the other women burst into loud laughter. It made him smile, too, and he turned toward the table. A stunning woman's eye caught his, her peripheral vision having detected his movement in response to their laughter. Still smiling at whatever the joke was, she said, "Oops! I guess we are being loud a bit."

"No, no, not at all," he replied. "I just wish I understood the rest of the joke. What language were you speaking?"

"Finnish."

"God," he thought. "If she's the finish I'd love it to be the start."

She held his eyes for a moment, then turned back to her friends. She said something to them, just a few words. He saw two of them raise their eyes toward him for a split second. He swiveled back toward the bar and ordered another drink. It was after 5, he realized, relishing the idea of a drink for less than $10. At regular bar prices in Manhattan, for the cost of two drinks he could just about buy a whole bottle to drink at home.

An hour later he wanted to go home. He hadn't eaten lunch and the Scotch was not having the effect he paid for. It wasn't getting him airborne. If he was going to walk home, now was the time to do it. One more drink and he'd have to hail a cab, doubling the price of that last drink. As he nursed the last one, more to change his position on the bar stool than anything else, he turned in the direction of the table of Finns. Whatever they were drinking, it was doing what his Scotch wasn't.

His eyes immediately focused on the woman he'd spoken to earlier. He had watched her make her way toward the restroom about twenty minutes earlier. Her blue skirt was not tight but it revealed the ass of an athlete or a dancer. When she reentered the lounge, he noticed how naturally her bare shoulders were squared. He averted his eyes before she got to the table.

"Do you want to join us?" She had stopped beside him, her head actually higher than his. "Since we're mostly talking about men anyway, it might be more fun to have a specimen at the table."

He didn't know which to admire most, her English or the lips that spoke it. Apart from his trip to Spain he had little experience of European women, yet this woman fit the generalization he was forming to a T.

European women were masters of minimal make-up. Why spoil a good thing, he'd said once to a friend when the subject came up.

"Sure you got room? I take up quite a bit."

"I think we can make room," she said as he stood up. "I see you are big. But it does not matter. We outnumber you seven to one." She pointed to a chair at a nearby table and he obediently slid it over, next to hers.

"So, what do you want to know about men?" he asked.

One of the other women, slightly older than the rest, spoke with the deliberation of someone who is speaking a foreign language or is trying to hide how much she has had to drink.

"Why do American men all wear hats, caps, what do you call them?"

Before he could answer, another asked, "Why don't you have a hat?"

"Wait, wait," said the one who had invited him to the crowded table. Her shoulder brushed his arm as she raised her hand to say "Wait." Turning her face toward him, mimicking a serious expression, she said:

"What we really want to know is this. None of the guide books answer this question. Are you ready?" She raised her left eyebrow.

Already he wanted to kiss her.

"Ready."

"OK, what the girls and I want to know is, we know that some American men make love with their socks on, but do they also make love with their trucker hats on?"

"That's right, Kaija. That's our question."

"Kaija? That's your name?"

"It is really Katariina. With two letter i's. But if you answer our question you can call me Kaija for tonight."

"For tonight?"

"Yes, for tonight, because we are going tomorrow."

"Where?"

"We are all flight attendants."

"Stewardesses?"

"Flight attendants," she repeated, with a hint of command in her voice. "And we fly back to Helsinki tomorrow."

"And if I decided to fly to Helsinki with you, what would I call you when we landed?"

"Intrigued."

If only she knew his credit card could barely get him to JFK let alone buy a ticket. However, the game was on, and she was dictating the moves. The tipsy, rapid, bilingual back and forth among the seven women rarely included him but they clearly accepted his presence. He belonged to their friend, Kaija. Her New York toy? So be it. "I'm not proud," he thought, enjoying the light touch of Kaija's arm repeatedly brushing his as she gesticulated. Her gestures weren't expansive and energetic like those of the Spanish he'd witnessed. If they were punctuation to her words, they were long dashes or ellipses.

By nine, five of the women had left, pleading the need to pack for tomorrow's return flight. Besides Kaija, the one other woman remaining was the youngest of the bunch. She said there was nothing much to pack and, besides, she wanted a drunk-in-Big-Apple story to tell someday. About an hour later, when conversation had all but died, she paid the waiter, slid her chair back and, before closing her purse, placed a tip on the table.

"What's that?" asked Kaija, feigning irritation.

"A tip. What else," said the young flight attendant.

"Well I think you got your — what did you call it — your drunken apple story. That's a one-hundred-dollar bill."

Immediately the young girl raised it to her eyes to read the denomination.

"This money's ridiculous! It all looks the same."

Subtly encouraging her colleague's departure, Kaija announced she'd take care of the tip.

"See you at the hotel."

"The hotel is...?" asked the woman, her arms extended like a swaying compass needle. Kaija gave her instructions in Finnish. All Kit understood was, "The Radisson."

"That's just a block from here," he said. "If your friend could leap buildings in a single bound she'd be right there."

"Can you do that, leap buildings?"

"Sure, I can even leap years."

"I don't understand."

"I was born on February 29th. We call that a leap year."

Though everyone else had left, they hadn't created space between their chairs. Their shoulders still touched from time to time. She chuckled at his little joke. "Come," she ordered.

"Where to?"

"The hotel."

"Where?"

"The Radisson."

"You're staying there, too?"

"We all are. It's the crew hotel."

She didn't give him a chance to pull back her chair. She didn't show any signs of being drunk, not that he was in any position to tell. Maybe she was always decisive. With an ass like hers, he thought, he'd always be happy to follow.

Outside the hotel, the doorman began to open the door for them. She waved him off and moved to the side of the entrance. From her purse she drew a pack of cigarettes, Marlboros. She offered Kit one. He shook his head. She lit her own and raised her eyes to his as she exhaled. He soon had the feeling that it wasn't so much a desire for a cigarette that stopped her outside the hotel but the chance to stand face to face with him, a final uninterrupted appraisal. They didn't speak. Suddenly she dropped the half-finished cigarette. His foot beat hers to it, crushing it. She chuckled again. She liked to play.

As the elevator climbed he decided he would kiss Kaija the instant they stepped into her room. By the time she found the key card in her purse, however, he had an urgent need to pee. Once the door was open his first words were, "The bathroom?" Without looking up, she pointed.

He realized he had not moved from her side all evening. Despite all the Scotches he had never gotten up to go to the bathroom. What was strange, and disturbing, was now that his bladder was empty the relief was also translating into a sudden plunge in his buzz. He put down the toilet seat and sat for a moment, collecting himself.

When he stepped back into the room, Kaija sat on

one side of the bed, wearing only a blue thong and a blue sports bra. He stopped in front of her and bent down toward her. He kissed her gently, and she clutched his hair, lightly. There was something about the way she did it that made him realize she was letting him know she could yank him down hard if she chose to. Still holding his hair with her right hand, she kissed him back as he unbuttoned his shirt. With her other hand, she undid his jeans.

She tasted like Scotch and, more faintly, tobacco. Though he never smoked, he was turned on by the taste of tobacco on a woman's lips. He hated the smell of smoke in a room, but loved what he tasted now. He moved his hands to her shoulders and started to push her back onto the bed but she pulled his hair to the right forcefully enough that his body followed, leaving him on his back. It didn't hurt but neither did it give him an option. Kaija let go of his hair and bracketed his head with her elbows. Her eyes were inches from his, unblinking. He ran his hand down her back and softly clutched the nicest ass cheek he'd ever kneaded. It filled his large hand. The firmness made him think of Play-Doh, warm Play-Doh.

He fought against her weight on his chest and she finally let him flip her over. With one hand he yanked his pants the rest of the way off, directing his lips to the tops of her breasts, turning her so he could release her bra. She grabbed his cock and he slipped his fingers under her thong. A moment later one finger entered her, then a second. She was already wet. She released her grip on his penis and let his hands and lips take control.

As his lips found their way to her left breast he began to feel dizzy. He didn't dare open his eyes. He wished she would grab his cock again. Work it hard. But she didn't. He had gone limp as week-old lettuce in the fridge.

As he stroked her, he slipped outside himself. His motions, his lips, his fingers, were becoming mechanical. He felt her magnificent body but no longer the desire to make it his. As the panic grew inside him, his fingers slowed their rhythmic caress inside her. She noticed and turned to her right side, pushing against him. She took his cock in her left hand and began working it, going deep to its base. He felt it start to come to life. Keep going, keep going, he thought, eyes closed, forgetting her body altogether. Suddenly she pushed him on his back and sat astride him. It was as if his rising erection had stopped between floors. He felt the pure male panic begin to invade again.

Had he been paying attention to her, he would have sensed her growing frustration. Her hand slipped his penis between her legs and she began to grind her hips hard. He felt her heat around the top of his cock but he knew he was barely inside her. He grabbed her ass with both hands, hanging on, hoping desperately to feel himself get sucked into her. He could hear her breathing harder. His cock was going nowhere.

It was then that he pulled her down to his chest with his left hand and began slapping her ass with his right, not ferociously but hard nonetheless. He felt her writhing under the first slaps. God, yes, he thought, holding her tight with his left arm. His cock was coming alive again. Suddenly, between slaps, he heard her voice.

"No. I don't like that. Stop."

She raised herself on her elbows, then her hands, looking down on him. Her tone was matter of fact. There was neither annoyance nor alarm. He stopped. In the moment that followed she remained motionless on top of him. He felt his cock go entirely limp. As it slipped out of her, she got off.

"I have to get some sleep," she said. "We leave early."

He walked to the bathroom and washed himself, wetting a second facecloth with hot water for her. When he brought it back he knelt on the bed and began to put the cloth between her legs but she slipped it from his hand and wiped herself. She tossed the cloth on the floor and turned on her side, away from him.

He turned off the light.

When he awoke, the sun hurt his eyes. The room was silent. She was not there. It was after nine. She had set the alarm for seven, but he'd heard nothing. His head hurt, as much from failure and guilt as from Scotch. He closed the curtains. He went to the bathroom to throw water on his face. He noticed the damp towel hanging from the shower door. He smelled traces of the shampoo she must have used while he slept. He turned on the water and adjusted the shower head to hard massage. The shower at his apartment was better suited to watering flowers than bodies. When he finished drying himself, he put his towel carefully next to the one she had used. He thought of taking it as a souvenir. But of what? A promising adventure that ended with an aborted take-off?

Returning to the room, he saw that she had put his clothes on a chair. There was a note.

"I think you missed your flight. Kaija."

. . .

The weekend he had so anticipated before being invaded by Finland turned out to be a write-off. His hangover didn't last beyond noon Saturday but the clearer his mind became the more sure he was that he had reason to feel uneasy. He couldn't define why. The uneasiness itself kept him from thinking. He couldn't get beyond a feeling of embarrassment. He felt like an actor who had forgotten his lines in the final scene of a play that, until that point, had held the audience and critics riveted. Disappointed, disgusted and unforgiving, they all walked out, demanding refunds. Even the stagehands left, not bothering to drop the final curtain to shield his shame. There he was, standing alone, on an empty stage in an empty theater, the houselights on high, the stage lights all focused center stage.

What had actually happened? He tried to be logical, detached. He took a pencil from a jar and laid a yellow legal pad on his lap. He needed a list. Short phrases.

Clear meanings. Lucid points he could visualize and memorize, and recite by rote when he began to question his own thinking later, as he surely would. Some things about himself, he knew. But Kaija had sprung a trap door beneath him.

The list:

- Couldn't get an erection.

He crossed that out and wrote:

- Couldn't sustain an erection.

- Reason: too much to drink, too little to eat, general tiredness

- Her fault?

Shit. He said it aloud, ripping off and crumpling the sheet. Kaija could have worn a nun's habit and still played his senses like a remote control changing channels on a television, volume up, volume down, volume up, volume down, just for her amusement. There wasn't a priest alive who could have remained chaste before a woman like that.

So what had happened? He tossed the pencil to the coffee table and watched it roll to the floor.

All evening — and surely this was also true in the hotel room, despite being in some degree drunk — he wanted to take her. All of him wanted all of her. She was a challenge. An exciting one. Her body deserved a statue, separated vertically down the middle by the meeting of two shades of bronze, one side light and feminine, the other dark and powerful.

Several times that weekend, his mind hovered around a notion but never nailed it to the wall. He was at his desk at the agency the following week when it crystallized. He had lost his erection because he sensed, as she lay on top of him early on, hands pinioning his chest, that something was wrong. The roles should somehow be reversed, but at the same time, and this was a first for him, he didn't want them to be reversed. As long as his embarrassment nagged at him, he kept thinking, if only there could have been a Take 2 for the entire scene, from the moment they were alone together.

As he stared at the wall behind his computer terminal, he toyed for a moment with the idea of pleading an errand to run so he could leave the office and cement the thought. But then he realized he didn't have to. Kaija had awakened something he thought had been a mere passing fantasy, engendered originally, to the best of his memory, by what he once thought must have been pornographic because the magazines were wrapped in plastic.

They seemed mostly to be from England. As an adolescent, when he first managed to buy one, he was intrigued. It was all new to him, but where was the porn? The images of women and school girls and governesses getting tawsed and caned seemed patently staged. His imagination wasn't really piqued until later when he read the series of erotic French novels. His mind provided the illustrations. The images it molded were infinitely malleable. They had a strange staying power. Even though he manufactured it, an image could pop up years later, as intact as an actual memory, even one that may have been reinforced by repeated viewing of an actual photograph.

As he recalled those images and the stirrings they spawned, the night's embarrassment became less acute. Spasmodic cringes gave way to daylight. In the light, he began to detect a thread to hang on to. It linked his adolescent fantasies with the remarkable presence that took him to her bed at the hotel. She must have been attracted to him, and he was certainly drawn to her at first sight, but he realized now that he didn't conquer her, he didn't win her over, he didn't orchestrate a single note that sounded during the course of the entire evening.

Now he realized she would have thought:

"Silly boy. Doesn't have a clue. You're mine. My toy."

Had he known himself better, he would not only have understood her assessment, he would have welcomed it. He would have nodded back.

"Lead on."

The desk phone he had picked up to appear busy as he thought of Kaija began to beep insistently. It startled him. Hanging it up, he turned to the list of client phone numbers pinned to the wall of his partition. He ran his finger down the list, pretending to find the one he was looking for. Looking back at the list twice, as if verifying the number, he dialed his home phone. As it rang, he was already thinking again about what really happened Friday night, about what was finally dawning on him. When his answering machine kicked in he said:

"Hi, have a couple of queries about the quarterly report translation. Do you want to say 'sales dropped' or 'demand softened'? Get back to me this afternoon if you can."

Convincing, he thought. Immediately his mind went back to the truth that was dawning about the night. Kaija was beautiful but she was a woman who didn't need men to confirm that. She didn't need to be wooed. As he looked back, he realized that part of him had sensed that. She had brought him, a perfect stranger, to her table. She had seated him beside her, possessively close. She had chosen when to include him in the conversation. Though she spoke in a normal voice, and with humor, the other women listened to her. And he listened to her. The evening flowed easily and he was perfectly content with his role, or would have been had he known he was playing that role. She was the perfect dominant, he realized, because she was a natural. At the table, in the bedroom, she didn't issue orders because she didn't have to.

If there was a tone of command at times, its existence was arguably ninety-nine percent inferred because, and this was the crux of his realization, he wanted her to command. All night, she led, he followed. And when he started spanking her ass in the hope of restoring his erection, what he really wanted was for her to be smacking his.

He remembered once dreaming he was drowning when all he needed was to get up and go to the can. Instead of fighting Kaija, charging ahead, holding his erection on high as battle colors, he should have surrendered to her. Just the thought of it, now, in his cubicle, changed the complexion of the day. What if he could see a woman like that whenever he wanted? Or, rather, when she wanted.

"Hi, I'm here, take me."

He'd happily check his macho at the door. Every visit would be like going on vacation from himself, impossible to do in any other circumstance he could imagine.

Work that day didn't let him pursue the line of thought. His project manager, a short middle-aged woman with far too much education for the job and the modest paycheck it afforded, called out his name and the two other translators who were working from French to English. There was a new rush job for a premium client.

"The one you're working on can wait."

It was just as well. The thought of Kaija in this new context had removed the embarrassment that had hobbled him since Friday night. Instead the image of her excited him, and he knew himself well enough to know that he would steal half the remaining shift from the agency by fantasizing about her rather than trying to figure out whether his sexuality was a lot more intricate than *Dick Has the Hots for Jane*.

As he left work the following Friday he toyed with the idea of going to the same bar where he met Kaija. He imagined her stepping out of a cab at the nearby hotel on 32nd Street, adjusting her flight attendant's uniform as she waited for luggage to be removed from the trunk. He didn't know what her uniform looked like. He wasn't even certain she worked for Finnair. But his imagination made it dark blue as he watched her buttocks move toward the hotel entrance. He pictured her in her room, showering away yet another flight. Was it as boring as his job? No, he concluded. For him, the act of boarding a plane, a train or even a city bus was an escape. The destination didn't matter, at least not until he got there. Being between A and B was his favorite place in life.

He didn't want to drink. By accident, he had been sober all week. When he returned home from the hotel Saturday morning there simply was no Scotch in the apartment. He had checked before returning to bed, too embarrassed to sit up and risk thought. When he awoke a few hours later it was raining again. He never summoned the will to get dressed that weekend, let alone walk to a liquor store three blocks away. In the following days, as his mind cleared, he began to feel he was on to something. He wanted to stay sober. And now it was Friday, stretching the streak to seven days.

Stepping onto the sidewalk, he began walking slowly south, toward the bar, thinking about what he would say to her if she were there. He ruled out "Nice flight?" He then heard himself confessing:

"I'm thinking I'm maybe not who I thought I was, or you thought I was, when we met last Friday."

There would be truth in that but he would have to get her alone to say it, away from the other stewardesses.

Click. Mental snapshot. He had set up Scene 2. There they were, standing between tables, him whispering as she stared back unblinking, uncomprehending. Damn, he would need another thousand words to sum up what he'd been thinking about for an entire week. The ice in her drink was melting. Scrap the scene. Couldn't work. He crossed the street, westbound, toward home.

Before he arrived he had rationalized that things had turned out well enough. By avoiding the bar he had completed a full week sober. Had he gone, he would have felt pathetic if he sat there all evening and she didn't show up. He also imagined her starting to enter the lounge, then, spotting him at the bar, turning quickly to her friends and saying:

"Let's go somewhere else. He's here."

No, he'd made the right decision. On Eighth Avenue, a few blocks from his apartment, he stopped at an Italian restaurant and treated himself to a take-out order of grilled chicken breasts atop a Caesar salad.

"Toss in some anchovies."

By the time he started climbing his stairs, he had shifted happily into fantasy mode. Without consciously directing the scene, he reshot his second meeting with Kaija. As in Scene 1, they stood between tables. She stared unblinking as he whispered his long sentence about maybe not being who either of them thought he was. In response, instead of the uncomprehending look and silence, Kaija said matter-of-factly, in the voice of Ilsa cutting through Rick's self-pity in *Casablanca*:

"So, what do you want me to do? Spank you?"

She hadn't whispered, but he didn't care.

He cleared a space on the coffee table for the take-out order. For a moment he thought of getting undressed, pulling out the bed and eating there, exposed to the anemic air-conditioning. No, slow down, he told himself. Savor the meal sitting up. If he ate it in bed he would wolf it down, in a hurry to masturbate to Kaija's question. He had all weekend for that. He felt the best he had all week.

He dug out his DVD of *Casablanca*, and Ingrid Bergman. Swedish. Kaija likely spoke Swedish as well.

CHAPTER 13

Obligatory Freedom

"I QUIT."

He was sitting across the desk from his project manager. It was six years and nine months to the day he had started working at the translation agency. He was thirty-nine. Although he was to always remember it as the day he saw the light and "just said fuck it," he had been given the choice of resigning or being fired.

He landed the job immediately after graduating. When he showed up for his first day of work, he hadn't had time to frame his certificate in translation. He thought he'd discovered the New World, a career and new life.

Now history needed rewriting. Columbus stepped ashore in the Bahamas, and the rest was history if you ignored the addenda attached to that history, such as the fact that he had actually hoped to land instead in Asia. Eighty-one months at the agency convinced him he also had made a navigational error. He had landed at Napoleon's Elba. If he didn't escape soon, he feared it would become his Saint Helena, his final resting place. At thirty-nine he was too young to settle for a bi-weekly paycheck.

In the past year he had begun to repeatedly fail to reach his word-count quota. He drank most nights and the first hours of the day felt like trying to run a one-hundred-yard hurdle race on a cinder track in bare feet. It was simply too painful to run fast enough to be able to hurdle the barrier each boring sentence presented.

He knew he was digging his own grave. He'd had a few warnings from the French projects manager but he had started to feel almost indispensable, not by virtue of meritorious service but by force of longevity. In the grander scheme of things, six and three-quarter years was a short duration. Yet in that time he had become the agency's second longest-serving, or longest surviving, translator. Translators, for the most part, were writers first and not cut out for factory piece work. And the salaries were too low to hold anyone with real skill.

In that time, he made one friend. Surprisingly it was the project manager, who was also unofficially office manager, the very woman who was now firing him. She was somewhere in her forties. She could have been early forties but a faintly lined smoker's complexion aged her. Her lips were pale. Her hair was long and marginally disheveled most of the time. Like everything else about her, it had no identifiable style. Her bangs reached the black rims of unflattering rectangular glasses with nine tiny white hearts where the arms met the frames. Most days she wore charcoal gray jeans and plain blouses or shirts. Everything about her, he recently decided, spelled resignation in both her professional and personal life. It scared him that while he wasn't there yet he was beginning to understand it. She wasn't someone he thought he would befriend outside of the office, but they chatted easily.

His sorry morning states had led to little meetings over time. As uncommunicative as she had first appeared, she surprised him eventually by admitting she identified with his malaise. The difference was she didn't drink. If she did, she joked once without smiling, they'd have to carry her out by noon.

"I envy your tolerance," she said, adding, "for alcohol."

She'd make a good drinker, he thought. Her predilection for precision would do her in. A pause to debate herself about the use of a semi-colon would justify a shot. By the time she ratcheted the debate beyond one of simple clarity to pretension in the 21st Century, she'd be pouring doubles.

"You're not only not making your quotas," she told him, "you've started getting sloppy."

"You mean someone around here actually looks at quality?"

"No," she replied with simple honesty. "But it happens from time to time that a client notices. Then I get shit."

He'd never heard her swear before. He took it as a sign of respect, or empathy, one of the two.

After a long pause, he said, "I'll crank it up."

"I'm afraid it's too late for that. Decision's not mine. It's made."

He let the news sink in. After a moment he stood up and spun his chair around one hundred and eighty degrees. He sat back down, resting his arms on the back support.

"OK, I'm fired."

"You could quit instead. Like, you know, if you were worried about how things would look on your CV."

He'd never heard her butcher "like" before. "Shit" and "like" in the same day. She cared.

"But I'm sure you know if you get fired you get benefits."

He knew he'd been sloughing off. He'd hated the job almost from the beginning. And when he realized he was almost the sole survivor among the people he first signed on with, he drank up and geared down.

"Gotcha!" They'd noticed.

He'd been asleep for so long he hadn't thought seriously about what else he could be doing. Now that he had been caught out, he felt relieved.

"Twenty-six weeks," she said in response to his stare. "It's not much, though."

In his mind he quickly did the math: thirty-nine years of age minus one salary, add in not much money at all for twenty-six weeks, and then add freedom. It added up to more of an existence than he had now. He'd freelance.

"Fire me," he said.

"With pleasure," she said, smiling. "You know that means you have to pack your coffee mug and get your ass out of here right now?"

He dismounted his reversed chair like a weary cowboy at movie's end, leaned across her desk and gave her a peck on the right cheek.

"Adios, amiga."

He didn't bother retrieving the coffee mug. He walked out the door and down the one flight of stairs to the building entrance empty-handed. After six and three-quarter years, there was nothing to take away that would prove he had ever been there.

When he stepped out onto the sidewalk, he looked up toward the sun, closing his eyes. It felt good. In the office he had just abandoned, there was no sunlight. Blinds were drawn to prevent it from interfering with computer screens.

Turning left, he began walking downtown, slowly. With almost joyous indifference, he realized his pace was probably irritating other pedestrians. Slowly, indifferently. That's how free people walked. No, a better word: ambled. He was always editing. With no course set, other than generally south, he ambled in zigzags. By the time he felt a sheen of sweat on his neck and forehead, he had reached Union Square. He sat under a tree. He could spend the remainder of the afternoon there if he wanted, with other independent men like Gandhi, Warhol and Lincoln, whose statues shared the park. He was in good company.

After he cooled down, his mind began to feel as still as the park's statues. The exhilaration of being fired for the first time in his life was slipping away, along with the one-sided chitchat about what shape that new life would take. Solitude sat down beside him on the park bench. He acknowledged it, but though his first instinct was to welcome it he almost just as quickly felt it as a void, an emptiness.

He had tossed away a job he hated and the bodies that accompanied it. Now, in a park encircled by traffic and countless people, he was alone, like the statues. Abe never chewed the fat with Andy. Gandhi probably shivered on fall nights.

As he had ambled downtown, the prospect of freelancing had charged his imagination with industrious images, up at dawn, bed left unmade, translated words filling his screen by the hundreds. He couldn't get down to work fast enough because now he was pulling his own wagon. The load was his to turn into dollars. It mattered little whether the texts were interesting. They bought him freedom from bosses and office hours. They bought him business cards that read, "I'm my own man." Though he would be translating texts not necessarily much different than the ones he churned out for six and three-quarter years for the agency, he was no longer a factory drone.

Solitude edged closer to him on the bench. It dawned on him that he had no clients. And he hated selling himself. He had little experience to peddle. At least, he thought, he had thirty-three years on his side. He could fudge his experience more convincingly than a 21-year-old graduate. What the hell, why not fill in a couple of years pretending he was doing what he always wanted to do but likely would never be able to afford to do:

"Translation, fiction — novel entitled blah blah by emerging Guinean underground author so-and-so."

The lie wouldn't be so farfetched, not like a business-man sprinkling his CV with an MBA graduation diploma bought online. There were lots of those downtown. Fur-thermore, he had translated novels, at least favorite pas-sages of novels, for his own pleasure.

By the time solitude sidled closer still and put its arm around him, he realized the void didn't begin and end with unemployment. He had far fewer friends than fingers. Though he sat on bar stools once or twice a week, he had no social life. The fact of going to an office and working with people whose names you knew, although you rarely spoke to them, passed as belonging to society. He could sit on a barstool and say, apropos of nothing except the image of a space shuttle on the muted TV on the far wall of the bar, "Well Samantha, you know who I mean, my colleague at work, Samantha, she thinks the space program is a crock," and his listener would unconsciously connect the dots and assume a full life was being lived.

He tried to remember the names of the translation agency's clients, the ones he knew from translating their documents. He wrote their names on the back of a paper bag he found in a trash can near the bench. He suspected some of them must be very large companies, some based in the States, with European subsidiaries, and others based in Europe and doing significant busi-ness in the U.S. The agency was getting only the dregs, voluminous dregs, but dregs nonetheless such as internal reports, minutes of meetings, organizational restructur-ing proposals.

An old blues song slipped into his head, something about "There's a man goin' 'round takin' names."

"That's me," he thought. If he didn't take those names, the names of the agency's clients, he wouldn't have any names. He wouldn't actually be stealing. Besides, he never signed any agreement preventing him from con-tacting those clients after his departure. He wouldn't be gunning for the agency's business. He was going uptown where the decision-makers had their hair cut. He wanted the documents that top-level managers signed off on, new marketing and branding strategies, ad campaigns, brochures for investors, the documents that went to advertising agencies that employed or subcontracted to their own list of translators.

Technically, he didn't have much cred to get himself in the door at those places, in New York or in Europe. But from what he knew about the agency's clients, and from what he probably could uncover with a little research, he could drop names. He could sound like he knew the ropes.

Warming to his own theme, he realized he would need to do some image enhancement on his own experience. He was the right age to have had his baptism a good number of years before, to have accumulated experience, yet not too old to have something in common with men and women on the rise. He had read somewhere that forty percent of CVs contained imaginary degrees or job experience. He'd fabricate experience for his twenties, make it impressively varied but lay no claim to managing anything. Instead of being his only post-secondary education, his time at NYU would become an ambitious and laudable upgrading of skills, specializing in niche translating. Someone would have to read the transcripts to know otherwise.

The more he thought about it the more he realized he had a workable plan of attack. He saw himself getting all cocky and pimped up and selling himself as a specialized translator, someone with a steel-like grasp of marketing and advertising communications, a master at making every document sound as if it were written with the conviction of the CEO himself. He'd sell himself as a word professional (where the hell, he wondered, did he come up with that term?). He would give the impression he had worked directly with the agency's clients, and at the highest levels. He'd hint that he got high on mission statements. Their goals were his goals. And even better than experience, he would remind them he was a Yank, based in New York City. Who better to speak the universal language that puts corporations on steroids? Who could have a finger closer to the pulse of business than a New Yorker born and bred?

For the first time in about eight years, in fact since he had sat in Heathrow Airport and made the actual decision to go back to school and become a translator, he felt purpose. He felt in control. He felt horny.

As he walked home, it was the horny part of his contemplations that most stayed with him. Was he not only becoming his own man but also becoming a new man? He wanted to conquer something, or someone. That's when men felt alive. It was a rare feeling for him, yet he felt this was how he should feel most of the time. He was suddenly so sure of this that he told himself he must have gotten so bored with his life that he'd forgotten his true nature.

Before he got home, he had put horny aside because, as usual, he had no options that evening. In its place he pondered the business cards he'd hand out at every opportunity, for clients and potential clients, and for girls at parties and in bars.

"Name, number, address. All there. Work for myself. Have my own company."

He couldn't make up his mind whether "Word professional" sounded too pompous to put under his name, "Translator and word professional." He decided it wasn't. Pretentious was currency among the clients he planned to seek out.

By early evening, the excitement about the future deserted him in the time it takes to change channels with a remote. He was exhausted. He wished he'd made notes about how good it had felt to walk out of his office as a free man that day. He fell asleep trying to regenerate the feeling.

CHAPTER 14

Bronx Connection

"I AM who I wanted to be."

In the year since he'd quit his agency job, when he found himself obsessing like a buzz saw with a jammed trigger about how inadequate life was, he would remind himself in one-syllable-at-a-time utterances that he was who he wanted to be, a boss-free man. He had taken to saying them not only aloud but also loudly as he looked in the bathroom mirror. But the words were sounding emptier. More often than not the voice sounded disembodied, like a voice traveling through the apartment building's ancient plumbing.

On one hand, he was indeed surviving materially. He did in fact have a career. He was absolutely his own man, at least to outsiders. But now that he had hit his forties an image had lodged in his head, a "me metaphor," he called it. It wasn't held there by some kind of crazy glue. It was cemented by truth. He was beginning to see his life as a vinyl record without a B side.

He had no girlfriend at the moment and he was tired

of reading how hard it was to nail down a relationship in New York. He had backed into a couple of relationships but they never seemed right after a couple of months at most. There was a hugely silly element involved in the pursuit. Gutsy pretense added to quiet desperation, the whole varnished with a veneer of "it doesn't really matter." It all added up to damn close to nothing. And the interludes between relationships were lengthening. It made sense. He was scarcely visible. He went out infrequently now. As time went by he liked contemporary music less and less and more often than not would have to be dragged to a concert. When he did go out, he spent less and less money because the roller coaster revenue ride that almost every freelancer has to grow accustomed to had taught him debt was anathema. He couldn't make monthly payments if he didn't have monthly income.

Because he worked at home, he didn't spend on clothes. He worked in sweat pants (or no pants) and T-shirt in summer, sweat pants, T-shirt and long-sleeved shirt in winter. Because he sat at a keyboard most days, extra pounds had been stalking him for several years. He was no catch, he knew that, and he turned to imaginary encounters with women too beautiful for the likes of him. That practice also made it easier to do-si-do into fantasy.

He had a lousy track record in reality. There was a marriage that lasted about as long as any year's Super Bowl commercials strung together, and there were a couple of relationships that managed to last more than a year but were so loosely constructed that other attractions wafted in through the cracks, on his side or hers until the relationships sank below the surface without a ripple.

There were a couple of intense Roman candle affairs as well, but the oohs and aahs hadn't lasted long. What troubled him now as he shuffled into his forties was the increasing frequency of duds, couplings without sparks, let alone fireworks. Was it him? The heavy drinking? His choice of women?

The fear surfaced during his last dry spell, that is, a dry spell in terms of work. He couldn't remember his last drinking dry spell. What he had noticed was that when he had no money, and started to think he never would, he was more and more often dipping his toe in loneliness. He couldn't afford to circulate, to see or be seen. He couldn't afford to sit on a bar stool and hope to strike up a conversation. He drank at home, and played sloppy sax.

On a May afternoon he found himself on Mulberry Street. The long walk to Chinatown was a restoration project. The month had been rainy and cold, almost as uncomfortable as winter, and holding none of the promise May was expected to bring.

This afternoon the air was too blossom-sweet to sully with Scotch vapors. He needed to get out of the apartment and move his body enough to make himself breathe a shade deeper than shallow. The day was perfect, warm but not humid. He would sweat off the booze slowly, without having to constantly wipe his brow and neck with bunched-up tissues.

On Canal Street he bought a bottle of black vinegar he needed for a dish of sweet and sour spareribs, a recipe he'd found that morning on the Web when his body was screaming for food. The purchase was one of only two things on his list for the day. The other item was "Party," with a question mark.

Deciding he couldn't become a new man in a single day, he abandoned his plan to walk back home for the exercise. On the train he decided he would go to the party. A friend had told him about it.

. . .

The walk to Chinatown had gotten the blood circulating. When he breathed, his chest moved perceptibly. Sometimes lying in bed after a heavy night's drinking he would watch his chest and wonder how it was possible to breathe without chest expansion. Today, he had felt so revived he immediately dozed off on the sofa when he got home.

When he awoke it was too late to inaugurate the Chinese ribs recipe. He showered, shaved and found a plastic bag for transporting his Scotch contribution to the party. He also threw in a bottle of water. It would take him a good hour to get to the party in Morris Heights, with two trains and a few blocks of walking.

He got off the 4 train at the Burnside Avenue Station in the Bronx. When he walked down the stairs to street level he rejoiced that the gods had placed a Burger King across the way on Jerome Avenue. It was still early. He'd have time to eat slowly and not arrive bloated. He order double cheese, rings and black coffee.

When he entered the hallway on the third floor of the five-story brown-brick apartment building an hour later he could hear the music. After climbing the stairs he paused to catch his breath. When he had recovered, he twisted the top off the virgin bottle and took a swig. He suddenly had the feeling the same old shit was starting all over again.

He knocked on the door. When nobody answered he let himself in. The reggaeton immediately drilled holes in the little reservoir of wellbeing he'd carefully stocked during the day.

It was early and only a few people, all girls, were dancing. Some furniture had obviously been removed for the night because a dozen other people he assumed to be guests were seated on the floor, leaning against the lime-green walls. They were watching images projected on the facing wall. He couldn't determine why. Maybe it was simply a poor man's emulation of a laser light system. If it was, it got his vote. He hated light explosions. Torture tools belonged at Gitmo, along with a lot of today's music.

He wandered through three other rooms, including the kitchen. The apartment was large and well kept. If he squeezed by someone, it would earn a perfunctory nod. He figured he had yet to rub against one of his hosts. They would have said hello, maybe asked him who he knew, how he came to be there. Since he'd only been invited by a friend of a friend, he wasn't sure how he would answer.

Rather than shuffle around looking lost he decided to become a man of purpose, someone who belonged and knew his way around. He made a beeline for the kitchen and rifled through the cupboards until he found a highball glass, although he later saw the plastic cups guests were meant to use. An ice bag had been ripped open in the sink. Instinctively he knew the day's physical restoration project, himself, had been cancelled. Rather than leave his Scotch with the rest of the liquor and coolers on the kitchen counter, he kept the bottle at his side.

From the front he heard sudden shrieks of welcome or surprise. By the time he navigated his way to the living room it was jammed. It was as if another party had transported itself holus-bolus. Bodies swallowed up most of the projected light. Faces appeared out of near blackness and disappeared. Someone turned up the reggaeton to compensate. Most of the new faces were Latino. Considering the music, maybe his host was too, not that it mattered much now. It was almost too loud to say hello.

As he drank, his ass got sore sitting on the floor. Holding the bottle carefully, he got to his feet. The music had by no means won him over but he decided he could live with it under the circumstances and he started moving to it, mostly a swaying motion, with a step or two thrown in now and then. Glass and bottle kept his arms near his sides.

His eyes had grown accustomed to the dim light and by standing he found he could put faces to the bodies he'd been focusing on, hoping the sexiest ones would stay in view. He kept looking for one in particular, a face to go with a body that wore a short, sleeveless, strapless purple dress with feet that moved about on sparkly silver shoes. He knew it was the effect of the booze and the now-hot room, but he was also afraid of finding the face. The evening would be ruined if she wasn't pretty. He wanted her to be not just pretty but very pretty. If she wasn't, he had resolved to leave. He'd already had imaginary conversations with that faceless body. He'd already touched it as it gyrated. Yes, he'd leave. He was getting too drunk to construct a replacement fantasy.

After a momentary silence the music switched to hip-hop. That momentary silence was enough to release the puppet strings that had kept him weightless. His body felt heavy and hot. To regain control, he forced his way around the room. It took concentration because the room was so crowded. By the time he'd completed one lap he spotted an opening in the hallway and strode towards the bathroom.

In the line, two bodies ahead of him, was the woman in the purple dress. "Turn around, turn around," he said to himself, trying to will it to happen. As she finally stepped into the bathroom he caught sight of her right profile. He realized he would see the left as she exited. Several minutes later, she emerged. She had done up her long black hair. Yes, yes, he voted. If she noticed him staring, she gave no sign of it as she pushed by. He wanted to follow her in the hope of striking up a conversation before she got swallowed up again in the living room crush. But shit, he'd been drinking for two hours at least and needed to pee badly. Would he even have realized the need had he not found himself in front of the bathroom door?

He leaned against the wall behind the toilet and rested his head on his forearm, eyes closed. Once his bladder was empty his head felt clearer and his breathing was easier. He sat down and opened his eyes. He picked up his bottle, which he'd placed beside the toilet bowl, reached forward to the switch beside the door and turned off the light. The darkness made the music and voices from outside seem louder. He had one thought:

was he too smashed to pursue the purple dress? Probably. Indeed quite likely. The next thought brought a small smile to his face. It made him feel clever. He decided play Chase the Skirt. The reasoning: being inebriated meant courage wasn't lacking and, more important, if he got immediately shot down in flames he mightn't even remember the rejection tomorrow.

Someone knocked twice on the door. He unscrewed the bottle cap, slowly took a swig, purposefully replaced the cap and stood. He felt fine. He switched on the light and opened the door.

By the time he edged his way back into the main room, the sound system was blasting Beyoncé. The press of bodies was even tighter because room had been cleared near the projection wall to make space for two women. He couldn't see their faces. Both were bent over, dresses hiked above their waists. A booty poppin' contest. A young man wearing shades despite the near darkness of the room rested his left hand on the small of the back of one of the girls. No one was declaring proprietorship of the other girl but occasionally a hand reached out of nowhere and tapped her gyrating ass for a bar or two. Sporadic shouts of approval rose over the music, as if in encouragement to a particularly inspired jazz soloist.

The instant he pulled his eyes away from the booty battle they landed on the face above the purple dress. She was barely a yard to his left. The roving light had caught her full face. Dark eyes, Latina face. And not a kid. Thank God. She was instantly back in shadow. He edged closer. Out of the corner of her eye she must have noticed his much taller presence beside her because she looked up and smiled quickly before turning her eyes back towards the grinding girls.

When the song ended he said "Hola" and raised his bottle as an offering. Another song began before she had a chance to answer. She pulled his hand closer to see the label on the bottle. She nodded and pointed toward the kitchen. He followed close behind. To occupy less space as she wormed her way through the people in the corridor she raised her arms above her head. The mini dress rose another inch. Another inch and he'd be looking at the skin of her cheeks.

He wasn't sure why they were headed to the kitchen until she reached behind two women in full embrace and retrieved a plastic cup, which she used to scoop up some ice from the sink. She then slid by him and proceeded to make her way back down the corridor. When she had to pause to wait for people to make room, he noticed her swaying motion was not in time to the music. She was feeling no pain either.

Turning the corner into the living room they found a small clearing by the wall. She turned to face him, holding up her glass. He poured a generous measure of Scotch. He had left his glass on the floor some time before and had given up trying to find it. After raising his bottle to clink her plastic glass, they both drank. He leaned close to her ear and introduced himself. She put her hand on his right shoulder and pulled him down to her level. "Alana," she said into his ear. Before she released his shoulder she planted a kiss on his cheek and turned toward the crowd of dancers. A sudden surge of bodies from behind pushed him against her. She turned and smiled. She raised her arms, one with her glass, and began dancing inches from his body. He reciprocated. As she danced, she looked down toward the floor, and he looked down on her body.

By the time she finished her drink, she still had some ice left in her glass. She gently took hold of his wrist with one hand and unscrewed the bottle cap with the other. She held the cap between her middle and index fingers and the glass between the index and thumb, and turned his wrist over. She released it when the glass was half full. He thought it was a remarkable demonstration of coordination.

Once again she turned away from him, but this time she backed her body against his, which was already against the wall. He lowered his free hand to her tummy as she leaned fully against him. A one-armed hug. Now and then she lightly swayed her ass against his groin, then would stop, content to just lean against him.

The room was tropical hot and they were both perspiring, and would have been even without the booze. He blew on her neck to cool her down. He realized he was issuing the long, controlled stream of air from the diaphragm, like the good woodwind player he wished he was. Alana pressed harder.

Finally she turned and pressed her breasts against his sweat-soaked shirt. Pinioned against the wall, he lowered his head. The kiss continued almost uninterrupted until they were on the street. It was good to be outside. There was a heel of Scotch left. He no longer had the bag he brought it in. She raised it to her lips. He laughed as her arm motion seemed to cause her to reflexively jut out the opposite hip. She left the last taste for him. He placed the empty bottle beside the building entrance and they walked toward Burnside to make their way toward Jerome Avenue and the train.

As they walked she asked where he lived.

"It's too late to go all the way back there. You're coming to my place," she said, suddenly pressing her hand against the small of his back to hurry him up. She wasn't shy about making decisions.

Just as the elevated tracks came into view, she suddenly stepped into the street and hailed a cab passing in the opposite direction.

"Come," she said, as if he needed prodding. "It's less than ten bucks to my place. Knock off the train fare and the cab's six bucks, with tip."

Tires squealed as the cab executed an instant U-turn. Before following Alana's irresistible purple behind into the cab, he saw the downtown train pulling out of the elevated station. It was almost 3:30 in the morning. The next train wouldn't arrive for twenty minutes.

CHAPTER 15

Answers

NOW, eleven years after that first booze-fueled night together, it was clear that Alana had simply had enough of K. The finality sunk in during the days after she defiantly told him she'd met a guy and gone to "fucking heaven." He had toyed with the idea that she was merely annoyed that he'd walked out on her the night he revealed his spanking fantasies and, possibly, implied that sex with her wasn't good enough.

She had a right to be hurt. He had gone about it all the wrong way. Had he managed to reach her first thing the following day he might have righted the canoe. Relationships weren't ocean liners with stabilizers. They were flimsy affairs. No, they were more dangerous than canoes. They were kayaks, two-seaters that overturned with every careless comment, each intimation of indifference. You spend half the time upside down, under water. It takes a lot of skill to get right-side up before the relationship drowns.

He was now history. Alana had kicked free and swum toward the surface without him. He had surfaced far away, alone.

Had he been pretending he was the only one who knew the relationship wasn't going anywhere? Had he assumed she was as weak as he was, content to tread water simply because it seemed safer than the alternative, taking a chance by drifting off alone in a world continually being reinvented for younger people? Probably.

How many times after an argument had he kept his distance until he started to sniff out the difference between alone and loneliness. When the latter settled in, like humidity in August, he would find himself obsessing again about Alana, trying to conjure desire that would join them forever. He kept hoping that by force of imagination he could reinvent himself so that he could burst through Alana's door fueled by so much new-born passion there would be nothing to work out and make right with the relationship. The Word Man wouldn't need words.

Now he knew that would never happen. He lunged out of his chair and went to his desk. Cleanup time. Fresh start. He put several language reference books back on the shelf and dumped some loose receipts into an envelope. They had been covering up a pair of earbuds he thought he'd lost. He then found an old crumpled-up list. Among the items on it was "Call A." He now remembered having tossed it toward the little black waste basket under the desk, then, days later, discovering that he'd missed. After picking up the piece of yellow paper, he had stood and tossed it back onto his desk for some reason rather than in the waste basket just inches away.

He now spread the note flat and blindly reached for the nearest pen. He crossed out the item "Call A," only to realize the pen he'd grabbed was a highlighter. It couldn't be erased, like memories.

. . .

Forcing his mind to the future, he typed:

Mistress, mistress / on the wall / who will be the first
to call. Ta-da, ta-da / da da da / ta-da ta-da ta da da.

It was cold and raining and he was restless. No work,
and no word from the two women, the two dominatrixes, who now exclusively fueled his fantasies in the
absence of Alana.

Four days later, the Egyptian Princess won the race.

**Back in the city. A bit tired though. Call me day after
tomorrow. Looking forward to this.**

PS... don't call before 11.

Her email had arrived in the morning. She must have
taken an early flight from Montreal. He called up her
website on his laptop. The images were almost becoming animated before his eyes. He had done this before
and discovered that if he stared at an image long enough
it eventually moves, an eye, a lip. He'd made the discovery years before while watching a documentary about
famous Indian chiefs who had stood up to hordes of
white settlers and soldiers. It was around four in the
morning. He was tired and he'd been drinking, but their
tragedy had bored deep into his imagination. He stared
at the proud defiance captured by 19th-century cameras
and painters. One by one the images budged, barely
perceptible movements that ended as soon as they began.
The blinks, the twitches struck him as signs from the
beyond the grave. The chieftains had not given in, even
in death.

He pictured the Egyptian domme sleeping, the big
dark eyes focused inward on her own dreams.

That evening, as if the two dommes were in
collusion, Felina emailed.

Call this number and tell me when you want a session and I'll schedule you. You must call me again one hour before the session to confirm. If you don't, I will cancel the session and you will not be granted another one. When you call to confirm, I will give you directions where to find my dungeon.

Already, he felt he had chosen well. Felina sounded as if she were all business, all dominance, which was the way things should be, he supposed. Dominance was her business, and that's what her customers were looking for in one form or another. But in contrast, the two email messages he had received from his Egyptian Princess — why was he already thinking of her as his, and was he reading too much into her words? — made him feel they were already friends. She sounded like any young woman he might meet at a party, or while waiting for prescriptions to be filled at Walgreens, a woman like any other woman, except...

That's where the sentence in his mind ended, at the word except. He didn't finish the sentence because he didn't know what came after except, except that he wanted to believe his life wouldn't be the same after meeting her. He had given up trying to change it himself. He wanted to offload himself, or more accurately, be offloaded. He wanted to back the 18-wheeler up to the loading dock, hop down from the cab, unlock the beast's doors and call out to anyone in the warehouse who might be listening, "Have at it. Take it all."

As instructed, he phoned her two days later, at 11:35 a.m. Hours earlier, over his morning coffee, he had written on his list: "Noon, call her." In the end, he was simply unable to wait the extra twenty-five minutes. He tried to emulate the tone of her emails and sound chummy. After introducing himself as the guy who'd written her a novel when she was in San Francisco, he asked,

"Catch up on your sleep?"

"Yeah. Well, no, not really. Don't know why I came back so friggin' early in the morning… OK, OK, let's see. Look, can we set something up for tomorrow instead? I want this to be good and that's not something that's likely to happen tonight the way I'm feeling. You OK with that?"

Since living out his fantasy of pulling on a pair of tights and being tied up and spanked by a beautiful, dominant woman was something he never thought he would ever do, waiting another twenty-four hours served only to heighten the anticipation. Just having actually spoken to her replaced impatience with inevitability. If he were told he had five minutes to live, he suspected happily that the anticipation he was feeling now would eat up four minutes and fifty-nine seconds, leaving just one agonizing second to wait for death.

"Absolutely," he answered.

"I'll email you the address. Call me sometime in the afternoon to confirm."

When he hung up, he went to the kitchen to get a glass. He had already dropped in two ice cubes before stopping himself. If he started drinking now he'd be sweating it out the next day while standing face to face with the only mesmerizingly beautiful four-thousand-year-old Egyptian Princess he'd ever met. To stifle the urge, he open-throated two large glasses of ice-cold water from the fridge.

He tossed his sax case on the sofa and looked for some sheet music. As soon as his eyes fell on the tattered Charlie Parker *Omnibook*, he grabbed it and put it on the music stand by the window. He had been trying to play some of the transcribed solos for years yet he still couldn't get even close to the required tempos on many of them, let alone nail the phrasing. That volume was an old friend, and a good enough friend to have told him straight out years ago that he would never be a good player. They made a deal, though. He could keep playing the pieces as long as it made him happy, and some days he felt he was actually getting closer. Other days, like today, too excited to sit, he'd say to hell with trying to get it right. He just wanted to fill that horn with so much air and so much sound he'd make it levitate, with him holding on, fingering like a madman and not giving a damn what it sounded like to passersby on the street below.

An hour and a half later, played out, he opened the sofa bed, turned on the TV, and lay down. He fell into a dreamless sleep. When he awoke an hour and a half later, he speculated that the reason he hadn't dreamed was that even his unconscious didn't know what came after "a woman like any other woman except."

. . .

Her email arrived shortly before 10 that night.

Where will you be coming from?

Chelsea.

Your lucky day. But you might not think you're so lucky after I finish with you.

The advantage of email was that he could read that threat as a warning or a seduction. He chose the latter. In none of the website photos was she smiling, but her body floated between a model's and a ballerina's. What was there to fear?

Her message continued:

I work out of two places, one in Soho, the other in Midtown. I'll try to line that one up for tomorrow. I'll tell you which when you call. Pleasant dreams.

When he turned off the light and closed his eyes, he smelled the fresh fall air that had been settling into his apartment all week. The humidity was gone, hopefully for the year. But when he awoke, fresh had become frigid. He closed the window and looked for slippers.

As he waited in the kitchen for the coffee to brew he turned on the oven, leaving the door open. It was far too early for radiators.

He had a small translation job that wasn't a rush, but he decided to finish it to help pass the morning. In the afternoon he ran a few errands, more to stretch his legs than anything. Against the chill, despite the sunny sky, he wore a T-shirt, a shirt and a jean jacket. He was glad he didn't drink the day before. Between the fresh air and the walk he felt almost healthy. He also felt like he would be soon going out on a date rather than submitting to a dominatrix who boasted of getting turned on beating men's asses black and blue.

He decided to get a haircut. Incongruously he had a macho urge to look his best for a woman before whom he was going to figuratively prostrate himself, and maybe literally as well. He didn't know. All he had to go by were barely remembered, decades-old French erotic novels. Who knew what the reality was? So far she didn't fit the stereotype. During the haircut, he became lost in anticipation. He was jolted back to reality when the barber spun the chair around so K could judge the result in the mirror. They hadn't exchanged a word. He pressed a larger than usual tip into the barber's hand.

The appointment had been set for 8 p.m., in the lower West 30s. She named an intersection and told him to call her from there for final directions. At 5:30 he got out of the shower. He had washed his hair again to destroy the overly neat haircut. Tonight he didn't feel that old. As he put on deodorant and aftershave, he realized his mouth was dry. He was feeling nervous. He sat on the toilet and cut his toenails. The bending left him slightly out of breath, but the nervousness had lessened.

"Shit," he thought. "I've got stage fright. I'm a fifty-one-year-old man going to see a twenty-something girl and I'm the one with stage fright." He stepped naked out of the little bathroom and opened his closet door. He had been planning on wearing his tights under his street clothes, in case stripping and changing in front of Egyptian royalty was not done. But would he be too hot? Would he sweat on the way there? He flicked on the weather channel. ... *and overnight we'll be dropping into the forties,* said the perky blond. *Not what you really want for post-season baseball.*

"But perfect for spanking," K said aloud, reaching for the tights he kept in a plastic storage bin on the top shelf of his closet, neatly folded under two winter scarves and a pair of gloves. He sat down on the edge of the sofa and stepped into each leg before standing to pull them carefully up to his balls. With his left hand he cupped his testicles and lifted them outside the tights to make sure he could raise the tights hard against his crotch. Releasing his testicles, he used both hands to pull the tights over his ass and then wedge them firmly between his cheeks. Then he pulled them up high enough to get his hands, and then his arms, into the straps.

As long as he remembered, the feel of cotton sent gentle shockwaves through his finger tips, like a vibrator that didn't need batteries. When wearing tights he felt like horniness embodied, looking for an excuse to happen. Even better, tights on a beautiful woman... marry me, marry me, introductions can wait. Tights were the ultimate and the subtlest bondage. As near to gossamer as they might be, with each movement they clutched like lips and fingers prodding, cupping and kneading his penis, balls, and anus. On a stunning woman latex and rubber could be riveting to his eye but the touch did little for him, or so he imagined. Ultimately, what disqualified them from fetish status were the materials. They did not seem fine enough and supple enough to ride up between a woman's cheeks, defining their voluptuous symmetry. They could never caress her anus the way the cotton could, or so fully transmit the warmth of her body as he and she wrestled about on the bed.

Christ, he thought, pulling his pants over the tights and doing up his shirt. In just minutes, after all these years of fantasizing, he would be removing these same clothes to stand firmly astride fantasy and reality, the reality of a living, breathing mistress, *maîtresse*, dominatrix, domme, seductress, amazon and, maybe just maybe, a lovely young woman who happened to be minted on the other side of the same kinky coin. "You top, me bottom. Nice to meet you."

He stepped into the fresh evening air and headed east, zigzagging toward the dungeon. The walk seemed to take forever. As he approached the appointed intersection, he phoned her. Though they'd never met, she was already on his speed dial.

"You're a block and a half away," she said, giving him the address.

When he got there, all he saw was a Jewish bookstore. On closer inspection he saw few books but a lot of knickknacks, kitsch and framed humorous sayings. Had he misunderstood the directions? He walked up and down the street hoping to see a more obvious building. He was minutes away from being late. She had told him she expected her submissives to be on time.

Returning to the address she'd given him, he saw what looked like a freight entrance. There were two buzzers. There was no response to the first one. The second buzzed back instantly. It was identified only as #2. The hallway was barely large enough for the little elevator with a silver metal door. He got in and pressed the 2nd floor. It rose so slowly that he checked his watch before, at last, it stopped with a thud. He pushed open the door and saw a reception counter, unmanned and in near darkness.

"Finally," said a voice with feigned impatience. He turned into the darkness, and there she was, his Egyptian Princess.

"When I saw the Jewish book store downstairs I thought I'd misunderstood the address," he said.

"I specialize in spanking rabbis. Come in."

He followed her a few steps until she stopped at a door. She pointed across the hall to another door.

"You can change there. There's also a shower if you want."

"No," he said, looking at nothing but the eyes he'd stared at on his computer screen. Although he sensed he had left the sentence unfinished, he raised his eyes from hers and took in the architecture of dark black hair knitted this way and that with chop sticks.

"I mean I've got my tights on underneath. I don't need to change," he said finally. "It's damn cold outside."

"Did you bring me a pair?"

"No, but I will. I didn't know what size to get you, or what color you might like."

He could smell the chill that clung to her black leather jacket. Earphones hung about her neck. She must have just arrived herself.

"Well, I've got to change," she said, opening the door behind her without turning around. With two fingers of her left hand she lifted the bottom of his black T-shirt, revealing his white tights. Seconds ago, he thought he had spotted a no-nonsense veneer on her young face, but if he did it was gone as the confirmation he was wearing the promised tights gave birth to a smile he thought he'd never forget. She gave his stomach a quick pat, then a little pinch.

"It's the first time," he said.

"The first time you've worn tights?"

"Both. No, yes it's the first time I've seen a domme, but it's not the first time I've worn tights. It's just the first time I've worn them outside. Outside my place."

It was so awkwardly said that he confessed:

"I'm nervous. Mouth even a little bit dry. I mean I'm a little bit nervous. Not a lot."

"Well you should be," she said, looking him in the eye before turning to enter the room behind her. "I'll call you when I'm ready." It was only then that he noticed the rest of what she was wearing: faded blue jeans, not tight, and clunky black goth boots with lots of buckles.

As she disappeared inside he wanted to keep talking, there in the dimly lit hallway, inches from her. After decades of bouncing around his head, the cage door was about to be sprung on his fantasies. Was the desire to stay there talking more a desire to preserve the moment than confront the risk he had worried about from the moment their appointment was confirmed? What if the real thing left him cold, and feeling ridiculous, and out $200?

He tried to wedge off his running shoes, forgetting he had double-knotted the round laces to prevent them from coming undone. He had to kneel to untie them. He pulled off his socks and stuck them into the shoes. He dropped his pants, then scooped them up and rolled them around his forearm. He then wrapped them with his T-shirt and shirt. He realized he should have wrapped the pants around the shirts. Just as he placed the clothes on the floor, he heard her say, "Come in."

For some reason, he decided to take the clothes into the room with him.

"Put your clothes over there, out of the way," she said, pointing casually to the corner with a riding crop. The crop was black like the teddy she wore.

"I hope this is OK," she said. "I don't have any tights." Before he could answer the obvious, she reached out with the crop and lightly brushed his balls and penis, bunched together by the tights.

"Cute," she smiled, turning her back and walking a few steps to a wooden, X-shaped cross. Her long buttocks were completely bared by the high-cut teddy, which made her legs appear even longer than they had in one of his favorite photographs on the website. In it, she was lying on a bed, on her back, propped up on her elbows. She wore a long skirt, dark green in his mind, but the color always changed as he pictured it, in the way his mind so often animated still photographs he wanted to live in. The skirt was raised past mid-thigh on her left leg only. The folds of the skirt fell so naturally it was impossible to believe the bare thigh was anything but an accident. Yet as his eyes traveled up it, they continued under the skirt to her crotch. Her panties were bordeaux, almost translucent. For an instant he allowed the three middle fingers of his right hand to graze between her legs. Warm and getting warmer. As he slowly withdrew his hand, he looked up to her face to see if she minded. Then he remembered he was imagining the photo. Her dark eyes looked at the camera, just looked. There was no smile, no transparent design to seduce, but he sensed the permission to approach was there, implied, if you dared.

Before he could make out the delicate dark tattoos on her back beneath the teddy, she took his left wrist and raised it near the top of the St. Andrew's cross, where a leather wrist cuff dangled. He felt her body against his as she reached up with both hands to attach the cuff. On the way to his other side, while holding his right wrist, she paused behind him to pass her nails lightly up and down the inside of each of his buttocks. As she attached the other wrist, he urgently wanted to free his arms, turn and wrap her slim body in them. Then it dawned on him, he couldn't. For the first time in his life, he was bound, attached, captive, fettered. And utterly vulnerable. His Egyptian Princess was squatting beside him. His eyes locked on to the back of her long neck. She tapped the inside of his calf, making him spread his legs wider, and in an instant his ankles were shackled. He had been so intent on tracing the lines of her body he had not been aware of what she was doing at his feet.

She stopped directly behind him. Taking the top of his tights in her right fist, she yanked upwards. It was if her fingers were pressing hard between his cheeks. He prayed she would reach around and grab his cock to complete the erection that was struggling with too many new sensations all at once.

She let go of his tights and stepped back. As she did he remembered the admonition on her website, and just about every other domme site: "No touching, no sex, of any kind." Surely she wouldn't leave him like this. He had only been with her five minutes and he felt more turned on than he had in years.

There was a full length mirror on the wall in front of him. For a second, no more, he felt he looked silly in tights, an old man spread-eagled and bound to a St. Andrew's cross in a sorry little room without windows. Then he saw her in the mirror, looking at him looking at himself. She had a flogger in her right hand. She held it vertically. With her left, she stroked the thin, broad tresses. She then began swinging them slowly back and forth, like a pendulum. She was no longer looking at him. She seemed entranced by the swaying flogger. He closed his eyes, for some reason hoping to memorize the image of her face lost in thought.

Thwack. The strands landed full on his right cheek. Not hard, but the thud was surprising. He looked up into the mirror just as she raised the flogger again, holding the tresses above her left shoulder, twisting them into one. This time he jerked as her backhand blow landed on the left cheek, harder than the first and slightly higher. She had his attention. For several minutes more, the flogger rose and fell like a slow dance. He felt the warmth seep deeper into his buttocks. Without realizing it, he was standing less upright, pulling down against the wrist cuffs so he could bend forward slightly, pushing his ass toward her after each blow, asking for more.

When she stopped, he was disappointed. It had been like making slow love. She was standing immediately behind him.

"So, you seemed to like my toy."

"I wish you hadn't stopped."

"Well, that's why I stopped," she said, punctuating her words with hand slaps. "You were liking it too much."

After nudging up his tights again, he heard the sound

of her high heels retreating. He had closed his eyes again. Being bound heightened sensation. When he reopened his eyes, he couldn't see her in the mirror. It seemed as if minutes passed. When she returned, she appeared out of nowhere. He hadn't heard her at all.

"I ditched the heels," she said, placing a palm on his back, on the skin just above his tights. "Hope you don't mind. I'll die before I get used to them." He liked the unpretentiousness. He forgave her for breaking the spell.

Thwack. Almost searing. He had trouble making out what exactly was causing the pain until she moved left a couple of steps. It was a brown leather strap, maybe an inch and a half wide. Harmless looking, but more serious than the flogger.

"This was what you wanted, isn't it?" she asked.

She'd remembered the time he'd sent her the email describing his fantasies, the part about wanting to be punished with a strap. His school had punished students with a paddle, but he'd read somewhere about schools that used straps. His imagination adopted the latter instantly. It went without saying the teacher wielding the strap was arrestingly hot, and untouchable because she was the teacher, he was a pupil, she was an adult, he was a kid. She was his favorite and she beat him every chance she got. She ordered him to stay in school to all hours so she could strap him to a young man's version of hysteria with no one around to hear. In time she ordered him to show up at night, at her home, for punishment in her basement. Because of the proximity of the furnace, she said, she had to strip down to bra and panties. She would tie him to a workbench. "No," she would say afterwards. "You cannot stay. Don't be ridiculous." With that she would give him a kiss on the forehead and send him home. The little kiss bought his silence. He would walk home in the dark, not thinking at all about the pain she had inflicted, only whether she was masturbating at that very moment.

The barefoot Egyptian Princess resumed.

"Can you do it harder?" he asked.

"I most certainly can." She sounded pleased, very.

He was glad when she finally stopped. She passed her hand over each cheek.

"Warm," she said, her lips close to his right ear. "Hot."

Like a boy, he felt proud of himself for taking the strapping, and like a man he felt happy this woman was pleased. Already he wanted to please her, like the teacher in his young man's fantasies. But now he wasn't too young and she too old. If anything it was the reverse.

For several minutes, she stood next to him, almost leaning against him, her left hand lightly resting on his chest while the right one reached behind and spanked. She was too slight for her hand to have enough strength behind it to hurt him but it was enough to bring his erection back, because of her hand on his chest as much as the one doing the spanking.

However he lost the erection instantly when he felt her unbuckle the cuff on his left ankle. Was the session over already? He had no idea how much time had passed. She freed the right leg, then the two wrists.

"Come," she said, leading him to a red-padded bench, shaped like a workhorse. "Over," she instructed, directing him to lie with his torso along the length of the bench. Again she attached his ankles. When she knelt in front of him to do his wrists, he stared down at her breasts. She sensed his stare and looked up, her face just inches from his. He laughed as best he could with his face mostly on the fake leather padding.

"What?" she said. "What's so funny?"

She stood up and he explained. Strapped down as he was, he felt like he was talking to her waist.

"While you were down there tying me up, your breasts made me think of something. That's all."

"Are you going to tell me?"

"It's silly." He explained how much he liked one of the photos on her website. She was braless. Her left hand cupped her right breast. Her right hand held a needle which she had just used to pierce her own nipple.

"I told myself right then and there I wanted to introduce myself to your right breast one day. Your left one is beautiful, too, but it's your right one I'm in love with."

She laughed.

"I hate to be the one to break the news but they come as a pair. They are BFF. Inseparable."

She moved behind him, her fingers walking down his spine as she went.

"I was going to strap you some more, but I think I need to enlarge your horizons." When she said that, the first thought that came to his mind was that she was going to work an outsized dildo into his ass. Where had that thought come from? He'd never so much as touched one in his life.

"You told me 'no paddles,' right?"

"Right." In his imagination, getting spanked with a strap gradually built up the heat until it magically passed straight through his buttocks into his penis. At the moment the pain became unbearable he came. Always. Right on cue. Perfectly synchronized. Without fail. The two sensations, the pain and the orgasm, were identical. At least, that's how he imagined it. There was no room for a brutal wooden paddle. Screaming and horny don't live on the same planet.

"And you want an introduction to my right boob, right?"

"Right."

"I'll tell you what. I might consider introducing you some day if you let me introduce you to my friend here." With that she waved a dark-brown-stained paddle before his eyes. His eyes first fell on her fingers. They seemed surprisingly long as she held the eighteen-inch-long toy, her index finger resting on top of the paddle. Inches before his eyes, the paddle loomed large and lethal, too big for her slim arms to wield with any authority.

Before he could answer — once again he'd been caught out staring at her body — she said, with mock horror, "What the hell am I doing? I don't make deals. You're going to try it."

For a full three seconds after the blow landed, covering both buttocks at their fullest part, he felt nothing. He had heard the impact and he expected to be in hell. Then, slowly at first, the tingle set in. Nice. Then before he fully registered what was happening, the tingle turned into burn.

"Well?" She stood by his head again, paddle in her left hand, her right on her hip. He talked to her fingers, the ones that had swung the wood.

"I think I could get to like that. The delay, that was amazing. Ouch in slow-mo."

She laughed.

"It's something else, isn't it?"

Had she tried it? Had someone been lucky enough to emblazon her ass with a paddle? Do dommes sub to other dommes? Was it a woman, a man? The questions he wanted to ask her piled up too fast to corral.

"So do I get to meet your breast?"

"I think you need a few more."

He suspected she wasn't swinging hard but after just a few minutes the paddle had left him swallowing low-pitched growls as he battled against the pain.

He felt the paddle being placed on his back, then her two hands massaging his butt.

"Very nice, my dear. Very nice."

By the time his breathing returned to normal, she was removing the ankle chains. Several times she had told him to breathe, but he kept forgetting. When he did remember, he felt he could bear another whack. He had things to learn.

"I'd say you've been spanked. At last," she said, undoing his wrists. "You did well."

He stood and felt his ass. His cheeks felt like cardboard, warm cardboard. He wanted to hug her but he walked to the corner and started dressing. She watched him for a while, and then started picking up her toys, wiping them as well as the spanking bench and the cross. His street clothes on, it was his turn to watch her for a moment. Finally, reaching for the door, he said:

"If I may say so, you are very beautiful."

She looked up from across the room.

"Thank you." Her voice was resonant. He liked the way she accepted the compliment. There was something gracious about it, like he'd expect from a Princess, not that he'd ever met one. He liked the slight contradictions, too. A princess who can't wait to kick off the high heels. A princess who says "Fuck" when she breaks a nail, as she did while detaching an ankle bracelet. A fine, delicate face that could suddenly don a no-nonsense veneer, only to shatter it a moment later with a huge, easy smile.

Adrenaline walked him home. He arrived so quickly it was if he'd only gone to the corner store and back. He immediately poured a Scotch, then pushed it aside. Before drinking he wanted to write down everything he could remember about the evening. And he didn't want the alcohol to numb the butt burn, not one bit. As long as he felt it the Egyptian Princess was there, in the room with him. He'd sleep with her.

He wrote for an hour, then opened his email program and wrote her:

Thank you so much for tonight. I mean it.

I could get addicted to this. Does that happen a lot?

I flew home.

Did I remember to say you're beautiful?

He hit Send and raised his Scotch to his lips. The ice had long ago melted. He drained the glass and went to the fridge for more ice.

He'd done it. Or rather, she had done it.

CHAPTER 16

On the Wagon

THE flood of emails began not long after their second session. He apologized to her not just for the number of messages, but in some cases their length.

I hope Manhattan's most beautiful domina is well.

Are you up for a longish e-mail? I haven't written it yet, so it won't descend on you in the next few minutes. Maybe not even for a few days.

It will likely be long because I'm not doing a great job of making my mind up about things these days, be it the kind of spanking session I'd like next, let alone the rest of my life. I want this, I want that, I can't remember what I want. Brain babble.

It will also likely be long because being at the keyboard with you in mind is the next best thing to having a conversation with you. You didn't tell me you'd be addictive.

I'm writing this note mostly because I just wanted to

reach out and say hello. In fact, I just said hello, out loud. I very much hope I can manage to see you soon.

Take good care

To his surprise there was a flood of email waiting for him when he got home that evening, but he couldn't read them right away. Though his bank account was getting so low the monthly user fees were threatening to bounce back in the bank's own face, he bought a bicycle that afternoon, an Italian mountain bike, refurbished said the owner of the bicycle shop on the Lower East Side off Grand Street. It was made up of parts from different bikes, and in places the paint job looked as if someone had used it for blow torch practice. That was an advantage, said the owner.

"That bike, new, freshly painted, would get stolen within a day. This way you should grow old together, even in New York."

It was a couple of inches too small for him but it rode well, and it cost him only $250 cash. He had taken to riding the West Side Greenway Path which ran along the Hudson all the way from the Staten Island Ferry up to the George Washington Bridge, not that he had ever gone that far, at least not yet. A few days before his second session with his Egyptian Princess, he quit drinking. After warning her about the threat of a long email, he'd gone riding. When he got home he cursed himself for not using his credit card to buy a folding bike. Carting it up the stairs to his apartment was more of a workout than riding it. Worse, it was in the way. To open up his sofa bed, he had to move the bike as well as the steamer trunk. He had already skinned his shin trying to navigate by it.

Before he could read her reply, he had to rub the sweat out of his eyes. Just receiving the message made him happy, and he found it endearing to see a Princess stoop to texter spell. What he most liked was the growing feeling that this pro-domme liked him.

you can write all you like. i'll read and respond if i can- though prolly not in as lengthy a manner.

anyhow- my boyfriends mom is coming into town tonight...i get to play tour guide, so i must be off...

thanks for all your compliments...i'll let you in on a secret- i don't handle them well.

take care

He read right over the boyfriend reference. He wanted to know everything about her but for now he would file certain things in the bottom drawer, at the back. Her boyfriend lived in San Fran. He wasn't well. That's all he knew. She must have been with him when she received his client-information tome. He preferred to imagine her giving West Coast subs a taste of the apple but there were days when even that image, if he let it take form, poked a jealousy-dedicated synapse.

Within three months, almost to the day, of their first session, he told her he was going on the wagon. She had never experienced him drunk, but he'd told her about drinking his way out of several relationships and a job.

He had told her that for their first spanking session, he stopped drinking twenty-four hours beforehand, so he'd sweat 100 percent pain, not 40 percent alcohol. She smiled at the challenge.

"I'll taste-test your sweat while I'm whipping your ass. If there's a hint of Scotch, the gag goes on and your ass is all mine."

Later, he imposed a forty-eight-hour policy. When he told her he'd been approved for a rehab program at an addiction center, she gave him a nervous little hug. He appreciated it, but he couldn't help noticing that when she wasn't in domme mode, in session, there was a tentativeness about her at times. He probably never would have noticed it had he never seen her in her dominatrix persona. The role fit her like a pair of tights.

His decision to enter the rehab program wasn't triggered by a recent drunken horror story. He hadn't added any juicy material for a future biographer's notes. He hadn't tried to kill himself, he hadn't torn up a rude client's check, he hadn't signed up for two years of non-refundable tango lessons. No, his only problem was that he was starting to feel happy instead of resigned. He didn't know how to deal with it.

He also needed money, and an ad in the paper one morning provided a possible six-month solution. The ad was addressed to lifetime drinkers. He qualified. He had started at fifteen. By military eligibility age, seventeen, he was drinking alone with stolen, borrowed and, occasionally, bought booze. The study would start with a brain scan to determine damage caused by booze. Afterwards, it would pay him $1,400, more than he would make in a particularly bad month of translating. It would be guaranteed income. He would sleep better, he thought.

However it wasn't to be. Just as he never won bets, never bought winning lottery tickets, he found out once again that he had no choice in life but to earn his own way, step by step, no free rides. He always rationalized that this lifetime of his was a karma payback gig.

He had torn out the ad with the phone number, which he called that very morning. Late that afternoon he got a call back from a woman. She said she was calling from a university but he didn't catch the name, hers or the university's. She sounded young. She said she was very sorry to have to tell him that he was not eligible for the program because being over fifty he did not satisfy the study's parameters. Her accent, he guessed, was East Indian. She sounded sweet.

"But, sir," she said, "I am guessing that you feel you require help. If that is the case I would be pleased to make an appointment for you to see someone at our addiction center and they can advise you what can be done. Would you like that?"

Why was he trying to build an image of her in his head? Her question came before he had time to complete the image.

"Yes," he answered.

Just over a week later, after being interviewed by a psychologist, doing some verbal and written tests, and then spending an hour with a psychiatrist, whose office walls were covered with paintings, her brother's, he was assigned to a group.

Stupidly, he felt sort of proud that he qualified, as if he'd passed an exam after weeks of hard study. For two weeks, they told him, he would attend sessions daily. During that time he would be on medication to help him rest and avoid anxiety that might lead him to a bottle. After those two weeks, if he stayed clean, he would begin a second stage that would last about a year and a half, with several group sessions a week, afternoon or evening as suited his schedule. Again, he said yes when asked if he wanted to continue.

As much as he wanted to see his Egyptian Princess, a session during the two weeks on serious Valium would be as stimulating as making love in a space suit. When he was promoted to Stage 2 of the program, he called her.

"Hey, guy, guess what?" she blurted out. "I'm going to Mexico. Two whole hot months."

"Shit," he thought. "Can I see you before you go?" He wanted to add, "I need you right now," but he was not her problem.

"I'm leaving in six days and I got a bunch of things to do. I've got to see my landlord about the rent, find someone to take care of Simon."

"Simon?"

"Yeah, Simon, my cat. Buy a bikini," she continued, "master Spanish, take salsa lessons. The usual. Look, I'll call you back if I can get my shit together in time."

Although it didn't sound likely she would find time

for him, he walked to Chelsea Market later that afternoon and bought an insider's guide to Mexico at Pos-
man's. When he returned home there was work waiting
for him, about two weeks' worth.

He felt his life was changing. It was something he
hadn't felt since he went to Spain as a young man and
came home with a career plan. He wanted a drink.
Instead he opened up the bed. It got dark so early in
December that he didn't feel guilty about it. He pictured his *maîtresse* wearing a bikini and sitting on a bar
stool in some place like Oaxaca. After masturbating he
thought for a second about using the money from the
new project to fly to Mexico and surprise her. Christ,
dumb ideas weren't reserved for drunks. He fell asleep
soon afterwards. He woke up at three in the morning,
more refreshed that he'd been in ages, and began work.

Three days later, she called.

"Saturday, six o'clock. I might try to make it even
earlier. I take off the next day. Does that work for you?"

CHAPTER 17

Ming Empress

THE session time actually ended up being later instead of earlier, 8:30.

"And it's not the usual place," she said at noon that day. "It's around the corner from you. If I beat the crap out of you, you can still limp home."

The pre-session taunts, threats and teasing provided the soundtrack for his day.

"It's between Seventh and Eighth. Find the door that says PB on it. It's downstairs. Tell them you're there to see me."

He arrived early. At first the blonde at the desk at the bottom of the stairs couldn't find a record or the appointment.

"Does she work for us, or is she an independent?"

"Indy, I guess."

"That means she rents dungeon space from us," she explained. She rummaged through some papers on the desk, pushed aside the magazine she'd been reading, and finally checked the computer.

"Nope. Nada."

His heart fell.

"I know it's tonight," he said. "She's leaving the country tomorrow."

"OK, honey. You said you're early. We're not booked big time tonight. If she doesn't show up you'll get your pick of our mistresses. Come here," she said, getting up, walking a few feet to her left, and opening the door to a tiny windowless room with dark green walls. He hesitated. He glanced downwards for a mini second at her high heels, and then back up her fishnet stockings which came to an abrupt end at a short black skirt. She held the door open for him. He had to brush by breasts to enter.

"There are some magazines on the table beside the chair."

Other than an old *Newsweek*, there were only nightlife listings and bondage and discipline ads, some European, some local, from glossy to newsprint. No stories, just photos of doms and dommes and dungeons with all the usual promises — he felt he was becoming an old hand at this — and contact information.

He stopped at one dungeon ad. It was for the dungeon he was now waiting in. He learned that PB stood for Pandora's Box. He remembered watching a TV show about it. Apparently it was famous. Though he was still in Midtown, he felt he had definitely gone uptown in dungeons.

After rifling through the other publications, he put them aside. There was only one domme he wanted to think about. He stood and did some stretching exercises. They got rid of the sway back that settled in after a day of sitting at a keyboard. Tights were unforgiving. The stretching also got him breathing deeply again. Seeing her had continued to be like Christmas morning as a kid, excitement holding his chest in a bear hug.

He had to inhale.

A knock. The receptionist poked her head through the door.

"She's here. She'll get you after she changes."

It was 8:37. He didn't know whether the clock was already clicking on the hour he would pay for. From a large Apple Store bag, he took out his tights. He'd be ready when she came to get him.

Minutes later, his Egyptian Princess ushered him into a vast room with a ceiling that must have been two basketball hoops high. At least that's how he was to remember it. Red walls, gold picture frames, jade-colored floors, gold dragons and pleasure couches, black cages, a golden throne. In the middle, dwarfed by the room, was a spanking horse. She stood next to him, watching his reaction.

"The Ming Empress," she said. "All the rooms have themes. Pretty cool, no?"

He looked down at her.

"More than cool."

She stepped behind him. He felt her hand grasp the top of his tights, making them snugger. Without a word, she tugged upwards and forward, propelling him toward the bench. She draped him over it, like a puppet. He knew the routine, but this time she didn't bind his wrists and ankles.

"I'm not going to go easy on you tonight."

He had to laugh. She hadn't gone easy on him since their initial session. She loved her work. It wasn't an act. Thanks to a mirror, he had once seen utter, unblinking concentration freeze her face before she launched a swing.

"This place is taking a big bite out of the tribute you're paying me. So I want my money's worth. And because Mexico is putting me in an exceptionally good mood, I'm going to make things tougher on you. I'm not tying you up and I'm going to come down on you hard. If you try to get off the horse, I'm going to hook you up there."

He looked up and saw some sort of suspension rigging between two pillars.

"Your shoulders will pop out their sockets while I whip you until you bleed. Yell all you want. No one will hear you." She seemed to make a point of uttering her most dire threats when she was within whispering distance. Her tone would be as casual as if she were informing him of tomorrow's weather forecast. Weather was inevitable. There was no point protesting.

She stepped in front of him.

"So, I'm sure you don't want me to have to do that," she said, digging her thumbs into his shoulders. "You're going to be a good boy. I just know it." She patted his head and moved behind him, warming up his butt with her hand.

Because he wasn't bound, after half an hour of flogging, strapping and paddling he couldn't stop himself from writhing precariously on the horse, almost sliding off on several occasions.

"This won't do," she said. "I'm going to have to hold you in place." In a second, she had lifted herself on top of him. She sat upright and straddled his back, facing his feet.

"Hold my ankles. Don't let me fall off."

Her right elbow digging into his back, she leaned backwards and dangled a new toy in front of his eyes, a thick, beautifully varnished hairbrush-shaped paddle.

After a moment, she sat upright again. He felt her warm buttocks on the skin of his upper back, above the tights. She placed her left hand on the small of his back. As she swung the brush down hard, he felt her cheeks roll on his back. The pain was excruciating. Desperately, he reached behind him, grasping her boots at the ankles. His eyes were watering.

"Breathe," she kept telling him, as if he were a silly person who couldn't follow basic instructions. He did as he was told, and tried to block out everything except her soft hot buttocks clinging to the skin of his back.

When she at last stopped, she told him to get down from the horse and pull down his tights.

She walked him to the golden throne.

"Bend over," she said. "Rest your hands on the arms of the throne." She took his camera out of the Apple Store bag and made a record of the evening's work.

"Something to warm my heart while I lie on the beach toasting the rest of my body in the sun," she said.

She had told him she didn't have a camera and he had offered to lend her his for the trip.

"Email them to me," he asked, deciding on the spot to build a collection of his own. He took the camera from her and photographed her sitting on the throne. For the first time, she appeared small to him. But her eyes looked black against the gold of the throne. She belonged there.

After changing, they stood in the corridor near the manager's desk. He gave her the Mexican travel book. She seemed sincerely delighted. For the first time, she threw her arms around his neck.

"Something tells me you'd like to come with me." She smiled up at him. With her hands still around his neck, he reached for his wallet.

"Let's see," he said, holding the wallet up so she could see. "Five dollars. Enough?"

"Hell. What a shame. Poor guy. I guess you're just stuck in the city."

Before they parted on the street, he told her he'd gotten a great contract that week.

"I can wire some money to you if you run out. No use going down there and not enjoying it all the way."

"That's sweet, but no. I don't like owing anything to anybody."

He kissed her on the cheek and they walked off in opposite directions.

CHAPTER 18

Rehab

JUST as K two months before had thought of showing up in Mexico as a surprise, he now thought of meeting her at the airport. Eventually, he had dismissed that idea. He had thought of her constantly, more intensely and for longer than he'd ever thought of a woman before, and that was reason enough to rein himself in.

He did not understand why she seemed to like him so much. Was he that starved for affection that he'd trip over anyone offering it? It wasn't his money that attracted her because she knew he had to save up for each session, canceling once because a small check from a new client had bounced.

It wasn't physical attraction. He was almost a quarter century older than she was. If he had seen her walk by on the street, not knowing she was a domme, he would have said, "Shit, that's beautiful." She would have no trouble attracting men her age. Although he was flattered by her "liking," he took it with a grain of salt, just as he had done during their second session:

"If I were just a little, little bit older and you were just a teeny bit younger, I'd shag you myself."

It was a while later during that same session, when he was bound hand and foot facing the floor and couldn't react, that she exclaimed out of nowhere:

"God I love anal sex. I love it!"

He never did remember in what context she'd said it, but from that moment on the image of having anal sex with her got equal masturbation billing with his spanking fantasies. It was no mean accomplishment.

In the end, her two months of absence weren't the eternity he feared. She had told him before leaving that she could arrange for another mistress to see him while she was gone. Quickly, loyally, he said no.

"I'm yours."

"I'll send you her name and phone number anyway." However, she never did.

After less than a month of rehab, he was ridiculously happy. For the first time in his life, or so it seemed, everything had become easy. He hadn't the slightest urge to get stoned despite spending hours with people who still had the urge to some degree or other. Some were the bravest people he'd ever met, scratching their way hour by hour in the belief that there was another kind of existence waiting for them. Others, often the ones he instinctively related to most, tripped, just disappeared, or ended up being sent back to Stage 1 or admitted to the hospital before their death wish could come true. Some had been going through the revolving door for years, as addicted to rehab as their substance of choice. Yet already he felt he could walk away without the slightest risk of falling into the hole again.

Every day, be it beautiful or bitter and windy, he walked and walked. A guess said it was around three miles to the addiction center on East Broadway. Most days he sold himself a return trip. One day, in an alleyway after a dusting of snow had fallen, he measured his stride. Not enough snow had fallen to distort his way of walking, but there was enough to leave footprints. He had so much energy to burn he could afford to be meticulous. He took ten measurements and averaged them: twenty-seven inches a step. The measuring put him behind schedule, but for the sake of accuracy he walked at a normal speed, counting the steps: 7,326.

When he arrived at the center, he was high from the rhythmic counting. His body and mind had been in sync for close to an hour. After less than a quarter of an hour, thoughts had stopped trying to slip in between the numbers. If his concentration started to waver, he counted aloud. When he was young he used to clear his head while walking by breathing to the tempo of portions of two Beethoven symphonies he loved, 3 and 9. Out for four beats, hold for four, in for four, hold for four. He got the idea from the conductor of a youth symphony he had once met. He had asked the conductor if it was particularly difficult to maintain an especially slow tempo. The conductor said his trick was to match his breathing to the tempo.

When he arrived at the sessions, especially at first, he continued to sweat, often for ten or fifteen minutes. A tall thin Englishman, aging faster than his years, would remind him in an exaggerated London accent that "this edifice is ever so thoughtfully furnished with shower facilities in the basement."

A young woman, a PhD candidate who discovered coke while lost in the end notes of her thesis research, liked guessing how much weight he'd lost. In two months alone he dropped twenty-three pounds. He hadn't been trying to lose weight, but when he saw it happening, and so quickly, he pushed himself to walk even faster. He'd picture himself in tights, a new man for the return of his Egyptian Princess. He dared hope she would see him as a younger man, too, a shag-able man.

Was that even possible? No. Nothing would ever happen between them no matter how fit he got. But he could no more stop fantasizing about fucking that delicate young body, weightless, half his size, yet impregnated with a power to dominate, than he could imagine returning to a vanilla world where sex had ceased to be his one great hope for salvation.

Sex had been the place to hide when nothing else in life resembled whatever it was that the boy in him had pictured life to be. He could never fully seize the old sense of anticipation about what life held for him, just around the corner, when he would be an adult.

As a boy, the anticipation filled him so close to the brim some days that he could barely breathe. He couldn't wait. Whatever life was really like, the boy thought, it would be danceable. At the very worst, he wouldn't be able to stop tapping his foot to its pulse. Then he became an adult, technically at least. And there were moments, danceable ones, but they came farther and farther apart. There were long stretches when life was almost flatlining. Only sex could fine tune the fibrillations of his heart. The pulse would return.

He would sit on a bar stool and watch his brain-function monitored on the big-screen TV between the shelves of bottles. Other patrons saw breaking news and sports on the lounge screens. He had his own signal. The screen was a depth-of-anesthesia monitor. It charted his evening, drink by drink. Sometimes when he asked the barman for another Scotch he also requested he switch the channel, the one with his heart monitor. In the bar's restroom, however, there were no screens. As he peed, he would wonder whether the overdue release of urine steadied or increased his heartbeat or registered brain activity. When at his stool, if the brain monitor went blank, he noticed the barman had a habit of suggesting he head off home.

Now the Egyptian Princess was his substance of choice. Imagining making love to her black eyes — they weren't truly black, but from a distance, in photographs or his imagination, they were — would send both monitors dancing. When he imagined her turning the tables and dominating him, tying him up and beating him, then leaving him bound while she fucked him, the graphs on the monitors would defy science. They would spike and plummet and describe long soaring arcs, as if they were plugged into the skins of five conga drums all urgently punctuating the world differently as the moment dictated. They would defy science because the feeling of being alive couldn't be measured after all. He just was. Alive.

He was in love. Thank God she was in Mexico. He knew if she even heard him think it she would slam the door on him. She hated "clingy clients."

LeBron had noticed the change.

"You play better sober," he said one day, without ever having asked whether his friend had actually stopped drinking. Since LeBron usually brought his own beer downstairs for their afternoons, he never had occasion to ask if there was anything around to drink. The answer would have been no.

"You're a wind-player. Booze messes up your breath control and that messes up your playing. It should mess up your talking, but unfortunately it never did. One of the mysteries, I guess."

On another occasion, when leaving for a music gig, he stopped in the hallway and turned to his friend.

"Nice to see you finally enjoying the life gig. It doesn't pay much, but what the hell."

CHAPTER 19

Bienvenido

JUDGING by the time of her email, and the time of her departure for Mexico, the message must have been the last thing she'd done before leaving for the airport two months earlier. He was touched by the fact she had written, not just because she seemed to care about him even though they had known each other barely three months before she flew south, but also because he knew she was a night person right down to her tattooed left foot. Her budget Aeromexico flight left JFK at 9 a.m. She must have been up all night to have written him at 5:22 a.m. He had printed out the email and carried it in his pants pocket every day since. It was no longer legible to someone who had not memorized the words.

It saddens me deeply to think of you so depressed... and without work...it also saddens me to think of you drinking as much as you have all these years- it makes me very happy to hear you have opted to get yourself some help. one less thing i can punish you for. I'm very proud of you.

He waited until the day after her return to call her. It was raining and cold. When she answered she was in Midtown, about to finish running errands.

"God, yeah, it was great."

He could hardly hear her over the traffic noise and the wind-swept rain although she was almost shouting.

"But I'm about ready to fucking faint. Got in around 11... at night. I've got to eat and I've got to sleep, and I've got to find some damned cat food for Simon. I'll eat it myself if I have to. I haven't been this cold in months."

"I've got a can opener."

"What?"

"I've got a can opener if you want to eat the cat food here. I've also got some things for you. Come on over. I'll fix you something. Split the cost of a cab, OK? I'll meet you downstairs."

He had given her his address but she said she was so tired she'd already forgotten the building's number.

"My place will be on the right. I'm going to put on my winter coat. It's red. You'll be able to spot me."

When they got upstairs twenty minutes later, she let him hug her. He held on to her for an extra moment. Her first word, whispered in his right ear, was "Food."

He retrieved a towel from the bathroom and tossed it at her from across the room, then put on a small amount of water to boil. Five minutes later she was sitting in his big arm chair, legs folded under her, eating Thai soup and a basic green salad with commercial Italian dressing.

"Man," she said when the last noodle was gone, "that was necessary. Thanks."

While she ate he had taken a cardboard box out of the trunk and placed it at his feet, between the sofa and the trunk, where she couldn't see. When she'd finished, as he took her dishes from her, he asked if she was ready.

"For what?"

She had forgotten he had "things" for her besides her first food of the day.

He knew he had overdone it. She wasn't someone you could buy. It wasn't like the compliments that flowed from his mouth, like a drinking fountain turned full force by a thirsty child who ends up drenched. She had said she didn't take compliments well but they drew the biggest smiles and he suspected the exasperation was feigned. She knew he meant them.

"First," he said, handing her an X-Acto knife and a rectangular box still in its USPS parcel.

She shook it. It was light. No sound. More patiently than he would have, she slit open three sides of the parcel and plucked out the protective wads of *L.A. Times* newspaper. Inside she found three wooden paddles, one round and about the size of a man's palm, and two rectangular ones, one medium-sized and one large, a foot and a half from the business end to the tip of the handle. They were stained black. She had admitted to him she had been domming only a couple of years and had few toys of her own. Despite her evident fatigue, enhanced by Tequila on the star-filled night before her departure from Mexico, she was tickled to get them.

"Light, but hardwood. No need to hold back," he said. Before she could respond he handed her another box, this one opened, its irregularly shaped contents covered clumsily by a piece of newsprint from the *New York Post*.

"Be careful," he warned. She lifted off the newsprint. Two cacti. "Chica and Chico," he said. Chica had two arms extending from the main stem of the plant. Chico was penis shaped.

"Engorged already!" she said.

"Call me Chico," he said.

The next gift was unwrapped. A red document folder. Inside were four documents, each several pages in length, single spaced and stapled. On top was a Table of Contents.

"What is all this?" she said, flipping through the

pages, then reading the Table of Contents.

"Short stories, very short ones. They just popped into my head while you were gone. They're all set in Latin America. I haven't played with fiction for years," he said. "Thought they might make your vacation last a little longer while you read them. Besides, they didn't cost a cent."

She looked at him for a moment as if he were crazy.

"Just one more and I'll let you go home to sleep," he said. He hated saying those last words because against all hope he was praying she would disguise her pleasure at being, as she would put it, "gifted" so generously by him and say something like, "I'm so beat I could crash right here, in this chair."

This gift, the final one, he didn't hand to her. He tossed it, startling her, but she made the catch. A pair of tights, the same style as his, a cotton unitard, but black instead of white.

"Cool," she said. "If they fit, if I don't look ridiculous in them, I'll wear them at our next play session, when, by the way, I intend to modify the meaning of 'severe' with one of my new toys."

She stood up, stepped over to the sofa and leaned down to give him a hug.

"Thank you," she said, looking into his eyes, before breaking away to say with disarming practicality:

"How am I going to get this shit home?"

"Home." Damn it, he thought, getting up and heading to the kitchen. He returned with a big plastic shopping bag with a handle. "Put the flat stuff in the bottom, then the box with the Chico and Chica, and surround it with everything else to keep it upright. Whatever you do, don't reach in without looking. They're a lovely couple but they'll prick your hand to shreds."

She had her leather jacket on before he could do it for her, but she turned at the door and put her hands on his shoulders.

"You're a sweetie. I'll call you when I've got myself together."

And then she was gone. He felt deflated. Fantasies had a shorter life span than cherry blossoms.

It was almost two weeks before she called. Giving up drinking had been a lot easier than leaving her alone for that time.

"Would you still like to have a session at your place?"

He didn't remember having suggested one, and he was convinced he remembered every single word she'd ever spoken to him. What he had said was that he wanted her to drop by his place again for a visit. He wanted a memory of her image etched into his room. He wanted the company, even if it haunted him like a ghost.

Though they were still in touch, LeBron had recently moved out of the apartment upstairs. Since then, K had few visitors.

When he was too tired to fantasize, he knew this amazing woman would never remain in his life for any-thing approaching long enough. It wasn't a thought he dwelled on, like the knowledge that he could never tell her fully how he felt about her.

Though in her presence he never felt it, he was old enough to be her father. He knew she "kind of liked him," to use her own words, expressed in an early email. He also knew that coming from her, those words were also understatement. Even with a young man, from the little he had come to know of her, she would be excruci-atingly cautious about declaring her feelings. Inside her being was either unshakeable independence or a cavern-ous fear of closeness.

CHAPTER 20

Ballerinas and Pirates

TWO weeks earlier, as she curled herself up in his wing-backed armchair before wordlessly devouring the soup and salad, she turned her head toward the adjacent kitchen.

"The trunk," she said.

"What about it?" he replied, bent over the counter trying to make out the water line inside the container of Thai soup.

"Will you leave it to me when you die?"

"If you're good to me in my old age, when my butt is too old to paddle."

"Won't happen. I'll find some other way of torturing you. So, can I have the trunk?"

Her matter-of-factness about his demise teetered on impudence. It turned him on. He felt young for a moment as he peeked at her from the kitchen, seeing her in left profile, the opposite one to the image that was engraved in his mind from the first sighting on the Internet.

He had an overwhelming desire to pull her over his knee and playfully spank her. The microwave timer rang. The soup was ready. He burned his fingers as he transferred it from the Styrofoam to a proper soup bowl.

Now that she was back for her second visit to his apartment, clearly rested, it would never have occurred to him to imagine her over his knee. She was in charge from the moment she let him kiss the evening chill on her cheeks.

He was hoping she would be wearing the tights he bought her but she wasn't. She politely ordered him to lie over the trunk, lengthwise. As he lay there, she undressed, down to a black sports bra and small black cotton panties with a white waistband. She slipped her high black goth boots back on, which made her seem to tower over him.

From a sports bag, she pulled out lengths of thick white rope. He felt its smoothness as she deliberately bound his ankles and then his thighs to the trunk. She moved to the other end of the trunk and began what turned out to be the part he remembered most from that night.

She knelt in front of him, her face inches from his, as she began lacing rope around one wrist, then the other. Her concentration was total, her eyes focused on her work. As for his eyes, they rode down her long fine nose, over her breasts, then along her forearms to her fingers and the rope she was manipulating. After binding each wrist, she bound them together and then ran the rope through the leather handle grip on the end of the trunk. She rose and passed the rope around the trunk to the other end where she reunited it with his ankles, finishing up by securing it through the leather handle at that end. She tested the rope, yanking it gently here and there, then smacked his ass with her hand.

"Trussed like a turkey," she announced. She sounded pleased with herself. Later she was to tell him that she had only started learning rope bondage the summer before. While in California, she attended a seminar by Midori. She said the woman was the priestess of erotic Japanese bondage techniques.

"The only thing I haven't succeeded in tying up is my cat."

To his surprise he didn't get to cry out, as she often put it, "like an angry bear" under blows from paddles, or hiss and squirm under the deepening sting of straps. For what seemed like twenty minutes she laid on a flogger, coiling it up, and then exploding her arm forward in a horizontal blow or from above. The pain was, in a strange way, not painful. The flogger, he decided, was the most sensual of the toys, to look at, to touch and to experience the business end of.

As if reading his mind, however, whenever she thought he was enjoying things too much she would suddenly send several blows raining down on his upper back and shoulders. His cries then were much higher pitched.

She finished the session with something new for him: a cane, light and whippy, the sonorous swish almost worse at first than its bite. She latticed his behind slowly and deliberately. She didn't have to swing hard. He imagined that the cane would have been far more uncomfortable had she started the session with it. Though he had deeply enjoyed the flogger, she had applied it for so long that it had left his ass slightly numb.

When she put the cane down on the sofa, she returned to his side and spent several minutes slowly running her nails over the little welted rows. Unlike the dungeon they had last been in, there were no large mirrors in his apartment to allow him to fix on her expression as she beat him, or, as he would have liked now, the junction of her right thigh and buttock, barely two feet behind his head and a few inches from his right leg.

When she knelt in front of him again to undo the ropes he was content as usual to watch her, mostly her face. It was so beautiful, but as always the dark eyes made him think there were many secrets behind that face. Finally, still kneeling while massaging his wrists, she looked him in the eye. Her eyes grew lighter and she asked, "Well?"

From his almost sleepy smile, she knew he had liked the session.

"I'm not always a mean bitch, you know."

Despite the percussion, it had been the most sensual session yet. He sat on the sofa and silently watched her pulling on her jeans. She was barely two hand lengths in front of him. By the time she was fully dressed and reaching for her jacket on the back of the door, he had a full erection. Amazed, he held his breath as he felt his erection climb against the tenuous friction of the cotton tights. He couldn't remember how many years, how many decades, it had been since he had desired a woman, while sober, and a dressed woman no less, so much that he got a spontaneous erection. As she slipped an arm into her jacket, he came to.

"Wait, wait," he said, urgently pulling a pair of jogging pants and a T-shirt over his tights. He slipped his naked feet into his running shoes and grabbed her toy bag. He carried it as they walked downstairs to the street where he saw her into a cab.

As he handed the bag into the back seat, he flash-dreamed he had a bag, too, and that the cab was taking them to the Port Authority terminal where they would board a milk-run midnight bus to anywhere. She would doze off and her head would slowly slide against his shoulder, like in the movies. He would sit motionless so as not to not wake her. At dawn, the bus would pull in to a diner, the one in Edward Hopper's painting. Then he remembered she didn't drink coffee and the mini-dream evaporated. The cab pulled into traffic without him.

The next morning, by the time he returned from breakfast on Ninth Avenue, his inbox contained three job offers. Since he had stopped drinking, he found himself with cash in the bank. He estimated that boozing had been costing him more than $400 a month, enough for two sessions with the Egyptian Princess. He hadn't even bothered factoring in the restaurant meals and take-out food he resorted to when his body sobered up enough to scream for food.

Even better, through no doing of his own, work had started to pour in on a regular basis. If a talisman could exist in mind only, the Egyptian Princess was his. It was about this time that she started becoming more than just the first woman to excite him sober. Watching the pain many out-patients at the addiction center were continuing to go through, he often felt like he'd been blessed with some kind of virgin sobriety miracle. He had suddenly been reborn sober without his life having totally disintegrated first. He wasn't religious. The only explanation was that, though her body had been far away on the beach at Oaxaca, the talismanic version in his mind had saved his life.

Now, as he stood in the bathroom washing egg yolk off his shirt, he was becoming convinced she had saved his sexual life as well. Many a time, particularly while drinking, he had concluded that mankind really dies when sexual drive dies. People may shuffle around for years afterwards, begging for money on the street or running corporations, but they are zombies all the same. The stain wouldn't come off and he threw the shirt in the laundry basket in the closet. He yanked a T-shirt from a hanger. If his domme wasn't Egyptian, he thought, she had to be Haitian or Jamaican or African, a loa, a spirit with the power to revive the soulless.

Because he had so much work, it was almost a month to the day before they saw each other again. Although more often than not he was spending twelve hours a day translating, there was no let-up in the letters he continued to write her. Some were getting so long he divided them for her convenience into chapters, with summary titles at the head of the message. She could read them bit by bit, he said, or jump to parts that interested her and ignore the rest.

He had suggested a couple of possible dates for sessions but she had gotten busy, too. The one date that would have worked for both of them, she had to cancel at the last moment. When she phoned to cancel, she said something about an out-of-town client who once put her up in a hotel in Philadelphia. He paid for twenty-four hours a day of her time for four days and gave her a generous shopping budget.

"We never even ended up having a session there," she told him. "He just wanted me around to impress his business buddies. Actually, he was a real prick at times. Rude. He was never like that when I saw him here. Like I was his slave or his fuck or something. I wouldn't touch him for anything."

So why had she just agreed to see him again?

"He likes to show off by slowly pulling wads of money half out of his wallet like it's his prick. He knows I don't do nudity. I don't do sex. I don't know a real domme who does. But like his money he's always accidentally showing his cock, you know? Suddenly he's got to adjust his shorts, or he's fucking itchy."

"Sounds like a trust-fund teenager."

"Yeah, a balding forty-year-old teenager. When he does that, I don't look at his hand. I just fix my eyes on his. He thinks he's seducing me. I'm thinking of how much cat food I can stock up on.

"I'll be back Thursday."

"Train?"

"Yes. Sometime in the morning."

"Would you mind if I met you? The station's just a short walk from my place."

The session they planned over lunch near Penn Station was the second at his place. She said she liked outcalls with clients she trusted because she didn't have to pay a dungeon fee. The Chinese fireworks at PB's had cost her $75 for the hour.

After the first apartment session, he had carefully noted that none of his neighbors had looked at him differently. However, they tended not to look at each other anyway. Few ever talked to each other. He guessed they probably heard nothing. The flogger and the cane weren't loud, or easily identifiable to the uninitiated, and she went easy on him so he hadn't even needed to bite on a face cloth or a gag to muffle his groans.

The light bulb in the hallway had burned out the night before and when she stepped in out of the gloom, he saw that her face was radiant. She was almost grinning. She let him hold her jean jacket as she slipped her arms out of the sleeves. Usually she didn't give him the chance. He thought it was a domme thing. Don't let men think they can gain any favor by holding chairs, opening doors and taking jackets. However as he got to know her, the person, he began to think a lot of independence from the old courtesies was just the way most young women were today.

"Come on, come on, come on!" she said. "Let's see those tights. I want to play."

He had them on already. He had put on jogging pants and a T-shirt when the door buzzer rang, just in case it was someone else. He wouldn't put it past her to send a pizza delivery to his address at the same time as their appointment on the chance he might answer the door wearing nothing but tights.

"And, dear, don't forget to tip." He could imagine her saying it as she slid past the pizza man and into the apartment, turning to watch his embarrassment.

As he began slipping off his T-shirt and pants, she leaned over the end of the trunk and used her entire one hundred and ten pounds to shove it across the room, under the window, out of the way. With that, she stripped off her own clothes with her back turned to him. Immediately his penis stirred. She was wearing the tights he'd bought her.

"Yes," was all he could think of saying as she turned toward him. His erection hardened as he saw how tightly the black cotton pulled against her box. Before he could detect whether the tights betrayed the impression of her nipples, she ordered:

"Stretching exercises first." As she said it, she turned the arm chair around and effortlessly lifted her right leg high enough to rest her ankle on its back. He could barely raise his to the arm of the chair, more than a foot lower than her leg.

"Come on. You wear tights, you must be a dancer," she chided. She dropped her leg and put her hands under his ankle and started lifting. He had to grab the kitchen door frame to keep from falling.

"That's pathetic," she said. "Now the other one, maybe the ham's not so tight." She grabbed his ankle as it got to her waist height and placed it against her tummy. She began taking little steps forward, forcing him to use his other leg to hop backwards into the kitchen. When she had him backed against the fridge, she let go, and then turned and told him to follow her back to the living room. His eyes followed her buttocks as she walked, then saw how her tights became almost transparently thin when she bent over to pull a pair of socks from her running shoes by the door.

"You'll need socks, too."

When he had his socks on, she said she wanted to see him do a standard ballet step, an *assemblé*.

"You're kidding. What's an *assemblé*?"

"You know, you just jump forward and touch both your feet together in the air. Do it."

"Shit." He had no choice. He took two quick steps to launch himself but immediately realized he wouldn't become airborne more than a micro second. He backed up and threw caution to the wind on his second attempt. He crashed to the floor so heavily that a reading lamp beside the sofa bed fell to the floor.

As he sat on the floor rubbing his hip and enduring her laughter, he demanded:

"You try it."

Instead of answering that she was the one who called the shots, she pursed her lips and sprung forward, weightless, her two quick steps making almost no sound on the floor. Her feet didn't manage to touch each other in mid-air but they came a lot closer than his did. However upon landing, her left foot slipped out from under her on the hardwood floor and she tumbled on top of him, laughing. Because of the way she landed on him, he found his right hand on her tights, on the inside of her thigh midway between knee and heaven. Had she not been laughing as she struggled to get off, he knew he would have stolen a kiss, probably ending the session on the spot.

In her role as ballet mistress that evening she chose one instrument, a fifteen-inch-long wooden paddle. She made him bend over the back of the sofa for the first round. Twice he writhed his way to the floor. Then she had him bend over the back of the arm chair for more. As she grabbed the top of his unitard in her left hand, she suddenly discovered the utter joy of the fulcrum effect. With the slightest tug forward, a much bigger man could be made to rock forward until his head touched the chair seat. She released him and he swung back, and then she yanked again. This time, as his torso descended the other side of the chair, she slid her fingers between his buttocks where the tights were strained to their limit, pressing against his anus, bearing his weight. *Whack!* His butt was stretched so tight, the blow all but landed on bone. Another ten and she knew he could take no more.

"That was so cool," she said. "Leverage rules."

"You sound like a stockbroker," he said, using the chair arms to push himself upright.

"Not nice! Stand in front of the door, facing it."

As he did so, she added:

"For your information, I was talking as a physicist, not a broker. I deal with them differently."

She stood behind him, her left hand pressed against his back, forcing him against the door.

"Hold on to the coat hook and don't move."

At the start of the session, after hearing how loudly the paddle blows rang out in the tiny apartment, she had reached into her bag, pulled out a CD and popped it in his computer. She had her own tiny external speakers. She plugged them into the mic jack of his computer, then got down on her hands and knees to crawl under his desk to plug them in. Later he wondered why she didn't ask him to get down on the floor to plug in speakers. He concluded that being a domme was as much about taking charge and making things happen as it was about sitting back and giving commands.

After popping to her feet with a dexterity he could never have rivaled even as an athletic young man, she cranked up the external speakers full volume.

"Maybe that will camouflage the sound," she said. The music was a playlist she had put together. Not one piece sounded familiar to him. It wasn't the fact that he didn't like it that bothered him for a moment, it was the realization that he was hearing further proof that they were from different generations.

"Come on, keep that ass out," she said after landing the one-hundredth smack.

"You know what? Now your neighbors know for sure what we're doing. So there's no reason for me to go soft on you."

It was hard, he discovered, to laugh and flinch violently at the same time.

Finally, she stopped.

"Believe me, I'd love to go on all night. I've never had a client I could spank this hard. Never. But I've got to go."

He turned around. She still looked radiant.

"You don't have to."

"I do," she answered. "Believe me, I'd love to pull down your tights and watch the bruises form. But I've got to see another client. He's in a hotel room on 58th.

I left him there before coming here. He just wanted to be tied up and gagged, then left in his room with the lights out. It's up to me when or if I go back to untie him. I have a feeling he wouldn't be pissed off if I left him there all night and he was found by the chambermaid in the morning. That how his fantasy plays out, at least in his head."

"So leave him and stay here."

"Can't. You know, what if he chokes, or the ropes cut off circulation? It's easy money. I'd like him to stay around for a while."

She was standing so close to him that his arms had no choice but to encircle her.

"That was a lot of fun. Gotta go." She didn't give him a chance to dress and walk her down in the dark.

He didn't bother pushing the trunk back to its usual place. Although it was only 9 p.m., he opened the bed and lay down to contemplate the hard leather she'd left on the surface of his buttocks. His cheeks were totally numb. She liked receiving damage reports in the days following a session. She wouldn't be disappointed with the one he would send tomorrow.

As the summer passed, the frequency of sessions didn't accelerate, for the most part because of his schedule or hers. Other times she "just felt tired." She never went into medical details but more than once she had said something about it being painful to sit for long periods, such as air flights to Mexico, or it being almost impossible to sleep comfortably for more than two or three hours at a time. She spent much of the night on her feet.

What was accelerating, to Autobahn speeds, was the frequency of daydreams that airlifted him out of reality for minutes on end. Writing her emails every two or three days was no longer enough. He looked for excuses to phone her. She never seemed to mind. Once she phoned him.

"I'm so fucking horny."

She had his undivided attention despite the street noise. When she phoned he was walking across Lafayette Street.

"Wait. Wait." He pushed his way through some people standing at the corner of Howard Street. They had the green light but weren't moving for some reason. He entered the first storefront he found.

"OK, what were you saying?" As he looked around him he saw that he was in a store that sold gems and crystal products. He heard her repeat that she was fucking horny. Instinctively, he thought if it sounds too good to be true it usually is.

"Can you afford to buy me a month's subscription to a website?"

He didn't recognize the name of the site. She said it had some good BDSM videos, girl on girl, or a bunch of girls and a guy.

"Just a month," she said. "I can download my fix." The problem, she said, was that she didn't have a credit card.

"Could you sign up and send me the password? I mean, only if you can afford it. You seem to be scoring clients like crazy."

He was and he agreed.

"As soon as I get home."

"Hugs. Lots." And she was gone.

Did she have any idea how much he desired her? Did she know that she was the only woman in the world who could make him feel like a whole man again? Or did he seem so old to her that the thought never crossed her mind? Why didn't she have a lover anyway? Before pursuing the thought, he left the store and let the street noise drown out the thought of her being with another man.

The next session grew from a playful exchange of emails about International Talk Like a Pirate Day in

September. Years before, he used to devour any novel about the age of sail, be it a naval adventure or a pirate tale. Though he was well-versed in pirate history, she was the one who told him about Talk Like a Pirate Day.

When he arrived for the session, at the studio dungeon where she had initiated him into the world of BDSM, she lashed him down along the length of a spanking horse while still wearing her street clothes. She then left the room for several minutes. A moment after hearing the door open again, he jerked as he felt water splash down on his back.

"Have some rum, matey!" She had entered the room with a mouthful of water and spit it out on his back. As she moved into view, he saw she was wearing a huge-brimmed black pirate's hat and an eye patch, leaving one utterly convincing black eye to glare down on him.

"I intend to amuse myself," she proclaimed, kneeling before him to tighten his wrist cuffs. Rising to the knees of her tights were black boots he'd never seen before. The leather looked soft. With her flogger draped over her shoulder, the tresses falling like hair over her left breast, she patted his shoulder with her right hand and announced, "Should you complain overly much about my little entertainment, you'll find yourself back in the Royal Navy pursuing your career as favored peg-boy of officers and midshipmen alike."

She was in fine form. For a quarter of an hour she flogged with abandon his back as well as his buttocks and the back of his thighs. It was hot work for thin arms like hers. At last she stopped. Standing before him, she removed her magnificent hat so she could lift off the eye patch.

"It's making me so dizzy I've got to sit down." She then put the hat back on and lifted herself up onto his back.

"That's better," she said. Out of her silver buckled sword belt, she pulled a hair brush. Slowly, she started tattooing his butt with moderate smacks. They stung but were more than bearable.

Although he had now known her for a year, he only now asked the question he wanted to ask from Day 1. Although he had called her his Egyptian Princess because of the first photo he saw of her on the Internet, she had never mentioned a homeland. Her speech was as American as his.

"Austin," she said. "Austin, Texas." She pronounced the state as Tex-ASS. When he said she looked Egyptian, she said:

"You're not looking at Egyptian. You're looking at Jewish. My grandmother on my mom's side was born in Morocco. My dad's side is all from here."

He had his answer. He silently blessed her grand-mother for her looks.

As she talked about growing up, the hairbrush landed less frequently. Then she would wallop him, as if suddenly realizing she had been neglecting him. Her father was an engineer, her mother a teacher.

"It is and always was the most dysfunctional family in history."

She punctuated the admission with a sharp descent of the hairbrush. When it landed he said,

"OK. I've had it."

"You've never given in before," she said, legitimately surprised by him ending the session.

"I want to hear what you're saying," he explained. "I couldn't lose myself in the pain any more. That damned hairbrush was interfering with your story."

She released the leg and wrist cuffs. When he stood up she took him to the back of the room. When she turned on a table lamp, he saw there was a double bed against the wall. The room was actually double the size he thought it was. She told him to lie down.

"If you want to masturbate go ahead," she said, settling herself at the foot of the bed. She made the same offer at the end of one of their first sessions but he declined.

"Masturbating in front of you would be an obscene waste of semen," he'd said. This time, however, he pulled his tights down and started masturbating. As he did, she went on talking, absent-mindedly running a crop up and down his legs.

She had gone to a private school, which he had guessed from her very British use of the word "shall" in her first email to him. While there, she learned to speak French and Spanish, which were facts he didn't know.

"When I was about twelve, we found out that Dad had been screwing another woman. He'd being doing her for twenty years. Can you believe that? Twenty fucking years. When my mom found out she went crazy. Literally. I mean, certifiably. She told Dad to get the fuck out, which he did happily.

"My sister, she's three years older. Majored in coke at school and dropped out by the time she hit fifteen. I went to live with a neighbor. Their son had had a crush on me and somehow convinced his parents I was in danger living with a crazy woman and a strung-out sister. He was a sweet kid, but, I don't know, just a kid. As dumb as most boys his age. It was OK. I was getting good grades, so the school never asked questions about what was going on at home.

"And your sister?"

"Eventually, she got my Dad to write the school a letter stating she was temporarily leaving school to get assistance with a substance-abuse problem. He agreed to write it because she threatened to move in with him and his girlfriend."

"A determined woman, your sister. Is she a domme now, too, like you?

"No. She's not really strong. It's what drugs do. You do what you need to get what you want. She got married eventually and she's still a bit messed up, although I think she's clean most of the time. Don't talk to her very often."

"I gather you didn't grow up and marry your little boyfriend at the time."

She laughed, looking at him, as he methodically kept his erection firm without letting it go into overdrive.

"He wasn't a boyfriend, although it was kind of cool to have a boy to push around."

"So it's in your blood."

"Yeah, domination is a genetic thing. A bright guy like you didn't know that?"

Just as she'd once told him she was uncomfortable accepting compliments, something in her manner told him she usually kept her life story to herself. He guessed that a half-naked old man lying before her on a table seemed a relatively safe receptacle to pour her story into.

"But I gather you didn't live happily ever after with Austin's family of the year?"

"Nope. The boy's dad felt me up one night. I was a kid, for fuck's sake.

"I told my sister. She was ready to kill. Two nights later we stole a whole bunch of cash my mom had stashed in the house. She always said she didn't trust men or bank machines. She was probably so out of it, and would probably have been so pissed off at the boy's father, she would have given us the money, but my sister was too wired to wait.

"We caught a bus to Chicago, where my sister said she knew someone. How I don't know. Anyway, we get there and he's a dealer, about thirty years old. He had money but my sister didn't want to stay long. Since he was trying to act as if she was his girlfriend all of a sudden, she played along long enough to use his phone to call Dad back in Austin. Didn't ask how he was, just told him she wanted money. She told him we were being taken care of by a rabbi and she had him send the money to a synagogue. Man, could she ever find the right buttons to push.

"Anyway, the next day she went there, the synagogue, to explain there would be a check coming for her. She didn't take me. She looked much older than she was and she didn't want a kid like me with her in case they asked too many questions.

"When the letter came with the money, there was a note from my father saying we had an aunt in Queens, in Astoria. My sister didn't want any part of it. I guessed she wanted to stay near her source in Chicago. I don't really know. Anyway, she wrote a letter to the aunt and signed our Mom's name this time. I was on a train to New York two days later. And here I am."

"Where does San Francisco fit in?" He couldn't help asking. He wasn't innocently trying to tie up loose ends of her story. "You wrote one day that you were playing tour guide for your boyfriend's mom, from San Fran."

"You're going to have to hurry up," she said, suddenly lowering her eyes to the floor, ignoring his question and using the crop to tap the fist around his penis.

As she talked, he had been masturbating slowly, staring at her face. Her right thigh was against his as she sat near the end of the bed. Suddenly she cracked the crop down on one thigh, then the other. The pain was searing. Her eyes bored into his. She then used her hand to turn his leg outwards so she could flick the crop on the tender inner side of his thigh. His erection was suddenly rock hard.

She stood up and he slowed down, wishing he could look into her eyes as he came. She was back in a minute, pulling a surgical glove on her right hand. She slipped her hand between his legs. First one finger found his anus, followed soon by a second.

"Raise your knees," she said, probing deeper. She found his prostate and he exploded. No one had ever done that to him. Her eyes followed the stream of come that landed all the way up on his left shoulder. She gave him a demure smile and slowly withdrew her fingers. With her left hand she tossed him a facecloth that had been on the bed behind her.

"Since I'm telling you my life story," she said as they entered the little elevator, "I might as well tell you we're almost neighbors. My girlfriend and I moved in with this guy in Tribeca. He's a med student. They used to date now and then. They're sort of weird together. He acts like he's her boyfriend but he's not, and he was the one who asked her to move in to help with the rent. She's got a regular job and everything. I think he gets some kind of student subsidy. She figured moving in — he's not a jerk or anything — would be the only way she'd ever get to live right in Manhattan."

As they stepped out into the evening, she went on.

"I'm their U Girl, their utilities girl. I take care of Con Ed and a few other things. I think this guy likes having two chicks sharing his place. But with me there my friend has more excuses to avoid him. Anyway, he's doing his residency and he's almost never there."

She lived on Desbrosses Street, near Hudson, which wasn't really close at all to his place. He didn't care.

"Can I walk you home?"

"I'd like that," she answered.

It was a clear fall night, warm, but the air tasted clean. When they stepped into intersections, he put his hand protectively at the small of her back. But in a way he was glad she set a good but effortless loose-limbed pace. It discouraged complicated thoughts and intimate talk. Mostly they didn't speak, apart from comments about people and places they passed. When they finally arrived she rescued him from his indecision by kissing him on the cheek before lowering her head to his chest for the hug that had become a habit.

It was the last time he was to see her for fifteen months.

CHAPTER 21

Break One

AFTER leaving her that night, K felt he was going to burst. If he did, no one would be able to make hide nor hair of the pieces littering the street. He didn't know what he was feeling, or he didn't dare admit what he was feeling.

He was out-and-out in love with her, the beauty and the beastly old man, and there was nothing he could do about it. Yet he knew with absolute deadly certainty that if he took one single step along the path to confessing his love for this woman more than a quarter-century his junior, with everything before her in life, it would be like stepping into a passion-red Lamborghini and spending the last 3.4 seconds of his life accelerating from 0 to 60 and driving straight into a cement wall.

He started to walk quickly. For a couple of dozen strides he broke into a jog that for a moment became a run. The hard breathing didn't clear his head. In fact, it seemed to amplify his thoughts, forcing them to career about his head and crash into the cochlea, which sent them booming back to him. For a couple of blocks he thought he would have to walk all the way back to Chelsea to get himself together. He did not want to talk himself into believing that, possibly, she loved him in return. However, it was late and the adrenalin had said goodnight. Instead he walked down Canal, past the Tribeca Cinemas, and then turned right at 6th Avenue where a few minutes later he boarded the E train home.

For the next few weeks he went out of his way to write neutral emails. She answered in kind, although her replies seemed shorter than they once were. In one of them she mentioned there was a big BDSM event coming up, some kind of party at a kink-friendly club on the Lower East Side. She might be giving some sort of show, a demonstration. She said she thought he might be interested.

Who knows. You might meet a kinky girlfriend there.

He stopped breathing. Her seeming afterthought paralyzed him. Was it innocent, an idle speculation that meant no more than what the words professed, as in: "Who knows. It might rain next week." Or was she sending him a message, indirect, kindly put? A gentle let-down, an alternative to "It ain't going to happen. It just ain't."

Had she seen through him? Was she telling him to back off? From doing what? But the instant he heard himself ask "From doing what?" he knew he was sounding like a boy caught red-handed rifling his mother's purse for Scotch money. He was guilty as charged. She wasn't dumb. Though he had been as circumspect as a man walking a tightrope could be, the rope quivered precariously. He had betrayed his feelings, probably scores of times in her presence and countless times in the tens of thousands of words he had written to her.

She had even said, "No one has ever written me letters like yours." She had also noticed how green his eyes became when he sat close to her, talking non-stop about anything that rushed into his mind, tossing in outrageous compliments apropos of nothing and reveling in her amusement at his unabashed exaggerations.

To save himself from drowning, he grabbed onto a passing albatross, the thought that there was a possibility, albeit faint, that she loved him too. No, no, no. Immediately he tried to hold the damn bird under water, but the thought had already taken hold. He simply didn't want to reason it away. So what if he truly was making a fool of himself, what if his circumspection and silence hid nothing from her? He hadn't declared his love, but if she knew anyway then he was already a dangerous commodity, an aging male well past a prime he'd let slip out of reach, never fully exploited, to his eternal regret.

But but but, wouldn't such a man also be a fool if he were to cast aside even a single moment of feeling in love? It's the one constant in human behavior that clichés can't snuff out. He would have to be mad to deny himself the fortress that being in love erected against those invading thoughts of mortality, the ones that kept attaching themselves to his being like yellow sticky notes. If being in love was hiding his head in the sand, so be it. How — and this is the question he wrestled with all day — could he straddle the line?

He was already close to her, but if he inched much closer she would push back. She sometimes seemed more afraid of intimacy than he was of losing it. To move too close to her now would be a suicidal act. She might, not just might, she very likely would reject him. But distancing himself from her would also be suicidal. He could no more stop being in love with her than he could stop dreaming while asleep. Walking away from love, foolish love or not, would be tantamount to self-infliction of a terminal disease. The heart becomes obliged to rot, slowly. That was not an option, he decided. The fact that she was young was beside the point. It was not his fault. He had fallen in love with her, and would have regardless what age she might have been.

When he sat down to write her that night, he was an unwilling soldier. He was exhausted by thinking about something that does not exist in the form of thought. He gave himself permission to stay in the trenches at least one more day. He simply didn't have the guts to go over the top and risk getting shredded by bullets. He ignored the girlfriend reference and wrote:

Never attended a BDSM party. Do people play? Would we play? Would it sort of be like a date, you and I? By the way, I'll be finishing a project two weeks from today. Session?

It was several days before she replied. She didn't say she hoped he was well, as she usually did. She didn't apologize for the delay in replying, which she would normally do.

Worst fucking day of my life. Lost $300 on the street on my way to put it toward a $400 phone bill. Talked to a runny-nosed cum laude kid fresh out of Customer Relations University who said the company would like to express its sincere sorrow for my loss but had to know when I expected to pay the bill. Got home and had three clients cancel on me. I don't know why I'm answering your email now. I'm out of cigarettes and I don't have a dime on me. Going to have to wait until somebody walks in the door. What party are you talking about? I've been a bit messed up of late.

He wrote back immediately, quoting her previous email.

No, it can't really be a date. I'm not even sure I'm going. Just thought you might like to. If I do, if there are other clients there I'll have to spend some time with them. Same with anyone who seems to be into the idea of becoming one. I don't even remember when the party is. Sorry.

No hugs at the end. No x's. No be wells.

For the first time since he'd met her, he felt annoyed. He felt he was just another fly for her to swat in her state of pique. He told himself being annoyed with her was a good thing. It allowed him to stay in the trenches a while longer.

The following week she wrote to say she'd been in a lot of pain again, agony at times, but still made no mention of its cause. The pain seemed so frequent and acute at times he once asked, "Are you dying?" She replied, "No, I'm not dying, but I have no intention of going into further detail."

As someone who rarely stepped out in the world without wearing earbuds, she was particularly exasperated at having accidentally just deleted all her iTunes music, thousands of songs.

Rebuilding it is taking more energy than I have right now. Do you still want that session on the 10th? I assume that's the day you meant.

He waited a full week before replying. If she'd written a sweet message in the meantime, he would have jumped at the chance to see her. But she didn't. Not a word. He entitled his email: "Maybe another time." The body of the message read:

I don't really feel like it at the moment. Anyway, rent's due.

Her reply came only hours later:

well, thanks very much.

take good care of yourself will you?

oh- CC has a great fondness for tights i've found out...
you may wish to contact her in the future.

best of wishes, now, forever.

And that was that. The domme had dismissed
her client.

CHAPTER 22

CC

WHEN K went to the studio above the book and knick-knack store near West 30th for his first appointment with CC, he assumed that having been recommended to her by a fellow domme would make the approval process a formality.

He now knew his way around. The receptionist knew him as well. As he got off the elevator he gave her a little wave and she indicated with her arm that he should go straight in. He stepped into the washroom and put on his tights.

After emerging, he knocked on the door across the hall and a voice said in French, "*Entre.*" Come in, enter. Second person singular, "*tu,*" used among friends or when speaking to someone much younger or an inferior. But a domme demanded "*vous*" in return. French was tailor-made for domme-sub relationships.

"*Assieds-toi. Non, là, à côté de moi.*"

She indicated a blue cushion next to her.

"*Tu es traducteur, non?*"

The first thing he noticed was the utter chaos of tri-colored curls that flung themselves from her head in all directions like corkscrew pasta. The fact that they crowned a face with an aristocratic bone structure seemed incongruous at first glance. What he noticed second were the coral red tights clinging to a gymnast's body. She was petite but the chestnut eyes betrayed an energy that more than compensated for her size.

When he continued in French, confirming that she had heard correctly, that he was indeed a translator, she smiled approvingly. It was a sweet smile, the haughtiness gone for a second. He thought he was surely in. Before he could congratulate himself, she bluntly asked how he felt about his former mistress.

It would take a book to answer her question. Somehow succinctness intervened. He didn't know how to translate, "I think the world of her," so he said *"Je l'estime énormément."* He paused, looking for another way to put it, then decided to stick with the first words that popped into his head. *"Oui, énormément. Je l'adore."*

That won him another smile from CC. She seemed relieved. It made him think the two of them were not just colleagues but close friends.

Then he added, "But I have absolutely no idea what's come over her. She's like another person."

"You were crowding her. She couldn't breathe." She said it with perfect command of figurative English but left her French accent hanging in the air. "That's why she can't continue to see you."

CC did not beat around the bush. She also made it sound more final than he had imagined. He was glad he acted immediately to fill the void by seeing CC, but suddenly he felt sad. He wasn't ready to hear that final judgment. Just as he lowered his eyes, retreating inside himself, a delicious little foot pressed lightly against his penis. Its toes wriggled playfully. He looked up and saw a broad smile on CC's lips.

"You can touch my tights if you want." She had been

well briefed.

He ran his palm slowly up her left leg. The same cotton as his. Her strong leg filled them beautifully.

"Would you like to kiss them?"

He bent forward. Unable to reach, he shifted to his knees. Quickly at first, then more slowly he advanced again up her legs, this time with his lips. As he arrived barely inches from her sex, he felt three fingers on his head gently define her limits. He sat back and her toes found his huddled balls and penis once more.

They talked about their mutual love of tights. She said she had every kind imaginable, all colors, all materials. She said she had another fetish as well. Gloves. She had scores of pairs, riding gloves, opera gloves and everything in between. As for sessions, she loved heavy-duty corporal.

"I like to feel tired when I finish with clients. I used to be an exercise instructor. I like to work out."

She then stood, revealing an exquisite ass, muscled enough to move jauntily with each step, the tights disappearing between her cheeks exactly as his fantasies scripted such details.

"But I'm afraid I have another appointment," she said. "Another consultation."

He was crestfallen. He thought a session was sure to follow.

"The fee for a consultation is $50," she said as he reached to his pants on the floor to retrieve his wallet.

As he handed her the money, she said:

"You and I, we're going to have fun."

The prospect was so hot, he wondered how he had allowed himself to think the world ended with an Egyptian Princess. He walked home, with much the same stride that had carried him to easy sobriety more than a year before.

CHAPTER 23

Women Are Smarter

"DON'T you dare!" he told CC one winter afternoon. As had been the case with his Egyptian Princess, he had learned from the months of sessions with CC that she had a highly developed talent for the unexpected.

"*Ne t'inquiètes pas*, I'd never do that to you. It's not your thing, I understand." There was something dangerously chipper about her tone. He had dropped by to deliver a mirror he'd found abandoned on the street, nice dark mahogany frame, about four feet tall. There could never be too many mirrors in a dungeon as far as he was concerned. He liked to watch her body's slightest movement as she beat him.

A dance supply store had opened half a block from the dungeon.

"That will be convenient if I rip your tights off some day," she said.

What concerned him, knowing her well by now, was the window full of tutus.

"By the way," she asked, after dismissing his fears,

"do you mind if I have a photographer shoot our session? It would be good for my website."

"Yes, if you can give me copies of everything on a CD," he said.

She tied his wrists and ankles to the St. Andrew's Cross. Then, standing on a chair behind him, she drew an old-fashioned gas mask over his head. He could see it in the mirror in front of him. It was grotesque.

"Can you breathe?" she asked.

He could but he didn't like the feeling of the mask.

"It makes you look cute," she said. "It brings out your personality. But something's missing. You look cute but not adorable. Here's the real you."

With that she undid his right wrist. He felt something being pulled over his head but the gas mask made identifying it difficult. She re-buckled the wrist and repeated the exercise with his left arm. She then grabbed his waist and pulled him toward her, his ass colliding with her stomach. By yanking him away from the cross she could pull the costume down.

"What do you think?" she asked, lifting up his mask.

"Damn you! Wait till I..."

"Until you what? In your position, I'd be careful what I said. Yes, you're almost adorable now." She pulled his mask back down over his face, then flipped the pink muslin of the tutu over his head.

"Philip!" she called. "We are ready for you."

CC barely gave the photographer time to set up before she started laying on laying on a strap, which she liked as much for the sonorous crack it made as for the effect on his ass.

CC loved the camera and kept the photographer clicking furiously. At one point she used her victim as monkey bars, throwing her arms around his neck and pulling herself up to get her legs around his waist. At one point she sat straddling his left shoulder, using the snout of the mask to twist his head every which way. She must have known he could feel her vagina on his shoulder, mere millimeters of cotton separating their bodies.

When the photographer left she took off his mask and tutu and took him to what he had learned was called subspace, the rhythm of her blows finally triggering endorphins. At least that's what other people said happens. Whatever was taking place — and it by no means always happened — it was better than any booze high, the opposite in fact. He felt beautiful calm despite an ass that barely acknowledged CC's percussion.

Like his Egyptian Princess, CC seemed to have endless imagination. If anything, she was more physical. The disparity in her size and his was a mere challenge. They even wrestled once. She actually knew holds.

"I'd thought you'd like this," she said during the wrestling session. "Tights rubbing against tights." She really did share his fetish for tights, except in her case her body looked beautiful in them.

He saw her for close to a year. She always told him when his Egyptian Princess was having a session next door. CC sometimes called her in to examine the results she'd produced on her former client's ass. Because dommes don't invade another domme's territory, the Egyptian Princess never called or wrote during all that time.

He still dreamed of her but life was good with CC taking him in hand. They usually spoke French, which made her happy, and he learned a vocabulary university didn't teach. One day he asked where she was from. Montreal, a forty-minute plane ride, she said.

"Your Egyptian Princess is Canadian, too. She was the one who talked me into coming here a little over a year ago."

"She's not from Texas?"

"No. She tells people that. I think she's just really private. I think her dad lives there now but she never did. I think the way it went is that she moved here from

Montreal after her parents split up. She lived with some rich relative in New Jersey."

"Not Queens?"

"*Non, je pense pas.*" Then she suddenly remembered where her friend's aunt lived. "Maple something. Not *sirop d'érable* maple. Maplewood. That's it. Maplewood, New Jersey. Sort of Canadian, *non?*

"She can get away with it because she was raised by her aunt here, but I'm not supposed to be working here all the time without a visa, which is a real hassle. Why don't you hire me as a translator and get one for me?"

She said it as a joke, but the idea of such a beautiful business expense got him thinking. And remembering. He had flash-imagined the same arrangement with Selita, the purple-haired juggler who had latched on to him after his musical debut a few years before. Returning to the present, he had to ask CC to repeat a question she'd just asked:

"Ever try CBT?"

"CBT?"

"Cock and ball torture," she said. Along with her reply came a gentle kick to his balls, delivered by a shiny black patent leather shoe with a precariously high heel. She kept her foot there for a long moment, her gymnast's training allowing her to remain perfectly balanced on the other high heel without the slightest wobble. Her demonstration complete, she continued to talk about her friend's roots.

"She likes to go back to Montreal fairly regularly. In fact, I'm going at the end of the month."

"Damn," he thought. "For how long?" he asked aloud.

"Don't really know right now. A friend has just opened her own dungeon there. She wants to hit the scene with really experienced girls. She's a domme, too. She used to do porn there, at home, and here in the States. But she likes domming more. She's really good. I've done double sessions with her. We have a ball."

CC was so enthusiastic about the prospect that the curls on her head seemed to tighten as they danced to her gesticulations. He felt happy for her. There was something genuine about her. Now her brown eyes were bigger and rounder than usual, the youthful whites whiter.

. . .

Within minutes of leaving CC, he felt a warning. The walk home seemed uphill. He wished he could snap his fingers and be home. He wanted to be away from the noise of the street so he could think about what he would do if CC left, even for just a month or two.

Dommes met all his needs except expressly sexual ones. The sessions were intimate, sensual and erotic. Some days he told himself there was some kind of advanced form of sexuality at play. But other days he just wished he had a woman to make love to, or at least wished it until he started wondering whether his erection would fail him at the last moment. That wasn't an issue when he was with dommes

The prostate message from his Egyptian Princess, he suspected, was an exception, something between friends or, for now, despite their separation, two people destined to be friends.

That apart, his need to touch and be touched, his need to take shelter in the security of body pressed against body, those parts of his sexuality had all been relit the day he activated his fantasies. Without the attentions of dommes, all the ingredients that made up a man's sexual nature would boil down into a stew, one that would eventually be left untended so long that the day would come when there was nothing left but the blackened remains, unidentifiable and stuck to the bottom of the pot. More than once in his life he had thrown burnt pots in the garbage rather than scrape and scour. Once badly burnt, they never come clean.

At the moment, CC was keeping him afloat. He usually saw her twice a month. The rest of the time she perched in his mind, like an exotic bird in a cage. And he still felt through CC that he had a channel open, albeit a one-way one, for her use only, to his Egyptian Princess. He liked to think he had one and a half dommes. If CC left, he would have nothing.

When he stepped into his apartment something caught his eye and he looked upward. On the ceiling, above the armchair he worked from, was a darkened patch of ceiling about a foot wide. The white paint was now yellowish. Beads of water were forming on one side of the patch. As it had done six months ago, the toilet upstairs was leaking. That time, the owner of the building told the super to repair it himself. No need to call a plumber. When he ran into the super not long afterwards, the super told him to expect showers in the near future. Meathead, the landlord, was too cheap to replace the toilet bowl.

"It's cracked and the floor is rotting under the bolts. Expect rain, my friend, yellow rain." Some people fantasized about golden showers. He didn't.

He now ran up the stairs to the top floor and banged on the neighbor's door. He shouldn't have banged so hard. It wasn't the neighbor's fault. The super answered.

"Bad at your place?"

"Not yet."

"I'll be turning off the water in the building. Called a plumber to fix this the way it should've been fixed before. Fuck Meathead."

He returned to his apartment and moved the chair out of harm's way. He put a small pile of old newspapers on the floor to soak up any drops that fell. He then opened the sofa bed and turned on the TV, cranking up the volume to drown out his own thoughts. He was too frustrated to figure out exactly what he would do if CC returned to Montreal for more than a few weeks.

That evening, LeBron phoned to say he'd scored two tickets to a Mets game the following Sunday afternoon. When K started to say he couldn't go, LeBron jumped on him.

"They're not just any tickets, K. I'm talking Subway Series, the good guys against Arrogance Inc., everything that's wrong with America, the nameless ones from the Bronx. It's epic."

The Mets had been hot. They'd just swept the Phillies. The headline in that morning's paper had been "Bring it on!" The story quoted a Met saying the Yankees could bring their best game but it wouldn't be enough.

K was going to say he couldn't go only because he couldn't imagine enjoying himself. Not only did he sense the sky was falling after leaving CC, he got home to find his ceiling was falling.

"I'll call you tomorrow," K said. "I might have to work the weekend." It was lie. He didn't want LeBron to think he was crazy.

The next morning CC called him. He'd left his laptop at the dungeon. He always carried it with him. It was his office. He rarely saw friends, and sitting in cafés people watching made him feel at least potentially social. Sometimes he wrote fiction, but the last short stories he'd finished were the ones his Egyptian Princess didn't read because they made her too sad (she said they made her think of "the boy" in San Francisco). Mostly he used it to surf the Internet. He had never before left his laptop anywhere. CC hadn't even left New York and he was already unraveling.

CC said she wasn't at the dungeon yet. The receptionist had called asking if the laptop might belong to one of her clients. CC had a white Mac, too.

"What I really want is that leather bag you use to carry it around," she said, "but I'll accept a *pain au chocolat* or a *madelaine* or two. I'll be there in an hour."

They met on the sidewalk. He had never seen her in

jeans, sandals and a T-shirt. She could have been any college student, still wet behind the ears, not a skilled *maîtresse*.

He'd found a *pain au chocolat* for her and bought himself two croissants at the same time. CC said good morning to the receptionist, who handed her the laptop, then plunked herself down on the dark blue waiting room sofa. He joined her with their breakfast. She pulled a couple of tissues out of her toy bag to catch their breakfast crumbs.

"You'd like Montreal. You should come for a visit," she said. Had she guessed he was upset about her going?

"Would love to," he said, "but I can't leave. I never know when work is going to arrive."

They sat in silence for a while, eating.

"Why," she asked, "why does it matter where you are? You say you get everything by email. You said you even had a client in France. That's a little bit farther than Montreal."

He put his unfinished croissant on the coffee table and looked at her. Women are smarter, he thought. With all the thinking he did the previous night, trudging down rutted pathway after rutted pathway toward inevitable misery, it had never occurred to him that he could pull up stakes for a while.

"You'd just have to find a place to stay," she said, as if she had been the one pondering his problem all night. "It's a helluva lot cheaper than New York, unless you want to stay at the Ritz."

He stood up and gave her a big kiss on the cheek.

"Hey, come back here! In Montreal we do both cheeks. Do it right, or else."

Today, home was downhill.

. . .

When he got home, the super accosted him in the hallway.

"Had to open up your place. The plumber says the leak is coming from somewhere else than the cracked toilet bowl, but he couldn't reach the pipes so we had to cut open your ceiling to get at them from below. You weren't home so…"

"Do what the hell you have to do. I'm going out of town for a while."

With that, he brushed by the super and almost ran up the stairs, taking them two at a time until he stumbled while nearing the third-floor landing. The mess was worse than he expected, but he uttered only a single sotto voce "fuck" as he took in the gaping jagged hole in the ceiling and the chunks of plaster and fine white powder that decorated the floor, his desk and the books on a shelf beneath the leak. The place smelled like a toilet.

Getting as far away from the stench as he could, he sat on the floor by the window on the opposite side of the room and opened his laptop. In the browser search field he typed "amtrak nyc montreal fares."

CC had lit a fire under him. Not only would he be going to her city, he'd be getting out of New York for the first time in two decades. Unlike Barcelona, he wouldn't be adrift, lying in a hotel bed fantasizing about having an adventure with a beautiful local woman. As soon as CC arrived, his gut told him, doors would open.

Within seconds the Amtrak site informed him there was a train leaving for Montreal at 8:15 the next morning from Penn Station. The station was only a few blocks from his apartment. He'd walk, and grab an early breakfast on the way.

The train was dirt cheap, $63 one way. Good, good, he thought, not just about the price but — and he was probably the only Amtrak customer to think so — the fact that the train took almost eleven hours to travel the 330 miles to Montreal, an average of barely thirty miles an hour. Addicted to research, and with an evening to kill, he learned that most horses could run short distances at more than forty miles per hour, and he determined that the Pony Express would have covered the same distance in one day, seven hours and forty-five minutes. But the train fare was not that much more than the cost of street parking for a day in Midtown and he needed the time to think. He had no idea what he was doing. He had no idea whether the idea was one of his stupidest. He just knew he wanted to get on board that train before he had time to change his mind.

He checked the next day's forecasted temperature for Montreal, 85 degrees and humid. It usually wasn't humid in late September, even in New York. He threw underwear, socks, jeans and T-shirts into a carry-on bag. He had put a pair of slacks and three shirts on the sofa-bed, hoping to squeeze them in as well to minimize his luggage to one carry-on and his laptop bag. They didn't fit.

He stuck his head under the clothes hanging in the closet and felt for a never-used suitcase stored under a box of old files, stereo and TV cables, assorted manuals and warranties for products that had long ago found their way to the garbage. Once he had wrestled the suitcase out, forgetting about the plaster dust, he sat down on the floor to daydream about CC on her home turf in the world's second largest French-speaking city. At every level of heart and mind he knew that nothing would ever happen between them, but he pulled out his winter coat, scarf and gloves anyway. He was in it for the long haul, whatever it was. The coat fit, barely, in the suitcase with the shirts and pants.

He opened the bed, then decided he'd better take a shower before going to sleep in case he woke up too late the next morning. On the way out of the bathroom he gathered his toiletries and blood pressure medication in a plastic bag.

Though it was still early, he dozed off immediately. When he awoke a couple of hours later, just shy of 11 o'clock, he did something he wouldn't be able to explain in a thousand years. He phoned Alana. Though they hadn't spoken in two years, he never got around to removing her from his speed dial. He was glad he didn't have to look up the number. He was groggy and he had a headache, probably from breathing in plaster dust.

"*Bueno?*"

"It's me," he said. "I was wondering how you were."

Ten seconds is a lot of silence on a phone. To his surprise, when she finally answered he detected no hostility.

"I'm just fine."

He waited but she didn't add any details.

"And you?" she said, ending the silence for him.

"I'm OK. I'm leaving the city for a while. I'm going to Canada. Don't know for how long and I wanted to let you know."

"Why? Why would you want to tell me? You ignore me for years and now you want me to write your name on my fridge calendar and say 'Out of town?' Do you want me to draw a sad smiley next to it?"

Her voice was calm but the resentment was surfacing in the cadences. They were edging towards Spanish. Her English was perfect, she grew up speaking both languages, but her temperament took wing in Spanish. He realized he had no idea why he called her, none whatsoever, but he didn't want to fight.

"I could use a change."

"Couldn't we all," she said, her voice neutral.

"It occurred to me I could probably make some money there. I'll be in Montreal. The province is French. They're bound to need a lot of translating. And there's no reason I couldn't keep working for my clients here. All I need is Internet."

He sensed he was making a speech, talking to hear himself talk, or thinking out loud trying to figure out why he was boarding a train the next day with a winter coat in his suitcase.

"Do you know anyone there?" she asked.

He started to say "No," then stopped himself. CC's face was front and center in his mind. He suddenly felt trapped and ridiculous at the same time.

"An acquaintance, not really a friend."

"Guy or girl?"

"Girl. Woman. What does it matter?"

"No *sé*."

Spanish again. This wasn't going the way he wanted. It was dawning on him that he wanted Alana to understand him. He had gone out with her longer than any other woman. She was the last woman he'd made love to. In sexual terms, that was a long time. She was the woman he chose to confess to. His world had changed so much since he left her that his own past had become almost foreign. Was he just trying to salvage something from it by calling her? Rather than tell the whole truth he decided to tip-toe.

"I'm going through some changes. I always thought that if I could explain them better, better than I did the last night I saw you, you wouldn't be thinking I treated you like shit. The changes are real. I know that now. It wasn't something I was trying to force on you. It was just something I was trying to understand, and then you got all upset."

"For a guy who makes money with words, you sure did a shitty job communicating."

He couldn't think of what to say except "I'm sorry."

"You said that last time, then disappeared. What do you want? What are you saying, you want to get together sometime and talk? Like this week, next week? What?" Her words fell out faster and faster.

"I can't. I'm leaving tomorrow."

"Then why the hell did you call? Now tell me," she went on quickly, "this acquaintance of yours in the frozen north, it's some hot French chica to keep you warm?"

"She's a woman, just a woman I know."

"This chica, what's her name?"

He swallowed hard. He didn't know. He made up a name.

"Sharon Zadine."

"Sharon Zadine?"

For a second he thought he'd made a smooth escape, but when Alana repeated the name he realized how unlikely it sounded.

"Yeah, her friends call her CC."

"Sounds like a stripper, from Vegas."

"No, no she's not some stripper." He sounded defensive. He knew it. She knew it.

"You know what?" Alana said after a moment. "I was right years ago. You're an asshole."

The line went dead.

. . .

Enlightenment came a few minutes past Poughkeepsie. The train was nine hours and twenty minutes from Montreal when he figured out why he called Alana. He wanted it all. He wanted to take her, conquer her, cave man, cave girl, he has the club, the sexual paradigm he grew up with. And he wanted her to take him, modern man, modern woman, she has the whip. He wanted it all in one relationship. He wanted to ride high on a skyscraper-high sexual pendulum that swung over it all. Not just sexual, he thought, sensual. If it had a sensation attached to it, it swam in the same river. Tops and bottoms tossed, turned and churned in the same current of being.

Poor Alana, he thought. How could she understand what he was only beginning to understand? At that first drunken party in the Bronx, Hermes met Aphrodite. At some point as their relationship sobered up, he metamorphosed psychologically into some configuration of Hermaphrodite. But it was only a part-time gig, which made him almost impossible to define even to himself. As the train crawled along the Hudson, he wished the transformation had come with a user manual. "Hermes is dominant on Mondays, Wednesdays and Thursdays of months with thirty days. Aphrodite rules the rest of the time. Sensual anarchy overrides all default settings in leap years."

He liked the analogy. He let the clickety-clack of the rails soothe his mind. Even though he knew he couldn't live with Alana, he still felt vaguely guilty about the way his ignorance had betrayed her. If the day ever came when she would allow him to speak to her again, he would push her latest collage to one side of the coffee table and lay the hermaphroditic explanation down before her.

As the train rolled on, he kept his eyes on the river that linked the sea and New York, and then Lake Champlain. Suddenly he turned away, startled. His imagination had been testing his theory on the fish in the river, churned by the currents until they transformed from tops to bottoms and back again in an orgy of sensations.

His mind then turned away from the river as he pictured an elegantly constructed nineteenth-century white frame house with a welcoming veranda, a manicured green lawn and a white picket fence. For some reason he felt the house was somewhere in the South. Over the double-door entrance was a large wooden sign, easily readable from the sidewalk.

It read: "100% Bio - Fair-trade Bordello."

Then, in smaller letters that could only be read after passing through the gate and taking a few steps toward the veranda:

"Naturally occurring, naturally nurtured practices warranted not to have adversely affected or disadvantaged any individual's well-being."

Suddenly, his mind went back to the river. He thought of the pollution in the waters that embraced the fish. He pictured new grotesque, deformed PCB-bred species quickly overtaking the hermaphrodite fish. What was this age doing to us? Somebody upstairs, he thought, was playing ping-pong with Yin and Yang.

"Next stop, Albany," said the conductor. "We'll be stopping for a while to change engines. You'll be permitted to detrain. Smoke 'em if you got 'em. The station has a food court. Just go up the stairs on the platform."

About seven hours to Montreal. The lights went out as the train's power was shut off. Most people were getting off. He took advantage of their departure to avoid the line for the restroom. When he exited, a schoolmarm-ish woman huffed that use of restrooms in stations was forbidden. "You are old enough to know that."

He felt like answering, "No, lady. I'm just learning."

CHAPTER 24

Montreal

CC HAD told K to try to find a room in some area called Le Plateau, near her friend's dungeon in central east Montreal.

"It's slightly like a mix of the Lower East Side and the East Village, but mostly French, and without the horrible rents," she said. "Lots of trees."

By the time he rode the escalator up to the station concourse, which was nearly empty, it was 8:30. The train was an hour late. "Normal," another passenger told him. "You never know how long Customs is going to stay on board."

When Canadian Customs asked him how long he planned to stay, he answered three to four weeks. As soon as he said that he wondered how he'd explain a winter coat if Customs decided to look through his suitcase. He had heard about American tourists showing up with skis in summer. He'd play it that way, he decided.

"You never know with the weather," he'd say. "Climate change and all that."

The train ride had been endless. It wouldn't have been, he thought, had there been an Internet connection. He just assumed there would be Wi-Fi. Even buses from New York to Montreal offered wireless. He'd planned to pass the hours finding a cheap hotel, memorizing streets around the dungeon, looking for Quebec translation organizations and forums for professionals, checking for projects from his existing clients in New York. One more good job and he could pay CC for a year's worth of sessions. He also wanted to email her to find out exactly when she was coming.

There was another thing his haste had sabotaged. He should have told LeBron to pick up his horn for safe-keeping while he was away. He owned nothing else of value. He also wanted to ask him if he knew anyone who might want to sublet the place for a while, maybe a visiting musician. LeBron knew he left a key to his place in a hole in the mortar on the side of the stoop. It was a habit from his drinking days. LeBron had once found him passed out on the steps at 4 a.m.

"Shit!" he said as he rode the escalator up to the station concourse. He was supposed to have called LeBron that morning about the Mets-Yankees ticket. "Priorities, K-Man," LeBron would admonish him. "Priorities. It's time you got your priorities in order."

K grabbed a coffee at a McDonald's in the station and sat down on a bench to drink it. He opened his laptop and saw immediately there was a wireless connection available through VIA, a Canadian railway.

He broke the news to LeBron:

Can't make Sunday's game. In Montreal. Season might be over before I return. More later.

He then started searching the Internet for a bed.

He typed in the dungeon's address, on rue

Papineau. It wasn't listed but Google provided the map he wanted. He then saw an office supply store at the far end of the station concourse but it looked closed. The new beginning was making him feel hyper-efficient. He had wanted to copy the map to a CD then print it out at the copy center advertised on the store window. That would have to wait for another day.

Keeping the map open in one tab on his browser, he opened another and searched for "B&B directories list plateau mont-royal Montreal". The first listings he checked out in detail made him shudder, $160 to $200 a night. He had planned to avoid hotels for two hundred reasons just like those. However minutes later he was finding what he wanted. Unfamiliar with the streets, it took him half an hour to cross-check the promising ones with the map of the area. In his head he was calling it the Dungeon District. Finally he chose one. He decided to phone instead of email because his ass was getting sore on the wooden concourse bench. He'd been sitting since morning.

Bingo. He'd thought his chances were slim because there were only four rooms, but the woman's voice said there was a beautiful room already waiting for him. He had addressed her in French, but she switched to English to tell him summer was over and most of the tourists had headed home.

"You can stop and window shop without being run over by people," she said. He told her where he came from they once put a line down the middle of a sidewalk, the store-front side for tourists, the other for New Yorkers in a hurry.

He closed his computer and started to make his way to the taxi stand, then realized he'd better eat before checking into the bed and breakfast on a street called De Bullion. It wouldn't have room service. He returned to McDonald's (which he detested by the time he'd hit puberty). Now that he'd solved the accommodation problem, he felt suddenly tired. He wished he could go to Shake Shack heaven back home. Tonight, though, McDo, as he heard a young French-speaking woman call it when he entered the restaurant, tasted almost refined after Amtrak's leaden menu. They must have counted on the train's movement to help passengers digest it.

He didn't know why but he was surprised the traffic seemed almost as slow as Manhattan's. The streets were teeming. The cab driver, a middle-aged Haitian, said the terraces were full because "everyone knows the warm days will soon be gone.

"The fear of winter fills them with passion," he said. "If I were young like them, the fear of winter would fill me with rum." He laughed as if such days were sadly behind him, then pulled deftly, and half into oncoming traffic for a moment, to get around the car in front, which was attempting to turn right across two lanes of stubborn traffic.

"As long as the temperature is above 25 degrees, minimum, I smile at everybody, even drivers like that one." For a second the thought of someone from Haiti smiling in 25-degree weather didn't scan, until K remembered he was visiting the land of Celsius. As he had once calculated the number of footsteps he took walking to the addiction center, he translated 25 degrees to Fahrenheit. He fudged, as he did many years before in Barcelona, multiplying the Celsius by two, instead of the more demanding but correct 1.8, and adding 32. The result was 82 degrees, from which he lopped off a few degrees to make up for his fudging. He settled on the upper seventies.

By the time he'd made the calculation, the cab had pulled onto a side street and stopped in front of graystone row houses. The one bearing the B&B's address had an orange door. There was a little garden, maybe six or seven feet deep, framed in front by a low wrought-iron fence and a row of orange flowers. He didn't know anyone with a garden and the only flowers he could identify were roses and tulips. As he got out of the cab, he noticed every door in the row had a different color, the one to the right of his being forest green. The base of the wrought-iron balconies above echoed those colors. A drinking man's dream.

As he signed the register, the woman he had spoken to on the phone, dark-haired, he could see now, and about his age, allowed him to continue in French. She made no comment about it since his French was obviously well beyond that of tourist phrase books.

It was amazing what a change three hundred miles could make. Graystones instead of brownstones, French instead of English, multicolored money instead of greenbacks, and room rates that were reasonable despite the bathroom being a shared amenity. When he got to his second-floor room, a vacation from his fourth-floor Chelsea walk-up, he threw his suitcase on the bed and instinctively reached blindly with his other hand to turn on the TV. There was none.

After a second's pause, he decided the absence of TV dovetailed perfectly with the emerging sense that he was embarking on something significantly ridiculous, or ridiculously significant. Ever since the night he became addicted to his Egyptian Princess and her sensual art, he felt his life had a focus, a well to drink from as needed, finances willing, a full-service gas station, a place to go to when he was running on empty. She had closed the door on him, but before she did, she had given birth to a new world inside him, and the door to that world was wide open. He wanted to explore it all.

He needed coffee for the laptop session ahead. The landlady downstairs directed him to the street corner just a few yards to the south.

"Turn right and take your pick," she said.

On the street sign at the corner he read "Prince Arthur Est." Pedestrians only. No cars allowed. Paving stones, imitation 19th-century street lamps, and wall-to-wall restaurants. It wasn't long before he found a coffee to go, but he knew he would probably return to one of the cafés with his laptop the next day.

Returning to his room, he wrote on a small notepad.

List:

- Write CC.

- Write LeBron.

- Draw map to dungeon.

- Dig up numbers of translation agencies.

- Write a phone spiel in French explaining why no experience in city, but am eminently qualified nonetheless.

On his laptop, he fine-tuned a spiel he'd written on the train. Upon rereading it, he judged it to be a nice little piece of fiction:

"I've just finished a long-term project for the marketing department at (note to self: find name of U.S.-based multinational with offices in Mtl). They needed a translator in-house so they flew me up. I've been here since spring. Love the city. Just love it. My New York operations pretty well take care of themselves. I rarely have to go back. If I do it's usually on a weekend. I'm seriously looking at settling here."

He dozed off shortly before sunrise. When he awoke, the clock-radio was still on. He'd found a 24-hour jazz station. The announcers were French. Though he needed another coffee, and would have to go out to get it, he said aloud: "That's cool."

He turned the volume up a bit while he got dressed and collected his shaving gear to take to the communal washroom. It was in use. He returned to his room and pulled a chair to the window. It was sunny, the sky a perfect blue, but the air entering the open window was chilly. He looked down and saw some people holding their jackets close to their chests and walking quickly. Had summer vanished overnight?

Map in hand, he found that the dungeon was a good twenty-minute walk northeast, maybe a bit more. On the way he stopped for breakfast. Instead of choosing among the countless restaurants on rue St. Denis, with boutiques growing below, beside and above them like so many vines, he settled for an unimposing one at the corner of avenue Mont-Royal. At first glance from outside he knew the menu: bacon, eggs, sausage, pancakes, home fries, coffee. He also noticed the gold old American Arborite counters and red booths. As he entered, he scooped up a newspaper from an empty table, rolling it as he walked to another empty table by a window. Upon unrolling the paper he saw a giant headline and a giant photo filling Page 1, the same tabloid formula he breakfasted with at home, except the paper he'd be leaving yolk stains on was *Le Journal de Montréal* instead of the *Post* or the *Daily News*.

CC had been right on about the Plateau. It was a Lower East Side mix of borderline pricey boutiques next to ma and pop stores, burger and dog places, fruit and veggie stores and restaurant menus with $5 breakfasts and others with entrées starting at $20.

There were also small storefronts with second-hand books and vinyl records. When he spotted one with some great old Blue Note and Impulse releases, he forgot about the dungeon and went in. He picked up a copy of a Freddie Hubbard album, *The Body and The Soul*. Although he hadn't owned a record player for a good twenty years he never missed a chance to go into a store and take vinyl in his hands, smell it, and reread the long liner notes.

In New York, he went every couple of months to a jazz record store squirreled away on the eighth floor of an old office building on West 26th. No sign at the building's entrance even indicated its presence, yet it held a treasure in its hundreds of bins of recordings. It seemed every time he entered, the owner was holding a fifty-year-old LP up to the light, then wiping away the last smudge with a cloth. The last time he was there, the album being polished was Lee Morgan's *Sidewinder*. Now in Montreal, the Freddie Hubbard album he held brought back the feelings he'd had while listening to it as a teenager, when he thought that the music and Scotch would imbue him with a veneer of sadness, like a grown-up, even though he'd never had any real experience in life.

Since the Egyptian Princess opened that new door inside him, he had become a stranger to that kind of sadness, as he had to Scotch. Hubbard's flugelhorn playing was still exquisite but parts of it no longer made him so sad he couldn't breathe. The recording he most wished he had now was Johnny Hodges playing alto on Billy Strayhorn's *Day Dream*. Its title alone made it his living theme song.

By the time he returned to the sidewalk the sun was warm, the earth coming to a standstill in its orbit beneath it, pausing at the crossroads of the seasons. He felt like a new man as he walked another fifteen minutes to Papineau, where he turned left. Half a block later, on his left, so nondescript he at first walked by it, was CC's dungeon, or rather, her friend's.

It looked like an abandoned storefront, a dark red velvet curtain blocking out curious eyes. Flyers were threatening to fall from the mailbox to the right of the door. Below it was an intercom button but no indication of an office or apartment number. He stepped back to the busy street and looked up. The two stone-fronted floors above looked like apartments, although he saw no lights or other signs of life. He had become enough of a dungeon rat to know not to expect flashing neon arrows to point the way. Looking at his watch he realized it wasn't even noon. The place was likely still closed. If Quebeckers partied late like their Latin cousins in Barcelona, high noon on the clock was still sunrise to them.

He would ring the little white buzzer, barely visible on the metal intercom, another day, when he knew CC had arrived.

He walked back south on Papineau, eventually coming to a large park on his right. Checking his hand-drawn map of the neighborhood, he decided to angle through the park southwards to a major street called Sherbrooke, which eventually intersected De Bullion, where he was staying. The park was large, traversing several streets with grounds for picnics and bocce, dog walks, baseball diamonds and finally a little lake, which forced him north again to circumvent it, finally taking him down the west side of the park, lined by mostly three-story row apartments, many of them elegant stone-fronted affairs with eccentric Victorian towers sitting atop them like party hats. A tiny block after exiting the park brought him to Sherbrooke Street, the bottom of the Plateau. He was cordoning off the Dungeon Zone — CC had told him there were others near hers. Streets to the south of Sherbrooke all seemed to plunge downhill toward the St. Lawrence River and the Old Port.

By the time he got to the orange door he was tired. A man greeted him and said he hoped he would join them for breakfast tomorrow.

"You left so quickly this morning, we couldn't invite you to the kitchen."

Once in his room, he kicked off his shoes and lay down. "Now what?" He decided to leave his work-seeking phone blitz until tomorrow. He turned on the radio, still tuned to Planète Jazz-FM, and fell asleep.

He woke up more than three hours later, just before five. He wished he had a little fridge in the room and a coffee-maker, although he had use of the shared kitchen.

He also needed to go to the bathroom. As he pulled on pants, socks and a T-shirt, he decided it was good that he had to dress first. He wouldn't waste the rest of the day in bed. While in the bathroom on the floor above his, he realized he hadn't checked his email all day. Had CC answered? He hurried back to his room and opened his laptop, which he'd stored in the closet under his empty suitcase. Shit, she hadn't.

He was still entirely on his own north of the border, he thought, before checking himself. Of course he was alone. What had he expected when he boarded that train yesterday morning? Was he thinking she'd be there at the station, waiting for him, suggesting he move in with her, that is, if he thought he'd like that? Some days he thought that with each passing year his fantasy life and idle day-dreams were sending him warning messages.

"Attention, the following program may contain material of an extravagantly fanciful nature and is not intended for rudderless souls."

He wished he could switch on a TV for distraction. After sitting for several moments on the end of the bed gazing dumbly at himself in the mirror above the dresser, he realized his laptop could serve as his TV. Immediately, he navigated to CNN and clicked on the first video link he saw. He was not sure why he chose CNN. He rarely watched it at home. Maybe home was where he wanted to be for a while, figuring this whole thing out as he should have done before precipitously packing his suitcase and hopping the first train north like a fugitive.

By 7 he was getting hungry but he was hanging on to watch the end of an episode of *Law & Order: Criminal Intent*. He'd read that the television set for NYPD head-quarters was shot in his neighborhood, at Chelsea Piers.

Before the show finished, an email notification popped up on his screen. Immediately he knew it wasn't from CC. There was no mugshot on the message. He'd linked a photo of her to his email contact list. He paused the TV show and read the email. It was from LeBron.

All is cool, kind of. My old lady left me so I'm stuck sleeping with your horn. Pretty baby but cold, K-Man. Did you know you have a honkin' big hole in your ceiling? I wouldn't want to be looking up when your neighbor's having a crap. I'm putting the word out about a sublet. Will let you know. Maybe my band will land a gig in Montreal some day. You're the craziest translator I know. By the way, the Mets took the series. We got braggin' rights. Later.

He had his shoes tied just as *L&O* finished. He put on a second T-shirt and a long-sleeved shirt on top, and went out in search of a restaurant on Prince Arthur. The night had turned chilly. He told himself he would buy himself a jacket for fall as soon as he nailed a translation project. He stepped into a small East Indian restaurant with warm yellow walls. In his mind he ran through the hotshot-translator-for-hire spiel he had translated into French. He would try it out the next morning. He pulled out a little notebook from his pants pocket and wrote a reminder for that night: recharge phone.

CHAPTER 25

Settling In

OVER breakfast K found himself with three other guests, all women in their forties from what a Tourism Québec brochure in his room said was the historic Saguenay region of the province. From one of the B&B's owners, K learned there were monthly rates available. His room would cost $750, enough of a saving that he knew then and there he could afford to stay long enough to make use of the winter coat he lugged from New York.

Immediately after tucking away his ham and eggs with a side of buckwheat *crêpes*, he pulled the owner aside and made the arrangement. A few minutes later, back in his room, he wrote in his journal that if LeBron found someone to sublet his Chelsea apartment from time to time he'd have clear sailing ahead. He added:

"Have the strongest feeling that little CC is going to get it through my head once and for all that there is still a whole lot of livin' to do." On rereading the sentence, he thought how strange music was, the way it can get inside you and take up residence for life. He realized the lyrics of a song had dictated the sentence, even though it took a minute for the actual music to sound in his head. "Christ," he wrote in brackets, "*Lot of Livin' to Do*, Sammy Davis Jr. 50s, 60s? CC probably wasn't even born the last time I even heard that one."

Stuffed from the large breakfast, he lay back on his bed, pulling the laptop onto his chest. He opened his email program and created a message template for work. After his signature, copied from a scanned JPG image, he added addresses for his Montreal and New York City offices. For his address on De Bullion, he changed *Chambre* #2 to a business-like *Bureau* 2.

When he caught himself closing his eyes and daydreaming about CC, he sat up. He had work to do, or rather work to find. After returning from a long shower upstairs, he hit the phone.

Twenty-one phone calls, seven live voices and one and a half hours later, he found he could verbally skateboard through his spiel as easily as he could recite his date and place of birth. Much as he had done when he sat on a park bench one day overlooking the Hudson River so many years ago planning his suddenly imposed career as a freelancer, he sold the fact that being New York-based meant he had the latest marketing buzzwords and nuances at his fingertips.

He liked to think of himself as a creative person, a writer, musician, a drawer of stick figures. Inside, he knew there was only a modicum of truth in that conceit, but even sober he wanted to believe in the notion that by imagining himself as this or that kind of person he could eventually become it.

Since venturing out on his own, his at-times desperate scramble to unearth business had revealed a salesman side to his nature. Mentally slipping into a gray suit with a red tie atop a crisp white shirt had become as easy as massaging pretentious documents, documents written by or for corporate executives who in turn would pretend they actually believed their own mission statements verbatim. These people paid good money for well-translated documents. They fretted over each word. Two thousand managers had to sign off on important documents that essentially said nothing.

His morning's efforts produced two promises to "add your contact info to our list of translators" and one proposal to meet the following week.

That evening he bought a whole pizza on a whim and hurried home. He had planned to eat out, as usual, but now that he was a resident, he wanted to kick back and feel at home. It didn't matter that practically nothing in the room belonged to him.

He was pleased with himself. While turning on the salesman persona was not difficult when the motor was running and when the stakes were high, he spent the vast majority of his time in a sort of no-man's land, waiting to have his life activated, fantasizing about and fabricating sensual and maybe sexual partners. Even in fantasy, he acknowledged he didn't know himself anymore. All he wanted now was to earn enough money to do nothing but buy opportunities for sensation. He viewed his initiative to contact his Egyptian Princess as a lifesaver. He owed her his life. And smaller initiatives like the one today, dialing phone numbers and acting a role, were far greater accomplishments than anyone could possibly guess.

Today, he felt the tortoise had indeed emerged from its shell.

An entire deep-dish pizza. He deserved it.

The next morning the sun was shining again. He still tasted the pizza and had no appetite at all, but the owner and other guests were the only people he knew in Montreal. He wanted them to scrape away the hesitancy in his spoken French. Yesterday they showed themselves too willing to fill his silences with English. He would set them straight this morning. He'd tell them to show him no mercy.

As soon as that thought occurred to him, in those

words, he remembered that he got a smile every time he said something similar to CC: "*Faites-moi mal, maîtresse!*" She would always smile but he was never sure whether it was because of the prospect of beating his behind or if it was because of his accent.

He'd first read the expression when CC showed him a photograph of the front page of an old issue of a Montreal tabloid. The paper had done a story on the dominatrix she was now hoping to go into business with. It was the kind of photo-story that allowed the paper to pretend to be shocked yet sell papers at the same time.

Now, as he dressed, he decided he wouldn't ask the tourists to hurt him if he made mistakes in French over breakfast.

As he was about to open the door, an email arrived from a New York client. Eleven thousand words needed within seven days. He wrote back: "Working days?"

The immediate reply was: "No, one week from now. A slam dunk."

"No problem," he lied.

He opened the attached text and scanned it quickly. Straight forward, a quick $2,200. His appetite had returned. It would also help pass the time until CC arrived.

Finding himself alone at the breakfast table, he lied to the owner and said he wanted to take a walk before breakfast. He returned to his room to get his laptop and left. Before stepping outside, he leaned into the kitchen and told the owner he was going to skip breakfast. No need to keep breakfast on offer just for him. Why had he lied in the first place? He had no idea. Lying was unsettling. It became easier and easier to do.

"Work does that," he thought finally.

In no time, he found himself within half a block of CC's dungeon. On his first visit he had spotted a nearby café with Wi-Fi. He entered and ordered a hot chocolate with whipped cream, another reward, this one for having walked off some of the pizza. He was feeling generous towards himself, a rarity, and he was feeling flush though he hadn't earned his money yet. After reading the morning paper, he ordered a croissant and started to translate.

By noon he was hungry and asked the girl behind the counter for a tuna salad sandwich in a wrap. Earlier she had come to his table to clear away the empty hot chocolate mug. She had long black hair, thick, eyebrows that rose in grand arches, and light green eyes. When he sensed her presence and looked up, he was so struck by her face he was actually startled.

"Where are you from?"

"Here," she replied easily. "Family's Persian. You're not the first one to ask."

Her shift ended before he had reached the quota of translated words he'd set for himself that afternoon. Without consciously thinking about it, he felt disappointed when he saw her leave, blowing a kiss to some of her co-workers as she went. Then he started cursing himself. He was doing it again. It had become a disease. He would utterly forget his age when looking at beautiful young women. It took a physical effort to step back and remind himself of his age, and how he must appear in their eyes. They were probably only nice to him because he was clearly old enough to be no threat. He was too old to hit on them. And he knew that. He knew that too well.

So how was it possible to look in the mirror while shaving day after day and not see the face everyone else sees, whether they're male or female, young or old, stranger, friend. It was as if the only change in his appearance that he had ever registered was that of boy to man. He guessed that the problem was that the voice in his head, the one that babbled about how beautiful the Persian woman was, was the same voice he had as a twenty-one year old, the same timbre, same resonance.

It was early evening before he reached his quota.

He had run out of steam.

At the corner, on the other side of the street, he boarded a westbound 94 Mont-Royal bus. He had to drop two toonies into the box, two $2 coins. The fare was $3, exact change. The overpayment for a ride home was worth it, although traffic made it a long one.

Looking out the bus window, he imagined CC walking along the same street. She said her mother once owned a fruit and vegetable store on it, and that she worked there as a kid. He also thought of his Egyptian Princess. In fact, even after more than a year apart, it was rare that a day went by without at least one image of her drifting through his mind. He wished he knew what elements in his mind conspired every day to shake the snow globe. When the flakes settled, there she would be, staring at him, her face neutral the way it was before he met her and never the smiling one that he suspected knew he was in love with her.

By the time he got home, he had decided to spend the next day in his room, putting in a marathon work session. He wanted the work out of the way. He wanted to be free to fantasize.

CHAPTER 26

Company

BY MID-MONTH he was almost ecstatic about his spontaneous decision to buy a one-way train ticket to a strange city for the sole purpose of staying close to a sexy little dominatrix with a penchant for having fun at his expense. Work arrived on his laptop at a more than livable rate, and he now had two Canadian clients to add to his U.S. clients. Nothing major, but one of the new ones made a point of saying plenty of projects would come his way in time. The client said it was just a matter of letting other managers know he did good work and could be counted on to be available on short notice.

The news from LeBron was even better.

I have a proposal for you. I told you my old lady left me. Same old story about musicians' hours and everyone else's hours. The problem is I can't cut the rent here on my own ($1,900 a month). In fact, I can't even come close.

I know you think bass players are not much above drummers on the evolutionary scale but we can have moments of brilliance. How about this... I move into your crib until you return. I can handle the rent and look after your place, forward the love letters you get from ladies in your dark past. I talk to your horn every night and I promise to continue. I can de-crib as soon as you decide to come back. Just give me a bit of a heads-up.

I'll tell the super I'm there at your request. Maybe you could send a letter saying that you're out of town on business or serving a ten-year stretch in Sing Sing and you want me to look after your place. He'll go for it because he knows me. Besides, I think he's tone deaf.

An immediate yes would be a life saver. I'd even be willing to give you my Mets hat. The overpaid bastards blew the season again. Do the papers up there cover this farce of a ball club?

Life was good, he thought. LeBron got his "immediate yes" with an email that day, allowing him to assume the rent in Chelsea, about one-third of what he'd been paying at his old place. The arrangement was perfect for both of them. The email included a reminder to have copies made of his door key so there would always be one hidden in the crumbling mortar, and a copy of his mailbox key. In his haste, he completely forgot that junk mail alone would have left the box overflowing by now. He also included an attachment, a letter giving LeBron permission to occupy the apartment in his absence.

The weather was turning. Leaden skies replaced sunshine for days at a time. Like Manhattan, Montreal invited walking, but he found himself staying in his room most of the time. That was bearable as long as there was work to occupy him. He was spending more and more time in the mornings chatting with the people who ran the B&B after breakfast. They were his only social contact.

The man, Robert, turned out to be the son of the other owner, Ghislaine. One day he confessed in English that "being an innkeeper is my daytime gig."

"Musician?"

"No, I sculpt. Come."

He led K to a small room with a large window facing a tiny paved backyard. His studio.

"I started with wood a long time ago. Now I work with stone," he said. On a shelf above a bench strewn with an assortment of mallets, chisels, rasps and whet-stones were some of his works. Although the colors were beautiful, greens, gold, reds and creams, a large number of them looked unfinished or abandoned.

"All failures," he said, laughing, "But sometimes what comes out surprises me. Those I want to keep. I don't even think of trying to sell my sculptures."

They had something in common. Only choice of instrument separated them.

"Most of those are alabaster. Before I die, though, I want to try marble. I tell myself it would be like playing classical music instead of contemporary. You know, breathing the same marble dust as the masters did. But that's a lot harder to work with. I'd need to buy better tools. They're not cheap."

When K returned to his room he wished he had his sax. The three other rooms were vacant that week and he now knew the owners would tolerate his playing. Work had disappeared a week ago. Despite the feeling he had new friends downstairs, he felt more alone than he liked.

He was irritable, and he realized the irritability had been showing its head off and on for days. He thought of "taking two aspirin," which was his shorthand for mas-turbating. He thought of returning to bed despite the early hour and getting off to an imagined scene with CC. After a moment, even that seemed too demanding.

It was then that it dawned on him that he was angry with her. She was supposed to be here, in Montreal, maybe even within shouting distance. He'd been writing her for weeks, asking when she was planning on showing up. Then he started writing just to ask if she was all right. He was getting worried something had happened to her in New York. During the year-plus that he'd known her, she always replied within a few days at most. She also initiated emails and phoned him out of the blue to suggest a session or announce she had a new toy to try on him. He hadn't heard a peep since he left New York.

Was the approach of the infamous Canadian winter stirring his impatience? Cold and solitude wouldn't make good bedmates judging by how irritated he was today. It was merely gray and bearably chilly. His own thinking puzzled him, since he knew CC would never be sharing his bed on a zero-degree night. Then he remembered how quickly he had acted when his Egyptian Princess dumped him, suggesting he contact CC. The Egyptian Princess had instantly filled a gaping hole in his life, though he had not been able to define that hole at the time. Making an appointment to meet CC that very day kept the hole filled, even sight unseen. The fact that she was a domme, and one with a tights fetish to boot, was enough. Later he realized that the gaping hole CC had unknowingly plugged was the bridge to a life he found worth living.

He took his laptop to the communal kitchen, put on a pot of coffee and started to write a note, not to CC but to his Egyptian Princess, his first in more than a year.

I hope you don't mind, after me not having been in touch for so long, if I ask you a favor.

Could you tell me if CC is OK? I've gotten quite worried that she may have had an accident, or something else bad has happened. She has suddenly stopped responding to emails, including my last one, more than a week ago now, saying that I would like her permission to look for another mistress.

If you know that she is OK, could you please just let me know? There's no one else I can check with. I'd also prefer it if you didn't tell her I was asking. It's her business if she doesn't want to contact me.

And... if you have a minute when you reply, I would very much like to know how you are. And, if you have two to three minutes, your complete take (just type fast, the hell with spelling) on your place in the universe at this moment in time.

I hope you're well.

Though he had braced himself not to expect a reply, he felt so happy to be writing his Egyptian Princess that he kept the unsent message on the screen, rereading it in his mind with different voices and intonations. Tears were jostling in the wings, preparing for their entrance, like a corps de ballet being herded by a nervous stage manager. Just in time, he smelled the coffee and hit Send as he got up to go to the counter.

The reply came two days later, another gray cold day. But he hadn't really noticed the weather. Writing his Egyptian Princess had recharged him, giving him another fantasy to pass time with. At the moment there was no work at either his Montreal or New York offices. He loved how nicely some BS sounded. He was waiting for a Montreal client to propose a long-term project and inquire about his availability. The test would be not to laugh as he said, "Let me check my schedule with my New York office and I'll get right back to you."

That morning, Robert had presented him with a flute.

"It belongs to a nephew, but he's just been kicked out of music class because he hasn't shown up since the first week of school. Someone should make use of it."

K had been testing out the flute when the reply came:

I am well, and as far as i know- cc is fine, though she didn't reply to my phone call yesterday. but i assume all is well, and perhaps she is just out of town, or busy with her various works. when she gets in touch, i'll let you know- not to worry...

if you would like a part-time, winter mistress, i can probably help you out... hehehe... but you'll have to come up to Montreal. I've been home since the end of summer... try it, you might like it.

CHAPTER 27

Reunited

"OH MY God, how are you?" When K heard her voice he felt he'd been an idiot, the densest man in the world. He understood nothing.

Though she was still on speed dial, it had taken him a full hour to press the number. His room was not big enough to pace. He went down the stairs, first to the kitchen, then outside without his coat. He turned onto Prince Arthur. Because of the cold he ducked into the first restaurant he came to and ordered a coffee to go. He took the first sips there while looking out the window. It was mid-morning, the street was quiet. Her email made it clear she would be happy to see him any time, although she didn't "want to cut CC's grass."

How long had she felt that way? Why had she dumped him in the first place? Could he have been with her all this time had he not been so desperate for her to treat him like a friend, who just happened to also be a client? In the last few emails, she had stopped making him feel special. She sounded impatient. She signed her messages without endearments. At the first sign of impatience from him, she got pissed off and pulled the plug.

"I'm here."

"What do you mean, 'Here?'"

"In Montreal. I've been here for a month. CC said she was coming here to work for a while for a friend, to help her open some new dungeon. I've walked by it several times. I've never seen any sign of life."

"No, no. It's open. They just make it look that way. Behind that big curtain it's really cool. I haven't sessioned there yet but I can't wait. I'm waiting for CC, too. The woman who runs the dungeon is her friend. CC's my introduction."

"So where is CC?"

"*Shizer!* I didn't tell you. She's OK. She's fine. She finally called me back last night. She didn't know you were expecting to find her already here in Montreal. She said you're crazy. She's flattered you'd follow her around the world. Those were her words. 'Follow me round the world.' Really flattered."

"That's me. Just put a fine ass in tights in front of me and you've got an unshakeable shadow all the way to Timbuktu."

"Speaking of which, I'm all out of tights, mister. I gave my pair to CC when we stopped seeing each other. You'll have to get me some."

"I can't wait that long," he said, instantly turned on. The idea of CC pulling on the tights his Egyptian Princess used to wear sent his fetish meter to melt-down levels.

"Back to CC for a sec. She said to tell you she's got some debts to work off first, and then she's got to find someone to take her apartment before she can move back. She said I can have you all to myself as long as I give you back in one piece when she arrives. I told her I couldn't guarantee the one-piece part."

"Did she say why she didn't let me know? I wrote

many times and left messages. I was really worried."

"No, but you have to know a lot of dommes are like that. They're different. They do things their own way. They don't mean to be rude. That's just the way they are."

She said she had a lot to tell him, but all that could wait until after they had a session.

"There's a dungeon right near my place. It's where I started a few years back. It's called Caro's and it's not expensive. Want me to find out when I can book a session?"

"Make it a double."

She laughed, then turned serious:

"You still not drinking?"

"Nope."

"Proud. Proud of you. I'll get back to you in a couple of days, tops."

Before hanging up she asked, "Where are you staying by the way?"

He told her.

"No way. I used to live on the next street, Coloniale. Shit. I don't believe it. Anyway, that's good because the dungeon I'm talking about isn't far. You can walk it in twenty minutes."

She gave him the intersection.

"I think I've passed it."

"Ciao."

This wasn't happening, he told himself. It just couldn't be. Time had reversed itself. She had gone home. He had left home. But hell, Egypt was still Egypt. He pulled on his winter coat and flew down the stairs like an adolescent, two at a time. He walked down to Sherbrooke, then east past the intersection she indicated on the phone. He tried to guess which building housed the dungeon. It had to be one of the old triplexes on the south side of the street. Their gray stone walls seemed to be brooding under the slate November sky. Whichever house it was, it would make for a cozy reunion.

He had energy to burn, so he turned north a block later, skirting Parc Lafontaine. His eye followed the grass sloping sharply down to the little lake. It had been emptied of water for winter. Much of it was filled with leaves. At the top of the park he walked its northern border, which brought him to Papineau. He walked north for two and a half long blocks and stopped in front of CC's dungeon. He stared at the velvet curtain. For a second he thought it moved, as if someone was adjusting it. But he couldn't be sure. It may have been wishful thinking, the way he made the portraits of long-dead Indian chieftains come alive on the television screen so many years before just because he wanted to talk to them.

He had walked hard, with purpose. It had been many days since he'd given himself a workout. On the way home he stopped on Mont-Royal for a pizza made with curry. Spice, he thought, that's what was back in his life.

. . .

She called the next day.

"Couldn't book a double session. A long time ago you offered to take me out for supper. Is the offer still good?"

"You'll have to pick. I'm new boy in town."

"Like Asian? I know one about five minutes from Caro's. They don't use meat or fish but if you can find anything on that menu that doesn't taste just like the real thing, I'll buy."

She suggested they eat before the session. He preferred after. In his dotage, he said, food made him sleepy.

"I could make sure you don't fall asleep, put you in a pillory and throw leftover Chinese at you, or hang you upside down or something. No, sure. We'll play first, and then I can watch you squirm trying to get your sorry ass comfortable while we eat."

Hearing her teasing him again after all that time was

bringing tears to his eyes. It was like being a kid again, back home, at the family table, food on its way from the kitchen, everything the way it should be simply because that's the way it had always been, at least until he got old enough to see his parents for what they were. Then everyone died and he hadn't felt at home since.

The sessions were usually an hour long. If he were a rich man he would have been happy to pay for the anticipation she created. If the session were a day away he'd feel he was in her hands for the whole twenty-four hours.

Caro, the owner, met him at the door.

"*Bonsoir, monsieur. Suivez-moi, s'il vous plaît.*" She was middle-aged at best. He was so intent on seeing his Egyptian Princess that he was unable to recall Caro's features afterwards beyond the attractive voice with a touch of built-in flirtatiousness. She led him into a darkened living room, and there she was, his Egyptian Princess, in the corner by an end table, butting out a cigarette.

"Right on time." She smiled and took his hand, like a girlfriend might. He wasn't going to spoil the moment telling himself to get real.

She was wearing the same black teddy, or one similar to what she wore on their very first session in Manhattan. And the black high heels she hated so much. He remembered how happy she was to kick them off mid-session. She opened the door to a steep stairwell leading to the basement. He offered to go first in case she stumbled because of her heels.

"In fact I hope you do. I would love to catch you. You'd owe me your life."

"Go," she commanded, accepting his hand for the final few steps at the bottom. She preceded him through a red door, revealing a spacious low-ceilinged room with a spanking bench. There was also a wooden affair to kneel on with eye-hooks for ropes or cuffs, and a low double bed to the left. He wondered whether that was the bed she propped herself up on for the photo on her website, where she wore a skirt, raised mid-thigh on one side, and stared right through the camera.

"Over you get."

She'd chosen the spanking bench.

"I'm out of shape and I don't want to have to deal with keeping you in position. Haven't had anyone I could really hit to my heart's content since I last saw you. You haven't gone all soft on me, have you?"

The fact was, he had, but not physically speaking. He kept his mouth shut. It turned out he would have been saved from himself anyway. She gagged him a moment later.

"There are tenants on the second floor. Caro said she heard them walking around a little while ago. I don't intend to go easy on you but you're going to have to eat the pain I'm going to lay on you. Besides, muffled cries... that's what I like best. Whimpering... Yum!"

Halfway through she stopped and sat on the bed. As she had done once before during a session, she lit a cigarette, leaned back on one elbow and stared at him, trussed on the bench. She had removed the gag for his comfort and brushed the hair off his face. He was sweating.

"Is it too hot in here? Or is that unmitigated fear, my dear?" she teased.

He was at his favorite stage in a session. His buttocks were almost numb and he was free to float. Sometimes he imagined he was actually in water, and that each stroke was the domme's hand pushing him upstream against a current of lukewarm water that lifted him almost above the surface, then released him until the next push. At times, it also seemed that at this stage there was a different kind of communion with this delicate woman who had the power to hurt him despite her size. She was more present. Often, he felt her fingers give a single-pass caress on the bare skin of his back or neck. Sometimes she would push down on his back for a moment with her palm, the pressure calming him if she caught him holding his breath against the sting.

Even though she had replaced the gag, she made him count the last twenty strokes, getting barely intelligible numbers in response. She swung a black paddle with much of her strength. At twenty, she tossed the paddle on his back and exclaimed,

"Yes! Hell, yes! That was the best birthday present I've ever had."

She'd celebrated her birthday just two days before.

As she had taken to doing every time she bound him in that position, she released his legs first, then knelt inches from his face to undo his wrists. If he extended his neck he was sure he could reach her eyelashes. He wanted her lips.

The evening was clear and cold. They walked quickly to the restaurant. For her main dish, she ordered one that was mostly noodles and vegetables. He ordered ersatz fish, first because he loved fish, secondly because he figured it would be harder to fake.

"The bet's still on."

She won. It was impossible to do what the chef had in fact done. Each dish was a masterful lie. He'd once asked himself if his love for this girl was a masterful lie he concocted for himself, just because the feeling was too good to be true. He debated the idea for a long time, but stopped when he realized he was smitten the instant he saw her. He didn't have time to concoct anything. He didn't have time to subtract her age from his. Being in love wasn't his fault.

Over the meal he learned his Egyptian Princess had become a student.

"Couldn't see myself making a living whacking asses for the rest of my life, although it sure beats an office job. I've been out of school for a long time now, and the only thing I've learned is that I'm more sure than ever that I wouldn't live to thirty if I worked in an office. So I've gone back to school. I'm in my second year at Concordia. That's one of the universities here."

"In?"

"Theater. Their theater program. I'm studying scenography, and costume design. I'll be a set designer someday."

How many other secrets did she have? He knew all about her dysfunctional family, including the fact they weren't really from Austin, and he knew about the love of her life, who years later still made San Fran her favorite city in the world even though it made her sad more often than not.

Even though she had moved on, she admitted now, she still wanted to see him again, "just to see him."

"Wouldn't that be painful?" he asked.

"You're not the only masochist in this room," she confessed, closing the book on the subject she probably hadn't meant to broach.

While he paid, she hurried outside. They'd spent more than two hours at the table. She needed to smoke.

"Would you like me to walk you home?" he asked, handing her the doggy bag she'd requested. "It's late."

"I'd like that." It was the second time he would walk her home, the first on her turf. He took the doggy bag from her with his right hand, and took her hand with his left. Unfortunately, unlike the stroll to Tribeca, she lived only a ten-minute walk away. She let him give her an easy slow hug at the entrance to her building. He hadn't forgotten that in Quebec both cheeks get kissed. She smiled up at him and turned quickly to the door.

He had heard Montreal was a romantic city. A voice inside told him he should get out of Dodge while the going was good. He couldn't bear to lose her twice.

CHAPTER 28

The Egyptian Room

WHEN K had quit drinking in New York, the transformation had taken place in winter, too frequently under gray skies, in damp cold, rain and snow, abetted by gusting winds. He had conquered. As winter drew nearer in Montreal, he almost welcomed it.

"Take your best shot." He felt damn near impervious to anything he didn't want to be affected by. He was in love again, the same love, only no longer on pause, where feelings get distorted as images did on VHS tapes when a film was put on pause. The resumption was not through his efforts or hers. But it was not mere serendipity. It was meant to happen, just the way VHS tapes automatically resumed playing after a set amount of time on pause in order to protect the tape from stretching.

Every day he rejoiced in the feeling, surer than ever he had been blessed with the benefits of some kind of mistake. The ability to feel "in love" was not a feeling programmed in humans to have a shelf life. Love, OK, in love, no. Somebody screwed up but he wasn't about to hand the feeling back. It was like finding a small fortune on the sidewalk in Westmount, or on the Upper East Side back home. No one would suffer much if he pocketed it.

The important thing was that he mustn't tell her. Since reconnecting in Montreal, he had already started teasing her again that the huge disparity in their ages was also a screw-up, and that she'd be stuck fending him off in his next life as well, when he would reincarnate as "young and studly," and living just down the hall. He said he would even be a few years younger than her but she immediately nixed that idea.

"A boy is the last thing I want."

His life's only difficulty was not resuming the tidal wave of correspondence he had instigated when they first met. The instant she said she was a writer too, and welcomed his words, he felt the door was open. But in retrospect he had gone overboard, by a lot. He needed an editor, an emotions editor. He had to be careful now. If only his fingers weren't too big to text messages on his cell. One hundred and sixty characters, a limit conceived to cool any passion, a limit better suited to hurting than loving. In his mind, he was constantly talking to her, and if his fingers got near a keyboard, a full-sized keyboard, she had mail waiting.

Work saved him from himself. He let her be for the most part.

She had told him she was already studying for end-of-semester exams. She didn't have to say more. She had told him she had always been an A-student, even when her mom was throwing furniture at her dad in the next room, or her sister freaking out on meth or tripping on coke. Now, at university, if she got a B average, she said she wanted to puke.

In early December he wrote a minuscule message:

Anything happening on Papineau yet? Just curious.

To his surprise she phoned that night, late.

"Can't do this anymore. Can't stop studying but I've stopped getting anywhere. I haven't slept for twenty-four hours, at least."

"Then take a break."

"Can't."

"Run around the block."

"I don't run. Ever."

"Skateboard."

"It's nighttime. Too many potholes in Montreal."

"Get laid."

"No BF."

"Don't believe you."

"There was a boy last summer. He sort of just hung around. We started making out one night, but I just couldn't. Same old problem. He was sweet about it, really sweet. But it's been months. I'm sure he gave up waiting a long time ago. I don't talk to anybody."

"Drink, then."

"Can't afford a hangover… Shit, shit, shit. Why didn't I stay in school? It used to be easy. I would have graduated years ago."

"Glad you didn't."

"And why not?"

"You'd be a scenarist and not a domme. And where the hell would my life be then? Don't be so damned selfish."

Finally, a laugh.

"Really, though, I've got to keep going, somehow."

"Can I help you study? Slap you around when you nod off, that kind of thing?"

After a moment, she said:

"Actually, yeah. Come to think of it, you can make me describe some shit out loud. Right now I keep reading things over and over again hoping they stick, but I don't know if they are."

He said he could be there in twenty minutes, but she said no. She needed the walk. It was uphill from her place on boulevard De Maisonneuve. And it was a cold night. She hated cold with a passion. It would do her good.

"I deeply admire your masochistic side. See you soon. Hey, remember, you can't smoke here. House rules, not mine."

When she arrived, her cheeks were pink. He rubbed her back with one arm as he hugged her with the other. A minute later she sat cross-legged on the bed. She tossed him some of her notes from which to ask questions. Her handwriting was smaller than the type used for side-effects on medication bottles. He had to go downstairs to ask Ghislaine if she had a magnifying glass. She did.

After two hours she abruptly announced:

"This isn't working. I gotta go."

From the window he saw her walking briskly back home. He felt he had failed her but didn't know how.

Around 1 a.m., she phoned again.

"You know what I need? I mean, everything else has failed. I need a session. I don't care if you can only pay the dungeon fee. I need to play."

Although her student allowance covered rent and a few essentials, she needed sessions to stay in cigarettes and Friday night sushi. With exams approaching, though, she had sworn off sessions and people. He was learning she didn't do anything by half measure.

"I got thinking on the way home. I never answered you about the place on Papineau. By the way, it's called CMF, Club Montréal Fétiche. It's open. You'll love it. I was going to wait until school was over for Christmas before taking you. But I want to go now, well it's too late for tonight, but maybe tomorrow. If I feel the way I feel right now you'll have laryngitis by the time I'm through."

She was sounding like her old self. He wished he could hug her again. Although he loved having his large hands on her young body, there was a fragile side to her that she hid well. When he spotted it under attack he wanted to sweep her up and shield her. On those occasions there was nothing sexual about the urges, and he didn't feel guilty about them. But she wanted no part of that. "You're not my father," she once snapped.

"Tomorrow it is," he said, accepting her offer for a session before correcting himself. "Today, I mean."

"I'll call you with the time. By the way, thanks for tonight. I'm just in an anti-social funk, I think."

When he arrived at CMF at 7 that evening, there was a string of small white Christmas lights around the top and sides of the red velvet curtain. They weren't meant as Christmas decoration, just illumination.

It was several minutes before someone answered the intercom.

"*Oui?*"

He said he had an appointment at 7. He heard a heavy door closing from inside, then a moment later the front door was opened part way. It revealed the face of a young green-eyed woman with long carrot-red hair. She wore a short black leather skirt and a simple white blouse.

"Please take off your shoes or boots. There's a coat rack behind you. Make yourself comfortable," she said, indicating a deep, leather-covered sofa on the side wall of the small foyer.

"There are some magazines on the coffee table. She'll be with you in a minute."

The deep red curtains, which looked somehow cheap from the outside, succeeded in creating an ambiance inside. The coffee table was in the corner, beside the sofa. On the wall facing the entrance, a great easy chair, higher than the sofa. It was also leather-covered. Beside it, a heavy wooden door, through which the redhead disappeared. On the wall facing the sofa, photographs of the *maîtresses*. On the top right was his, looking down on him.

An instant later she appeared, easing her way through

the heavy door, then, once free of it, all but launching herself into the narrow space that separated his left side and the arm of the sofa. She was excited.

"I'm so happy you're the first customer I'm bringing here. I've been telling them all about you."

"Which of my many secrets have you been betraying?" he asked, feigning shock.

"None of the juicy stuff," she said, mimicking his alarm, then adding, "Just the fact that you're distinguished. You're a gentleman. You're clean. You can put two words together. You're not greasy. You're not an asshole. You're not slimy."

He realized her profession wasn't as glamorous as it seemed.

At that point a stunningly sensual black woman, who looked six feet tall, appeared in the doorway.

"It's all yours," she said with a slight accent, smiling hugely at the two of them. As the two rose from the sofa, she threw her coat on, pulling the collar high, and waited for them to start to enter the dungeon before she let in the cold air on her way out. Before the heavy door had a chance to close fully, she called out to them:

"*Bonsoir. Amusez-vous bien les amoureux!*"

What had his Egyptian Princess been saying to her colleagues?

Barely several steps inside the big door she leaned on him, directing him through a beaded curtain into a room about the size of his Chelsea apartment. It was called the Egyptian Room.

CC knew he had called his first mistress his Egyptian Princess, and she had told him about the room when her friend created the dungeon in Montreal. And now that he was back with his Egyptian Princess the endearment had become a bit of a running joke, mostly because while she was Jewish her family had no connection whatsoever with the few hundred Jews remaining in Egypt. She confessed to having misled some clients who asked about her exotic looks. She said she came from Moroccan Jewish origins that went far back, almost to prehistory.

He said he liked that story but preferred his pharaonic version.

Immediately inside the door was a wicker throne on a pedestal. Mats and cushions lay below saffron walls and fake Egyptian bronze ornaments, huge peacock feathers, a pharaoh's bust and a long single-tailed whip. On the floor was a low wooden bench with eyes for binding bodies. She sat on the throne, almost dwarfed by its high back, watching him take in the room as if it was the source of his personal Nile.

"No, I wasn't born in this room, so don't ask. Off with your clothes, on with your tights."

With a crop that came out of nowhere, she pointed to a curtain on his left. It opened on a walk-in closet, full of hanging costumes, extravagant boots and at least a dozen pairs of shiny black, red or gold high-heeled shoes. Because it was cold outside, he had worn his tights under his street clothes. In a minute he stood before her. She was still on the throne.

"Get down on the floor. I don't want you looking down on me."

She got up and slowly extracted white ropes from her bag. When she found the lengths she wanted, she motioned for him to get over the bench. She bound not only his wrists and ankles but his waist, severely limiting his ability to wriggle out of harm's way.

After twenty minutes of increasingly heavy flogging that included his shoulders, applied unfailingly just when he was getting too comfortable with the rhythm of blows to his buttocks, she tossed the flogger to the floor as if bored. She clinically felt his ass for a while but he didn't know whether she was pleased with her work.

He then felt something new. He looked up to the mirror in front of him and saw that she had squatted down astride his left leg. She had positioned her crotch on his calf muscle. In her hands she had three paddles, two wood, one leather. She started with the latter. A microsecond before each blow landed he felt her crotch move against his tights. As she settled back preparing for the next stroke he felt her buttocks wrap around his calf. Apart from a pause to switch her seat to his right calf, the barrage continued for an unusually long time.

She didn't talk, tease or bait as she often did. And he had a focus that devoured him. He could feel the heat of her vagina and he was sure it was wet. Later he realized the sensation could have been felt in combination with his own skin, warm and wet from simple contact and cotton-soft friction. He preferred the former explanation and had no intention of asking her if she came. However, she did volunteer that she never "thought that position would be so comfortable."

After she untied him, she said:

"Show me your ass. I don't want to wait for your morning-after report."

After passing her soft hand over his now-naked cheeks and flanks, she said only:

"I guess that will do."

When they had dressed she showed him the dungeon's other room. Every square foot of wall space was chrome silver and draped with punishment toys on silver hooks fixed to wire mesh. Straight ahead was a spanking horse, to the right a St. Andrew's cross with a pulley system rigged above it, and on a raised floor to the right of the entrance, a medical examination table with stirrups. Near it was an old wood-and-glass cabinet with two shelves of dildos of impossible sizes, condoms, cleaning supplies, wipes and rubbing alcohol, and disinfectants.

"When they speak of the dungeon, this is the room they mean."

Upstairs, she said, was a bar and lounge for play parties.

"Cool, no?" She seemed to say that when she knew he

was getting off on something as much as she was.

They decided to share a cab to Sherbrooke and St. André, which would leave him a seven-block walk home. She would continue south a few blocks to her place.

"I think I'm too tired to study now."

"That's good," he said, giving her hand a squeeze. They rode in comfortable silence, once again skirting Parc Lafontaine. Despite the fact that the approach of winter had stripped the trees of leaves, the park was becoming an oasis in a city that was still mostly unknown to him. Fertile things seemed to grow nearby. He gave her hand a kiss and got out of the cab at a red light.

As he walked he told himself he couldn't ask for more than he had in his life right now. When had he ever felt that? Probably never. In the glow of the evening he had just experienced, he told himself he could live without having sex with her as long as she stayed in his life. She got off spanking him, he got off afterwards, thinking of her face and her touch and sometimes her ass, but mostly just the soul that lived behind those dark eyes.

More and more often, at least in his mind, her body found an excuse to press against his. He was perhaps too big for her to give him much of a hug but he always felt free to hug her because she "really liked them." Why, he asked now, did he spend so much time regretting that he probably would never have sex with her? He was just too old. He knew it. She knew it. He had everything now. Sex would probably end up destroying that. If she had sex with him she would hate herself for it afterwards, and probably him as well. And he might hate himself for drawing her closer to a man who had relatively little time on earth to share with her. She ought to be with a young beautiful man to live out her best years.

Yet he wondered anyway. Was the urge too primal to ignore under any circumstance? Was he just kidding himself?

The interrogation occurred frequently but it seldom lasted long. It tended to arrive and depart like a leg cramp in the middle of the night. He was simply too happy to drill deep. He felt alive, a rarity in his life that he was only starting to appreciate.

Although he could be pedantic about language, he had taken to mimicking dommes in their use of the word *session* as a verb. As her exams approached, they had stopped sessioning. To his surprise, he didn't feel deprived in the slightest. He discovered that seeing her was enough. Although he continued to write long emails, he didn't send them out of respect for her obsessive studying. Instead, he began making brief visits to her apartment, breaking her studies with foot massages or a meal he would deliver personally from one of the restaurants on Prince Arthur.

Each time he walked back out into the night, he marveled at how haughty and domineering she could look during a session but how sweet and small she could appear at home, in T-shirt, pajama bottoms and immense fuzzy blue slippers. The only constant was the black eyes.

She said she didn't have the energy other people had. That was why she had to shut out the world to study, so she could use every waking moment. Those waking moments, he remembered, were too infrequent because of the pain that woke her every few hours. She never spoke of it, and he had never asked after being told testily that a) she was not dying, and b) she had no desire to discuss it further.

It was also during these interludes in her studies that she confessed she was more sub than domme in her personal relationships. She could be annoyingly private at times, then uncommonly open.

"In the sack I'm pretty passive."

He had gone to bed with sexually passive women in the past. It always ended badly no matter how beautiful they were. The older he got the more he wanted to be aggressed. For a long time he thought the change was likely physical in origin, a result of too much booze, too little exercise, a little too much weight. He had his testosterone levels checked at one point.

"Normal, normal, normal...," said the doctor. That supposedly good news was an open invitation to overthink.

Was he picking the wrong women? Even he couldn't be wrong that many times. It had to be the fantasy. It needed tending too. It had to be included in the mix.

He still didn't know what portion of the mix it had to comprise. In fact his Egyptian Princess, who made him happier than he'd dared think possible, was sabotaging all his calculations. He was becoming as confused as he was before the first Internet sighting. Their sessions kept his fire lit, but he was now wrestling with the realization they weren't enough. His penis answered to her, and seemingly her alone. And now that he knew she was "passive in the sack," instead of his desire turning tail and running, his penis was slipping into warrior pose. He wanted to conquer her. He wanted to take her. He wanted to dominate her. He was becoming the male he used to think he was, the one he grew up thinking he was supposed to be.

In bed at night, the confusion increased. It would have been so much simpler if he could have been content being dominated by her. Now either prospect tripped his imagination but he didn't know which to choose. Submit to her, with her one hundred and ten pounds, or fuck her, with his 200 pounds? Either way he'd roar. Some nights he watched a double feature.

The dilemma was rich. It had all the elements. It summed him up. And she could swallow all of him.

But that joyous thought always had to be shunted onto a siding. He could never have her, at least not the way that would make him whole. Continuing to see her in the face of such impossibility, was that the very reason he chose her? Was it the ultimate masochistic act? He knew he was doomed but he also knew he would stay on board the train until the track ran out.

In the middle of exams, she phoned him at 5:30 one morning. It was dark and would be for almost two more hours. The first snow had fallen two days before, not much but it made winter official.

"I want to go back to Mexico. During break."

She had been up since 3, cramming.

"There's no more room in my head. God, it's so fucking small." If her head stored information as compressed as her handwriting, he thought, it could hold about three times what his large head could. She had an exam at 10.

"Then go to Mexico," he said.

"No money." She reminded him she didn't even have a credit card.

Immediately, he offered to lend her the money and immediately she refused.

"I hate debt. More than that, I hate owing people anything."

"But you're in desperate need of mescal, or sun, or both."

"Something like that, and in that order."

Despite the hour, an idea was starting to take shape in his head.

"We hold the mother of all sessions. At your place so there is no dungeon fee. We eat, beat and... I don't know what else, but it goes on for six hours at least, three sessions strung together. Then I reach inside your tights and stick $600 between your breasts. Which reminds me, you still haven't properly introduced me to your right breast."

"Oh shit, can you really afford that?"

He had to think. He had money due him. He calculated roughly how much. What he never knew was when he'd get paid.

"I'll tell you what," he said. "I'll just put the flight on my credit card. I should have gotten some checks by the time I get billed."

"You sure?"

"Yes. Except I don't get to meet your right breast that way."

She laughed.

"I never said you could."

"OK. OK. Here's what we do. After you beat me silly you make me give you a whole body message over your tights. I've been fantasizing about that for ages."

"Deal," she said. "The mother of all sessions. So be it."

Before she went back to her books, they worked out possible dates. She'd need a day's rest after exams, and he had to go back to New York the coming weekend to take care of what LeBron described as some official-looking mail.

CHAPTER 29

Mr. Potato Head

JUST north of Yonkers, he opened his eyes as the Amtrak conductor announced there would be a delay arriving at Penn Station. There was some sort of accident on the bridge leading onto Manhattan Island.

"The police have closed the bridge. That's all we know at the present time. However it doesn't look like we'll be on our way any time soon."

The conductor sounded like Jimmy Stewart. It was almost 10 p.m. and the train was already an hour late, but Jimmy Stewart wasn't a messenger most people would consider shooting. Nevertheless cell phones were being drawn from holsters with gunslinger speed. Connections were being missed to suburban trains. When was the last ferry to Staten Island? Would AMTRAK hold the train to Washington? Hotel check-in times were in peril, and families waiting at the station were being told to stock up on doughnuts and coffee.

He closed his eyes again and tried to visualize LeBron remembering to return his key to the hole in the side of the stoop. LeBron had emailed to say he could mostly certainly find "alternate accommodations" for the weekend.

"LeBron is in demand these days," he wrote.

LeBron was always in demand, it seemed. The alto player wondered what it was like having the bass player's sex life. Was it a succession of Selitas, good sex, no relationships to speak of, desire always showing up for the party, and complications and psychology, under their own or any other name, heartily discouraged?

LeBron had been a loyal friend for years, his best friend. Was he the same for the women he left behind? He couldn't help wondering whether that was ever possible once sex was involved.

It was shortly after midnight when he got to his place. Trying not to look suspicious, his fingers fished out the key from the stoop. As he climbed the stairs inside, he realized the light bulb on his floor had gone out again.

"It's not burned out," the super had kept saying. "Must be a loose connection or something, and I'm no fucking electrician. Complain to Meathead if you can find him."

Inside, apart from the space shrinkage caused by LeBron's magnificent double bass and his electric bass and an amp, the apartment looked unchanged. Even the ceiling had been repaired. He poured a glass of water and sat down to look at the mail LeBron had laid out on the trunk.

He had trouble figuring out what nasty official-looking stuff LeBron had been referring to. Finally he found three letters from the New York State Department of Taxation and Finance. Citing Schedule SE (Form 1040), they all said the same thing: they'd failed to receive the quarterly estimated tax payments that self-employed people were required to make. He didn't mind parting with often much-needed cash to make the payments because he had learned the hard way that scrambling for the money at the end of the taxation year always meant borrowing money, which banks weren't happy to do because his income was low and inconsistent. One year, while drunk, he made the payment with a credit card cash advance. At 20 percent interest, the next tax year had already arrived before he managed to pay it off.

Since he had no intention of declaring income from his "Montreal operations," he would low-ball his estimate. He'd figure out the amount in the morning. He went to bed picturing his Egyptian Princess falling asleep fully dressed, on her bed, with her books and notebooks.

In the morning, he walked over to Ninth Avenue for breakfast. He brought his checkbook and the tax department's return envelope with him. He'd have to buy a stamp later. While waiting for fried eggs and hash browns he manufactured anticipated revenues for his worst year ever.

He'd forgotten to pick up a paper but found a copy of the *Daily News* on an uncleared table two booths down. Breakfast out was still his favorite moment of the day. It felt good to be home.

It was a mild day. The sun was promising to break through, and he decided to stretch his legs after the long train ride. After finding stamps at a fruit and vegetable store and mailing his check, he started to cross 23rd Street. On the cement island that prevented cars from venturing into the bike lane, he stepped aside to avoid a surge of pedestrians coming the other way. His right ankle twisted sharply as his foot slipped off the cement into the earth in the empty city flower bed. His body twisted as he fell forward, landing hard as if tackled from behind. His head ricocheted off the pavement. Dazed, he rolled slightly onto his right side. His left forearm was numb. With his right, he pushed himself into a sitting position, then to his knees. A young man, maybe still young enough to be still in high school, helped him to his feet.

"You OK, man?"

"Yeah, OK. I'll be fine. Thanks." Despite the shock of the hard fall, K couldn't help wondering whether the boy would be that nice a person once he'd lived a little longer.

Slowly the pain in his left wrist mounted. He couldn't move it. It was twisted, angled like the baseball cap on the head of the boy who helped him up. End of walk. He had to get home. He took one step and nearly fell again. The pain in his right ankle was excruciating. Petrified of falling, he made his way to a lamp post and leaned against it. He could tell his ankle was swelling rapidly. Let it be a sprain, he almost prayed. As for his wrist, he had no idea.

He wanted to hail a cab, but after several agonizing minutes he feared a driver would never see his raised right arm. He needed to lean out into traffic but he didn't dare move away from the lamp post that was supporting most of his weight.

When a cab finally stopped, the driver eyed him warily as he hobbled to the door. He managed to get it open, then pivoted on his left foot and let himself fall backwards onto the seat. He got his left leg inside, then had to use his right hand to grab his pant leg and pull his right foot in.

When he gave the driver his address, the cabbie asked, "Sure you don't want to go to a hospital?"

The driver was right. He'd never make it up his four flights of stairs.

He waited five hours in emergency before seeing a doctor. At least they'd put him in a wheelchair.

The verdict: clean break and a half cast for the wrist, and a Velcro brace for the severely sprained ankle.

When a cab finally deposited him in front of his building, the hardest part was getting up the steps to the entrance because there was nothing to lean on. Once inside, using the railing, he hauled himself one step at a time, sitting on a step at each landing. With two limbs on opposite sides of the body out of commission, each movement required thought. Right hand goes here, left foot goes there, then the right, and then push off back to the left foot as fast as you can. Don't let go of the railing.

Fortunately, he hadn't made the bed that morning in his haste to enjoy a Saturday morning breakfast out. He worked his way around it to get a glass of water to help swallow the painkillers, which he then deposited on the floor beside the bed. He slept with his clothes on.

Other than going to the bathroom and grabbing a new package of sixteen cheese sticks from the fridge on the way back, he spent the next twenty-four hours in bed. Sunday evening he arranged for a cab to pick him up at 7:45 the next morning to take him to the train station. Luckily he had returned to New York with only a carry-on bag. It had a strap so he could carry it hands-free.

. . .

They let him sit in the car next to the dreaded dining car so he wouldn't have far to struggle. AMTRAK called it the dining car. He called it the microwave car. Nevertheless, he ensconced next door for half the trip, during which he read most of the remainder of Isabel Allende's *Island Beneath the Sea*, the book he'd bought in Montreal for the trip home. It was the only good thing about the weekend. It was the title that first made him reach for the book. How much of his own being had been beneath the sea before meeting the Egyptian Princess, or for that matter, before LeBron dared him to really play his horn?

He wasn't sure things would get much better in the coming days. Before the train even pulled out of Penn Station he realized he should have stayed in New York for a doctor's follow-up. He was also supposed to see a physiotherapist for his ankle, which had now become the injury he cursed the most, especially while trying to turn on his side at night when the sheets had it solidly ensnared. He was also supposed to lie on his back with his wrist raised above his head but he had never been able to sleep on his back. He rigged a pile of pillows on which he would rest his wrist as he lay on his side.

However, it wasn't until he had regained his room on rue De Bullion, and after receiving effusive expressions of concern from Ghislaine and Robert, that he realized he couldn't work with one hand. He had been doing well, very well because of the new Canadian clients. In fact, he wondered often why he hadn't sought them out before while still in New York. On a French-speaking island in an Anglophone continent, the demand for translation was insatiable. Quebec and Canadian terminology banks set the standards for language resources in Europe.

How long could he hold out without working? The doctor told him it could take three months for his wrist to fully heal, barring complications.

"However, while skateboarding may not be recommended, you'll be keyboarding before then, not very fast perhaps but you'll be able to do some work."

As he eased his shoulders against the headboard, he saw a flash of silver lining in the cloud that now hung over him. His masturbating wrist was unharmed. The thought sent his mind off in search of his Egyptian Princess, and then to their plans for the mother of all domination sessions, the one that would buy her escape to Mexico. He couldn't hold the thought. His eyes tripped down his body, over his cast, and then down to the brace-wrapped ankle.

There was a knock at the door. It was Robert, with a quiche his mother had made.

"Since you're in no position to cut up your food, we figured you could manage a quiche with a fork only."

Eating with one hand forced him to eat slowly. The quiche was so good he knew he would have wolfed it down otherwise. Maybe that's how you earned the right to be French or French-Canadian. You had one of your arms tied behind your back so you could learn to eat slowly and savor. That way you learned to distinguish what was good and what was crap.

At the risk of interrupting her studies, or worse, waking her from her rare sleeps, he hit her speed dial number. It would have taken him forever to dial the ten digits with his big right thumb.

"Oh no," she said when he broke the news. After he had assured her he would survive, she said she'd been looking forward to the monster session.

"I have my last exam tomorrow. It would have been the perfect way to celebrate."

Apologizing that she had to study, she promised to call him.

"Not tomorrow because I'll be drinking with some of the other kids from school, but the day after."

Though she was in her late twenties, she often included herself among the kids she studied with. He wondered if, being back at school, she was reliving a time when many things seemed possible in life, like the way he might be doing now, allowing himself to feel in love with her despite his age.

It was apparent she relished the chance to make up for what she missed by fleeing her messed-up family before going to college. He had noticed it before but never ceased to be amazed at how she could so convincingly revert to being the sophisticated, worldly domme that so easily occupied a large part of her being. It wasn't an act. The shoe fit. But the more he got to know her, the more he saw her in different environments, the more he suspected her personality had a host of distinct chambers, like the stage settings she was learning to design. Act 1 and Act 2 could be worlds apart. Someday, he hoped, he would get to find out how they came together in her Act 3.

When she entered his room two nights later she laughed at his predicament, his ankle and forearm looking like they had been hurriedly and crookedly stuck onto a Mr. Potato Head. There would be no "Poor you, poor baby" from her unless she said it with a mock gravity.

"I'm done!" she said, flopping onto her back on the bed beside him. His eyes took in her body. Had she done so knowing he was physically incapable of doing what he most wanted to in life, roll over on top of her? She welcomed his attention but, apart from hugs, she always managed to dance gracefully out from under overly long looks or away from a hand that lingered on her shoulder or her cheek after a good night kiss.

"Fortunately for you," she said, propping herself on her left elbow, her face close to his, "there's nothing in my contract with my conscience that prevents me from beating up cripples and invalids. I checked. In fact, I give them reduced rates because they give me so much satisfaction in return. You and I, we shall do what we can do. We will improvise. You shall feel enough pain to make you forget your wrist and your ankle but no more than that. Think of it as physio."

She then suggested having the session at her place, the following Saturday afternoon. "If I took you to a dungeon looking like that they'd call the cops themselves."

Before she left he told her to look under the bed. He had ordered a gift for her from the States. It arrived just before he left for New York. She pulled out a cardboard box and placed it on the bed.

"Do you have a knife," she asked, "to cut the tape?"

He told her not to open it there. It would be easier to carry home unopened.

"But I'll tell you what it is. It's that Midori book on Japanese bondage. There's a bunch of different ropes and a CD to help you figure it out. I guess I'm no longer in the running to qualify as a model for your practice sessions."

"You never were in the running," she said with her usual frankness. "You're not flexible. I can't twist you inside out. I'd like a lithe young woman to work on. Know any?" If she were in range, his right hand would have found her ass at that moment, no matter how much pain the gesture would have cost him.

She lowered her face, close to his, and looked him in the eye. "Seriously, seriously thank you, first of all. I've wanted this book forever, and secondly, this book will give me some seriously fun ideas for Saturday. Fear not."

Before leaving, she lightly pressed her palm on his chest. He found the gesture intimate. After she'd closed the door behind her, he remembered someone telling him that gesture was also a good one to calm a baby, to reassure it.

CHAPTER 30

Mother of All Sessions

"THE girls who live upstairs are out and I just found out the couple across the hall are in Europe, and the jerks downstairs are probably just getting up, which means they're going to start blasting metal any time now. It goes on before the coffee. So you can scream all you want and no one is going to run to your rescue."

K handed her a little white cardboard box with a gold ribbon. Six chocolates, all different, handmade by a chocolatier on Mont-Royal, near the CMF dungeon.

She sat down on the arm of a sofa and took one out with her long, fine fingers. Her lips closed around the tiny bite she took from one of the chocolates.

"Oh my God! These are too fucking way good to melt and pour over you."

While she finished the piece, he took off his street clothes. He wore his tights but only to his waist. "You'll have to help me get the cast through the arm hole and pull them over my shoulders."

Before arranging them, she gave him a taste of the chocolate on her thumb.

"Very nice. Thank you," she said, adding, "But I'm not going to share."

When she had adjusted his tights, he handed her a CD. He'd quickly thrown it together in New York, a collection of salsa pieces, some traditional, some pop.

"To help you get in a Mexican frame of mind," he said.

With him following, she went to her computer on the long pine dining table and put on the CD. He then gently nudged her aside and sat down in front of her laptop.

"I know you usually refuse to sit on men's laps but we need to buy your ticket together."

He raised the arm with the cast to give her room to nestle in. If he hadn't had the cast he would have wrapped his arms around her for life just to keep feeling her soft cheeks on his lap, black tights on white tights. Warm, so nice and warm.

She had already bookmarked the Internet travel site where she had found the best price for Mexico. As she typed, her lower body moved ever so slightly. He felt an erection beginning.

"Credit card. Credit card," she said, as if impatiently knocking on a door.

He already had it in his hand. As he passed it to her, he leaned forward, looking over her shoulder, his head next to hers.

"Here," she said. "Hold the card for me while I type in the numbers."

A message popped up on the screen stating that the name on the credit card did not match the name on the requested ticket. It asked for a phone number for the cardholder to confirm the purchase. She typed in his cell number.

"Got your phone I hope."

"Yes, but it's in my coat."

When she got up to fetch it for him, he felt naked. He had been imagining them fused together. If she had told him she wanted to stay on his lap for the next six hours, he would have gladly bought the ticket anyway.

The phone rang five minutes later and he sealed the deal. She was good for Mexico.

For the next hour they chatted as she played with her ropes, trying different knots and testing them, rifling through the book for other ideas, and finally deciding how she wanted to truss him up.

"I think I know how I'm going to do this," she said. She tossed two outsized pillows onto the long sofa. It was early 20th-Century, patterned with an elegantly curved dark-stained back, rescued from a sidewalk the day before garbage pick-up. She told him to put his knees on the sofa's edge.

"Lean forward now. Put your neck and arms over the top of the sofa. Good. OK, get up."

She started by wrapping rope around his good wrist and passing it under his shoulders and around his back, linking up with the wrist again. From there she ran the rope between his legs and up between his cheeks. He couldn't see what she was doing but after a few false starts she had fashioned a harness that she slipped over his balls and penis, pulling it tight but not painfully. The rope then looped around his waist and back up to the shoulder harness she'd created. One long end dangled to the floor.

She made him put his knees back on the edge of the sofa and lean forward against the huge pillows, leaving his back slightly arched. She helped him place his armpits on the top of the sofa, elbows and head hanging over the other side. As he leaned forward, he immediately felt the rope pulling taut between his buttocks and the noose around his sex tighten. When he reported this, she said, not half-proudly, "That's the whole idea."

She then used her leg to push a hassock close to the sofa. "Ease your knees off the sofa edge. Just hold on to the sofa with your elbows."

He felt his shins come to rest on the hassock.

"Perfect."

He heard her walk away. The music suddenly blared joyous Latin rhythms. Then he felt her hand separate his legs a bit, tapping the inside of his thighs. She sat on his left calf, her left leg outside the hassock, he right in front of it, between his thighs.

The paddle landed, and kept landing.

She was seriously enjoying making him jump with the occasional extra-forceful blow. He had once used a little camcorder to film a portion of one of their sessions, and it was there that he noticed her eyes suddenly magnify a second after she'd landed an especially meaty blow, like a kid when the birthday cake is brought into the room, candles lit.

In her left hand she held the trailing rope end and used it like reins to pull him back into position. When she yanked on it he felt as if the soft rope was going to cleave his buttocks even deeper. He had never felt more immobilized or vulnerable.

As always, he didn't want it to end. Although she frequently asked if his wrist was comfortable, she stretched the paddling out in an almost leisurely fashion. There were long periods when neither of them made a noise. There was just the music and the paddle's thwack. He wondered at one point whether she was decompressing from her exams or focusing on the feeling between her thighs. As always, he had lost his erection as the paddling went on but his entire body felt like it was on another plane, eager and primed for anything she might want to do to it.

When she finished she told him to stay put, as if he had any choice. She returned with a camera and photographed her rope work from every angle, once giving another yank on the portion between his legs for good measure.

She finally kneeled on the sofa beside him and reached over him to start unlacing the rope around his shoulders. He felt her breasts on his shoulders. She removed the big pillows from under him and with a hand on one shoulder guided him back from the top of the sofa and into a kneeling position in order for her to access the rest of her rigging. She gave his penis a feather-light flick with the back of her nails.

"Asleep?"

Because of his broken wrist and still swollen ankle, they agreed they wouldn't be able to put in a marathon session of corporal punishment. In the days leading up to today, he'd been thinking as much about giving her a full body massage as the prospect of receiving CP from her. Since she'd be wearing her tights, his hands — actually, now, one hand — would become conduits for the greatest torture imaginable as they caressed every nook and cranny of her body, warm and soft, but ultimately denied to him by the thin layer of cotton.

She had walked over to the table to get her cigarettes. At the same time she turned off the music. The silence felt good because it allowed him to listen to all the sensations his body was babbling about.

He sat next to her in the middle of the wide sofa as she smoked. When she finished, he asked if she was ready for her massage. As she exhaled the last bit of smoke, she said yes, but the voice caught a bit. He thought it might have been from the smoke she was exhaling. To make room on the sofa, he slipped to the floor. With his right hand he reached to her waist and gently started to direct her to lie down.

"No, my legs, yes, but not above." She seemed suddenly ill at ease. He studied her face as he gently passed his hand up the outside of her thigh. She didn't quite meet his gaze, which was unlike her. She could stare down her cat.

Soon he was beginning to feel almost ill with disappointment. After barely a couple of minutes, he stopped. It was pointless to continue.

"That's fine," he lied. "No point if you're not in the mood." He tried to make light of it.

"Sorry."

She lit another cigarette.

"I'm not the cuddle person you'd like me to be, or I'd like me to be."

The room felt very hot. He knew she kept the thermostat high because she detested being cold. But this time it was either the effect the tobacco smoke was having on him or his own disappointment that had left him flushed. He felt the session was over. He said he was too warm and was going to get out of his tights. She agreed it was a bit warm. She said he could open a window if he wanted.

He went to the bathroom to change. Her apartment was large but her bathroom was as small as his in New York. He would change instead in the kitchen, where he could lean against the fridge. Then he realized he would need her help getting the straps of his tights over his arms. She helped him without saying a word.

When he returned to the living room she had found her smile again. She seemed relieved.

"Come, sit down," she said, indicating the cushion next to her on the love seat. "I'm really grateful for what you've done, about the ticket and all that. I really need to get away."

"Chinese food sound OK?"

She looked at him as if she had forgotten that people have to eat from time to time. "God yes. I'm smoking so I won't faint." All she'd consumed was a single bagel and bottle of orange juice ten hours before.

He asked if she had a takeout menu.

"Don't need one," she said. "What do you like?"

"Anything."

She picked up her cell and dialed. A few seconds later she was rattling off a combination of dishes.

While waiting for the food to arrive she went into her bedroom and changed into jeans and a short black cotton dress with a picture of Batgirl. With a cigarette in her left hand, she walked around putting away her percussion toys and rearranging the pillows on the long sofa, sitting down there finally to slowly coil her ropes. They were soft and she clearly liked stringing them through her fingers.

When she had put everything away, she returned to the small sofa. He could see that she was tired. He knew she'd had only three hours sleep the night before, but until a little while ago it didn't seem to affect her. He expected only the smallest of small talk from her until the food came to the rescue. Instead she said, "I really like guys but I just can't..." She stopped. After a moment she drew her feet under her and leaned her side against the back of the sofa, hands between her thighs. He wondered whether she was trying to stop herself from reaching for another smoke.

"... can't let go?"

"Yeah."

He was curious, and a voice inside told him it was not the time to press her, but he wanted to know whether her intimacy problems dated back to losing "the boy" she loved so much in San Francisco whom he suspected was her first lover, or to the time after she fled her parents' home and moved in with the family of her schoolmate, so wonderful and welcoming until the father came to her bed one night.

Or was the whole thing physical? From their very first session years before, he knew she suffered from some physical problem. His original fantasy had been to start a session OTK, over the knee, and end it that way with everything in between being up to her. She did just that, but a few days later in an email she had written that as much as she liked the intimacy of OTK she sometimes suffered leg pain that made it impossible. He knew pain kept her awake at night and made sitting for three hours on a plane hell, and once he heard her say, "I hate my body." It was then that she told him she had been on a waiting list for more than a year to see someone at a pain clinic.

It took forever for the food to arrive. Before it did, her body had become agitated. She couldn't get comfortable, and her eyes betrayed moistness.

"Shit, where's the food? You've been shrinking me since I ordered. Can we stop?"

When the buzzer rang, he apologized about interrogating her. She got up to get the door.

The food revived her immediately. While punctuating her words with slashing chopsticks, she talked about Mexico, and how she would love to stay there forever if it weren't for the hell of mastering indirect object pronouns in Spanish.

"If I could get that down, I could pass for Mexican." And she could, he thought as he watched her fingers manipulate the chopsticks. Egyptian Princess, Moroccan Jewess, Latina lover, and a complexion born for hot sun.

The afternoon with her, the session, had been wonderful. The evening? He had left not long after they finished eating, and as he walked home he felt frustrated. He couldn't decide whether he was frustrated with himself because he had upset her with what must have seemed to her like an interrogation, or the fact that it produced few answers, or whether he was just plain frustrated sexually. He wanted to dismiss the latter because until meeting her, he had all but resigned himself to that state. His days as a conquering lover were long over. For that matter, he was honest enough to know he had never really been one.

As he lay on his bed half an hour later he started shrinking himself. Who was he kidding? How much time had he spent fantasizing about the long intimate massage his hands would give her body during that session, all the while telling himself it was innocent because those very

tights that betrayed every nuance of her body and radi-
ated its warmth would ultimately stamp his arousal with
a single word, DENIED? It wasn't innocent, especially
not tonight. Somewhere along the line, he had hoped
against hope that his touch, while supposedly acting out
his fetish-driven fantasy about tights, would turn her on
so much she would scream at him to fuck her.

Incredibly, he had also forgotten that he would be
entering the mother of all massage sessions with only
one hand. His fantasizing prior to going never reflected
that fact, just as he could look in the mirror day after day
while shaving and never see his aging face.

Before going to sleep, he tried to masturbate but
couldn't.

He let two days pass before writing her. He said the
first part of the session was a joy but there was nothing
even remotely BDSM about the remainder of what was
supposed to have been a mini-marathon to pay for her
Mexico flight. He repeated his apology about grilling her
like a psychiatrist while they waited for the food, but he
also said he had to come right out and say that he didn't
get what he paid for.

She wrote back a couple of hours later saying he had
every right to feel that way. She said she'd been horri-
bly tired from the outset, her period was just beginning,
and school had drained her. How did he want to square
things? The last thing in the world she wanted was to
lose him as a customer. The way she saw it, she said, was
that she owed him two sessions. She was not comfortable owing him, but there was little time left before her
departure.

It pleased him that she didn't want to lose him as a
customer, but the word "customer" grated all day. She
was right, there wasn't enough time left for sessions. He
couldn't take it physically. He also realized he wasn't in
the mood to play. That evening he wrote back:

What I really feel like is just spending time with you before you go. I don't know, maybe walk around town, shop if you want, have a nice supper somewhere. If you're down for that, we're square.

That's what they ended up doing, even though the weather had turned colder than he ever thought possible, and his ankle forced them to walk at tortoise tempo. The weatherman said minus twenty Celsius. She said, "No way, minus thirty, at least." In his head he settled on twenty below Fahrenheit.

She bought a silver bikini that afternoon, which she said she would model for him when she got back. She took him to a warehouse store in the garment district in search of bargain-priced jeans. Her need for a cigarette forced her to abandon the search after an hour of trying pair after pair. She bitched again about having no hips. She accepted his arm against the cold as they walked back to a major thoroughfare. It was too frigid to wait for a cab in that area on a Saturday.

She also asked him if he could afford to buy her something she always wanted, an authentic priest's shirt. They ended up finding one at the Centre d'apostolat liturgique on Sherbrooke Street, a few minutes' walk from Caro's dungeon. Although the first-floor store selling religious items was small, she said she read its annual sales were somewhere near a million dollars a year. No one went to church anymore but the people must be finding some use for them. If Montreal were Florida, she said, people could use the items as lawn ornaments. She confessed to having her own small collection of plastic Jesus figurines like those on sale in the store. She bit her hand to keep from laughing disrespectfully as they tried to determine which was the kitschiest. The nun behind the counter didn't appear to notice their amusement.

When they left the store, it was still far too early for supper and too cold to continue walking the streets. Supper would have to be another day. For now they opted for a hot chocolate. Since they weren't going to go through with their supper plans, she said she would take advantage of being in the area to visit a girlfriend and probably sleep over to avoid going home in the cold.

"Would you like to walk me there?"

It was out of his way but keeping her warm with his arm was better than supper. On the way, they stepped into stores several times to get out of the cold. One was a costume shop. She loved costumes and said she might find some fun stuff for sessions there. They also went into a hardware store, where she informed him a poor domme could equip herself cheaply with things like big wooden rulers, doweling and rope.

"And who knows, maybe a nipple clamp or two."

She stopped him in front of a simple-looking restaurant with a bistro menu. It was called Au Cinquième Péché. As he read the menu, she said:

"I'd like to come here with you some night. I knew a guy who worked here as a busboy. Apparently the food's great."

"Like a date?"

"Yes, a date. It would give me the excuse to dress up."

He reminded her he didn't even own a sports jacket.

"No, not that kind of dressing up. Not formal. I just meant I would have fun spending a couple of hours picking out a whole bunch of things to wear, you know, play with what goes together."

It could have turned ten degrees colder and he would not have noticed.

"Then it's a date," he said, nestling her under his arm again.

Five minutes later they were at a windy intersection kitty-corner to her friend's apartment building. Despite the cold she detested, she turned to face him, waiting for her hug. He made it a long one, just like the kisses to her cheeks.

As he walked home he imagined they were lying naked in bed together, letting their bodies warm them up. The fantasy was innocent, he told himself. He was in love and he just wanted to leave it like that. When he got home he went on the Internet to find out which *péché* was the fifth sin. He learned the Church didn't officially number the sins. Some people said it was gluttony. One site defined gluttony as "The inordinate desire to consume more than that which one requires."

He required all of her.

CHAPTER 31

Much Much Much Love

TWO weeks later, on the day the Egyptian Princess was to return from Mexico, he sat in a café in the Quartier Latin on rue St. Denis. The mid-January morning was mild and almost painfully sunny, an odd day to choose for making a will.

He wasn't feeling particularly mortal or morbid. In fact, the New Year seemed full of promise: he had a date. The fact that he would have to wait three months for it didn't matter. That's when she would begin her spring break. She had decided she needed to bear down harder on her studies during the winter semester. Sessioning was fun, and it increased the amount of sushi on the table, but she feared her marks were slipping as a result. She wasn't going to play until spring break. No parties, no tequila on Friday nights.

He said he would do his bit. He would continue writing her but he would stop thinking of every excuse he could to drop by. He had written:

Seeing you for just ten minutes would be worse than
not seeing you at all.

He would be returning to New York shortly to have
his cast removed and he felt in his bones that business
would start to boom again. Apart from thoughts of her,
being one-armed had defined boredom as he had never
known it. It was hour after hour of sitting, and it saddled
him with extra pounds. The weeks during which he
couldn't type for more than a few minutes at a time had
led to work drying up. Clients had gone elsewhere.

Other than his hosts on De Bullion, he had no friends
in Montreal. Knowing that his Egyptian Princess would
be stepping through Customs into the Arrivals section
at Aéroport Montréal-Trudeau early that evening was
enough to fill him with the belief that all was well on all
fronts, or at least would be soon.

He felt like spring cleaning his world. When he
flipped open his laptop he half expected his fingers to
auto-construct one of his more elegant lists. He sipped
from his large mug of the boldest coffee the café had to
offer. Suddenly he realized he had nothing to list. He
wasn't doing anything that needed organizing. He was
in waiting mode. Had he been home in New York, he
would use down time to practice sax and read. Now he
found fantasizing far easier than turning pages. Finally,
a few letters appeared on the screen:

"Make will."

Other than making love to his Egyptian Princess,
what better way could there be to address his fear of
dying. If he made love to her, even just once, he wouldn't
care anymore about mortality. As it was, he had all but
stopped worrying about it since she had come into his
life. During the year and a half after she dumped him
as a client, shuffling him off to her friend CC, he once
let her know that being apart was difficult at times. She
replied that she was always there for him, "in the ether."
It was a notion he then kept in his back pocket, ready to

haul out when he started to think about being alone on his deathbed. Once he imagined her visiting him as he lay on that bed. He announced, "I'm dying." Without missing a beat, she replied: "No you're not. I'm not finished with you yet." Death would have to wait. The domme said so.

If he made his will, he would be at least acknowledging it. He would have a picture in his mind of the world post-him, his funeral, his absence witnessed and recorded in memory by someone still among the living, his last wishes being tended to. Preparing for the end would be a mature thing to do.

Because of the sun pouring through the window of the café, he had to adjust his laptop screen to view it clearly. He began to search for examples of wills, then templates for doing your own without legal expense. He also got a copy of *La Presse* from the counter and turned to the obituary announcements, substituting his name for those of the recently deceased and much loved.

From the Internet he copied and pasted what seemed to be the basic requirements with regard to estate and wishes with regard to dispositions in the event of mental incompetence or being kept alive artificially, and finally what he wanted done with his now useless body.

He started with the latter. Cremation. Ashes to be disposed of in New York Harbor. Whether they floated up the Hudson toward Lake Champlain and Montreal or out to sea would no longer be a concern of his.

He then jumped to the head of the list and thought about his estate. He had only a few thousand dollars in the bank, and at the rate he was going that would be gone soon enough. He ran his inner eye through his Chelsea apartment: sax, flute, stereo, TV, Italian cookware set, T-shirts, jogging pants, and ...? That was about it. Did that even constitute an estate? It was only when he realized he had nothing to leave that he also realized that he had no one to leave all that nothing to. His parents were dead, he had no siblings, and the only cousin he actually still knew had disappeared from his life long ago.

For a second the thought was sad, but then he saw the bright side. His passing would be a simple, bureaucracy-free affair. He would arrange for his cremation and the posting of death notices when he next returned to New York. As for the last will and testament, he typed:

"I, _____, the undersigned, declare on the _____ day of the month of _____ in the year _____, that after the payment of any debts existing at the time of my death all my money and possessions be left to (my Egyptian Princess) _____, resident of the city of _____, in the state/province of _____ , _____."
Witnessed by: _____ [name in capital letters]
Signature: _____
Date: _____"

He made a note to find out whether a second witness was required. The next time he went to the library he would make a printout and fill it in. Robert and Ghislaine could serve as his witnesses. Or he could wait until his next trip back to Manhattan to buttonhole his apartment building superintendent and LeBron. He wasn't sure if the witnesses had to be from the U.S.

His one-item checklist was complete. As he stood in line to get another coffee he tried to imagine his Egyptian Princess's possible reactions to learning she was his beneficiary, the dying wish of the crazy older guy she had as a client off and on over the years. Or would she smile and shed a tear?

Late that night he received an email:

Dear Weather Office:

please kindly fuck off. there is no way in hell i will ever remain in Canada with weather predictions like the one I just heard on the radio. i'm trying to reacclimatize myself, not end up in a coma...

i have a bunch of stuff to do this week, and to be honest, my head is nowhere near a space to be working in right now, but we'll keep in touch about dinner, deal? i hope all is well with you my dear.

much much much love

The weather was indeed turning glacial. His heart was another matter.

CHAPTER 32

Break Two

THE cast was off. The final X-rays showed the ferocious break had healed well. K's first thoughts were about the pleasures of taking a shower without a plastic bag over his arm and being able to scratch an itch behind his right shoulder.

He also used his liberated left arm to hold on to the overhead bar on the train that took him to the Brooklyn Bridge/City Hall station where he walked to a funeral home on Madison Street. They were less effusive about his death when he explained there would be no funeral service and no burial, just cremation. However, they assured him the $4,000 he was putting on his credit card now was, considering his relatively modest years, an excellent investment against inflation, and one that ensured that his loved ones would bear no unnecessary burden upon his demise. The word "death" was never uttered.

LeBron was on the road with the band, but he got the super's signature on his will. He had also decided to make LeBron his executor, but the bass player didn't know it yet.

While waiting for LeBron's return to New York, K used the time to call translation agencies in the hope of getting on their lists of freelancers or, better yet, tumble onto one that just landed a major project and could use all the help it could get.

He also walked incessantly, enjoying New York's less frigid temperatures, relishing the rhythm of having both arms in motion, and exercising the feeling of being more in love than ever, and far less old. He had utterly abandoned the haunting notion that his being in love with a woman not yet even thirty years of age needed any qualifiers. It was what it was.

He remembered the first time he had ended an email to her with the word "love." It was a couple of months after her first return from Mexico. He had taken the liberty of attempting it after she had confessed "I kind of like you." He had couched its use with an explanation that it was more efficient than constructing, message after message, a phrase requiring twenty-five or thirty words to express bottomless fondness. She had replied that using the word "love" was his prerogative but that she would choose to ignore it.

Now, as he walked, he found himself often repeating the four words that ended her last email: "much much much love."

No woman had ever said anything to him that touched him so deeply. He felt he was atop a ten-foot high unicycle pedaling like a happy fool around and around a circus ring, a thousand people cheering above the band blaring *da da dadada da da daa da, da da dadada da da da daaa da, da dadada da dadada dalelelela!* That he could keep his balance defied all logic, but there he was anyway, riding high with nothing to hold on to, waving back at the smiling faces. Did she have any idea what she had enkindled?

He descended into Penn Station three weeks later, after LeBron's overdue return to the city. He had never written it on paper, but the to-do list in his head contained the item "my death." Next to it was a flamboyant checkmark in gaudy yellow marker. He knew the notion was somehow a twisted one, but that checkmark was giving him so much relief and satisfaction that he wondered whether his death was destined to be his greatest achievement.

On his return to Montreal he found that winter was just going through the motions. Snow sometimes turned to rain and slush. He almost preferred the cold.

He sent his Egyptian Princess an email simply announcing his return. He had vowed to let her be so she could concentrate on her studies. He wasn't surprised that he didn't receive a reply for almost a week. When it came, though they hadn't seen each other for almost a month and a half, the tone was as if they'd been chatting only minutes earlier before the call had been interrupted by someone at the door.

She had received all her marks from the previous session. They were "so-so" by her standards, so she said she was right in opting to be an "anti-social B" until the end of the current semester. She had a huge paper to hand in shortly and she was shattered that her best study aide had disappeared. What kept her going for hour after hour, she explained, was having episodes of a TV show playing next to her on her laptop. The series had just ended, "the best TV show in history," she said, an HBO police series called *The Wire*.

"Think you could find it on the Internet and make me a copy? I half-listen when I'm reading but it does the job... it works, like white sound."

Since he still had no work, her request was a welcomed project. He found torrents for all five seasons and, after downloading all sixty episodes, he set to making DVDs for her. While waiting for the computer to encode the downloaded torrents, he began watching Season 1. She had great taste in white noise. He was hooked by Episode 2.

When the DVDs were completed he went shopping on a prematurely spring-like morning for her other request, cigars. He found an elegant shop downtown on Peel Street and another not far away on St. Catherine. He had gone in search of a second store because of the intimidating prices at the first. Both were purveyors of "authentic Cuban cigars" and they sold other luxury items such as wood and leather designer humidors.

In the first he saw an attractive box of twenty-five San Cristobals, for only $600. There was nothing like a liquidation sale at the second store either. In the end, he settled on a five-pack of Cohiba Exquisitos for $54. He continued west on St. Catherine until he came to a post office near Guy, near the university she studied at. He found a box just large enough for the DVDs and the cigarillos and mailed it.

The following Saturday morning, Valentine's Day, he switched on his computer. Despite the early hour, she had sent him an email not long before. It must have been the first thing she'd done after getting out of bed.

happy singles awareness day.

i hope all is well with you my dear.

xo

In early March he put together another DVD package, this time of movies. One of them was *Breakfast at Tiffany's*. When his Egyptian Princess was at her softest, light years from her domme persona and wearing PJs and fuzzy slippers, she reminded him a bit of Audrey Hepburn, not so much in looks but in the combination of a delightful but strong personality bundled up in a delicate body. He had meant to tell her that but the movie would do a better job.

But the message he most wanted to communicate was to be found in a more recent movie, *The Curious Case of Benjamin Button*. He would have loved the film even had he not known her, but here was a fantasy that reworked his promise to reincarnate as a young man she couldn't resist. While watching, he became Brad Pitt on his backwards journey to birth while the rest of the world continued to age. It wouldn't last but he and his Egyptian Princess would have a good decade where they were close enough in age for him to have his greatest wish.

She later wrote that she loved the *Benjamin Button* movie but he was never to find out whether she viewed it the way he did. As the calendar entered the final week of school, his impatience got the better of him. He began sending little messages of encouragement that ended with allusions to his building excitement over their dinner date. The date of her final exam passed, a Friday. On Sunday, he phoned. She said she was still recovering. He suggested meeting on Tuesday. She said she'd have to get back to him because some friends were planning to visit from out of town.

This was not what he had expected. He waited out the week, then sent a text message. He told himself his words were meant jokingly, but he was agitated as he wrote them, struggling with the tiny keys on his cell and feeling like he had crawled on his hands and knees for three lonely months through a narrow dark tunnel only to find the other end blocked.

If u r in the arms of a lover it will be a while b4 I can say I am happy for you but I promise to recover in time 2 attend ur graduation

There was a knock on his door and before answering he hit Send. It was Ghislaine asking if he would join them for supper. He declined.

He felt sick to his stomach.

Two more days passed without word. He texted again:
What r u up 2?

Sleeping.

Two days later, she wrote an email message.

I feel very much like I owe you an explanation. I'm in a bit of an awkward place right now- with a lot of things in life, my dealings with males especially, and perhaps more so because of the original nature of our relationship. I was really put off by the feeling of pressure I got from your text, and it made me want to avoid the situation altogether. i feel it's probably best for me to focus on other things in my life until I'm able to communicate clearly, and not feel pressured or uncomfortable. I don't believe I'll be doing sex work any time soon- Your Egyptian princess is a piece of me that's retired for awhile I should think. I think it's also in your best interests to focus on finding a mistress you can be loyal to. I'm sorry if this makes you upset- but I feel as though I need to set more limits for, and around myself these days, and I didn't really realize that until this week.

I truly hope you are well, and continue to be so.

He made his way upstairs to the bathroom and tried to vomit. He failed.

CHAPTER 33

When All Is Said

IT WAS dawn before he stopped writing. He doubted he had ever written so many words in a sitting. With all his might he was trying to do the mature thing, the loving thing: respect her wishes.

In that light, this was the last chance he would ever have to express his heart. He retraced their history, and admitted parceling out his feelings of love for fear of chasing her away. He told her how much he had always wanted to make love to her, and in the same sentence said he knew how utterly repulsive the prospect must be to someone barely half his age. At this juncture, though he was certain she knew it, he was not going to pretend his passion for her was anything but what it was.

He told her how easy it had been to stop drinking solely because of her. He fell in love with her and that saved his life. And, he asked, did she have the faintest idea what it felt like to fall in love at an age when every young couple walking by conspires to remind you how necessarily empty your soul will remain to the end of your days? Of course not, he said, because she was young enough to fall in love again.

He tried to make her understand that while he would never do anything to bring her even a moment's unhappiness, and that in a perfect world he would have found the strength to remove himself from her life, leaving behind only a note that thanked her for giving him back his life, he was not that man. He was helpless.

For well over an hour afterwards he felt he had said everything, but the knowledge that the next few words would likely be the last he would ever speak to her constricted his throat painfully, despite the fact that it was his fingers that would have to speak those words. He walked up and down in front of the bed for several minutes, a passage shorter than he would find in a cell on death row. He noticed the rising sun for the first time, and also for the first time became aware of what a fool he'd been to allow this to happen. He typed:

Whatever you decide, I will love you always.

In case a dream revealed a way out of the tunnel, he decided not to send the email immediately.

He awoke in the late afternoon, surprised that he had been able to sleep so long. He had not undressed. As he sat on the edge of the bed, he realized that he could all but quote from memory the thousands of words he had written that night. He took two steps to the chest of drawers where he'd left his computer and clicked on Send.

He tried to play flute, hoping sound would give him something to hang on to, but it didn't. He was too shaken, and for the moment there was nothing he could do but let her news take root in reality.

He pulled a sweatshirt over his T-shirt and went out in search of a burger. He ended up walking for half an hour, all downhill, and stopping only when he reached Old Montreal on the shores of the St. Lawrence River.

On rue St. Paul, he ordered a small quiche in a bistro with a zinc counter. He started to walk up a street named St. Laurent, also known higher up the hill as The Main. Halfway before reaching Sherbrooke Street he hailed a passing cab to take him home.

Not long afterwards, she replied. For a moment he felt hope that she would retract her dismissal as the product of yet another "anti-social funk." Instead he read the most astonishing, unexpected, painful words he could ever have imagined. In large red, underlined letters were the words:

Not Fucking Cool!!!!!!

Then, in regular type with no punctuation she damned him to hell for his passive aggressive attempt to manipulate her feelings.

She was too angry to even sign the email.

At 10 o'clock the next morning he walked into a liquor store for the first time in more than four years.

The first few days, his body and mind screamed foul. He'd lost the tolerance he once had. He fought the relapse, and some days he won. After sleeping off a losing day, he phoned her. He got her voice mail. He said:

"You're killing me. Call me please."

He assumed she'd ignore his call. For a second his heart leapt when her name popped on the screen of his cell phone.

She sounded impatient. Yes, she said, she'd read his letter, but she offered no further comment.

"You sound angry," he said.

"I am."

After a long silence, he said he'd started drinking again.

"I suppose you blame that on me?" she asked.

He took his time before answering, and finally said "No."

After another silence, he asked if she was going to call someday.

"I don't know," she answered, still refusing to offer any words of explanation or hope.

"Goodbye," he said. The word came out softly. Before his thumb found the End button he heard her say "Take care."

He was understanding less by the minute.

In the following days, he drank non-stop. If he played flute in his room, he hugged the shrill third octave. When Robert had lent him the instrument, he had purchased several studies and collections of sheet music, mostly for 17th and 18th-century sonatas. But Bach, Telemann and Handel betrayed no ferocity in their notes.

She had yanked him off the wagon. She was making him drink. When he told her, "No, you didn't make me drink," he was lying. He was hiding behind Rehab Speak: only you are responsible for your actions. Bull-shit. He should have told her:

"It was you who put the revolver on my bedside table. I just pulled the trigger."

Since January, when she was no longer giving sessions, and with her blessing, he had been occasionally seeing the striking black dominatrix who had brushed by them on their first night at the dungeon on Papineau. She didn't work under the name Voodoo Goddess but it was a pet name he had given her in his mind because it easily inhabited the same fantasy sphere as Egyptian Princess.

While chatting after their last session, the Voodoo Goddess had said something about the desire to domme being only part of her nature, a curious and passion-ate part, one that may have been there since childhood even, but only a part nonetheless. As an example, she cited the fact that she was a very happily married woman with young children.

"I'm a mother like any other mother," she said.

"I go to parent-teacher meetings." Her laugh came from deep down and her face lit up with delight at the thought of the other parents and teachers realizing what she did for a living.

Back on De Bullion, he thought about that conversation. It occurred to him that the duality his Voodoo Goddess had spoken of might be of use to his Egyptian Princess. He wrote her, just a note. He apologized for invading her privacy, but felt compelled to share something from a former colleague of hers that she might find useful.

The reply was almost instantaneous.

Appreciate your reaching out but what part of no contact don't you understand?

CHAPTER 34

Return Ticket

WHEN the alarm clock spritzed his mind with radio static at 6 a.m. on a chilly June morning two years later, his eyes were already open. Without looking, he reached out with his left arm and turned the alarm off. He rarely used it, and when he did he would set it to wake him up with classical music. At some point when dusting, he must have nudged the dial off station. He had set the alarm so he would have time to pack and take a cab to the station for the morning train to New York. But he hadn't slept. The decision to leave served only to convince him there were reasons to stay.

It wasn't the first time he'd called Amtrak and bought a ticket, only to let the train pull out with an empty seat. Over the past two years he kept telling himself he had to get out of "her" city and return to his own, but the decision-making process sputtered when he realized he had little to return to.

As he sat up and shredded his yellow and white train ticket, he wished he could find a new phrase to describe the precipitous end to the relationship with the Egyptian Princess, but, as usual, he had to give up. There was no way around the fact that it was the greatest mystery of his life, bigger than existence. He wouldn't have said that about a woman when he was twenty-five, but now even the platonic love of a beautiful woman trumped the metaphysical. At times, he suspected she may have acted for reasons he was too smitten to discern, but that didn't lessen the mystery, or the hurt.

When he bought the ticket he had just finished shredding he had written LeBron to let him know he'd have to find somewhere else to live. But he never heard back. It had only been a month and it was possible LeBron was playing out of town.

He'd never told LeBron about his Egyptian Princess but he had told him he'd fallen off the wagon. LeBron — who would probably regard a scientifically confirmed Doomsday date as little more than a fortuitously long break between sets, like a ConEd power failure during a heat wave — didn't miss a beat when he got the news.

As much as LeBron hated to mention the Yankees, he wrote that Mickey Mantle hit a ton of home runs not only when hungover but also when drunk.

So dust yourself off, straighten your cap, hitch up your pants, vigorously adjust your jockstrap, pick up your bat and look straight into the nearest TV camera. There's always one in the dugout. Let the world know that your having bloodshot eyes is a congenital thing and that you're still very much in the game. Spit if you want. I don't really care for it but it's an option for ballplayers.

Once outside, K realized he had no appetite for breakfast. Instead he walked downhill to the subway and rode the Honoré-Beaugrand train to its destination, then crossed over to the westbound tracks and returned downtown. During the ride he decided he had no choice but to run away. He smiled at the realization that, at his age, running away now meant running home, back to the familiar, and maybe back to the bearable.

He would write LeBron again, offering him as much notice as he needed to find another place to live. He decided he would remain in Montreal until the first snow fell. He liked the indefiniteness of the deadline. He wouldn't find himself counting days. The first snow could fall in November or January.

Work had been profitable in Montreal, and he still had his Voodoo Goddess. She had a knack for healing.

As strict as she could be as a mistress, she was naturally affectionate. They had quickly become so comfortable with each other that she knew she had carte blanche for their sessions. She directed his movies. She chose the soundtracks.

"It works for me too," she said one afternoon when they were talking about ad-libbing the sessions. He'd dropped by just to chat. Talking to her on a workday afternoon felt like hopping a stealth flight to Neverland. "There are days when you don't want to follow a client's script, believe me. You do it because you're getting paid to do it, but I didn't learn to domme because I wanted a paycheck. I get off giving the way you get off getting."

Sometimes her sessions amounted to little more than percussive massages to the sound of hypnotic African drumming, her dungeon illuminated with scores of candles to deepen the trance. The ambiance she created made him imagine they were in a dusty hot village with palm trees and the scent of the sea. She had placed him, bound, on a four-poster bed and sat on his back as she used his cheeks as another conga drum. Eventually, in his imagination, she would surely yield to the drums and fuck him, right there in the dirt.

Other times, he trudged up the long narrow staircase to her dungeon feeling dead to any kind of emotion, good or bad. She was a safe port in his storms. There was nowhere else to go. Invariably, although he couldn't explain it, he left feeling she'd somehow found his On switch.

Several times he tried to stop drinking and brought her the remainders of bottles. She'd told him to call her day or night whenever he felt he was going to fall off the wagon. It was an offer AA couldn't top, but he never called her. He didn't want her to see how weak he was. The irony of that feeling didn't escape him. With her, during sessions, he wanted to be weak. He wanted to cede control.

He did manage to stay sober for three and a half weeks, and the fact of being sober, like the first time he quit, made him feel like he had a new toy to play with. The toy was a desire to go out into the world and taste it.

His first sortie was to attend a party hosted by his Voodoo Goddess. Though he was vaguely tempted to play in public, he had never attended any of the several other regular play parties in the city. He told himself he'd be too old for the crowd, too overweight, too ridiculous. Being open about his fantasies with a pro-domme in a single room was one thing, but in public with strangers was another.

The Voodoo Goddess's party turned out to be the grand opening of her dungeon as a party and play space, two floors of 19th-century Montreal architecture, twelve-foot ceilings, oak-paneled walls and decorative moldings that smiled down knowingly on what lay below. The opening had drawn more than two-hundred-and-fifty people, too many. There was no room to play. It was almost a relief, but he went home that night knowing he had no reason to fear sticking out like a sore thumb. Young, old, fat, skinny, dressed, undressed, there to play, there to look. There was room for him, he decided.

He was soon a regular. Although no other place tempted him because no other place had a Voodoo Goddess to greet him at the top of the stairs, he learned it wasn't unusual for several places to be competing for much of the same BDSM-fetish community on the same night. He had trouble remembering their names because dungeons rarely had a long life. Few make any profit.

One night while sitting at a kitchen counter that doubled as a bar, he talked with a middle-aged man. Originally from Egypt, the man had once managed clubs in New York before moving north. They had met several times before and often talked of dommes. The Egyptian was passionate about the subject.

"On the one hand, my friend, the city is swarming with young mistresses and masters, and that is good," he said. "The young people have fallen in love with fetishes and fashion. But, you know what, my friend? Many of them are not who they say there are. Just because a beautiful young woman gets a beautiful photo taken of her wearing beautiful high boots and latex, that does not make her a domme"

They were seated next to each other on stools looking at bodies, some fully dressed and masked, and others naked or all but. The urbane Egyptian gestured toward them with his left arm.

"There are probably not more than one or two real dommes among them, dommes who know what they're doing, dommes who not only are skilled with the toys but who, I don't know..."

His voice trailed off as he searched his memory.

"Yes, I've got the example. You, you and I, we once talked about a woman we used to see. She was magnificent. Refined. She knew how to make a man do things. She was Moroccan, that's right, Moroccan. What was her name?"

"I don't remember her name either," K answered. "I used to call her my Egyptian Princess."

"That's good. That's a good name for her. I have a weak spot for Arab women," he laughed. "But our mistress, she was Moroccan. Jewish, I think."

When K told him she was Canadian, he said with finality, "No, no, you're mistaking her with someone else."

After the Egyptian left him, K reached across the

counter and filled a tumbler with yellow rum. When he started drinking, the forty-ounce bottle was more than half full. It was empty half an hour later. He staggered into the cloak room to change from his tights back into his street clothes.

Before he gave up his room on De Bullion and returned to New York, his Voodoo Goddess told him she could see in his heart it was time for him to go. She handed him a slip of paper with the phone number of a friend of hers in Manhattan, a young dominatrix who saw only select clients.

"She may be only five feet tall but the devil himself likes to surf her imagination. I've written her. She knows all about you."

As enticing as her friend sounded, he wondered whether he was a fool to leave his Voodoo Goddess and the city. In just a few months in Montreal he could claim more acquaintances than he'd ever had in Manhattan.

The train ride to New York would have taken forever had it not been for the surprisingly strong effect several bottles of Samuel Adams had. He slept solidly from 5:30 to 9 p.m. He took a cab home and fell asleep not long afterwards. Before he did, he thought of making a list for the next day but he couldn't think of anything to write.

CHAPTER 35

New York

FOR the first few months back in the city, K told himself he was happy rebuilding his old routines, the pot of coffee to start the day in his own room and not downstairs in someone else's kitchen, his own shower, breakfast on Ninth Avenue, morning work if there was any, and sax in the afternoon. He no longer read much, mostly because there was no optical prescription for Scotch vision.

He hadn't invented a nickname for the little dominatrix he was now seeing on the recommendation of his Voodoo Goddess. They slipped into an easy relationship from the very start. He saw her usually once a month, depending on his revenues. New York prices seemed to have escalated to $250 and up. He was afraid that giving her a nickname would somehow let him pretend he could replace his Egyptian Princess once and for all. There was little chance of that happening. The truth was he had never seen another domme without at least once imagining during a session that the blows were coming from the hand of his Egyptian Princess.

Apart from LeBron, who was absent most of the time, on the road playing bass, or playing house with a new girlfriend, he had no friends. He had returned to the bar he drank at as a young man, but not as often as he used to because it seemed paying bar prices had become a pastime for trust-fund kids only. In time, though, the new faces on the adjacent stools were becoming familiar. They had first names.

Not long after he'd marked his first year back in Manhattan, he phoned Alana. To his surprise she didn't hang up and she didn't sound annoyed to hear from him. He talked a bit about Montreal and he mentioned that he took a drink now and then. As for her, not much had changed in her life, beyond aging, she said with a hint of laughter. It was good talking with her again, he thought. However when he suggested they meet she declined.

"I haven't had a drink in two years. Still do a little weed but no booze. I do what I can to never be around it. I'm afraid you're included. When I think of you, this won't sound nice but it's the truth, when I think of you I remember waking up with you in my bed and not having a clue how you got there or what your name was. So, us getting together is not a good idea. It won't happen."

After he put down the phone, he felt more alone than ever. He had no right to think Alana would want to see him but he realized he was disappointed at the finality of her rejection. He understood about the booze. He'd been there. But the verdict was still rejection. It didn't help to remember that he had laid the foundation for it.

Although his break-up with Alana was far in the past, and his break-up with his Egyptian Princess wasn't even technically a break-up since they'd never been a couple, he felt like he was going through two divorces simultaneously. One, let alone two, was considered grounds for insanity. Memories of affectionate moments, and a web of what-ifs, more than once segued seamlessly from one woman to the other. In his nobler moments, he tried to convince himself that some of the blame lay with himself, but those thoughts didn't survive long.

That winter, after the fifth snowstorm of the season, dropping more snow by mid-January than Montreal got all year, he took his bike downstairs. He hoisted it onto a snow bank and chained it to a lamp post. Returning to his apartment, he poured a drink and pulled a chair to the window where he had a clear view of the bike.

The dumping of the bike had started with a question that popped into his mind from nowhere, but it intrigued him: "Who in their right mind would bother jacking a bike in a snowstorm that made streets impassable even for cars?"

He had his answer five hours later, just past midnight. Two guys, one skinny and tall, one fat and short, made the bike theirs. He couldn't make out faces because they wore hoodies under their winter jackets. The job was so easy he barely saw the bolt cutters. The short guy carried the prize on his shoulder. The hours of waiting, then the action that lasted mere minutes, were still better than that night's TV would have been.

He was happy to be rid of the bike. It took precious space in his room and he no longer had the energy to ride it, let alone cart it up and down stairs. He was getting fat. Pipe dreams about an attractive woman walking into his bar and sitting beside him no longer flew. He avoided looking in the mirror, even while shaving.

Some days television could feed his need for company although on his little walks, more than once he slowed his pace when approaching a young girl sitting cross-legged on cardboard on the sidewalk with a tuque in front of her for change. He would debate asking if she would like to get warm for a while and watch some television with him. He would lean down and deposit whatever coins he had into her hat. As he did so, he would try to gauge the look on her face before posing his question. But not once did he ever dare ask it.

The young women wouldn't understand he was just lonely. They'd think he was some old pervert and tell him loudly where to go. As he walked on, though, he would talk to some of them in his mind as if they'd accepted his invitation. He would explain to them that feeling alone in the city was one thing, feeling alone on this earth was another. Maybe they were too young to understand.

Having no one else to think about, most of the time the words in his head were congregated around his Egyptian Princess. With time, those thoughts and imagined scenes had mingled carelessly with memories of events that had actually taken place. The line between them blurred. Imaginings could be recalled just like real events. Together they were becoming his revised history.

. . .

The instant LeBron stepped into the apartment he smacked into a wall of sullenness. It was as if K didn't recognize him. Finally K motioned him in with his arm before sitting back down heavily in his chair.

"Drink?"

"Yeah. I think I've got some catching up to do," LeBron said.

"What do you mean?"

"First of all, you look like shit. Booze or women in general, or a woman in particular?"

"You psychic?"

"At your age life shouldn't seem so complicated," LeBron answered. He had poured himself some Scotch instead of the usual beer. Something told him he might need to be a forty percent-er that evening.

"It's been my experience," LeBron said, "that life sucks pretty well as much as you let it suck. Melodrama is for daytime TV."

"I don't watch soaps."

"But something tells me you're in one. Dangerous stuff. It's like looking at life with cheap 3D glasses. Everything blurred, nothing clear. Gives you a headache but you get addicted anyway."

"What the hell are you talking about, LeBron?"

"Around the time we met you had a lady, a girlfriend. But since then..."

LeBron looked at K and shrugged his shoulders. It was minutes before he resumed. K's eyes fixed on him occasionally but his head was elsewhere.

"You're almost never connected and I'm almost never disconnected. Yet you get turned inside out, K. Me, I stay me, at least most of the time. You know how?"

"By taking out-of-town gigs when things get heavy," K interrupted. He was mad at the world, even LeBron.

"Nope. By not romanticizing the journey. That's something I learned way back in the seventies. It works. I don't have it tattooed on my ass or anything but neon lights start flashing when I drift too far from it."

When his friend didn't reply, LeBron explained.

"It means you're a little speck of something and you're not much more than you are at that particular minute. You can love that moment or hate it but one thing you're not is the past, and the present, it isn't your future. Your life isn't a novel, a play, a symphony. Loose ends don't get tied up at the end. Nagging questions don't get answered."

"I don't want that kind of life, LeBron," K said, more loudly than he'd intended. "I want it to be a movie. When it's all over, I want to walk out onto street feeling I got my money's worth."

LeBron put down his Scotch. Evidently his friend was still sober enough to think. He decided to drop the lecture.

"So, K-Man, tell me a story." LeBron leaned his lengthy frame back against the sofa and cradled his glass of Scotch in two hands.

He told LeBron about his Egyptian Princess, his kink and everything. It was a three-intermission movie.

When he finished, LeBron raised his glass to his friend.

"You lucky bastard!"

"Lucky?" K said, screwing up his face as if looking at a mad man.

"You fell in love for God's sake! Lucky you. Damn right. Shit happens, love happens. Love goes. You don't get to choose."

K stared at his friend. He'd blurted out his life's biggest secret and LeBron hadn't missed a beat, hadn't juggled with judgment for a second. K felt the bitterness, the self-pity, whatever it was, subside. His friend had pulled the plug.

"I didn't think I'd ever feel that way again," K said, his tone now matter-of-fact.

There was something sober in his voice, LeBron thought. Maybe it was just simple truth.

"In fact, at first," K continued, "I didn't even want to give it a name."

"Most of us don't get a second shot," LeBron said. "Some guys never get a first one. I envy you."

"So why do I hate my life?"

It was a long time before LeBron answered. It wasn't a question someone else could answer, but his friend was fading again. He was staring at the floor. His breathing had become audible, slow, like sleep. Before his friend's eyes closed, LeBron answered.

"You fell in love with someone safe, someone you couldn't have, someone you could never disappoint in the sack, someone who could never cheat on you."

"Where are you getting all this from? Some book?"

K said it accusingly, as if LeBron had slapped him on the back of the head with a pop psychology paperback, but an instant later he knew what LeBron was saying made some kind of sense. When LeBron didn't reply, he said:

"Sorry. Maybe I don't want the mystery solved." He smiled, apologetically. "Go on."

"Well, I think, not that you knew this was happening,

I think you fell for someone who would never be around long enough to see you're not all what you seemed to be at first. I'm not shitting on you. You're just like everybody else. I'm sure this girl was beautiful. She turned you on when you thought you could never get turned on again. But you knew you could never have her, or she'd never have you. Right?"

"Yeah, of course."

"No, not of course. You knew it but you wanted to pretend it wasn't true for as long as you could. And believe me, you didn't turn her on no matter how much you talked about sex. Look at us!"

LeBron pretended to hold up a mirror to his friend's face. Then, when he reversed it to mirror his own face he began scatting Ellington's "Things Ain't What They Used to Be."

"But I really felt she loved me," K said.

"Maybe she did, for whatever reason. Maybe she didn't. But it wasn't the kind of love you're talking about. I know that."

When LeBron didn't get a reply for what could have been minutes, he swallowed what was left of his Scotch. As he reached for the bottle, he spoke quietly.

"Ground control to Major Tom..."

K raised his eyes, for a second surprised to find someone else in the room.

"What if she played me? What if I was never more than a client to her? That's the one thought that makes me sick. It's a million times worse than never seeing her again."

He'd torn out the long-metastasizing tumor and slapped it down on the trunk.

"Hey!" LeBron interrupted, hands raised to halt a runaway train. "That's crap, K-Man. How could she be screwin' you around? It's not as if you were making her rich. Hell, I'm sittin' here drinking your Scotch. Am I playing you?"

"I don't mean financially. I mean, was she really a friend? She knows I'd do anything for her."

Suddenly K clapped his hands, hard, as if he were trying to pulverize a fly that buzzed and buzzed but was too stupid to fly out the window. He was angry.

"How could she just slam the fucking door? I wrote and wrote and she never answered. I said things that no one could have ignored, that no friend could have ignored. Could you do that to a friend, LeBron? Close the door, slam the door, just like that? No, no, no. No one could. She treated me like shit. If she was never really a friend, this has all been farce. That's the one thing I need to know before I die."

"Let it go," LeBron said. "Don't let your head go there. You had a great flight in your big sexy hot-air balloon. So what if it crash landed at the end. You walked away from it. The flight was good. Let it go."

K ignored LeBron and the booze sucked him back into a wave of feeling he'd been victimized, made a fool of. He babbled on again. When the word "betrayal" slipped out, he stopped talking. He was too drunk to know how to put it in a sentence that made sense.

"Let it go." LeBron said it more softly than the first time, and his friend looked him in the eye.

"I don't want to. Simple as that, I plain just don't want to. I'd rather die feeling the way she once made me feel than die pissed off with my feet on the ground. Realistic is another word for counting the days until you die. I wasn't afraid of dying when I was with her."

"Well, my friend, before you run out of days to count, I strongly suggest you get yourself another lady. Scoop up the first one who looks sideways at you. Sweep her off her feet, take her home and start playing house."

"That's your secret?"

"Kinda."

K looked at LeBron for a long moment, unblinking, thinking.

"Christ almighty," K said at last, smiling crookedly. "Bass players."

CHAPTER 36

The Clock Is Ticking

THE next morning, K couldn't remember a whole lot of what LeBron had said but he knew he'd gone to bed thinking it was important. Sitting down with his first coffee, he put his glasses on and looked at the screen of his laptop. In one-inch-high letters were the words "LET IT GO."

Some days he felt he was finally managing to do what LeBron told him to do, at least the letting go part, but other days he thought of his Egyptian Princess most of the day just because he had to fill his mind with something. Sometimes the imaginings and memories left him at peace, thankful for the world she'd opened for him. Other days he thought he'd suddenly discovered maturity. On those occasions, he'd chastise himself for grieving something that never was and never could have been. How absurd was he capable of being? From the first moment he realized he was in love with her he knew they could never have become lovers, so why indulge the drama? But whatever that insight was worth it failed to eradicate the days when anger made even Scotch taste bad.

One Saturday afternoon, while mindlessly surfing Internet sites during commercials on TV, he joined two social networking sites. In both cases, within minutes of signing up, email arrived telling him there was someone who wanted to be his friend. The notion was ludicrous. He opened the messages anyway. Both were from someone representing the site, welcoming him aboard. Why couldn't they just say that? He'd never used an Enter key to seal a friendship. He went to bed that night without having accepted either request. He made both wait overnight in their browser windows. He woke up depressed.

As he sat down and stared dumbly at the laptop screen, he hit Enter on both social networking sites, then wondered why he did that. Were there no other friends to be had? What was the attraction? The coffee was bitter but needed.

Time Magazine said digital befriending was a global phenomenon. One of the sites he'd joined was Facebook. He started poking about and clicking. He saw what people ate for lunch that day, and the people they got drunk with the night before. Bosses were wasting countless hours browsing Facebook to find employees to fire for having lives outside of work.

Suddenly he realized how the disease spread. Facebook was asking him if he wanted it to find people who might be friends or potential friends. It wanted to crawl into his laptop, find his address book, and kidnap each and every entry.

OK, go for it, find me a friend, I dare you. He said the words in his mind, but his lips moved as he slapped the Enter key. He had no expectations, not even when the photos and names of five possible friends first flashed on the screen. He left the laptop to find a cloth to clean his glasses. He finally found one on top of the fridge. He had no idea why he would have left it there. Returning to the computer he glanced at the tiny photos. His eyes came to rest on the one in the middle of the five. His Egyptian Princess.

He stopped breathing and his eyes didn't blink. Slowly he pushed the little table away. He took off his glasses, reaching forward to place them next to the computer, then leaned back in his chair. The screen was almost a blur but he saw her face crisp and clear. His mind had engraved the image so deeply that it filled in the details his eyes couldn't make out, as if it had a zoom button and auto focus.

For days he waited, debating. What was over was over. Leave the girl in peace. God she was beautiful. God he was an idiot. He could hear LeBron saying, "Amen to that, K-man." Had she been truly angry with him, or just insisting on space and time? Had she simply never read his last letter, the way she'd never read his short stories for fear they'd remind her how sad relationships can be?

One afternoon, sober and knowing full well that he was stepping into outer space untethered, he typed her name into Google's search bar. He found three mentions of her full name. One was a page from the university theater school site in Montreal. The other two were newspaper theater reviews, one of which perfunctorily praised her set design, while the other rejoiced that her vision was a *"perfect example of how a minimalist approach to set design can maximize the creative possibilities at the director's disposal."* Deafening silence, he thought, that was minimalistic.

It was only in rereading the last review that he noticed it was a New York review. Was she back in the city?

He picked up his sax and walked up and down the room blowing scales as loudly as he could, starting with the cycle of fifths, then switching to chromatic scales, stopping and starting, each time trying to play faster and louder. He wanted to reach the half-tone fury of the "Flight of the Bumble Bee."

When he put down his horn he forced himself to

clean it methodically before pouring himself a drink, first the mouthpiece and the reed, then the neck, cleaning it inside and buffing it outside, and finally the body. The cleaning ritual calmed him. After gently placing the horn back in its case, he poured the drink, but wouldn't let himself take a sip before he found a CD to listen to loud. He found several he wanted to hear.

By the third one, an Aretha Franklin album, he was well on his way to being drunk. When she sang the first two syllables of "Skylark," Tom Hanks ran out of the dugout begging him not to cry. K listened to the song three times, thinking of his Egyptian Princess, somewhere out there, in the valley, through the mist. Could she hear its song?

He opened his laptop and searched for an MP3 of the song. After finding it, he returned to Facebook and called up her page. He wanted to send her the song as an attachment. He chose "Send Message." Seconds later he learned that he had to send a friend request first. Twenty minutes later his Egyptian Princess answered the friend request.

OMG. I've thought of you often.

please don't be offended when I say no to your friend request. It's my own little world. It's very private. do you need a mistress? I know a girl.

let me get back to you by Gmail.

hugs

He was beside himself but too drunk to even half absorb the possibilities that were invading his head. Daring to think his life was at a turning point he opened the sofa bed and, short of breath, sat down on the edge. The metal leg that supported that side of the frame suddenly gave way. He rolled off onto the floor. He lay there, thoughtless. Finally his eye fell on a rigid plastic box in which he kept his extra sax neck straps, reeds, cleaning kits and mouthpieces. He shoved it under the edge of the bed. The fit was perfect. He had a leg to lie on.

Unbelievably, when morning came, he was not hungover. It must be adrenalin, he thought. He stared at his regular email program, trying to will an incoming message via Google. He still felt like crying, but out of happiness.

By midday there was still no word from her. He couldn't sit still. He started to write a new email, he had to explain in more detail the baggage he had because it had to be talked about, but he didn't want to scare her off. Mostly he wanted to let her know how happy he was to be in touch again. He joked about how much older he had gotten waiting for her. He proposed a date, two days away, and a place, "under the clock in Grand Central. OK?"

. . .

When his Egyptian Princess saw his email she felt angry without having read a word. Why couldn't he have waited? Damn him. When she read it she felt his old intensity. Metaphor tripped over metaphor. She used to find his letters beautiful. Now the images he evoked didn't translate into meaning and understanding in her mind. They felt like sandpaper loitering on a cut.

She reached for her cell and called CC. They hadn't spoken in a while, but she was the only person she'd ever confided in about the client they both knew well. She was also the only person she'd really opened up to about how she'd liked guys but was afraid when they liked her too much in return.

When she heard CC's voice, she didn't say hello. She didn't ask how she was. Immediately, she uncorked a bottle she'd hoped would become dust covered.

"He's back, CC, and he wants to see me. Right away. Why am I angry?"

"*Attends, attends.* Back up. What the hell are you talking about? Who the hell are you talking about?"

She listened patiently but not much made sense. She waffled.

"I don't know. It's not as if he's been bugging you all this time. You shut the door and he didn't knock once. You even told me once you wondered what he was doing these days. How come you're pissed off?"

"I know, I know. I was so happy to hear from him, I really was. Then he ruined it all. He told me how much I'd hurt him but then said he was sure the anger would vanish the instant he saw me. CC, he's in love with me still! I can just tell. When he writes he knows how to make everything, even heavy things, sound like he's joking, but it's there. I know it's there."

"What's there?"

The Egyptian princess remained silent long enough for CC to finally ask if she was still on the line.

"Are you OK?"

"It's like all this emotion, all his needs, the two together, it's like a wave coming at me. I can't swim for Christ's sake. It's like I'm OK walking out until the water's up to my knees. It feels great, warm. The water's beautiful. But then I feel an undercurrent and get scared. He's a beautiful man but he'll drown me. I know it."

"Sounds to me like you might be panicking in a wading pool. See him. You two have got some history. You said yourself you're happy to hear from him."

"No, you don't get it. He's got a hole in him he wants me to fill. I can't do it for him. I smile and give him a hug. But the undercurrent keeps sucking me away. Why can't people love someone without needing them?"

"I don't know. I'm not like you. I like being told I'm beautiful. I like men falling for me. I get sad when they stop coming by. You get sad, too, I know, but you also feel relieved. Doesn't make a lot of sense."

After hanging up, she smoked two cigarettes in succession while thinking about what CC had said. It wasn't the smoke that was suffocating her. She felt just like she did when he texted years before about the dinner date she'd backed out of.

She clicked on REPLY.

I didn't mean to hurt you and I'm sorry if I did. But you're doing it again. Why couldn't you wait until I replied like I told you I would? I can't believe you're asking to meet right away. So no. I hope you have a happy life.

· · ·

When he read her email he was too dumbfounded to take his eyes from the screen. He didn't reread it. He only stared. He was beyond not understanding. What planet was she on when she wrote that?

His whole being refused to let her words penetrate.

Finally, he started typing. He prayed her message had been written in a fit of pique because he hadn't let her dictate how he might reenter her life. He prayed she was still at her keyboard, regretting her outburst.

He made it simple.

You were happy to hear from me, and you know I felt the same. What could it matter if I wrote back before you replied? I had something to say. What other reason could there possibly be for getting in touch if it wasn't to see each other again?

See you under the clock at 10. Can't wait.

He couldn't admit to himself that she might not come, but when he finally tried to make some sense of her email his fear deepened. What did she mean, "I didn't mean to hurt you?" If she read his letter two years ago, when she told him "no contact," she knew she'd hurt him because he'd written that no other human being had ever treated him so shabbily. That was the word he used, shabbily. She knew her request to be left alone made no sense, at least with regard to him. He'd explained he hadn't even seen her for three months at that point. If she cared for him at all, how could she have ignored that letter?

He never truly believed she hadn't read it. You don't do that to people, not friends. But if she'd read the letter there was no way she could stand having him think she treated him shabbily. She would have hurried to reassure him. But she hadn't. Suddenly he wanted to shout. At her.

If she had ignored his letter, her silence had been an insult worse than if she'd walked up to him in the street and spat in his face. Every day of silence was now an insult. He'd made a fool of himself, in his own eyes. All those days. He calculated quickly. More than eight hundred of them spent stupidly trying to understand her, stupidly missing her, stupidly believing she would soon pop out of her self-healing bubble and embrace his kind patience.

No, she could not possibly have read the letter. Nothing else could explain her innocent delight at hearing from him after all that time. She would not have responded that way if she knew he was upset with her.

In little more than an hour, his barely describable joy had dissolved. She didn't give a damn. If she thought of him often, as her Facebook reply said, why hadn't she contacted him? She was the one who closed the door so it was up to her to open it again.

Then he reversed himself. She had read the letter, of course she had, and didn't want to see him right away because the baggage he described in the email heralded confrontation, the one thing she couldn't abide. The hysterical yelling bouts between her parents had hardwired the dread. Why did he have to ruin things by bringing up the past? He could hear her saying it because she had once said something similar describing a former boyfriend. She had said she still liked him but whenever she'd drop in to see him he would always bring up the things they used to argue about. She stopped going over.

"Why would he keep doing that?" she asked. He had shrugged his shoulders, unable to believe the old boyfriend wouldn't have welcomed her with open arms. But now it was suddenly different. If she asked him that question again he'd have an answer, and he would shout it at her: "Because people have a right to understand! You had no right to leave him tangled up in unfinished business, as if you neglected to untie a client after a bondage session."

When he calmed down, he realized he was incapable of believing she could knowingly be unkind. But she had a temper, he thought, though almost immediately he realized he'd never seen it. He corrected his memory. She could be sharp-tongued. If someone annoyed her she could get on her high horse a little too fast. But both traits were always fleeting, probably leftovers from her adolescence when by her own admission she was bossy.

His mind returned to her welcoming words on Facebook. Now they shimmered in schizophrenic contrast to the message he'd just received. When he was her client, he'd never encouraged her delight in performing cock and ball torture. CBT was not for him, he'd pleaded. Now she was kicking him in the balls, hard. Why? If there was any credible reason, it certainly wasn't in her email.

Had she joined her generation in sidestepping relationships by hiding out in a cyber-circle of friends, most of whom they've never met and never would, all disposable with a click of the mouse, acquaintances and former lovers alike succumbing to new verbs like *unfriend, unlike?* Had she become so rutted in glib, caustic, bubbly 10-second keyboard eruptions that the idea of stepping outside the cyber-bubble was a risk no longer worth taking? He then remembered a young neighbor telling him his girlfriend had texted to say their year-long relationship was over, all feeling and investment in another human being annulled within 160 characters, punched out while listening to an iPod.

Tired of not understanding a single thing about her reaction, he decided to err on the side of hope. He went out and had a steak dinner. If he was going to stay sober he needed to eat. If only he'd kept his bike he could have easily sweated out the booze of the past few days.

After eating, he walked down to 23rd Street and east to the Chelsea Cinema. He shoved across $13 for a ticket to what looked like an adventure movie. He didn't catch the title. He only wanted to pass a couple of hours without the possibility of drinking. When he got home that night, he stood for a long time under the shower, using alternating hot and cold to stop his mind. He slept well, much better than usual.

The next day passed more easily, and a small translation project sucked up much of the day. He laid out fresh clothes for the following morning.

He awoke to a downpour forceful enough that rain was spattering the floor by his open window. He dressed quickly and decided to have his coffee at the station. He'd have to take a cab to stay dry, but a check of his wallet, and the pockets of the pants he wore the day before, revealed only five dollars and change. He didn't have to leave for another forty-five minutes, and he hoped the deluge would at least let up by then. It didn't.

He was soaked by the time he walked the block and a half to a bank machine in a drugstore. He got wetter still as cab after cab passed occupied. When he arrived at Grand Central the clock read 9:53. He moved closer to it, scanning the marble steps and landings at each end of the station as he walked. He couldn't spot anyone who even resembled her. When he reached the clock, he slowly paced around its four opal faces, hoping to actually see the big hand advance a minute closer to 10. Then he remembered she was, as she put it, "not anal about arriving on other people's dots."

At last the clock read 10. He felt it took forever to stare hard yard by yard to the depths of the station, then across its width in the hope of spotting her. By the time one scan was done she could have appeared anywhere. He prayed his height made him stand out. A swarm of little children, all attached by cords, brushed by him, forcing him to turn around. When he looked back, the future had taken a step away from him. The hand had just settled at 10:01.

Once again he gazed the length of the concourse and let his eyes climb the far set of stairs to see if she was there, peering down from the second level, watching him. That is something she would do in those wonderful days when their relationship was playful, intentionally make him think she was late, and eventually so late he would think she had stood him up. She would enjoy seeing him pace.

Hoping that's what she was doing, he put his hands in his pockets and ambled to his left, where he leaned against the wall next to the ticket windows for suburban trains. Then he realized that if she was watching from the second level, she would not be able to see him now. Fearing that she would think he'd given up and left, he pushed his way by people to get back to the clock.

It was 10:04. How long would she figure it would take him to believe he'd been stood up? He pictured her phoning him later, confessing her stunt and laughing. He was so practiced at animating her in his imagination that daydreams got confused with reality in no time at all. When he looked at the clock again it was 10:14.

Thinking other people must suspect something was going on, he looked around and realized there was no one within fifteen feet, something that doesn't often happen in New York. He was clearly in view. She was not there. At 10:51 he left.

He walked vaguely toward his place. The rain had stopped. After zigzagging southwest, he turned north for no reason. A half hour later he was standing next to the bike rentals on Central Park South. There were no takers on a day like this. No one even tried to sell him on the idea. He had to ask for a bike. He bought an hour.

There was a time when he would have enjoyed her poking fun at him. Now it felt like a knife blade. Why after all this time? He had been long gone from her life until two days before. He had left her alone as she had asked. Why did she send him hugs, then cast him adrift again?

Within minutes, the rain returned as hard as it had been that morning. Utterly drenched, he rode the bike hard. And he rode his anger. Damn her! Damn her! He was yelling into the rain. Adrenaline made his legs young. He peddled harder and, changing gears smoothly, he stopped talking to the rain. He redirected his words to her, yelling. Damn you! Damn you. Fuck you! How could you? Fuck fuck fuck fuck you!

By the time he'd crossed the top of the park and reached the Great Hill, he was so out of breath he could no longer shout. He pulled over to the side of the pavement and sat on the wet earth under a tree. He saw a bench about thirty yards further south. He had trouble making it out. No, he realized, he couldn't make it that far. He stayed where he was, seated on the wet earth.

He couldn't think straight. He knew that, yet he allowed himself to think she was still playing a game with him. That she really would call and end the game. But he was hating the game. He felt sick to his stomach from trying to pedal up the Great Hill. He didn't dare stand up at that moment for fear he'd fall over. Then for no reason at all he heard LeBron's bass voice quoting Charlie Parker:

"Don't play the saxophone. Let it play you."

"Shit, LeBron, what the fuck do you think I'm doing right now? I'm getting played, man, fucking played, and I'm tired of it."

He didn't know whether he'd said that out loud or not.

CHAPTER 37

Wordless for Once

WHEN LeBron spoke to the nurse two days later, she explained that his friend had suffered a stroke, a bad one. Apparently, she said, he had lain on the ground in Central Park for several hours before being discovered. The rain had become so heavy that it wasn't until it stopped that someone spotted a rental bike on the side of the road with no rider nearby. She said it looked like his friend had probably been trying to get out of the rain when he had his stroke. LeBron's phone number was in his wallet. It was the number of his new girlfriend's place. LeBron always gave K the numbers of his girlfriends to make sure they could stay in touch.

The nurse couldn't say what his friend's future held. He would likely be sent to a rehab center. At the moment he was paralyzed on one side. Maybe therapy would help, maybe not.

LeBron told the hospital his friend had no family and they said they would notify him when he could speak, and if he was transferred for rehab. After he left the hospital, LeBron headed to Chelsea. He dug out the key from beside the stoop. He didn't feel like going home to see his girlfriend. He wondered whether he should take the alto sax for safekeeping.

The next few months produced no improvement. LeBron visited less and less frequently because while K seemed to recognize him he had no recollection of what they talked about the previous visit. Most of the visits were now conducted in silence. LeBron brought him magazines but the only ones that interested him seemed to be girly magazines. K would often start masturbating with his one good hand while he was still there. LeBron wondered whether arousal was the only thing he was now capable of feeling. Was that how life ended?

When LeBron wanted some alone time, which he usually spent practicing, he took to hiding away in his friend's apartment. He had moved his double bass back there because he was called on to play only electric in his current band. He had also signed for his friend's clothes at the rehab center, as well as his wallet and cell phone, and brought them back to the apartment.

One day a young woman with purple and pink hair showed up at the door asking for K.

LeBron remembered her.

"Juggler?"

"Yeah." She smiled. "How did you know?" Without waiting for an answer, she said she hadn't seen K for a long time but she was in a music store the other day and suddenly wondered whether K had ever recorded with the group she saw that night in Brooklyn. "Something to remember him by," she said. "It was a fun night."

"No," he said. "There's no recording of him." She seemed disappointed. After a moment, he added:

"He was supposed to have been on one of our CDs about a year ago, but the studio date got changed at the last minute and he couldn't make it. Yeah, it would have been nice to have him on record."

It was a lie. He wasn't sure why he said it. Maybe he just wanted to embellish her memory of his friend. Though he was still alive, his existence was now ninety-nine percent in the memory of others.

He told her about the stroke. For some time she looked up at LeBron, her mouth slightly open. Then, with a quick little smile, she said:

"Well, when he comes home, tell him Selita dropped by. Tell him I'm a really good juggler now."

Soon after that K's phone rang. It was a woman saying she was supposed to have met him one day but got tied up at the last minute. She said she'd been emailing constantly to set up another meeting but never got a reply, and he never picked up his phone.

LeBron asked if this was personal or business.

"Personal. We go back."

"You might want to come over."

He wasn't comfortable talking to a stranger on the phone. She arrived about two hours later. When she heard the news she sat stock still and said nothing. She looked directly at him but he knew she wasn't seeing him. He didn't interrupt her silence. Oddly, he felt relieved. He was just somehow glad to find that K's mystery woman cared enough about him to worry. His friend hadn't imagined it all after all. LeBron wanted to ask her a lot of questions, the questions that tormented his friend, but now wasn't the time. She wasn't his business.

CHAPTER 38

Reunited Again

WHEN the Egyptian Princess asked how K was doing, the nurse replied there hadn't been a change since the day he was brought to the center. He fought, physically fought, with his one arm, any attempt at rehab. She said he also hit a nurse one day when she was trying to bathe him.

"Hi mister," she said softly, stepping toward the bed.

His eyes fixed on her face but she couldn't tell if he recognized her. He looked so much older. He didn't look exactly fat but skin sagged under his jaw. His black hair had gotten a lot whiter. In a different light it might look almost all white. His mouth moved as if he was going to speak but he suddenly looked away and remained silent.

"I'm sorry I missed you at the station," she said. Even if he didn't understand, it was important for her to say it to him. He had remained motionless while she spoke the sentence. After a moment his left hand moved inside his hospital gown. He started to masturbate. LeBron had warned her.

She watched his hand and remembered him masturbating while she fingered his prostate, to his great
joy. She had enjoyed it, too. She had never done that to
another client. And she had marveled at the distance his
come had traveled. Throughout the massage and at the
moment he ejaculated his eyes had been locked on hers.
It had been a communion of sorts, he said later, and the
come had been the host. Maybe Catholicism wasn't so
evil after all, she thought.

But now his eyes were inward as his hand stroked and
jerked, the rhythm regular then ragged.

She began to feel certain he was totally blind to her
presence, the person whom by his own admission he had
been utterly obsessed with for years and years.

After what seemed to her like minutes, she could bear
his masturbating without her no longer. She placed her
right hand lightly on his. Instead of stopping, he wrested
his hand away from hers and resumed.

She placed the palm of her left hand on his forehead.
Slowly, he stopped masturbating. She switched hands,
putting her right palm on his forehead. With her left, she
lightly tousled his hair. He had always loved that. She
would do it to him when he was tied down on a bench,
after she'd pushed him hard.

His eyes closed.

Shit, she thought. She felt tears coming. She was never
cool with her own tears. She was always afraid once they
started they would never stop. She told herself that she
felt that way about anyone who was probably dying,
even strangers. And the now-immobile body before her
seemed like a stranger.

Leaving her left hand clutching his hair, she removed
her right palm from his forehead and replaced its soft
touch with a gentle kiss. Her lips remained on his skin,
then pushed down in another little kiss. As she did this,
her eyes closed.

"You know I never heard you play. LeBron says you

weren't half bad. He says you were too fucking dumb to know that, and you always would be."

Her left hand moved down to his left ear, then stroked his cheek.

"Maybe all this shit... maybe it wasn't your fault."

She kissed his right eyelid. Before the feather-light suction of her lips released it, she felt, barely, a flutter.

"Maybe one of us was just born at the wrong time, like in that movie you sent me, you know?"

Before opening her eyes his Egyptian Princess turned away, and then she walked off the ward. Long strides. Measured. Slow. Graceful. Like the night she wore the black teddy and led him into his first dungeon.

As she stepped through the door to the hallway, she stopped suddenly. LeBron was towering over her. Neither spoke. Each looked at the other expectantly. Finally, LeBron spoke.

"You OK?"

Her hot black eyes held his soft brown ones. Finally she took a short breath and answered.

"Why wouldn't I be?" She looked at him a minute longer, then turned and walked down the hall.

. . .

In the weeks that followed, LeBron would close his eyes and try to recapture her face at the very moment she proclaimed indifference to his friend's fate. Sometimes he was sure her eyes were moist. Other times he just couldn't tell whether his friend had been played or not.

On a bitterly cold spring day, LeBron did what he hated to do. He took a cab when he could have walked. He'd rather spend his money on a good time. But he woke up that morning, actually it was closer to noon, thinking about the expressionless face of the woman that caused his friend to slash and hack away at the remaining ties he had to the outside world.

For the first time in months, LeBron wanted to see

his friend K. He had told himself more than once that he would never go back. There was no point. There was no recognition, not even for a moment.

After paying the cab, he walked into the rehab center.

K's eyes were open but not moving. For once in these last two years on this bed, his good hand was still. LeBron touched him on the shoulder. His friend blinked. After a few seconds he turned his head on the pillow and looked up.

"Hey, K-Man."

K was still looking at him.

"I've been thinking, about your girl. You know she came, right?"

LeBron waited for a nurse to pass by, on her way to another bedside.

"Been thinking about that night when we sat at your place yakking, when you spilled out all the shit about masochists and sadists and beautiful women. You probably don't remember. You were drunk. Anyway, since the last time I saw you, I've been trying to figure out if she played you like a mark with bucks or whether you were special to her somehow.

He paused.

"I don't know how you'd be special to a woman like that. Man, look at you. Old and all that, like me for Christ's sake. Old and ugly. That's us."

LeBron looked around the ward. He saw a chair by the window. It had arms. He pulled it over to K's bed. It made noise on the floor but no one seemed to notice.

He took off his hoodie and the sweater underneath and sat down. For a while he leaned back in the chair, his long legs stretched out in front of him, disappearing under K's bed.

"Like I said, I've been thinking about the last time I saw her. I couldn't read her. One day I'd think I saw this, the next day I'd think I'd seen that. Come to think of it, I guess that's what drove you crazy. I'd be the same."

LeBron sat forward, his face a foot from his friend's.

"You wouldn't know it, but it's a shitty, angry day outside. But I came out because I had a thought. I thought about you seeing this picture of a woman, and for God knows what reason, you thought she was everything life had to offer, all rolled into one funky fine body. To you she was life everlasting, or whatever that book says."

LeBron sat back in the chair and closed his eyes. When he opened them again, he said something he was sure K had never thought of all that time he was crying inside. This time, LeBron didn't lean forward. He didn't put his elbows on his knees, and he didn't put his face inches from his friend's. Because he was still leaning back in the chair, slouched, he had to speak louder. In fact, he spoke much louder in the hope that his friend might finally hear something from outside himself.

"I think you were lucky, damned lucky, the luckiest bastard in the world. You're lucky because she yanked the lever on the scaffold. She stopped you from trying to love her. And that was right. In fact, that was righteous. If she had taken you to her bed or gone around the world with you, splitting everything fifty-fifty, proving beyond all doubt that she wasn't taking you for a ride... I'm just being out there for a second, pretending that your young princess could fall in love with you... you would have learned that she wasn't a princess, she wasn't everything all rolled into one, she was just a girl... OK, a woman. But what I'm trying to say, you stubborn bastard, is that she was just a person.

"Yeah, you would have learned that."

LeBron looked at K who seemed to be looking back at him with the same expression as before. LeBron stood up and put his sweater back on, pulling the hoodie over it. With his right hand he flipped the hood up. It made his eyes seem darker, the lines under them, and around his mouth, more creased.

"You know, and I know you're going to tell me I'm full of shit, but I think your soul..."

He stopped and closed his eyes. His skyscraper frame rocked slightly, the way it did when he was on stage playing bass. He wanted to get the words right. When the words came, they came from the bottom end of his vocal cords, slow and steady, like a walking bass line.

"... I think your soul... got turned off... just in time. I mean, just in time before you found out she could never be... what that fucked up, fantasizing head of yours wanted to believe she was.

"You'd probably tell me I'm full of shit if you could. But, believe me — are you listening, K-Man? — everything between you and that princess of yours, you know... it worked out fine. Just fine."

. . .

For several minutes after LeBron left, K's eyes remained fixed on the spot where he had been. Then they closed.

Reviews Welcome:

Authors always appreciate receiving reviews of their
work. If you would care to write one for the novel you've
just read, here are links to sites where you can post your
review, or simply type "he & She" Wayne Clark with
quotation marks in the webpage's search box.

Amazon.com — United States
http://www.amazon.com/he-She-Wayne-Clark/dp/0992120209/

Amazon.ca — Canada
http://www.amazon.ca/he-She-MR-Wayne-Clark/dp/0992120209

Amazon.co.uk — United Kingdom
http://www.amazon.co.uk/he-She-Mr-Wayne-Clark/dp/0992120209/

Amazon.fr — France
http://www.amazon.fr/he-She-Mr-Wayne-Clark/dp/0992120209/

Amazon.de — Germany
http://www.amazon.de/he-She-Mr-Wayne-Clark/dp/0992120209/

Amazon.in — India
http://www.amazon.in/he-She-Mr-Wayne-Clark/dp/0992120209/

Goodreads
https://www.goodreads.com/book/show/18516006-he-she

Smashwords
https://www.smashwords.com/books/view/369947

. . .

he & She is available as an e-book at most online retailers.

About the author:

Wayne Clark is a Montreal writer. For more than 35 years he has made his living almost entirely from words, from journalism to copywriting. He wrote fiction throughout most of those years, when he was sure no one was looking. *he & She* is the first novel that he convinced himself to publish.

Connect with the author online:

Web
www.wayne-clark.com

Twitter
http://twitter.com/@Wayne_Clark_1

Facebook
www.facebook.com/pages/Novel-he-She/704231929586837

Goodreads
www.goodreads.com/author/show/7276091.Wayne_Clark

Smashwords
www.smashwords.com/profile/view/WayneClark

www.ingramcontent.com/pod-product-compliance
Lightning Source LLC
Chambersburg PA
CBHW051527250626
47156CB00001B/263